Raves for the Esther Diamond series:

"Sexy interludes raise the tension between Lopez and Esther as she juggles magical assailants, her perennially distracted agent, her meddling mother, and wiseguys both friendly and threatening in a well-crafted, rollicking mystery." —*Publishers Weekly*

"Fans of Charlaine Harris's Sookie Stackhouse series will appreciate this series' lively heroine and the appealing combination of humor, mystery, and romance."
—*Library Journal*

"Seasoned by a good measure of humor, this fantasy mystery is a genuine treat for readers of any genre."
—*SF Chronicle*

"With a wry, tongue-in-cheek style reminiscent of Janet Evanovich, this entertaining tale pokes fun at the deadly serious urban fantasy subgenre while drawing the reader into a fairly well-plotted mystery. The larger-than-life characters are apropos to the theatrical setting, and Esther's charming, self-deprecating voice makes her an appealingly quirky heroine. The chemistry between Esther and Lopez sizzles, while scenes of slapstick comedy will have will have the reader laughing out loud and eager for further tales of Esther's adventures."
—*Romantic Times*

"A delightful mélange of amateur sleuth mystery, romance, and urban fantasy."
—*The Barnes and Noble Review*

"A paranormal screwball comedy adventure. Light, happy, fantastically funny!" —Jennifer Crusie,
New York Times bestselling author

D0030339

The Esther Diamond Series:

DOPPELGANGSTER
UNSYMPATHETIC MAGIC
VAMPARAZZI *

*Coming soon from DAW Books

UNSYMPATHETIC MAGIC

Laura Resnick

DAW BOOKS, INC.

DONALD A. WOLLHEIM, FOUNDER

375 Hudson Street, New York, NY 10014

ELIZABETH R. WOLLHEIM
SHEILA E. GILBERT
PUBLISHERS

http://www.dawbooks.com

Cover images by Dan Dos Santos

DAW Books Collectors No. 1518.

DAW Books are distributed by the Penguin Group (USA) Inc.

First Paperback Printing, August 2010.

1 2 3 4 5 6 7 8 9 10

DAW TRADEMARK REGISTERED
U.S. PAT. AND TM. OFF. AND FOREIGN COUNTRIES
—MARCA REGISTRADA
HECHO EN U.S.A.
        PRINTED IN THE U.S.A.

For my cousin,
Mildred Diamond Mailick—
whom I call Poppy

Author's Note:

The Mount Morris Park watchtower and its setting in Harlem are very similar to what is described in this novel, though I have taken a few liberties with it. And I sincerely hope that the inhabitants of several high-rise buildings that are near the park would, oh, notice and call the police if the events depicted in this novel actually took place there! The park itself was renamed Marcus Garvey Park in 1973, though some current maps still label it as Mount Morris Park, which is also the name of the historic neighborhood surrounding it.

Just as Vodou is an oral tradition, Creole, the language of the faith, is primarily an oral language. Consequently, I found up to *ten* different accepted ways to spell some of the names and terms used in this novel. So the spellings I chose to use in *Unsympathetic Magic* are not "correct" or definitive, they're just . . . what I chose.

The syncretic religions of the New World, including Vodou, developed among Africans preserving and adapting their spiritual beliefs under the yoke of slavery while also gradually absorbing (often under duress) the European religions of their captors. This humorous fantasy novel cannot (and does not attempt to) convey the history and complexity of these religions. For a short list of further reading, please visit the Research Library page of my Web site at www.LauraResnick.com.

Finally, I wish to convey my thanks and gratitude to the following people: the heroic team at DAW Books, and particularly my editor, Betsy Wollheim; Daniel Dos Santos, the artist who created the wonderful cover for this novel; April Kihlstrom, whose advice I sought in the nick of time; and many friends who offered practical and/or moral support while I was wrestling this book to the ground, including (but not limited to) Mary Jo Putney, Zell Schulman, Jerry Spradlin, Cindy Person, and Toni Blake.

Esther Diamond, her friends, and her nemeses will all return soon for their next misadventure in *Vamparazzi*, wherein will we finally learn what Max's issue with Lithuanians is.

1

As summer in New York City ripened into a sweltering stench of suffocating heat and humidity, I found myself arrested for prostitution, menaced by zombies (yes, zombies), and staked out as a human sacrifice. I also nearly got Lopez killed—again.

Although I realize this isn't exactly the sort of stuff that happens to *everyone* on a bad hair day, I nonetheless maintain that these events were not my fault.

Well, not *entirely* my fault. I do feel responsible for what happened to Lopez. Cause and effect. If I hadn't gotten him involved in my problem, then he wouldn't have come so close to meeting the Lord of Death.

And I got him involved because I didn't want a prostitution arrest on my police record. Indeed, I didn't want a police record at *all*.

Getting picked up for prostitution, though . . . now that was *not* my fault. That, obviously, would have happened to anyone who happened to lose her cell phone in a struggle with deranged gargoyles (yes, gargoyles) and trip over a living corpse in Harlem at midnight while dressed like a hooker.

Oh, if only I were making this up.

I was in Harlem in the middle of a muggy midsummer night because I was working. I'd been cast in a guest role on *The Dirty Thirty*, the latest success in the *Crime and Punishment* franchise of prestigious police television dramas. Affectionately known to fans as *D30,* this was the *C&P* empire's most controversial spin-off to date, a gritty, morally ambivalent show about rampant police corruption in the Thirtieth Precinct a.k.a. "the dirty Thirty."

After being rejected by *C&P*'s regular network because of its raw subject matter and antihero protagonists, *D30* had premiered on cable TV the previous summer, and it had soon become a critically acclaimed cult hit with a steadily growing audience. Some New York City cops condemned and boycotted the program, while others reputedly provided much of the show's material from their own experiences on the force.

The show's second season had begun airing this summer, when the competition mostly consisted of reruns, and ratings and reviews were good this year, too. So getting a guest role on *D30* was a good opportunity for me. Especially since I had no other real work (i.e. acting work) lined up and had been "resting" (i.e. waiting tables fifty hours per week) for the past couple of months.

It was also a terrific role. Granted, my mother wasn't thrilled about the prospect of my appearing on national television as a homeless bisexual junkie prostitute—but my mother is seldom thrilled about anything I do, so I let her oh-so-subtle comments about this job roll off my back. My father had declined to offer an opinion—though whether that was to avoid an argument with me or with my mother, I have no idea.

My parents live in Wisconsin and rarely visit New York—a city which, besides being an international epicenter for my profession, has the advantage of being eight hundred miles away from them.

However, parental dismay notwithstanding, Jilly C-

Note (not her real name), was a challenging and satisfying character to play: tough, bold, ignorant but shrewd, impulsive, completely amoral, sometimes cruel, and prone to occasional moments of twisted compassion. The script for the episode was smart, tight, and full of well-crafted surprises. My costume was uncomfortable and a little embarrassing, but this wasn't the first time I'd worked for long hours in tight clothes that left a lot of my character's skin exposed (and thinking of my body as belonging to my character rather than to me is one of the ways I get comfortable in the strange array of costumes that I wear in the course of my profession).

This was a terrific job, and I was delighted to have it. Even though I couldn't stand the regular cast member with whom Jilly had most of her scenes.

After five days on the same set with actor Michael Nolan, who played one of the dirtiest detectives in the Thirtieth Precinct, I'd already fantasized multiple times about stomping on his genitals with one of Jilly C-Note's high-heeled boots.

Dating actors is an exercise in masochism, which is why I don't do it. That's a long-standing personal rule. But I normally like *working* with actors—indeed, I normally like it so much that it's among the many reasons that I *am* one. Whatever their personal twitches and foibles, many actors, in the practice of their craft, are generous, engaging, and cooperative, and they care about doing what's best for the overall production.

Michael Nolan, however, was the *other* kind of actor. He was temperamental, narcissistic, rude, and primarily concerned with doing what was best for himself, and the rest of the production be damned. On the other hand, though it galled me to admit it, he was also talented, and the same qualities that made him so difficult to work with actually translated well to his *D30* role as Detective Jimmy Conway, an edgy, tightly wound, morally decayed cop struggling with alcoholism and (since getting shot in the first year's season finale) post-traumatic stress disorder.

In this episode, Detective Conway was shaking down Jilly for sex and information in exchange for not arresting her on suspicion of murdering her pimp. The script didn't reveal whether or not Jilly was actually the killer. Sticking with the dark tone that was typical of the show, the cops of the dirty Thirty didn't care that a pimp had been murdered; they were just looking for ways to benefit from the killing—such as blackmailing the chief suspect, Jilly, for information about other criminals in the precinct. This might well get Jilly killed, and the cops didn't particularly care about that, either.

Tonight was my final night of work on the episode, and despite how much I had enjoyed the script, the role, and the rest of the cast and crew, it was a relief to know I wouldn't have to deal with Michael Nolan again after this.

We were preparing to shoot the most awkward scene in the script—for me, at least. I didn't know if this scene's shoot had been scheduled last as a courtesy to me or for other reasons entirely, but I was glad either way.

In this scene, Detective Conway was questioning Jilly about an illegal weapons deal while making her perform oral sex on him. The physical aspects of the scene would stay (just barely) within the boundaries of what could be shown on a commercial cable network, but it was the sort of scene that's uncomfortable for two actors to perform the very first time they work together. By now, however, my fifth day of shooting, Nolan and I had already done a number of dialogue scenes together, as well as a grimly post-coital scene in a filthy outdoor stairwell. So, although I didn't like him, I was accustomed to working with him and no longer anxious about kneeling before him with my face in his groin for a couple of hours.

Heigh-ho, the glamorous life of an actress.

To his credit, Nolan was very professional about this sort of thing—as I knew from the thirty minutes (on-and-off) that he'd spent pumping his hips against mine in a dank stairwell the night before. (Scenes that look embarrassingly intimate onscreen are usually technical and choreographed, and so it was in this case.) When the cameras were rolling, what Nolan wanted most was to be admired for his work, and that meant that he focused on doing it well; this, in turn, allowed me to focus on doing my work well, too.

We were shooting in the East 120s tonight. Although that's in Harlem, like the Thirtieth Precinct, the neighborhood is not actually part of the Three-Oh. In fact, although I'd spent four of my five *D30* working days on location (since the death of her pimp, Jilly was homeless and most of my scenes were filmed outdoors), we hadn't gone anywhere near the Thirtieth. I gathered from the crew that this was because the cops of the Thirtieth unanimously hated the show. During its first season, they had tried (unsuccessfully) to prevent *D30* from getting any permits to film on location in their precinct, and there'd been some unpleasant incidents on the few occasions that the show had done location work there. So the producers decided it just best to film elsewhere thereafter. Since then, every episode contained some establishing shots filmed in the Thirtieth (which reputedly galled the real-life cops there), but no actual scenes were filmed in the precinct.

The night before, we had filmed in another part of town, where the location scouts had found a filthy, urine-scented basement stairwell that they liked. In that scene, a quick bout of impersonal, fully-clothed coitus between Detective Conway and Jilly came to a sudden halt when Conway had a debilitating flashback to being shot the previous season. He then exchanged some confessional dialogue with Jilly in which he came close to treating her like a person. Jilly, slightly mellowed by sharing Conway's flask of scotch, experienced an unexpected moment of compassion for the corrupt cop who was victimizing her. It was a great scene, and I had really enjoyed doing it despite the humid heat, Jilly's uncomfortable clothes, the overwhelming odor of urine, and Nolan's tantrum about the lighting.

Tonight's scene contained more strong writing. Having opened up to Jilly (ever so slightly) in the previous scene, Conway now resented her for glimpsing his vulnerability. So in this scene, he would make her get on her knees before him in a darkened street; it was an attempt to put her back in her place as a hooker, a junkie, and his stooge. And while forcing her to pleasure him sexually, he would stay focused on asking questions about criminal business—in particular, questions that could get Jilly killed.

The characters' previous scene had been a personal, even slightly touching encounter, in a grim, dreary setting. In tonight's scene, by contrast, Conway's deliberate attempt to demean Jilly would occur in attractive, romantically lighted surroundings. And in the final moments of the scene, Jilly would give as good as she got, humiliating Conway, in turn, with a few well chosen words, now that their previous encounter had given away his weakness.

Last night's scene had probably been the most challenging one for me and Nolan, since it required us—two actors who didn't like each other—to find an emotional connection between our characters, however brief and subtle it was. Tonight's scene, by contrast, was ideally suited to the adversarial energy that existed between us as people (and that seemed to exist between Nolan and *most* people). While waiting for the crew to finish their lighting and sound checks, we were running lines together, and it was going well.

The makeup artist touched up my face while I recited some dialogue about a pending sale of automatic weapons and cop killer bullets that was due to occur somewhere in the precinct. I looked in the mirror that the makeup artist handed me, then nodded to show that I was satisfied if she was. The pale skin, shoulder-length brown hair, brown eyes, and good cheekbones were my own. The heavy, smudged eye makeup, the ill-advised lipstick color, and the stringy, unkempt hairdo were Jilly's.

Then the makeup artist tried to touch up Nolan's face. With an irritable scowl, he shoved her hand away and finished saying his line. Without glancing at her, he then grabbed the mirror from her and looked into it.

"Christ, I look so *red*," he said. "What the fuck did you put on me?"

"Actually, I've been trying to tone down the red ever since you got on set," she said patiently. "Your color is really heightened tonight."

She was right. It was. I realized I had unconsciously assumed they'd rouged him heavily for this scene— maybe to emphasize Conway's emotional conflict.

"Of course, it's heightened," Nolan snapped. "It's so goddamn *hot* out here tonight." He said absently to me, "Aren't you hot?"

"Uh-huh." It was early August, so it had been hot every night of the shoot. These were the dog days of summer.

Nolan dragged his forearm across his forehead, smudging his makeup. I saw that they had indeed powdered him quite a bit tonight in an attempt to tone down his heightened color.

"Jesus, I'm really sweating," he said. "It's like a steam bath out here. There's no damn air."

Actually, here in East Harlem, we were close enough to the river that a slight breeze was coming down the street to us from the water. And since we weren't surrounded by the stench of urine tonight, I thought this was a distinct improvement over our previous night's location.

But Nolan said, "I feel like I'm going to throw up. Have you got something for that?"

The makeup artist signaled to a production assistant, who in turn spoke into her walkie-talkie, asking someone to bring something to "Mr. Nolan" for his nausea. The makeup artist went back to trying to tone down the color of Nolan's face, but he brushed aside her hand again, irritably insisting that she wait until he felt better.

I sighed and went to find a chair, since standing around in Jilly's high heels for any length of time made my feet hurt.

As I expected, Nolan's queasy stomach led to delays while he rejected various remedies offered to him, then threw a tantrum about the crew's failure to have on hand the exact product he wanted. A production assistant was sent to 125th Street, a few blocks away, in search of an open shop where the correct item could be purchased for poor Mr. Nolan's aching tummy. I resented the delay—especially after having been through numerous delays this week, always because of Nolan—but I also didn't particularly want him vomiting while I was kneeling right in front of him. Besides, I was just a guest performer, and an unknown one, at that. So I sat quietly, the perfect picture of patience, and endured the lengthy wait that ensued before Nolan finally felt ready to work.

By then, I was pretty sweaty. The breeze from the Harlem River notwithstanding, it *was* a hot night, and Jilly wasn't dressed for this weather. (Based on a line in the script about her needing to find someplace to stay before the weather turned cold, I assumed the episode was set in autumn.) I was wearing a low-cut leopard-patterned Lycra top with sleeves that came down to my elbows; an uncomfortably short, tight, red vinyl skirt with a studded belt; purple fishnet stockings; and black high-heeled boots. Completing Jilly's ensemble was a curly lamb vest. Wearing that vest in this weather was unbearable, so it always stayed on the garment rack until just before I stepped in front of the cameras.

Now that Nolan was pacing around in front of the cameras and revving up for the scene, I let the wardrobe mistress slip the pale, furry vest over my arms and onto my shoulders. A few minutes later, Jilly's immense purse, containing all her worldly goods, was slung over my shoulder. A production assistant stood nearby with some knee pads, which I'd be using later; I would only have to kneel directly on bare cement in the master shots where my legs would be visible.

In the opening portion of the scene, Conway and Jilly would exchange a page of dialogue face-to-face before he'd rough her up and force her to her knees. We had already worked on the blocking for this, and now I joined Nolan in front of the cameras so the crew could verify all our marks. Television and film work tends to involve a lot of technical considerations, such as making sure you're in focus, in the frame, audible, and correctly lit on every shot, as well as ensuring continuity from take to take of the same scene being filmed from multiple angles.

Finally ready for our first take—a mere ninety minutes behind schedule—Nolan and I now stood face-to-face, waiting for the director to call, "Action!"

I was close enough to see that, under his recently freshened layer of makeup, the actor looked even redder than before. But our lighting for this scene was so shadowy, I supposed it probably wouldn't matter.

"Action!"

Nolan turned into Conway in a nanosecond. He grabbed me and shook me, his hot breath brushing my face as he demanded I tell him what I knew. I struggled and prevaricated, pretending I knew much less than he supposed, but I didn't waste any breath trying to appeal to his compassion. My resistance infuriated him. He shoved me away—so hard that my heel caught in a crack on the sidewalk and I staggered sideways before I fell back against the wall. He pursued me, closing in on me. I knew we were off our marks now, as did he, but the scene was working so well that we kept playing it. As he leaned into me, though, I could see that he was even redder now, and sweating again.

An instant later, Nolan tripped over his lines. He tried to save the moment, but then he swayed dizzily, closed his eyes, and put his hand to his forehand.

He shook his head and, completely out of character now, said, "Nah, I lost it. Let's go back."

"Are you all right?" I asked.

"Yeah, fine," he said tersely.

He didn't look all right. He looked . . . well, not all right, anyhow.

I said, "Are you sure? Because you look a littl—"

"If you could manage to hit your fucking marks, that would be a big help," he snapped.

I fantasized about stomping on his genitals with my high-heeled boots.

We started the scene again. This time I fell backward into the wall exactly where I was supposed to. But when he pursued me and leaned into me . . . I saw that his eyes were watery, and his gaze was blurry. Nolan uttered Conway's next line with a thick, clumsy tongue. I kept going, whining Jilly's dialogue at him. He blew his next line completely, stumbling over a few disjointed words then falling silent.

There was a long pause. My tormentor just stood

there, gripping my shoulders, looking dazed and sweaty. In contrast to his deep flush only moments ago, he was now sickly pale, as if suddenly drained of all his blood.

"Are you okay?" I prodded at last.

Nolan gave a little start, as if suddenly realizing I was there. He let go of my shoulders, staggered back a step, and mumbled, "I think I'm gonna . . ."

A moment later, he vomited all over the sidewalk, splattering my boots.

2

Jilly's boots were a nuisance to put on and take off, so the wardrobe intern who got assigned to clean Michael Nolan's vomit off them told me not to bother removing them. I took off Jilly's curly lamb vest, then went and sat in the wardrobe van, where the intern sponged at my leather-clad feet.

After getting sick on camera, Nolan had been escorted into an air-conditioned location trailer, where he awaited the attentions of a medic. It was hoped that, now that he'd evidently gotten something nasty out of his system, he would be able to finish the night's work after a brief rest. Meanwhile, though, we were all stuck waiting around, and it didn't take long for people to start getting bored. Also hungry. And since Nolan, who'd just tossed his cookies all over the sidewalk, had eaten food from the catering van earlier, no one wanted to eat *D30*'s catered fare now.

When I emerged from the wardrobe van, one of the other cast members told me that the production intern who'd purchased Nolan's stomach remedy on 125th Street had seen an eatery there which boasted the best fried chicken in Harlem. The cast and some of the crew had gotten permission to go there for a meal while waiting for the verdict on Nolan. They had strict instructions to be back within one hour.

As they walked down the dark street, headed toward 125th, I debated the wisdom of eating anything, let alone fried chicken, if I was going to be on camera later tonight in this tight, revealing outfit. However, simply hanging around the set waiting for Nolan to get better wasn't an enticing prospect. Especially not with the other actors fleeing to a restaurant for the next hour.

"I suppose *one* piece of chicken won't show up on camera," I murmured, trying to suck in my Lycra-clad stomach where it spilled over the waistband of Jilly's extremely tight skirt. "One *small* piece."

I don't have the svelte or surgically enhanced body of a Hollywood leading lady, but I do watch my weight and try to stay in shape, given my profession. And the camera adds weight and enhances puffiness, so I'd been eating carefully in preparation for this role.

On the other hand, excessive self-denial is just morbid.

And now that I was recovered from the mild revulsion of witnessing Nolan's gastric episode up close and personal, I was feeling a bit peckish. Especially when I contemplated the prospect of working until dawn, thanks to these delays.

So I called after the departing actors, "I'll get my purse and catch up to you!"

I went back into the wardrobe trailer, collected my purse, and promised faithfully that I wouldn't get any stains or splotches on Jilly's outfit. Then I went back out into the hot, humid night in pursuit of my coworkers and a satisfying piece of fried poultry. I was already more than a block behind the others and didn't really know where they were going, so I walked at a brisk pace, despite the height of my heels.

Trailing that far behind my colleagues in Harlem

around midnight wasn't as foolhardy as it might sound. We were filming directly east of Mount Morris Park, which is a nice neighborhood, one that reflects the almost-frenzied renovation and rehabilitation projects that have characterized real estate development in Harlem for the past decade or so. In fact, much of Harlem is increasingly inhabited by white yuppies, a somewhat controversial state of affairs in the nation's most famous black neighborhood.

The main drag that I was headed toward, 125th Street, was at the forefront of this controversy. The famous commercial avenue of Harlem is now home to a large number of national chain stores and corporate-owned businesses. Fewer and fewer black merchants and small Harlem businesses are able to pay the skyrocketing prices for commercial space there these days. Harlem had changed a great deal in recent years; and whether that was ultimately a blessing or a curse, it did at least mean that I didn't feel anxious about being alone in this area after dark.

A moment later, however, I realized that might be naive of me. As I passed a narrow alley between two apartment buildings, a sudden noise startled me. I jumped and gasped. This, in turn, startled the individual who was poking around the Dumpsters there. The person whirled to face me, moving with noticeable grace in the murky shadows.

At the same moment that I saw he was a young African-American man, I also saw that he was armed! I made a choked noise and staggered backward, my eyes on his—his—his . . .

"Sword?" I choked out, scared and stunned.

He looked down at the long rapier in his hand, as if surprised to find he was pointing it at me.

I backed up a little farther, wondering whether he was an underconfident mugger, an armed robber with equipment problems, or someone attempting an anachronistic gang initiation involving seventeenth-century weaponry.

"I'm not looking for trouble," I said, taking another step backward.

"Chill," he said, lowering the sword. Enough light from the streetlamps crept into the alley that I could see his tense posture relax as he released his breath. "This isn't for you."

His voice sounded cultured, his consonants well articulated. Now that I felt safe taking my eyes off the sword, I saw that he was probably in his late teens, wearing dark pants and a dark tank top, and had close-cropped hair. He was too far into the shadows for me to see his features very well, but I got the impression of a well-proportioned fellow with good bone structure.

"What are you *doing?*" I said, now that I wasn't afraid that he intended to run me through with his sword.

"Hunting," he said tersely.

"Hunting?" I had a vision of rifle-toting guys in bright orange vests tromping through the woods in search of deer. "In *Manhattan?*"

"What are *you* doing?" He had evidently taken a good look at me by now. "This is a good neighborhood. We don't want crack whores turning tricks around here."

"I'm not a crack whore," I said without rancor, since his mistake was understandable. "I'm with the TV crew that's filming on the next block."

"Filming? Oh. So that's why that street's blocked off."

"Yes."

"You're an actress?"

"Yes," I said again.

"Well, you shouldn't walk around here alone at night, miss."

"Why? Do you think I might get attacked by a guy with a sword?"

"There's dangerous shit around here," he said seriously.

"I thought you just said this is a good neighborhood."

"I don't have time to talk about it." He sounded impatient now, as if I'd interrupted him in the middle of work. "But you should go back to your people. Right now."

"My people have gone for the best fried chicken in Harlem," I said. "That's where I'm going, too."

Despite the darkness, I could see that he was shaking his head. "It's after midnight. Miss Maude's is closed by now."

"Is that on One Hundred Twenty-fifth Street?" I asked, feeling my stomach give a disappointed rumble.

"No. But it's the best fried chicken in Harlem."

"I see. But that's not where my friends are headed."

"Well, you'd better catch up to them," he said, brushing past me. "And watch your back."

"Er, what *sort* of dangerous sh . . ." But the young man's purposeful strides were already carrying him down the street in the direction from which I had just come. I watched him disappear into the night. "Okay. Never mind."

The encounter, and particularly his comments, made me a little uneasy. But, after all, he seemed pretty young, and the sword certainly suggested a love of melodrama. In fact, the street that I continued walking down now was much nicer than the street I live on in the West Thirties near Tenth Avenue. However, I kept my eyes open, just in case.

On the next block, getting closer to Mount Morris Park, I walked past beautiful turn-of-the-last-century row houses that displayed crisp, ornate stonework, freshly painted trim, and polished wooden doors in the glowing light of the streetlamps. The sidewalk was free of litter, the street was quiet, and the garbage cans that had been set out for the following morning's trash collection were arranged in tidy clusters.

My footsteps slowed when I saw a shadowy figure dart across the dark street directly ahead of me. It was much too small to be a man, so I was more curious than concerned when an identical figure followed it a second later. I frowned. A couple of children out after dark, perhaps? *Small* children, though—too small to be outside this late at night, let alone out here without adult supervision. Still walking, I glanced around the street for an accompanying adult, but I didn't see one.

Then I heard some growling up ahead of me. I wondered if the two small figures had run across the street in pursuit of a dog. If so, that didn't seem like a good idea. The growling sounded angry. Dangerous. *Vicious,* I realized.

"Dangerous shit?" I muttered.

I halted, peering ahead. The street was adequately lit for walking, but not for seeing that far away, and the figures were immersed in shadow.

Then I realized I heard *two* dogs growling. Was that what I had seen crossing the street—a couple of dogs? I had thought the figures were upright, not running on all fours . . . but the shapes had been only a faint blur in the dark, and they were indeed low to the ground, so I might easily have been mistaken.

The growling seemed to be coming from behind a cluster of garbage cans directly ahead of me. I supposed a strong scent in the garbage had attracted a couple of stray dogs, and now they were fighting over food that someone had thrown away.

Vicious dogs on the loose in this neighborhood explained the young man's warning to me. It also explained his reference to "hunting." Apparently he'd been poking around the Dumpsters in hope of encountering these dogs so he could dispatch them—though why he'd chosen a *sword* as his weapon remained a mystery.

I decided to give the snarling dogs a wide berth. I was just about to cross the street to avoid them when I heard the clatter of tumbling garbage cans. Looking in that direction again, as the growling got louder, I saw a large figure trying to rise from the ground, flickering in and out of the shadows.

I gasped as I realized that the two dogs were *attacking* the larger figure, growling furiously as they flung themselves at it. The larger figure was trying to rise, moving clumsily under the onslaught of the two growling animals. One of the dogs seized an appendage and tugged, keeping the large figure from moving freely.

As I saw it silhouetted in the faint light of the streetlamps, I realized that the appendage in question was . . . an *arm*. A human arm.

"Oh, my *God!*"

I didn't think, I just reacted. I raced down the street with a horrified shriek. When I reached the struggling human's side, I swung my purse from my shoulder and whirled its not-inconsiderable weight directly into the head of one of the attacking dogs with all my might.

In the same moment that my blow knocked the growling creature backward and off its feet, I saw that it wasn't a dog at all. It was . . .

"A *gargoyle?*" I said incredulously.

It was about three feet tall, with two arms, two legs, and a hideous, menacing face, replete with long, ugly fangs and eyes that glinted red under the streetlights. It also had pointy ears, sagging flesh that looked sickly green in this light, and extremely hairy legs. If it had genitals, I didn't see them—but, then, I wasn't looking at its crotch. I was looking at the sharp claws on its hands as it hopped to its feet with an enraged growl and reached for me.

Terrified and flooded with adrenaline, I clobbered the thing with my purse again, and it fell down again. We did this once more with feeling, and I was just starting to think the gargoyle was reassuringly stupid when it changed tactics and, instead of attacking me, now attacked my purse.

The other creature, also a gargoyle, was still struggling with the large human figure nearby. I didn't have time to take a good look, but the size, like the deep grunts and moans, confirmed that the vicious creature's victim was a man. In my peripheral vision, I could see that he was trying to get away, but was moving clumsily and staggering around in evident confusion, tugging ineffectually at the arm that the growling gargoyle clung to.

"Hit it!" I shouted at him, while I played tug-of-war for my purse with my own adversary. "Kick it!"

The creature wrestling for possession of my purse was surprisingly strong for its size. I was fighting with all my might to keep the thing from ripping my purse out of my hands as we scrabbled around on the sidewalk, circling unsteadily with it caught between us. The gargoyle's growls were rabid and enraged, and its breath was so foul I thought I'd be sick from the stench. I had a feeling that letting it scratch me with those filthy claws would be a big mistake, so when it tried to do so, I reluctantly let go of my purse and jumped back. With a foamy-mouthed shriek of triumph, the creature turned around and ran away, clutching my purse to its chest like a war trophy.

I turned to face the other gargoyle, the one that was still attacking the man staggering around the sidewalk. Remembering the ruthless boots I wore, I raised a leg and kicked the creature in the back as hard as I could, striking it mercilessly with Jilly C-Note's long, sharp heel. The creature screamed loudly in pain and rage, whirled to bare its terrifying fangs at me, and then—to my relief—also turned and ran off.

The struggling man, freed of his attacker, staggered into another garbage can and fell down.

"*Dangerous shit,*" I choked out, panting with fear and exertion.

Shaking, I found myself in a sitting position on the sidewalk without quite knowing how I'd gotten there. I stayed there for a few moments, catching my breath and trying to absorb what had just happened. Then I turned to look at the prone figure nearby. He was lying there in a heap, not moving. I crawled over to him.

"Hey, are you okay?" I said, my voice still breathless.

He moaned pathetically.

"Did they bite you?" I asked. "Or scratch you?"

Dangerous shit, indeed!

He said, "Unnng . . ."

"Jesus, what the hell *are* those things?" I said. "Do you know?"

"Ba . . . ka . . ."

"What?" I said.

"Ba . . . ka . . ." he said faintly.

The disjointed syllables meant nothing to me. They probably meant nothing, period. And that wasn't important right now, I realized. "Are you hurt?"

In response, he moaned again.

"My name is Esther Diamond," I said, trying to sound much calmer than I felt. "Can you tell me yours?"

He was a black man, tall and well-built, with a neatly trimmed beard. He looked very ill and smelled weird, but he was wearing a well-cut tuxedo, though it was a little worse for wear after his struggle.

"Your name," I said. "Tell me your name."

He seemed so dazed, I was afraid he might not *know* his name. But then he said, "Da . . ."

"Da?"

"Dari . . . Darius."

"Darius! Excellent," I said encouragingly. "Darius what?"

"Mmm . . . Ph . . . Phelps."

"Okay, Darius Phelps." Since he seemed unable to tell me whether he was hurt, I said, "I'm going to check you for injuries now. All right?"

He neither protested nor agreed. After a moment, I started my search for injuries in the obvious place: the arm that the greenish gargoyle had been attacking with such ferocity while I fought its companion.

I also *stopped* my investigation there, since I immediately saw that the hand had been torn off the wrist and was hanging by just a thin shred of flesh.

I gave a choked scream of horror. Then I tried to get control of myself so as not to alarm the wounded man.

I steeled myself to look again . . . and saw that the hand was *moving*. I uttered a sharp cry of shock and threw myself backward, flinching away from the active appendage.

Darius grunted, evidently wondering what was wrong.

I heard myself panting with panic and revulsion. My hands were shaking. My heart was pounding frantically.

Calm down, I told myself, unwilling to look at Darius' dismembered appendage again. *It's just a spasm or something. Like a chicken running around without its head.*

I needed to get help for this man. Right away!

I reached for my cell phone so I could call 911 . . . which was when I realized that my phone was in my purse, and my purse was in the clutches of a demented gargoyle.

"Shit!" I said.

No reaction from Darius. I checked to see if he was still conscious. His eyes were half-open, his dazed expression unchanged. I thought he must be in shock.

I tried to pull myself together and *think*.

My first thought was to go find a hospital or a police station.

I was already on my feet before I realized that wasn't a practical plan.

"No. A *phone*," I muttered. "I need a phone."

I turned to Darius and forced myself to speak calmly. Or at least, I tried; I probably sounded as confused and scared as I felt.

"Darius," I said loudly, "I've got to find a phone so that I can call for help. I won't go far. And as soon as I find a phone, I'll be right back by your side. In the meantime, don't try to move. That's very important, all right? *Don't move.*"

Darius moaned pathetically again, which I interpreted as acknowledgment of my instructions. I repeated that I'd be right back as soon as I found a phone.

Then I tried ringing the doorbells of a couple of nearby row houses. No one answered in the first one. In the second house, a resident shouted down from the second floor that he was calling the police.

"Yes!" I shouted back. "Call the police! A man has been hurt out here!"

"Get away from this house!" he shouted back. Which convinced me that he might not call for help after all. I rang his doorbell a few more times. No response.

Then I heard a siren wailing. It sounded like it was only a block or two away. I followed the noise, moving as fast as I could in those cruel boots, and I reached Lexington Avenue. There were a number of businesses there, but it was past midnight on a weeknight, and they were all closed. I didn't immediately see any pedestrians, either, but at least there was a modest quantity of vehicular traffic on the street.

I started trying to wave down a car, hoping I could convince someone to stop and let me use their phone.

But the cars on Lexington just kept careening past me. I was terrified that Darius would die from his wound before I got help for him, or that those vicious gargoyles would return to attack him as he lay on the sidewalk, alone and helpless. Frustrated, confused, and panicking at the prospect of Darius dying because of my failure to summon help, I waded out into traffic, boldly—or quite stupidly—trying to force cars to stop if they didn't want to be responsible for running me over.

Only later did two important things occur to me.

The first was that, considering my costume that night—which I had by then completely forgotten about—my behavior was bound to be drastically misinterpreted.

Indeed, it didn't take long for two cops in a squad car to find me. Given the way I looked, my misunderstood aggression toward the passing strangers whom I stopped, my lack of ID, the crazed things I was babbling, and the fact that, in my frustration, I struggled physically with one of the cops, the results were probably predictable: They cuffed me, arrested me, and tossed me into the squad car.

The second important thing that finally occurred to me, as I was being taken to the Twenty-fifth Precinct to be processed and locked up, was that despite the gruesome severity of Darius' injury, there had been no blood at all.

3

I was leaning against the cool bars of my jail cell in the Twenty-fifth Precinct, exhausted, angry, crazed with worry, and also plagued by a vague feeling that I should start singing the blues ... when Detective Connor Lopez entered the detention area.

He flashed his gold shield at the female cop on duty, introduced himself, and said he'd like to talk to me. She grinned and said they'd all been looking forward to his arrival. Then she announced she was taking a coffee break and tactfully left us alone. (Well, "alone" unless you count my only cell mate, who seemed to be sleeping off quite a bender.)

Lopez looked roughly the way you'd expect a guy to look after being hauled out of bed by an urgent summons in the middle of the night. His straight black hair was rumpled, he needed a shave, and there were circles under his blue eyes. He had evidently dressed in a hurry, just grabbing the first items at hand when he'd staggered out of bed: cut-offs, a faded SUNY T-shirt, and flip-flops. Oddly, the overall effect of his untidy fatigue made him look younger than his thirty-one years, more like a grad student during exam week than a police officer dragged from his bed to bust me out of stir.

He'd inherited exotic good looks from his Cuban immigrant father and clear blue eyes from his Irish-American mother. I noticed that his golden olive skin was darker than usual. Maybe he'd spent some time out at the beach this summer, or maybe he'd been helping his parents with yard work at their home in Nyack, just north of the city and across the Hudson River. Or perhaps he had taken a vacation since the last time I'd seen him. Which had been in May. When he had told me he couldn't date me anymore.

My relationship with Lopez, though short-lived and unconsummated, was complicated. So I had been *extremely* reluctant to ask him to come to my rescue tonight. By the time I had decided to do it, I was out of other feasible options.

Besides, he *had* said that if I ever needed his help, I should call him.

And this was certainly an occasion when I needed his help.

Lopez's thick-lashed gaze traveled over me now, taking in the black high-heeled boots, purple fishnet stockings, and embarrassingly short vinyl skirt. When he got to my tight, leopard-patterned top, he lingered on my well-exposed cleavage, which looked noticeably more impressive than usual; one of the things that made Jilly's costume so uncomfortable was the push-up bra beneath it.

"Eyes front, soldier," I said irritably.

His gaze shifted to my face, where Jilly's makeup was probably making me look like a tubercular raccoon by now.

"Sorry." Lopez gave my overall appearance another quick appraisal, then said, "Are you really that hard up for money?"

"Oh, don't be ridiculous," I snapped.

He smiled wearily. "I take it you got a job?"

He meant an acting job, of course. As a detective in the Organized Crime Control Bureau, as well as a personal acquaintance of mine, he presumably knew that I still waited tables regularly at Bella Stella, which had been my day job in recent months (though it mostly involved working nights). It was a famous restaurant in Little Italy that was owned by a woman with close connections to the Gambello crime family. Lopez had been involved in investigating a Mafia murder that occurred there in May. I had witnessed the hit, and the subsequent strange events surrounding that murder had ultimately led to Lopez breaking up with me—before we'd even really started a relationship.

"Yes, I got a job," I said. "A TV guest spot. One week of work."

Stella Butera, owner of Bella Stella, had given me the whole week off for *D30* without any fuss or complaint. Stella was good about letting her singing servers schedule our restaurant work around our professional opportunities, and it was one of the reasons I liked working for her.

"TV, huh?" Lopez tilted his head. "And you're playing—let me guess—a Benedictine nun?"

"Yes. I suppose the outfit gives it away," I said sourly, recalling some of the insulting comments that the arresting officers had made tonight, assuming that I was exactly what I appeared to be.

"Well, I'm glad you got work, Esther. But the sixty-four thousand dollar question is," Lopez said, "why were you wearing your hooker costume and soliciting tricks on Lexington Avenue?"

"I was *not* soliciting tr—"

"I got a call from the desk sergeant here saying—"

"I *told* them what I was doing!"

"—that a crack whore who claims to be a friend of mine was stopping cars on Lexington and reaching into the windows to grab the drivers' crotches."

"I was not grabbing crotches!"

In my agitation, my voice got loud. I shushed Lopez, stopped speaking, and glanced over my shoulder to see if I had woken the other resident of my cell, an over-weight young African-American woman who was lying on a bench and snoring loudly. She had been like that ever since I was put in here, and her tough appearance made me very reluctant to risk disturbing her.

Lopez folded his arms across his chest and leaned one well-muscled shoulder against the bars of my hold-ing cell. "One man told the cops that you tried to steal his phone."

"Well, I did do that," I admitted in a subdued voice.

He sighed wearily and ran a hand over his face. "I as-sume there's a perfectly logical explanation for all this, Esther?"

"I got you out of bed, didn't I?" I said with regret.

"Nah, I was out shooting hoops when my phone rang in the middle of the night."

"I'm really sorry about this."

"What the hell were you *doing?*" he said.

The mingled exasperation, bewilderment, and concern in his tone were all too familiar to me. It was the essence of why he wouldn't date me: He thought I was crazy and possibly felonious. And although that was completely inaccurate, he nonetheless had some justification for thinking it. Moreover, I had to admit that involvement with me seemed to be bad for him. In order to protect me on previous occasions, he had done things that vio-lated his better judgment, his duty, and his honor—such as concealing evidence in a homicide investigation, lying to his superiors, and filing false reports. Lopez didn't like the choices he had made to shield me, and he was afraid he'd make more of them if we remained involved.

And now I was going to ask him to get the charges against me dropped and expunged. They were bogus charges, of course; but it was still a lot to ask, all things considered.

I said to him, "Look, you're the last person in the world that I wanted to drag into this. And I swear to you, I really tried *not* to."

"Oh, I'm glad you called. I wouldn't have missed your outfit tonight for the world. But the desk sergeant here must lead a sheltered life." Lopez's gaze dropped to my cleavage again. "You look *way* too healthy to be a crack whore." After a moment, he met my eyes again and smiled as he added, "But much too obvious to be an escort, of course."

"Perhaps we could discuss my character's position in the hierarchy of the oldest profession *after* you get me out of here?"

"Ah. Which brings us to the point." There was a little regret in his expression as he said, "If you want me to get you out of this, then your story had better be damn good."

"Why?" My gaze flickered anxiously to the door. The night-shift cops of the Two-Five were somewhere on the other side of it. "Are they going to be difficult?"

"No, *I'm* going to be difficult, Esther," he said irritably. "You got picked up while playing in traffic in Harlem in the middle of the night, dressed like a hooker and acting like a lunatic. And it's going to take a really good explanation to convince me that arraignment, remand, and a psych evaluation aren't the best things for you."

"What?" I gripped the bars. "No!"

My cell mate grumbled in her sleep and rolled over.

"Shh," I said to Lopez.

"I'm not the one raising my voice," he pointed out.

"Lopez, you've got to get me out of here," I said desperately. "And you've got to get them to delete any record of my arrest! I don't want it on my record. I don't want a record at *all.*"

"Start talking," he said implacably.

"First things first," I said. "*Please* get them to send a squad car to look for this guy I found tonight. He's severely injured."

"They sent a car, Esther. There's no sign of the man you described."

"What?" I frowned. "That's not possible! Darius was hurt too badly to get up and walk away. The cops must have looked in the wrong place."

"No, they looked in the right place."

"How do you know?"

"The two cops who went over there to check it out, in response to your story, turned on their cherry top—"

"Their what?"

"Uh, the red light on the roof."

"Oh."

"And that attracted the attention of a resident who came downstairs to ask if they were looking for the drunk hooker who'd been ringing his doorbell and shouting up at him a little after midnight."

"I wasn't drunk," I said wearily.

"So that sounds like the right place?"

"Yes. But Darius must have crawled into a doorway or something. He couldn't have gone far. The cops just didn't look hard enough."

"They were thorough, Esther," Lopez said patiently.

"They didn't even believe me!"

"No, they didn't," he agreed. "But it's a slow night, and you claimed you saw a man who'd been, er, attacked and maimed, which is serious stuff. So, just in case you're not quite as insane as you seem, they decided to be thorough."

I looked at him suspiciously. "You didn't waltz right in here as soon as you arrived. You talked to the cops out there first, didn't you?"

"Uh-huh."

Shit. While waiting for Lopez to get here, I had planned what to tell him: a version of the night's events that was close to the truth, but a tad more plausible.

He lifted one brow. "A man with a sword? A severed hand? *Gargoyles?*"

Too late now.

"That's what I saw," I said defensively.

"Sadly, I don't find it hard to believe that's what you *think* you saw," Lopez said. "Which is why I'm not so sure that getting you out of here is such a good idea."

I tried to control my frustration and focus on the most important thing. "Fine, let's forget about that for a minute. But, please, you've got to get them to find Darius."

"Esther, he's not there," Lopez said firmly.

"Then check the local hospitals. Maybe—"

"He's not at a hospital, either."

"How do you know?"

"We'll talk about that in a minute. For now—"

"But—"

"For *now*," he said, "I want you to tell me what happened. As clearly and rationally as you can."

"All right." I took a breath and tried to calm down. "That's fair."

"Glad you think so."

I started by explaining that a lead actor had fallen ill on the set tonight, which disrupted the shoot.

"Where were you filming?"

"East of Mount Morris Park."

"Did you tell the cops this?"

"I tried, when they were booking me." I shrugged and admitted, "But by then, they seemed so convinced I was crazy, I gave up before long and just asked for my phone call."

"It's not that I don't appreciate you thinking of *me* when you're locked up for being a demented hooker," he said, "but I'm wondering why you didn't just call the set and ask them to come confirm that you are who you say you are."

"All the phone numbers I need are in my purse, which was stolen before I was arrested. And I'm just a guest performer, so I don't even know most of the people's full names. When the cops let me have a phone book, the only number I could find was the show's regular production office. And when I called it, all I got was an answering machine. The office staff isn't there at two o'clock in the morning. Go figure." I sighed. "Next, I called my agent's cell, thinking he could come here and straighten this out. But he didn't answer, either."

I rested my head against the bars for a moment, feeling depressed. "I was supposed to be back on the set hours ago. They've got no idea where I am. I'm in *so* much trouble." I would be very lucky if the producers didn't fire me.

After a moment of silence, Lopez put his hand on mine and squeezed sympathetically. He knew how important my work was to me.

"What's the show?" he asked, trying to be nice.

"The Dirty Thirty."

He flinched and removed his hand. "I *hate* that show."

"It's a really good script," I said morosely, still thinking about how I was bound to be fired. And probably banned from all *Crime and Punishment* sets. "I play a homeless bisexual junkie prostitute being blackmailed for sex and information by a corrupt cop."

"Whatever," Lopez said sourly.

"I mean, that's what I'm playing *if* I've still got a job now."

"So some actor on a totally fabricated, insulting, bullshit TV show," he said, "got sick on your location shoot. They sent for a doctor, and filming came to a halt. What happened then?"

"Oh. Well . . ." I continued my story, explaining how I had wound up walking through the neighborhood alone in the dark in my costume, and what had happened next.

Lopez said, "And this guy had a *sword?*"

"Specifically, a rapier."

"How do you know that?"

"Because I'm an actress. The rapier was a common weapon in the sixteenth and seventeenth centuries, and it's used in the plays of that period."

"Did he threaten you with it?"

"Not really," I said.

"What does 'not really' mean?"

I explained that I had startled the young man, who lowered his sword as soon as he recovered from his surprise. I recounted our conversation, his departure, and what happened next.

"And this is when you saw the gargoyles?"

"Could we not focus on that?" I said irritably. "The *important* point is that I saw this man being attacked. And maimed." I continued my story.

Lopez soon interrupted to say, "The man was wearing a *tuxedo?*"

"Yes." Seeing that he was looking at me as if this required an explanation, I said, "What's so strange about that?"

He shrugged. "It just seems a little odd. Never mind. So this man . . ." Lopez's tone concealed something. I wasn't sure what. "He told you his name was . . ."

"Darius," I said. "Darius Phelps."

"You're sure?"

"Yes." Since he just kept looking at me, I asked, "Why?"

"Besides the tux, what did he look like?"

I described Darius.

Lopez lowered black lashes over blue eyes and stood

there silently for a few moments. He seemed to be thinking.

Finally, he said, "So you saw him being attacked. Go on."

I described the scene that ensued. And since Lopez already knew I thought the attacking creatures looked like gargoyles, I decided not to waste any time or energy prevaricating about that.

"Wait, you did *what?*" he said.

Caught up in my description of the struggle with the growling, befanged thing that had *stolen my purse*, by the way—"And is anyone here doing anything about *that?* Hah!"—I was taken by surprise when Lopez suddenly slipped his arms through the bars of my cage and slid his hands around my waist.

He drew me as close to his body as the cell bars would allow, rested his forehead against mine, and closed his eyes. "You saw a stranger being attacked on the street at night, and you jumped in to help him?"

"Well, um . . ." It felt so good to be touched by him. So good to feel the warmth of his skin and the soft tickle of his breath on my cheek. I had tried—with varying degrees of failure—not to think about this since he had broken up with me. And it was the last thing I had expected to experience tonight, given the circumstances.

"Esther, that's . . . dangerous," he said quietly.

I tried to snuggle closer, frustrated by the iron bars between us. "More dangerous for Darius than for me, as it turned out."

"Listen to me," he said, his hands moving from my waist to my forearms, stroking my flesh. "I'm very serious about this. When you see something happening—something like that, I mean—it's much better to call nine-one-one than to go diving in like that. Do you understand?"

"Nine-one-one!" I pulled away just enough to meet his gaze.

"Yes." He touched my cheek. "I know you want to help people, but—"

"No, I mean, that's why I ran out to Lexington Avenue and, er, bothered people. Darius was severely injured, and that creature had stolen my phone, which was in my purse. I was trying to find a phone to call for help!"

His expression cleared. "So that's why you were wandering in traffic on Lexington?"

"Yes," I said with relief, realizing it actually sounded sensible this time around, now that I was explaining it with relative calm to someone who didn't think I was a violent crack whore. "No one would stop to help me. Because of the way I'm dressed, of course—but I was so freaked out by what had just happened and so focused on getting help for this guy, I totally forgot about what I look like tonight. So I got desperate. And then the first person I stopped was so abusive, it kind of sent me over the edge. The next driver who stopped wanted me to, um, gratify him—"

"What?" Lopez's spine went stiff.

"I notice that *he* didn't stick around to complain to the cops," I said. "The next one after that is probably the guy who claimed I was grabbing his crotch."

"You were trying to grab his phone," Lopez guessed.

I nodded. "And I did try to steal the next person's phone—he was actually a pedestrian, not a driver—because I was frantic by then. But then the cops arrived, and, well . . ." I sighed and let my shoulders sag a little. "I wasn't coherent or courteous, I have to admit."

"And since you looked like a hooker and had no ID . . ."

"It didn't go well." I shook my head, recalling the ludicrous scene. "Anyhow, then they brought me here and they booked me. And when I was finally allowed to make a phone call . . ." I shrugged. "After my calls to the *Dirty Thirty* production office and to Thack didn't get me anywhere—"

"Thack?"

"My agent," I said. "Thackeray Shackleton."

"That can't be his real name," Lopez said.

"I have no idea. Anyhow, then I phoned . . . um . . ." I stopped awkwardly.

He looked puzzled for a moment, then made an exasperated sound, released his hold on me, and stepped away from the bars of my jail cell. "You called Max," he said in resignation.

"Yes. I called Max." And, I realized irritably, I had no *reason* to feel awkward about that. Max was a trusted friend who had saved my life. The fact that Lopez mistakenly thought he was demented, dangerous, and probably drugging me was one of the sources of tension between us. But since Lopez wasn't dating me anymore, I owed him no explanations about my friendship with Max. "But Max has only got one phone, and it's in the bookstore, on the main floor. At this time of night, he's probably upstairs and asleep, like everyone else. So he didn't answer." The other possibility was that Max was in the cellar beneath the bookstore, working in his laboratory all night long, as he sometimes did; he wouldn't hear the phone down there, either.

I said, "So, you see, I really did try to avoid dragging you into this. But I didn't know who else to call. And the last time that I saw you . . ." Which had been at the funeral of an evil Catholic priest who'd used his supernatural powers to commit murders and to try to start a mob war, and who had messily killed himself when his vicious scheme was thwarted.

"I said I wanted you to call me if you ever needed my help." Lopez sighed and nodded. "And I meant it, Esther. God help me."

"But I don't know your number by heart." I hardly knew any numbers by heart; and I hadn't had occasion to dial Lopez's number in well over two months, after all. "And you're not listed. I knew the cops here could get your phone number, of course. But they wouldn't give it to me."

"Go figure."

"So I asked them to call you."

"And that was the icing on the cake. They thought that was hilarious. A cop involved with the crazy hooker in their tank." He smiled wryly. "It's like an episode of *The Dirty Thirty*."

"Sorry."

He waved aside my apology. "Look, all things considered, you did the right thing, calling me tonight."

"Does that mean you're going to get me out of here?" I asked hopefully.

He didn't seem to hear me. He frowned suddenly and murmured, "An episode of *The Dirty* . . ." His voice trailed off and he stood there silent and motionless, a faint frown on his face, staring off into space. Thinking again. Piecing together things scattered in his head and making a coherent pattern with them.

After a moment, still frowning slightly at something I couldn't see, he said, "You're sure you told the cops here that you're with the production that's filming near here tonight?"

"Of course I'm sure," I said. "I was trying not to be charged, after all."

"Did you tell them what the production was?"

I thought back. "No, I don't think so. I was more focused on trying to convince them to send help for Darius."

Lopez shook his head and murmured, "But they must have known. It's their precinct. Of *course* they knew."

"Knew what?" I said.

He looked at me, his gaze clear now. "That the production filming in their precinct tonight is *The Dirty Thirty*."

I frowned. "So?"

"So that's a strikingly strange story that you're tell-ing, Esther," he said. "A guy with a sword uttering vague warnings. A couple of *gargoyles* attacking a man in a tuxedo. A severed hand . . ." He shook his head. "My guess is that you got caught in the middle of an elabo-rate practical joke."

"What?"

"And since you were alone in the dark in an un-familiar neighborhood, your imagination helped it along." He paused before adding, "You do have a vivid imagination."

"But why would anyone play such a gruesome practi-cal joke on me?"

"I doubt it was intended for you. It may not even have been intended for anyone in particular."

"I don't understand. Why would—" I gasped as I re-alized what he was thinking. "You think cops were play-ing a joke on *The Dirty Thirty* tonight? On the crew or cast members?"

"I'd say that it seems more likely than a young man in Harlem hunting man-eating gargoyles with a sword." He shrugged. "Don't underestimate how much cops hate that show."

"I heard there'd been some unpleasant incidents last year, but no one mentioned anything this . . . *creative*." I frowned. "So you think the cops who arrested me were part of it?"

"Maybe. Or maybe they just came to the same con-clusion after running Darius Phelps' name through the system." He shook his head. "I was pretty thrown by that, but since a prank has occurred to me, it's probably occurred to them, too."

"Thrown by *what?*"

"You supposedly saw a walking corpse." He looked at me. "A Harlem resident named Darius Phelps, exactly fitting the description you gave, died three weeks ago."

4

To my relief, Lopez made my arrest go away, as if it had never happened. The cops of the Two-Five released me with far more merriment than contrition; but since they were letting me *go*, I didn't care.

I decided against reporting the theft of my purse, partly to spare Lopez more embarrassment (I shrewdly sensed that my description of the assailant would cause further amusement on the night shift), and partly because I was so eager to get back to the set of *D30* right away and find out whether I still had a job. I was also skeptical that filing a report would improve my chances of getting the purse back, all things considered.

Lopez escorted me outside the precinct house, where a patrol car waited to drive me home; this was apparently the NYPD's idea of fair compensation for imprisoning me. A young black cop in uniform was leaning against the driver's door of the waiting vehicle. He straightened up as I approached, opened the rear door for me, and introduced himself as Officer Thompson.

When I asked to be taken to the place where I'd first begun my long night, though, he shook his head.

"If you're going to that film set, Miss Diamond, you're too late," Officer Thompson said.

"Pardon?"

"Yeah, they shut down and packed up a couple of hours ago."

"What?" I cried.

Thompson nodded. "They're gone."

Because I was missing! Because I'd gone AWOL! Because they couldn't keep filming without me!

"Oh, *noooo!*" I leaned against the squad car, wearily rested my face against my forearm in bitter defeat, and drummed my fist on the vehicle's roof. "I'll never work again!"

I heard Thompson say doubtfully to Lopez, "Are you *sure* you want to spring her, detective?"

"Not really," Lopez replied. "So what happened? Did the film set get rampaged by gargoyles and a guy with a sword?"

"What *happened?*" I said, my voice muffled by my arm. "They couldn't find me! *That's* what happened!"

Thompson said, "That guy had a heart attack."

"What guy?" Lopez said.

"That actor."

"Actor?" I lifted my head. "*What* actor?"

"Uh . . . Nolan something."

"Michael Nolan?" I straightened up and looked at Officer Thompson.

"Right! That was the name. Michael Nolan."

"Nolan had a heart attack?" I said sharply. "*That's* why they shut down production?"

"Yes, ma'am. I guess he's the star or something. So they couldn't keep filming without him."

"Oh, my God!" I said. "Nolan had a *heart attack?*"

The young cop nodded. "Uh-huh."

"A heart attack!" I punched the air in triumph as I gleefully shouted, *"Yes!"*

Given the chaos and anxiety that would undoubtedly ensue when the show's lead actor had a coronary while on location, the director and the production team might not even have realized that I was missing! And, in any case, my prolonged absence tonight had made no difference to the shooting schedule and wouldn't get me fired!

I am not a religious person, but I threw my arms up and looked skyward. "Thank you! Thank you! Thank you!"

Then I smiled exultantly at Lopez and Officer Thompson.

They were both looking at me as if I had just urinated on the steps of the precinct house.

"What?" I said to them.

Thompson glanced uncertainly at Lopez, who was still frowning at me. I suddenly realized why.

"Oh! Uh . . . Is Nolan alive?" I asked politely.

"Yes," said Thompson, still giving me a peculiar look. "I guess they called in a medic right away. And since this happened only a few blocks away from North General, they got him to the ER fast. Even though he kept saying he wanted to go to Mount Sinai, not to—you know— some *Harlem* hospital." Thompson smiled and added, "My buddy was at the scene when they were loading Nolan into the ambulance. I hear that actor's got a mouth on him that would make a gangsta blush."

"So that must be what was wrong with him," I said, recalling Nolan's behavior on the set that night. "He was red as a beet and too hot, then nauseated, then he was dizzy, then white as a sheet, then he threw up . . ." The siren I had heard while seeking help for Darius might even have been the ambulance that was taking Nolan to the nearby hospital.

"Yep, heart attack," said Thompson. "Happens that way sometimes. But they probably caught it early enough that he'll be okay."

"Not that you seem all that worried about him," Lopez said to me.

"Oh, give me a break," I said. "I've had a rough night.

Anyhow, if you knew Nolan, you wouldn't be all that worried about him, either. Besides, Officer Thompson says he'll be fine. Right?"

"Well, who knows?" said the young cop. "A heart attack can be a scary thing, even if it's not too severe. My dad took early retirement after he had his. So maybe Mr. Nolan will decide to slow down after this. Give up acting. Quit the show. And without its star, maybe *The Dirty Thirty* will be canceled."

"Wishful thinking," Lopez said morosely.

"God, I hate that show," said Thompson.

"Did you guys know *that* was the show that was filming around here tonight?" Lopez asked casually, as if commiserating.

I recalled his theory that I'd been the victim of an elaborate prank.

"Sure, we knew. They don't go to the Three-Oh anymore, but they still come here." Thompson snorted. "*Television* people." He blinked and added, "But I swear, detective, we didn't think your girlfriend was one of *them*. We all thought she was just a crazy hooker. God's honest truth."

"Of course," Lopez said wearily.

I said, "I'd like to leave now."

"My partner and I will take you home, Miss Diamond," Thompson said.

"No, not home," I said.

Lopez gave me a suspicious look. "Where are you going?"

"I have to go look for . . . for someone."

Lopez's gaze locked with mine. I could see him trying to decide whether it was even worth arguing with me, and whether he could trust me if I gave in and agreed to go straight home and stay there. He came to the inevitable conclusion, sighed, and said, "All right. Fine. I'm coming with you."

"You don't have to—"

"It's the middle of the night, Esther." He shoved me none too gently into the back of the squad car and got in beside me. "And you've already been arrested once in that outfit. As well as attacked."

"Darius was the one who was attacked. I just—"

"Whatever."

As Officer Thompson and his partner—a slightly chubby white man whose name I didn't catch—got into the front of the car, Lopez motioned for me to tell them where to take us.

When I did, though, the two cops in the front seat balked.

"Miss Diamond, we're the ones who searched that area after you were picked up. Your friend isn't there."

"He's not my friend," I said. "And I need to see for myself."

"But, ma'am, there's no—"

"Let's go," Lopez said firmly.

He was wearing shorts and flip-flops, and he was from outside the precinct, but he outranked them, and he spoke with authority. The cops shut up, and the squad car pulled away from the curb.

"Thank you," I said quietly to Lopez.

I heard him mutter, "I don't even get sex for this."

"You'd have to *date* me for that," I snapped.

"Huh?" He looked at me in surprise. "Oh. Sorry. Tired. Didn't realize I was talking out loud."

"Hmph."

I folded my arms and stared out the window while we rode the few blocks between the station house and the dark sidewalk where I had last seen Darius, not far from Mount Morris Park. Since the streets were practically empty, it took almost no time to get there. As we approached, I recognized the spot and said, "This is it! I'll get out here."

"We'll get out here," Lopez said.

"We'll *all* get out here," Officer Thompson said, bringing the car to a halt. "My orders were clear, detective. I am to make sure Miss Diamond departs this precinct. So I can't leave her here."

"Great," Lopez said to me as he nudged me out of the car. "Now there's a whole precinct that doesn't want you."

Ignoring him, I exited the car, frowning as I examined the site. "These garbage cans were all tumbled over when I left here."

Thompson's plump partner said, "We straightened them when we were looking for the dead guy." When we all looked at him, he added, "Darius Phelps."

While the cops hung around the squad car looking bored, I showed Lopez where Darius had been lying when I went to get help.

"You're sure this was the spot?" he said.

"Positive."

He glanced over his shoulder at the cops, then said quietly to me, "Then you didn't see a severed hand."

"I did," I insisted.

"Not a real one." Still keeping his voice low, he said, "It was only a few hours ago. If you saw a real dismemberment here, there would still be blood all over the sidewalk. It would be dry by now, but there'd be a lot of it."

"Oh." I blinked in surprise, suddenly remembering the absence of blood as I had gazed at the terrible injury. *"Oh."*

"You see my point?"

"Yes." I lowered my voice, too. "But I'm telling you, those gargoyles were real. I fought with one of them."

"It sounds like a very good costume worn by someone chosen—maybe even hired—for their size."

I looked at him. "You mean a little person?"

"Could be. I think the staging sounds too elaborate

to have involved young children." He continued reasonably, "It was dark. You were startled and scared. You'd already had an ominous warning from the guy with the sword. Everything happened fast. So you saw what someone wanted you to see. What the whole scene was orchestrated for you to see."

"A prank . . ." I mused. Lopez was making it sound very plausible.

"A well-executed one." He gestured subtly to the cops waiting by the squad car. "Thompson didn't sound too happy about *The Dirty Thirty* filming here. Maybe some of the guys in this precinct decided to discourage the show from doing more location filming here. Or maybe someone else is messing with the show, and the cops are just willing to look the other way." He paused before saying, "Anyhow, whatever the original plan for tonight was, it probably went off course when filming stopped unexpectedly after Nolan collapsed and you all started leaving the location."

"So these various, er, people that I encountered . . . You think they were improvising? Trying to squeeze something out of the evening, so to speak?"

"Probably."

"But why use a dead man's name?"

Lopez shrugged. "Maybe it was supposed to be the punch line: You report what you saw, you find out the 'wounded' man has been dead for weeks, and you realize you've been had."

"Hilarious," I said sourly.

"But, of course," he said, "they didn't count on their victim getting arrested, which put yet another kink in whatever the original plan was."

"Hmm." I thought over the whole episode. "You could be right."

He sensed my lingering doubt. "But?"

"But Darius—or whoever he was—seemed genuinely injured. Or disoriented. Or *something*. Not at all well, anyhow. And the attack on him seemed so vicious! So genuine."

"You of all people should know that disorientation, injury, and vicious attacks can be convincingly simulated," he pointed out. "Haven't you 'died' onstage?"

"Well, yes . . ."

He was making a valid argument. I supposed that the pranksters' violent interaction with an unwitting, unrehearsed audience member—*me*—was also a feasible part of the theory. After all, participatory murder mystery weekends, where actors following a plot interacted with paying guests who didn't even *know* the plot, were a popular form of entertainment. And despite my own perception that I'd been in real danger when fighting the gargoyles, I hadn't been hurt at all—just scared.

I looked at Lopez, feeling a little embarrassed now. "I guess I really got played, huh?"

He smiled and smoothed a strand of hair away from my shoulder. "Well, it sounds like they put on a hell of a show."

"It was so *real*," I murmured. Even now, I couldn't shake off my shocked fear upon confronting those growling gargoyles, or my horrified panic upon seeing Darius' severed hand.

After a moment, Lopez asked, "Can I take you home now?"

I nodded and turned toward the squad car as he took my elbow. But after a few steps, I halted, recalling Darius' prone, helpless body and his dazed voice. I closed my eyes, struggled with myself briefly, then gave a sigh and let my shoulders sag.

"I'm sorry," I said. "I can't go. Not yet. I have to . . ."

"You want to look around for him?" Lopez guessed.

"Yes." I said again, "I'm sorry."

"It's all right," he said. "This was upsetting for you. If

searching the area will make you feel better, then that's what we'll do."

"Thanks."

He gave my arm a gentle squeeze, then told the two cops that we were going to have a look around. They declined to assist us.

I started walking down the dark street, with Lopez at my side, looking in every stairwell, poking around every garbage can, and peering under several SUVs, as if I might find Darius' large frame concealed there. Rather than merely watching me, my companion looked in stairwells and under SUVs, too.

Given the various strange problems that had beset our short-lived relationship, Lopez was so often exasperated with me that I sometimes forget that patience was actually one of his virtues. He was obviously convinced there was nothing here to find, but nonetheless willing to poke around the dark street as long as it would take for me to feel more comfortable with the bizarre images that the night's events had inflicted on me.

And considering how rattled I still was, I appreciated his calming presence.

Lopez and I had first met when he was a precinct detective handling a missing persons case; Golly Gee, a surgically-enhanced, D-list pop star had vanished in the middle of an off-Broadway musical that I was in.

During those events, I had also met Dr. Maximillian Zadok for the first time. Max was Manhattan's resident mage and local representative of the Magnum Collegium—a secret, worldwide organization dedicated to fighting Evil. (Yes, Evil.)

The circumstances of Golly Gee's disappearance were deeply weird—and the ultimate explanation for her disappearance even weirder. Eventually, Max saved half a dozen lives—including mine—by defeating the

demented sorcerer who was causing a series of supernatural disappearances throughout New York City.

As one might suppose, those events drastically al-
tered my previously mundane worldview.

Lopez, however, thought Max's theories about the
case were crazy. He also thought that *I* was crazy—or at
least alarmingly gullible—for believing those theories.

A lot had happened since then (such as Max and I
subsequently getting involved in a series of supernatural
mob slayings in Little Italy shortly after Lopez was trans-
ferred to the Organized Crime Control Bureau), but one
thing remained constant: Lopez thought that Max was
dangerous—especially to *me*—and that I might be insane.

This had put quite a damper on our abortive attempt
to have a relationship.

Meanwhile, when I say that Max "defeated" the sorcerer who had tried to make me, Golly Gee, and a number of other performers vanish in a permanent and fatal
way, I mean that Max killed him. And I helped.

This was something that I was perpetually anxious to
keep secret from Lopez.

In fact, what Max had done to Hieronymus, the demented sorcerer (and, incidentally, Max's apprentice),
was actually "dissolution," not murder; but since Hieronymus' life was over, either way, I tended to view that
distinction as being theoretical rather than—oh, for
example—*legal*.

There was also no denying that, while more recently
trying to avert a mystically-manipulated mob war in Little Italy, I had said and done some very strange things.
In context, those things made perfect sense—that's my
story and I'm sticking to it. But since Lopez didn't accept the context, he simply thought Max and I were . . .
well, *lunatics*.

So, all things considered, it was pretty nice of him to

humor me tonight—after I had dragged him out of bed, embarrassed him with other cops, and told him such a bizarre tale—by searching a darkened street in Harlem in the middle of the night for a body or some other evidence that he was certain didn't exist.

Despite the haunting images in my mind, I was also starting to doubt there was anything to find. I was just beginning to entertain the idea of telling Lopez I was ready to quit when I rounded the bumper of a car and startled a small flock of birds that were gathered near the vehicle's curbside front wheel. I flinched and made a sound halfway between a gasp and a shriek as they cawed and flew away in a noisy flutter of black wings that gleamed darkly under the streetlights.

Lopez quickly rounded the other end of the car to see what had frightened me. "What it is?"

"Nothing." I put a hand over my pounding heart as I looked down at the spot the birds had just vacated. Feeling silly, I added, "Some birds. Crows, I think. They were eating something."

Lopez was standing on the sidewalk staring at the same spot. "Eating . . . something."

The peculiar tone of his voice made me take a closer look at the small, inert object lying in the dark shadows. I leaned over, trying to see it better.

He stepped forward. "No, don't."

The instant I recognized the object, I screamed.

Lopez pulled me away from the sight of Darius' severed hand, mangled by carrion feeders, lying on the sidewalk. He pressed my face against his shoulder as he turned his head and shouted, "Thompson! Over here! And bring a flashlight."

Shuddering with revulsion, I tried to get control of my frantic breathing as I heard footsteps approach us.

"Find something, detective?" It was Thompson's voice.

"Look." Lopez tightened his hold on me and added, "Not you," as I reflexively moved to look again at the *thing* lying on the sidewalk.

I squeezed my eyes shut and kept my face pressed against his shoulder as one of the cops drew in a sharp breath and the other let out a startled exclamation.

Lopez said coldly to them, "You're the ones who searched this area?"

"Uh . . ."

"Um."

"Nice job, officers," Lopez said.

"Hey, detective," Thompson protested, "we were looking for a *body*. Or an injured guy."

"And that makes it okay that you overlooked a *severed hand* lying on the sidewalk?" Lopez said.

"Well, er—"

"A severed hand that I believe Miss Diamond mentioned in the statement that she gave after being arrested for trying to get help for the victim?"

Even *I* winced at his tone now.

"Look, detective, we . . . um . . ."

"Call it in," Lopez snapped. "And you can thank your lucky stars that Miss Diamond isn't going to make your precinct's mess any bigger by filing a complaint about tonight."

"I'm not?" I said against his shoulder.

He goosed me to make me shut up. "I'm taking her back to Lexington to find a cab."

I lifted my head. "I can't take a cab. I don't have any money."

Thompson said, "We can call another squad car to take her home."

The chubby cop said, "So do we need to search the area *again* for the dead guy? Um, the injured guy, I mean?"

"Everyone *shut up*," Lopez said.

We all felt silent. Pressed up against his body, I felt him take a deep breath as he struggled to control his temper.

"You're not looking for an injured man," Lopez said with forced patience.

"We're not?"

"Take a good look at that hand. It wasn't recently attached to anyone *living*."

"Oh?" Thompson said.

I looked up to see the young cop bending over the hand, studying it curiously as he trained his flashlight on it.

His partner stood a few feet away and squinted at the appendage, clearly reluctant to get any closer to it. I suspected that squeamishness was a bit of a handicap in his profession.

Lopez continued, "And if a hand *had* been torn off someone's arm here, there would be blood. Plenty of it."

"Oh. Right," said the chubby cop. "I knew that."

Thompson squatted down to get an even better look at the hand. "So you're saying this came off a corpse?"

"Yes," Lopez said.

"Hmm. Any idea how old?"

"Probably a few days. Less than a few weeks."

"How can you tell?" Thompson asked curiously. "Especially now that it's partly eaten?"

The other cop made a sound.

"No decomposition," Lopez said. "It looks fresh, and it doesn't stink."

I swallowed my revulsion.

Still absorbed in his study of the mangled body part, Thompson said, "But what if—"

"Call it in," Lopez ordered again. "I'm going to put Miss Diamond in a cab, and then I'll be back." He added, "*Right* back."

The chubby cop said, "But we might need her statement."

"You've *got* her statement," Lopez said tersely, turning me away from the scene. "Let's go."

As soon as we were out of earshot, I said to him, "So I *did* see . . . see . . . Uh, *what* did I see?"

With his arm around me as he hustled me toward Lexington Avenue, he said, "You saw exactly what we talked about. Only whoever pulled this stunt went way too far."

"Well, *yeah*," I said. "They stole my purse!"

"They also desecrated a corpse."

"Desecrated . . . Oh!" I realized what he was saying. "That hand! It was real. And it was from . . . from . . ."

"From someone's body." His voice was tense.

"Oh, *yuck*," I said with feeling.

"So where the hell is the rest of that person?" He sounded as if he was thinking aloud. "And who is it?"

"*Was*, you mean?"

"Was," he agreed.

"Do you think some jerk raided the morgue to add a disgusting touch of reality to this whole thing?"

"That's one of the possibilities."

"You really think some cops did this?" I asked, appalled now.

He shook his head. "I sure hope not. Scaring a woman alone in the dark and then stealing her purse was bad enough. But snatching body parts? And leaving a severed hand lying around on the sidewalk where any neighborhood kid might have found it in the morning, if you hadn't insisted on searching the area now?" He said grimly, "There had better *not* be any cops involved."

But now it bothered him, and he had to know for sure. So he was going to go back to where we'd found the severed hand and work the crime scene, whether or not the local cops wanted him there.

Given the late (or very early) hour, we had to wait a couple of minutes on the corner of Lexington before we saw a cab. I was exhausted, and Lopez was preoccupied, so we didn't talk. Then, in response to Lopez's wave, a cab pulled up to take me home. The driver smirked when he saw Lopez hand me twenty dollars, which made me realize once again how I was dressed.

Lopez kissed me absently on the cheek and told me to go home and go to bed. "I'll take care of this. And I'll let you know if I find your purse. Okay?"

"Okay."

I got into the cab. And he returned to the scene of the crime. Which is how he got involved.

So if I hadn't called Lopez to come get me out of jail, then Baron Samedi, the Lord of Death, wouldn't have come looking for him on the dark, windswept night of thunder, terror, and angry spirits that would soon follow.

5

I awoke to the pain of a stiff neck, the irritation of light in my eyes, and the revulsion of a huge canine tongue washing my face.

I opened my mouth to protest against all of these sensations—and immediately had to spit out Nelli's tongue, which was still sweeping across my face.

"Ugh! *Blegh!*" I sat bolt upright, wiping my face in disgust and shoving at the dog. "Stop that!"

Nelli panted cheerfully, happy to see me awake. Her long, thick, bony tail wagged back and forth with reckless abandon. Given its size, density, and current speed, it could probably bring down a sapling. Or kill a gargoyle.

"Is she awake, Nelli?" Max called from the back of bookshop.

Nelli gave a little crooning bark, then swiped her paw at me affectionately.

"Ow!" I looked down at the broad red marks she had just made on my forearm. "Your nails need cutting."

Nelli was Max's mystical familiar. She had emerged from another dimension in response to his summons for assistance in fighting Evil. Max had been in dire need of help, since (brace yourself for a shock) New York City was proving to be a busy battleground between the forces of light and darkness; and Max's previous assistant, the apprentice Hieronymus, hadn't really worked out so well—what with being the maniacal, murderous summoner of a virgin-raping, people-eating demon and all.

I wondered if the daunting size of her mission accounted for Nelli's own daunting size; because apart from whatever advantage her physique might give her in combating mystical forces, she was an inconveniently *large* animal to keep in Manhattan. Easily as big as a Shetland pony, Nelli was well-muscled beneath her short, smooth, tan fur. Her massive head was long and square-jawed, and her teeth were so big they might look terrifying if the immense size of her floppy ears wasn't such a distraction from them. Her paws—which, like her face, were darker in color than the rest of her—were each nearly the size and density of a baseball bat, and the skin of her feet was as rough as coarse sandpaper.

Nelli's long, pink tongue hung out of her mouth as she gazed at me with uncomplicated good cheer.

"Max?" I croaked sleepily.

"Coming!"

It was morning. I was in Max's establishment, Zadok's Rare and Used Books, which was in a townhouse on a side street in Greenwich Village. After coming here in the wee hours, I had fallen asleep in one of the prettily-upholstered chairs in the reading area near the fireplace.

The shop had well-worn hardwood floors, a broad-beamed ceiling, dusky-rose walls, and rows and rows of tall bookcases overflowing with volumes about all aspects of the occult. Some of the books were modern paperbacks, many were old hardback volumes that smelled musty, a few were rare leather-bound books of considerable value, and they were all printed in a wide variety of languages.

The bookstore had a small customer base and got some foot traffic from curious passersby, but it was basically just a modest beard for Max's real work—protecting New York and its inhabitants from Evil—so he didn't concentrate on increasing its revenue. Meanwhile, I didn't know whether he had invested wisely over his long (*very* long) life or whether the Magnum Collegium, which had sent him here, paid him well. Either way, Max always seemed to have a healthy cash flow.

He thoughtfully kept a small refreshments station in the bookstore, stocked with coffee, tea, cookies, and snuff (yes, snuff) for his customers. It sat near a large, careworn walnut table with books, papers, an abacus, writing implements, and other paraphernalia on it. I was about to haul myself out of that chair—which was comfortable for sitting and reading, but which had not been designed for sleeping—and make a pot of coffee when Max ambled around the corner of a bookcase and greeted me. He was carrying a breakfast tray.

"Good morning! When Nelli and I came downstairs and found you here, sound asleep, I thought perhaps you would like some breakfast when you awoke. You looked rather, er . . ." His gaze moved briefly to the generous amount of cleavage exposed by my tight leopard-print top, shifted awkwardly to my short red skirt, and then moved to my hair—which was probably a rat's nest by now. He frowned with concern. "Are you all right, Esther?"

"Coffee," I said in a gravelly voice.

"Of course!" He set down the tray on the end table, within my reach. I saw that he had brought me mini-bagels, cream cheese, and orange juice as well as coffee.

"Thank you," I said gratefully.

"Delighted!"

Dr. Maximillian Zadok (Oxford University, class of 1678) beamed at me as he sat in the chair near mine. He was a short, slightly chubby, white man with innocent blue eyes, longish white hair, and a tidy beard. Fluent in multiple languages, he spoke English with the faint trace of an accent, reflecting his origins in Eastern Europe centuries ago. Although he didn't look a day over seventy, Max's age was closer to three hundred fifty years. In his youth, while apprenticing to a master of alchemy, he had unwittingly drunk a potion that substantially slowed his aging process—a potion which neither he nor his colleagues had ever been able to reproduce. He wasn't immortal, but he'd be around for a few more generations—unless the Big Apple finished him off sooner than that.

I used the little milk pitcher on the breakfast tray to pour some milk into the large mug of coffee, then lifted the mug gratefully to my lips and took a long, deep swallow. Luckily, it wasn't too hot.

"I was working last night," I began, aware of Max's concerned and curious gaze, "and—"

"Working at . . . ?" He lifted his brows inquisitively, evidently realizing I wouldn't have worn this outfit to wait tables at Bella Stella in Little Italy.

The Dirty Thirty.

"Ah!" His expression cleared as my physical appearance this morning began to make more sense. "This is the costume of the unfortunate woman whom you're playing in the television drama?"

I nodded. "And I got, er, mugged."

"Esther!"

"Purse gone, wallet gone, phone gone . . ." I sighed and ran a hand over my matted hair. "Hairbrush gone." I took another swallow of coffee, hoping I would soon start feeling human. "Anyhow, after a pretty eventful evening"—including two gargoyles, a prison cell, my ex-would-be-boyfriend, and a *severed hand,* thanks—"I was in a cab on my way home, it was the middle of the night, and I realized that I couldn't get into my apartment. *Keys* gone." And, genius that I was, I kept my spare set of keys *inside* the apartment. "So I told the cab driver to bring me here." He had smirked (again) at me when I paid him with Lopez's twenty dollar bill. "And I let myself in. I hope that's all right."

Since Max couldn't keep track of his keys, he locked the front door by using a spell that kept out strangers when the shop was closed but allowed him access at all times. Since I was a regular visitor, Max had modified the spell so that I, too, could enter the shop at will.

"Of *course* you came here, my dear," Max said soothingly. "You should have woken me!"

I shook my head. "It was so late. And all I wanted to do by then was close my eyes."

"But you could have come upstairs." Max lived one floor above the bookshop. "Nelli doesn't mind giving up her bed for a friend."

Nelli's bed, which was the couch in Max's sparsely furnished living room, smelled heavily of Nelli and was liberally coated with her hair.

"I didn't want to disturb Nelli," I said tactfully. "Or you."

"Nonsense! Anyhow, I was barely asleep, I assure you." He added, "There is also Hieronymus' bed, in his old quarters on the top floor."

"No!" I said more sharply than I had intended. Max blinked. I said, "I'm sorry. I didn't mean to snap at you. It's just that . . . Well, after what we did to him—even though he deserved it . . . I mean, since Hieronymus *left* . . ." Although we had, in fact, killed him, this was the phrase I had asked Max to agree to use whenever we referred to what had happened to the young sorcerer. It seemed safer than carelessly voicing the facts. Especially since we numbered a police detective among our acquaintances. "I just wouldn't feel comfortable sleep-

ing in his bed," I concluded. All things considered, even
the idea of *touching* anything that had belonged to Hieronymus repelled me.

Max nodded in understanding. "Well, in any event, I
hope the chair was not too incommodious last night."

"I wouldn't want to make a habit of sleeping in it." I
rolled my head around as I tried to ease the kinks out of
my neck and shoulders. "But it was a blessing to be able
to sink into it a few hours ago, believe me."

"I am most distressed by your misadventure, Esther!
Did your assailant harm you?"

"My assail . . . Oh, the mugging." I paused in mid-
stretch to meet his gaze as I recalled things about those
gargoyles that disturbed me all over again: the dirty
claws, the fierce growling, the rotten breath, the physical strength . . . "Max, the strangest thing happened
last night. Lopez thinks it was a prank, and maybe he's
right—but it all seemed so real!"

"Lopez?" Max sat up straighter. "Detective Lopez
was present?"

"That was later. After the mugging. He was helping
me."

Max lowered his eyes and absently patted Nelli on
the head as she sat beside him, her wistful gaze fixed on
the bagels and cream cheese. "And, er, how was Detective Lopez?"

"Fine," I said, trying to figure out where to start my
account of the night's events.

"Ah. Good. I'm glad to hear it. Good." Max kept
his gaze lowered as he asked, oh-so-casually, "And he
was . . . much like his usual self? You observed nothing . . . unexpected?"

I shrugged. "Well, it was about three o'clock in the
morning, so he wasn't *quite* his usual . . . Oh!" My dry,
sleep-deprived eyes flew wide open as I realized what

Max meant. *"Oh."* Staring at his face, I took another long sip of my coffee. "Oh."

"Hmm."

I said, "You mean . . ."

"Yes." He met my eyes. "Well?"

I thought it over. "No . . ." I shook my head and said more firmly, "No."

"I see."

"So you still suspect . . ."

Max and I hadn't talked about it. Not since the last time we had seen Lopez, when he had told me he couldn't date me anymore. I had occasionally thought about it since then, of course; but I mostly tried not to think about Lopez at all, and when I did think about him . . . Well, I'm only human, so, in all honesty, *that* wasn't what I thought about. But looking at Max now, I realized that . . . "You've been thinking about it."

"Yes." He nodded. "However, since the young man caused you some heartbreak, it seemed to me that my mentioning his name would be insensitive. And since my thoughts on this matter, in any case, are mere speculation based only on suggestive circumstances . . . Well." He gave a little shrug. "But since you happened to see him last night, I must admit to some curiosity."

I again remembered that night, more than two months ago, at the Church of St. Monica in Little Italy. I was in the clutches of a ruthless murderer who was handling me brutally and threatening to kill me unless Lopez allowed him to flee to safety, with me as his hostage. The prospect of stopping the killer was thwarted by the pitch blackness inside the church, where all the lights had been disabled. . . .

I was choking, close to blacking out, with my captor's hand around my throat as chaos ensued in the darkened church, with Lopez frantic to find me. I heard his voice . . .

"Esther! Goddamn it, where are you? Esther!" And then Lopez screamed, *"I want LIGHTS!"*

And the lights came on, blazing throughout the church.

That sudden shift from darkness to light may well have saved my life that night.

There was no logical explanation for how or why the deliberately sabotaged electrical system had revived at the very moment that Lopez demanded light. Max, however, thought there might be a mystical explanation for it: The sudden illumination could be the unconscious imposition of Lopez's will on matter and energy at a moment when he feared for my life.

(He cared about me; he just wouldn't date me.)

"As I confided to you during the funeral of our enemy at St. Monica's," Max said to me now, "I believe we need to keep our minds open to the possibility that Detective Lopez has talents of which he is unaware."

"I wasn't thinking about that," I admitted. I knew that on a good day, Lopez would be amused and dismissive if I mentioned Max's vague suspicion to him. And on a bad day? He'd go back to threatening me with remand and a psych evaluation. "But apart from estimating the age of a severed hand, he didn't evince any unexpected talents last night."

Max blinked. "A severed hand?"

"Yeah," I said. "That has a lot to do with why the subject you mention didn't cross my mind. Other things were claiming my attention."

"Whose hand was severed?" Max asked, aghast.

"Well . . ." I shrugged. "He told me his name was Darius Phelps."

I recounted the night's events to Max. He listened with focused interest, interrupting only to ask for clarification or additional details, a faint frown of concentration on his face. When I was finished, I realized I was hungry, and so I picked up a little bagel and started spreading cream cheese on it. Nelli's eyes followed my movements as intently if the fate of this dimension depended on what I would do next with that bagel. Avoiding her gaze, I bit into it and chewed while I waited for Max's reaction to my tale.

"I don't wish to alarm you . . ." he said slowly.

"Too late now," I said. "A guy with a sword, an attack by gargoyles, a severed hand, arrest, and imprisonment kind of took care of alarming me."

"What you experienced may not have been, as Detective Lopez thinks, a mundane prank."

"Actually, he thinks it was an elaborate prank."

Max shook his head. "By 'mundane,' I mean—"

"Ah. Right. The opposite of mystical."

"Yes." He stroked his beard as he pondered the ramifications of my misadventure. "What intrigues me is that the man you met is reputedly dead."

"That intrigued the police, too." I paused, recalling the cops' merriment as they released me last night. "Well, no, I suppose 'intrigued' is the wrong word."

"Your encounter with Darius Phelps may not be unrelated to the thorny problem which has lately been keeping me awake until late at night and making my sleep restless."

"Oh? Is this problem the reason you say you were 'barely asleep' when I got here around four o'clock in the morning?"

"Indeed," Max said. "There has been a recent change in the normal current of mystical energy here. The familiar flow seems to be . . ." Max made a vague gesture, trying to explain an esoteric sensation in ordinary terms. ". . . Turning in the wrong direction. Or being turned."

I took another hearty swallow of coffee and thought this over. "Max, I have no idea what you've just said."

"That's understandable, since I'm finding it difficult to explain it adequately."

Nelli watched with mournful longing as I finished my bagel.

I said to Max, "Well, I know that you can sense things that mundanes can't—such as supernatural disturbances in this dimension."

"Strictly speaking, the word 'supernatural' is inaccurate. Virtually all phenomena are natural, but some are mystical and some are not."

"Yes. Whatever." We had talked about this before. "What I mean is, I realize that you're sensitive to phenomena that others don't even know exist."

Max's ability to sense mystical changes or imbalances in his environment had saved me from a fate worse than bad reviews. We first met when he had prevented me from becoming the next victim in a series of mysterious disappearances. He had sensed a disturbance in the fabric of this dimension when performers began involuntarily vanishing during disappearing acts onstage, and this had led him to me—right before I would have become the next disappearee.

So if Max was again experiencing a sensation that he identified as a disturbance in the mystical energy of this dimension, then I took it seriously. Even more so if he thought it related to what I had seen last night. So I urged him to take another stab at explaining it.

"Picture the energy of life," he said, "as a river that flows steadily in one direction, ever onward, from its source to the sea. It may become a dangerous torrent in spring, it may dry up during a drought and nearly disappear, it may swell and flood the surrounding landscape after heavy rains, but it always continues flowing in the same direction."

Unable to withstand the burden of Nelli's longing gaze, I slipped her a bagel as I said to Max, "Go on."

"Now imagine that while boating on the river, or fishing in it, or while wading through it at a ford, you notice that certain portions of the river, against all experience and logic, are suddenly moving in the opposite direction. From the sea to the source, as it were."

Nelli finished gulping down her bagel, wagged her tail, and gazed hopefully at me. "No," I said to her. And then to Max: "Okay. I get it. If this is happening to the river of life-energy, so to speak, then that means ... Um, what does that mean?"

"Instead of a consistent flow of energy traveling, as it should, from birth to life to death, some energy lately seems to be moving in the reverse direction."

I frowned. "From death to life?"

"Yes. I cannot explain it or account for it. But that is what I sense."

"And then last night ..." I shuddered as a sudden chill passed over me. "I spoke with a man who has supposedly been dead for three weeks."

"Hence my suspicion," Max said, "that your strange experience may be related to this mysterious mystical matter, and that Detective Lopez, though an undeniably astute young man, is quite possibly mistaken when he characterizes last night's events as a prank."

"You think the man I saw last night was really dead?" I said with dread. "Even though he was, you know, moving around and talking?"

"No, my dear, I don't think he was really dead."

I sighed with relief. "Thank goodness." I found the idea too disturbing.

"Not anymore."

"Huh?"

"I suspect it would be more accurate," Max said, "to classify him as reanimated."

"What?" I was disturbed all over again.

"Or perhaps resurrected? Though that word has religious overtones which it would perhaps be best to avoid. I had a most unpleasant encounter, you know, with the Spanish Inquisition in Sicily. It was still relatively early in the eighteenth century, not long after I realized that I was aging at an unusually slow rate and, though in my seventies, I still looked like a young man. And the experiences which I endured in Palermo have made me wary, ever since, of—"

"Max," I interrupted. "So you're saying that you think Darius Phelps was dead? But, er, making his way back? Traveling in reverse, so to speak?"

"Based on what you've told me—a disoriented man matching the name and description of a recently deceased person who experienced dismemberment without bleeding—yes, I think that may be the case."

"Recently deceased," I repeated faintly, remembering something else now "He, uh . . . he smelled weird."

Max looked at me intently. "Can you be more specific?"

"I'm not sure," I said. "It was an unfamiliar smell. I suppose it was a bit like . . ." I felt queasy as I realized what Darius' odor brought to mind. "Like when you pull food out of the fridge and realize you should throw it away. It doesn't smell rank yet, but it just doesn't smell quite right anymore." I decided not to eat another bagel.

"Hmm."

"But I don't really know what a dead person smells like. Or someone not quite dead. Let alone some who used to be dead and isn't dead anymore." Now I wished I hadn't eaten even that one bagel. "Oy."

"I'm puzzled by the involvement of the gargoyles," Max mused. "Did the individual whom you encountered seem harmful or malevolent?

"No." I shook my head. "Darius seemed endangered, not dangerous."

"Despite their grotesque appearance, the traditional function of gargoyles is to protect us from evil spirits or harmful forces—such as demons."

"Well, keep in mind that I'm not expert on supernat— uh, mystical creatures, Max. Those hideous beasts reminded me of gargoyles, but that doesn't mean they *were* gargoyles."

"Ah. Yes. That's an excellent point. Nonetheless, it's well worth asking: Did Mr. Phelps seem demonically possessed, by any chance?"

"My knowledge of demonic possession is limited to what I've seen in movies," I said. "But at a guess, I'd say no. The man I saw seemed dazed, confused, and helpless. If he were possessed by a demon, wouldn't he—I don't know—pulverize the little creatures that I managed to fight off and chant the Latin Mass backward, or something?"

"Well, yes. Although generalizations are misleading, it's nonetheless true that impressive strength is a common attribute of demons. Then again, perhaps Mr. Phelps—or some entity possessing him—had already been weakened by an encounter with the sword-wielding young huntsman whom you encountered elsewhere in the vicinity."

"I didn't see any sword wounds," I said. "But it was dark, of course."

"And we can postulate, based on your observations of his severed hand, that there would have been no blood to alert you to a sword wound."

"Yes, thanks to the bloodless dismemberment that I was lucky enough to witness, we can indeed postulate that." I groaned with regret as I saw Lopez's comforting theory about a prank beating a fast retreat. "I really did see what I thought I saw, didn't I?"

"I believe we must investigate the possibility," Max said, patting my hand. "Mr. Phelps may be in need of aid.

Conversely, the gargoyles or the armed huntsman may be in need of aid. Or all three parties may be forerunners of some sort of apocalypse that needs averting."

"Wait a minute! How did this go from being a prank to an apocalypse?" I said crankily. "I haven't even finished my coffee yet."

"Bring your cup, if you wish," Max said briskly, rising to his feet. "We must leave immediately."

"We must? Why? Where are we going?"

"The library."

"The what?" I said blankly.

"The public library. In fact, I think our time will best be served by going to the outpost located in Harlem, so that we can also investigate the scene of your encounter. I may be able to identify clues to the incident that the police overlooked."

"But Max," I protested, "I want to go home. Change my clothes. Shower. Call *Dirty Thirty*'s production office. Start canceling and replacing the things that were in my stolen purse—ID, credit cards, cell phone . . . And I need you to let me into my apartment." Max's talents included the ability to unlock doors without a key.

"Of course, Esther," Max said absently, as he disappeared around the corner of a bookcase. "We'll do all of that. Immediately upon conclusion of our urgent business in Harlem."

"But Max, I can't go around town wearing this outfit and—"

He reappeared, wearing a jaunty straw hat that suited him well and holding Nelli's pink leather leash. "Shall we?"

Nelli leaped to her feet, tail wagging in eager anticipation of a field trip.

"We can't take a dog to the public library," I said firmly.

Nelli gave me a wounded look.

"Don't say 'dog,' " Max reminded me anxiously. Nelli was a mystical familiar, and Max considered it a solecism to refer to her as a dog.

"We can't take a canine familiar to the public library," I said.

Nelli whined.

Even getting her all the way up to Harlem would be a challenge, though we had by now learned that some cab drivers were open to monetary persuasion with regard to transporting Nelli. As for the subway, that was out of the question. The rules about animals on public transportation were strict and specific, and (as we had also learned) the Manhattan Transit Authority was not amenable to making an exception for a carnivorous mammal that outweighed many adult women.

"Oh, dear." Max said apologetically, "I'm afraid Esther may be right, Nelli."

She looked at him reproachfully as he set down her leash on the old walnut table.

"I will give you a full account of our findings when I return," he assured her. Lifting the receiver of the heavy old telephone that sat on the table, he added, "I will also ascertain immediately if Satsy is available to watch the store and take you out for your midday perambulation, since Esther and I may be gone for some time."

Satsy was "Saturated Fats," a three hundred pound drag queen who had assisted us in solving the problem of the mystical vanishings in spring. Satsy was an occult enthusiast who had already been a regular customer of the bookstore when we became acquainted, and now that Max had, as it were, a pet to care for, Satsy occasionally babysat Nelli and the bookstore in exchange for free books.

After a short telephone conversation, Max announced that Satsy would arrive within an hour of our departure. Nelli's tail wagged with renewed good humor, since she liked Satsy, who was a kind-hearted companion—and also a pushover who fed her too many treats.

As we exited the store, Max said cheerfully to Nelli, "I'm sure I can count on you to assist any customers who enter before Satsy's arrival!"

My guess was that when encountering Nelli alone inside the shop, most people sensibly turned right back around and left. But there was no denying that in the jumbled chaos of Zadok's Rare and Used Books, she was uncannily good at helping people find obscure Latin volumes on alchemy and witchcraft, when asked.

Once we were outside on the street, and my Lycra top, leather boots, and vinyl skirt caused the bright muggy heat of the day to hit me with full force, I opened my mouth again to protest and insist that we go to my apartment before doing anything else today.

But Max spoke first. "Which direction is it?"

"What?"

"The subway train to Harlem," he said. "Where do we find it?"

I blinked. "*You're* getting on the subway?"

Raised in an era when a horse-drawn carriage was the epitome of fast, sophisticated transportation (and would continue to be so for another two hundred years), Max had an unmitigated horror of modern moving vehicles. He preferred to walk to most destinations, and he sometimes paid (outrageous sums) for the slow-moving horse-drawn carriages from Central Park, popular with tourists, to transport him. He only chose to travel by mechanized means when he considered speed imperative.

"Our destination is some distance from here," he said.

"Well, yes. Seven or eight miles, I'd say."

"Therefore, although I do not by any means look

forward to the journey, a subterranean train is the best means of traveling to Harlem, is it not?"

"Yes. Especially on a weekday morning." Today was Thursday, and midtown would be clogged with traffic. "We can catch the train at Washington Square, change at Forty-second Street, and get off at One Hundred Twenty-fifth Street in Harlem."

"And the library?"

"There's a branch not far from there. Also not far from where I met Darius. But Max . . . why are we going to the public library?"

"To look for local obituaries from three weeks ago. We must find out who Darius Phelps was and how he died."

6

"**D**arius Phelps died of a ruptured intestine?" I stared at the computer screen in the Harlem branch of the New York Public Library while Max sat next to me and read over my shoulder. "That doesn't sound mystical. It sounds messy. And painful."

The library was housed in a beautifully renovated, ivy-covered, neoclassical building from the early nineteenth century, with a pale stone exterior, tall windows, and high interior ceilings. It was on East 124th Street, directly across from Mount Morris Park and only a few blocks away from where I had found gargoyles attacking the late Darius Phelps in the dark.

"It's unfortunate that there is no photograph of him," Max said. "We might be able to determine if this is indeed the individual whom you saw last night."

Phelps had evidently not been an important man, in worldly terms. His obituary was short and impersonal; I found it listed in several sources during the week he had died in July, but the information was identical in each instance.

He had died suddenly, at the age of thirty-seven, and no survivors were listed. He was originally from Chicago, had an MBA from Roosevelt University, and had moved to New York several years ago to work at the Livingston Foundation, where he was employed at the time of his death.

"The Livingston Foundation," I murmured. "Why does that name ring a bell?" I thought I'd heard of it before, but I couldn't place it.

"I believe that if you ask this machine to do so, it can provide information about the Livingston Foundation," Max suggested helpfully.

I typed the name into the search engine and clicked on the top result, which opened the page to a Web site. There was a photo of a large redbrick building, a navigation menu, and a mission statement about this private nonprofit foundation:

"The Livingston Foundation, created by the late Martin Livingston, fosters the dreams, nurtures the education, and supports the ambitions of young African-Americans. The foundation offers cultural and educational programs; administers grants, scholarships, and small business loans; and organizes community projects in Harlem."

I clicked on some of the links, and Max and I read the information there. Martin Livingston was a successful businessman who had retired as a billionaire at the age of fifty and announced he would devote the rest of his life to putting his fortune to work for the people of Harlem, where he had been born and raised. Thus, the Livingston Foundation was born, and Martin had spent the next dozen years turning it into an influential center for African-American education, culture, and community outreach. The Web site had numerous photos of him receiving leadership awards, giving speeches, writing checks, and shaking hands with people. Livingston had died two years ago, at the age of sixty-three. The foundation was now managed by its board of directors, in accordance with his legacy and his wishes.

"If *he* died of a ruptured intestine, too," I said, "then, as a safety precaution, we are not eating any of the famous fried chicken advertised in the windows of Harlem's dining establishments."

The text didn't say how he had died, but he was such a prominent man that the information should be easy to find if we did a search for his obituary.

"The Livingston Foundation must be here in Harlem," Max said. "Given the scant information about Mr. Phelps that we have thus far obtained, perhaps we should pay a visit to his place of employment?"

"That should be easy," I said, after clicking on the "Contact Us" link. "According to this address, we're about a sixty-second stroll away from it." The Livingston Foundation was on this same street, barely a block east of the library.

Max popped out of his chair. "Excellent!"

I logged off the computer and rose to follow him out of the cool, quiet library and into the midday heat. "Man, it's another scorcher today." I fussed with the Lycra that clung suffocatingly to my torso, then I lifted my tangled hair off my neck.

"I assume the Livingston Foundation will be climate-controlled," Max said soothingly. "Shall we?"

He could afford to be soothing, I thought crankily. He was wearing loose linen trousers, sandals, a short-sleeved cotton shirt, and a hat that kept the sun off his face. I, on the other hand, was wearing hot, uncomfortable, synthetic clothing that had already been through far too much activity to be sanitary even *without* the effects of this stifling heat.

I took his arm and proceeded down the street with him, walking parallel to the park. We were in the Mount Morris Park Historic District, a large and beautiful nineteenth-century neighborhood that had blossomed during Harlem's recent resurgence through the renovation of historic buildings and the revitalization of such great Harlem institutions as the National Black Theatre.

Thinking about that theatre made me think about work, which made me think about Michael Nolan, presumably still lying in a hospital bed only a few blocks away from here. That, in turn, made me think about the need to find a phone and call the *D30* production office.

"What a nice park," Max said, nodding in that direction. "And so big! One doesn't really think of there being such big green spaces in Harlem."

"No, I suppose not." The park, which was framed by an attractive wrought-iron fence, covered the space of about eight city blocks. The grass looked well-tended, there were a lot trees and some paved paths, and I saw many young children in the nearby playground, supervised by parents, elder siblings, or babysitters. Beyond the playground, the park looked more overgrown and lush, with shrubs, boulders, and dense thickets. At the distant southern end of the park, atop a steep hill covered by trees that appeared to be thriving in the summer heat, and surrounded by a thick fog of heavily leafed, sky-reaching branches, I saw the very top of some sort of skeletal metal tower. "What do you suppose that is?"

Max looked in the direction I was pointing. "Interesting. It almost looks like very old scaffolding, doesn't it?"

"Ah, here we are," I said as we arrived at the Livingston Foundation's redbrick edifice. It was indeed only about a minute's walk from the library. It was quite a large building but had relatively few windows. The architecture was charmless, but sturdy. Over the entrance, embedded in what appeared to be brass letters, was a quote from Dr. Martin Luther King, Jr. that appealed to

Max: LIFE'S MOST PERSISTENT AND URGENT QUESTION IS, "WHAT ARE YOU DOING FOR OTHERS?"

I, however, was less enthusiastic than Max about passing beneath this admirable motto and entering the building. He wanted to question people at the foundation, but I was uncomfortably aware that I didn't present a credible persona, dressed as I was. I thought perhaps I should wait outside for him. Max was trying to assure me, without noticeable conviction, that I didn't look quite as disreputable as I thought, when a tall, slim black man with a shaved head approached the building and tried to get through the doorway that we were blocking while we talked. He seemed to be in a hurry.

"Excuse me," he said, his gaze on my cleavage as he moved to step between us and enter the doorway.

"Oh, sorry. I'm in the way, aren't I? Max, we should move."

The man glanced sharply at me as I spoke, which made me look at him in return. He was about thirty, nice-looking, clean-shaven, and . . .

"Oh, my God," I said slowly. The cue-ball head had made him look like a stranger at first glance. He'd had close-cropped hair back when I knew him. "Jeff?"

He frowned, then looked thunderstruck as he recognized me. *"Esther?"*

"Yes." I smiled. "Jeff!"

"Holy shit! Esther Diamond!" He grinned and embraced me. *"Man,* it's been a long time!"

When he released me, I said, "I haven't seen you since you went on the road with that show. That was—what? Three years ago?"

"Four."

I said to Max, "It was a musical version of Idi Amin's life." Then to Jeff: "How did that go?"

"It died on the road."

"Go figure."

"But that was a long time ago. How about you? How've you been?" His gaze moved over me and his expression froze in an awkward smile. "This is . . . a new look for you."

"It's a costume," I said wearily. "I was working last night, and I haven't been able to get my own clothes back or go home yet. Long story." I gestured to his bald head. "This is a new look for you, too."

He ran a hand over his shiny bald pate. "What do you think?"

Rather than answer that, since I saw no reason to mar this unexpected reunion with an honest opinion, I asked, "Is it for summer? Or a job?"

"A job. They wanted a certain look. I'm playing an athlete." He flexed his shoulders. "I've been working out for it, too."

"You look fit." And that was true. Jeff was slim and long-limbed, not bulky or muscular. He wore a tank top and shorts in this heat, so it was easy to see that he was well-toned, his skin stretched smoothly over taut muscles and glowing with good health. "What's the job?"

Jeff didn't answer. Examining my outfit, which was looking the worse for wear by now, he asked, "So where were you working last night?"

"On location here in Harlem. A nighttime shoot for *The Dirty Thirty.*"

"Whoa!" His eyes widened. "I love that show."

"*Thank you,*" I said with feeling. "Er, I mean, I'm glad to hear that."

"*The Dirty Thirty,* huh? Well. Hmm." He smiled again. "Hey, good for you!" His gaze moved to Max and he introduced himself. "Hi. I'm Jeffrey Clark."

"Oh, I'm sorry!" I said belatedly. "Jeff, this is Dr. Maximillian Zadok, who's a good friend of mine. Max, Jeff is an actor and . . . an old friend."

Actually, Jeff was a former boyfriend. But that's a

phrase which implies old complications, and it seemed like too much information in the current circumstances.

"I'm delighted to meet you," Max said, shaking Jeff's hand. "Were you on your way into this establishment?"

"Yeah. I work here."

"Oh, of course!" I slapped my forehead, then looked at Max. "*That's* why it sounded familiar to me." I said to Jeff, "Now I remember! You used to teach workshops here."

"I *still* teach workshops here," he said.

"The Livingston Foundation." I nodded. "I knew I recognized the name from somewhere." I had never been here, but I now recalled that, staying true to the Harlem roots he had always wanted to have (in fact, he came from a middle-class suburb of Columbus, Ohio), Jeff took pride in teaching acting workshops to young people at the Livingston Foundation.

"Since you're employed here, then perhaps you knew Darius Phelps?" Max asked, leaping right into the breach.

"Darius?" Jeff shrugged. "Sure. He worked here." He looked at me. "Is that why you're here? You knew Darius?"

"Not exactly," I said.

"We have some questions about him," Max said. "Perhaps you can help us?"

"I didn't know him that well, but, sure, I can try."

"First of all—"

"Not right now, though." Jeff glanced at his wristwatch. "I've got a meeting, and . . . and . . ." His gaze was fixed on me, and he started smiling. "Oh, *man*. This is lucky."

"What?" I said.

Then his smile faded and he looked uncertain. "Actually, maybe you won't . . ."

"*What?*" I prodded.

"Do you want some work?"

He was speaking my language. I asked, "What kind of work?"

"I know you've got this *D-Thirty* gig and all, and this wouldn't pay much compared to that. But it also doesn't take up that much time, and it's a way to—you know—give something back," he said in a rush. "Plus, you'd really be helping me out."

"What kind of work?" I repeated.

"You'd take over some of the workshops I'm teaching here. This job I got—the athlete role—has some scheduling conflicts with my work here. I thought I had it covered, but I got an angry call from the boss this morning. The guy who was substituting for me here turned out to be a flake and hasn't shown up for a couple of days. I'm on my way into the boss' office to do a mea culpa and promise to clean up my mess." He let out his breath. "She was really pissed off, Esther. So it sure would help, when I go in there now, if I could introduce her to my new replacement."

Actually, I thought I might enjoy teaching some acting workshops. Meanwhile, my working in Darius Phelps' place of employment might be a fruitful avenue for investigating his fate, if he was indeed the individual whom I'd seen last night.

However, I was a little concerned about my outfit. "I'm definitely interested, Jeff. But do I really have to meet your boss? *Now*, I mean?"

"Since my previous replacement has crapped out on her, yeah, I think she's going to insist on meeting you. And then you and I can teach a class together today, so the kids can get to know you."

"Like *this*? But—"

"Come on." He gestured to the front door. "It'll be fine. I'll explain to her about the outfit."

I glanced at Max. He was frowning. But when I lifted

my brows in silent query, he gave a little shake of his head, indicating that he didn't want to discuss whatever was troubling him. Not in front of Jeff, anyhow.

"Okay, let's go meet your boss," I said to Jeff. "Oh! Wait!"

"What's wrong?" Jeff said.

"Before we do anything else, I have to make a call. Can I borrow your cell? Mine was stolen last night."

"Stolen?" Jeff reached into his pocket.

"Yes. I'll explain later. But this call is important. I should do it right now. Thanks." I accepted the phone from him . . . and then realized I didn't actually know the *D30* production office's number. I'd have to phone directory assistance first. "This will just take a few minutes."

As I walked a little distance away from the two men to make my calls, I heard Max say, "So you are a fellow thespian. Is that how you and Esther met?"

"Yeah. We did *Othello* together," Jeff said. "She was Ophelia. I got to strangle her."

And on many occasions after we started dating, I wished it had been the reverse.

Max was a Shakespeare fan, so he plied Jeff with questions about that long-ago production while I got directory assistance to connect me to *D30*. The production office's phone rang a few times, and then someone answered it just long enough to put me on hold.

Jeff had always been his own best publicist, and from the bits of his conversation with Max that I overheard while on hold with *D30*, I could tell that this hadn't changed.

That production of *Othello* had been a non-Equity cooperative showcase, meaning we all did it for free so we could list another role on our résumés, and so we could try to attract some attention (from talent agents, for example). The income from ticket sales barely covered the cost of the small, shabby performance space that we rented above a bar in the East Village. But based on what Jeff was saying about that production now, Max was probably getting the impression that we had performed the play at Lincoln Center and that Jeff had only narrowly missed being nominated for a Tony Award.

Playing Ophelia opposite Jeff had been my first good role after coming to New York. After graduating from Northwestern University, I had moved here with two other classmates, and we had gotten lucky and secured the rent-controlled apartment that I still lived in. We mostly paid our bills by waiting tables, telemarketing, and doing office temping. My first "acting" job in New York had involved dressing up as a bear and wandering the streets, handing out leaflets for a toy store at Christmas. I was subsequently cast as a singing rutabaga in a one-act play that toured local schools to teach children about nutrition. (The rutabaga, an unjustly neglected root vegetable, contains vitamins A and C.)

After that, I was determined to play an actual human being, even if I wasn't paid for it. So I went to the audition when I heard about the *Othello* showcase. The project was being coproduced by the director and the lead actor—Jeffrey Clark. Jeff had been in New York longer than I had, he knew the ropes better than I did, and he was tremendously talented. He was also very attractive, and he thought *I* was tremendously talented. Before long, our flirtation turned into a serious relationship.

We were together for almost a year, and we had some good times. Jeff was a decent man, as well as one who shared and understood my vocation.

On the other hand, he was also the reason that I had decided never again to date an actor.

Now, while I waited for *D30*'s production office to speak to me, I could hear Jeff telling Max about some of the other roles he had played since the Moor of Venice.

Moving a little farther away from them, I muttered, "But enough about me. What do *you* think about me?"

Then, finally, someone picked up the phone at *D30* and spoke to me. As soon as I gave my name, the woman at the other end of the line cried, "Oh, my God! *There* you are! I've phoned your apartment *and* your cell. Twice! *Each.* Where have you *been?*"

I took a deep breath. "I'm really sor—"

"We've been *frantic* to get a hold of you."

"I can imagine. And I want to start by say—"

"We were getting so worried!"

"I know," I said. "And I—"

"We are all *so* sorry about this, Esther!"

I blinked. "Pardon?"

"Have you seen the papers?"

"Uh, no, but—"

"Never mind. That's okay."

"Thank you. I mean—"

"As you may have heard—or maybe you didn't—Mike's gastric episode last night turned out to be a heart attack. A heart attack! So suddenly there were medics and doctors and ambulances and cops and hospitals and chaos and panic and—and—*and!* You know?"

"Um. Uh-huh."

"So we were at the hospital all night. All night! We left a skeleton crew to pack up the location shoot. And we totally forgot—I mean *forgot* until, like, this morning—that some of the actors had gone off to get something to eat!"

"Oh?"

"But now I know what happened to you, Esther!"

That seemed unlikely. "You do?"

"You poor thing! We had no idea until this morning that the actors were wandering around Harlem in the middle of the night wondering where the show had gone, and that the few crew members who were still there weren't very helpful. I can only imagine how *scary* that was for you!"

"I was pretty scared last night," I said truthfully.

"I'm *so* sorry," she said. "We're *all* so sorry."

"Oh, these things happen," I said kindly. "And I'm fine. So don't give it another thought. Really."

"You're *such* a pro."

I was very glad that someone on the staff of a successful television show thought so. "So tell me how Nolan is. Uh, Mike, I mean."

"He's, er, not very happy. But, well, I guess that's to be expected."

Based on my limited exposure to him, I doubted that he was *ever* happy.

She added, "He'd like it if you visited him. He's at North General in Harlem. He wanted to go to Mount Sinai, but—"

"I can't visit him," I said. "I hardly know him." Yes, we had simulated the act of sexual intercourse together in front of a TV camera, but we were scant acquaintances, at best.

"He wants visitors," she said firmly.

"It's probably not a good idea to tire him out with visits from casual acquain—"

"There's a sign-up sheet. When shall I put you down for?"

I supposed that if the star of a successful television show told the producer that he wanted visitors, then he got visitors. Even if we had to be bullied into it.

Since I was in Harlem anyhow, I said with resignation, "I'll go today."

"Afternoon or evening?"

"I don't know. I'm a little bus—"

"Pick one," she snapped.

"Afternoon."

She was in good cheer again. "He'll be delighted to see you!"

That seemed doubtful. But I wanted to stay on good terms with *D30*, so I would do my duty and go visit their star. "How are his nurses coping?"

"Mike wants to get out of the hospital as soon as possible," she said. "And the nurses are, uh, trying to help him with that."

I'll bet they are, I thought. "But he's going to be all right?"

"We sure hope so. He's been ignoring the warning symptoms for months, ignoring his doctor's advice, and refusing to modify his lifestyle or change his habits. Personally, I think what happened was inevitable, and he's lucky it wasn't worse. So let's all hope this incident is a wake-up call, and that he listens to it. Or we're going to lose a fine actor and special human being."

Whatever.

"So what are they going to do about this episode of the show?" I asked. My unfinished scene wasn't the only one that Nolan was scheduled to film.

"They're talking about doing some rewrites that will eliminate him from the rest of this episode and account for his absence from the show for the next few episodes, too."

"That makes sense."

"But Mike is furious about that and refusing to agree to it."

It came as no surprise to me that even a heart attack didn't make Nolan willing to surrender the spotlight for a few weeks.

She added, "He says he can be back at work in a few days and continue shooting the show the way it's been written. But the doctors are advising against it." She sighed, slowing down now and starting to sound like someone who had indeed spent all night at the hospital.

"We're shooting around his scenes for the time being, but we'll have to make a decision soon. So if you can just stand by, Esther? One way or the other, we'll need to re-schedule you, either to shoot the unfinished scene with Mike, or else to do a new scene the writers will draft—probably one where Jilly C-Note gives that same plot information to someone else in the Three-Oh."

"Of course I can stand by," I said. Because I am *such* a pro. "I've still got the costume, after all."

"Oh, that's right! The wardrobe mistress was asking a little while ago what to do about the missing costumes from last night."

"I'll get it cleaned." Possibly fumigated. "And I'll bring it with me to the next shoot."

"Great. I will make a note of that."

"Oh, and I've lost my cell phone," I said. "Until I re-place it, use my home number."

As we ended the call, I realized that I had a lot of ad-ditional practical matters I needed to take care of, with regard to my stolen purse.

Meanwhile, it sounded as if I'd probably get at least one more day's work on *D30,* which was good news, and it might be without Nolan, which was even better news.

When I returned to the entrance of the Livingston Foundation, I found Max alone.

He asked me, "Is all well?"

"Yes, no problems with the job. It's all sorted out. But we're going to have to go to the hospital later." I ex-plained the situation while lifting my hair off my damp neck for a few moments, in the doomed hope of catching a breeze. Then I asked, "Where's Jeff?"

"He was concerned about being late for his meeting," Max said, "so he went inside and left me with instruc-tions. We are to ascend to the second floor and seek the office of Dr. Catherine Livingston."

"Catherine Livingston?" I repeated, pulling the

sweat-dampened Lycra away from my chest for a moment as a trickle of perspiration ran down between my breasts. Jilly C-Note's push-up bra was starting to feel like a form of torture: ordeal by undergarment.

"Dr. Livingston is the founder's widow, according to Jeffrey," Max said. "Shall we go inside?"

"Wait. First tell me what's bothering you about this."

"Oh. Well, it may be nothing . . . but I'm wondering why the substitute teacher has ceased to come to work."

That hadn't even occurred to me. "It probably *is* nothing, Max. At almost every job I've ever worked, there's a problem with employee attendance. A lot of people are flaky and unreliable; and actors are flakier than most. Like Jeff, the replacement might have gotten an acting job that conflicted with his teaching schedule. Or maybe he just didn't like this job and, instead of quitting, he simply stopped showing up. People do that sort of thing all the time."

"You are no doubt correct. Nonetheless, without further information, I am somewhat troubled by the fact that an employee has stopped coming to work, without explanation, precisely when—we currently suspect—another employee is roaming Harlem after dying and being reanimated." He concluded, "It's troubling."

"Well, put like *that,* it's certainly troubling," I said.

"If you become an employee here," he said, "you should maintain an alert attitude and take no risks. And I, of course, will be vigilant on your behalf."

"Agreed." I turned to enter the building. "Now let's go inside."

After my initial surge of relief at feeling the artificially cool air of the interior on my hot, damp skin, I noticed that the inside of the Livingston Foundation was a pleasant surprise after the impression created by its generic exterior. The halls were painted in bright colors, African batiks and Caribbean art decorated the walls, there were beautiful mobile sculptures hanging overhead, and the furnishings were eclectic and interesting, rather than institutional. An elderly African-American man at the reception desk in the lobby greeted us with a friendly smile and, at our request, directed us to Dr. Catherine Livingston's office, saying that Jeff had told him to expect us.

We ascended to the second floor by way of a stairwell, then turned left, as directed. We entered a narrow hallway where the walls were painted a soft apricot color. One wall was decorated with vibrant textile artwork, each piece depicting figures and symbols in bright patterns.

"These are very pretty," I said, looking at one that portrayed a big red heart which contained smaller hearts created out of silver and gold sequins. It was set against a field of tropical foliage, also studded with sequins, and surrounded by multicolored abstract symbols.

The cloth hanging next to it, created out of shiny fabrics quilted together, was divided into four panels, each containing a large geometric symbol depicted in contrasting colors. One of the symbols appeared to be a cross decorated with flourishes and abstract motifs; next to it were the letters L E G B A. Another of the symbols was a triangle with curly lines sprouting out of it. The letters next to this one were O G O U N.

Max was studying these hangings with intent interest, a dawning expression of . . . *something* on his face. I wasn't sure what.

"Max?" I prodded.

"They're drapeaux," he murmured, his tone implying that this was significant.

"What are drapeaux?"

"Flags," he said, still staring at the artwork. "Ceremonial flags. They're carried at the beginning of a ritual to salute the spirits and start the ceremony."

I frowned. "What sort of spirits? What kind of ceremony?"

"Vodou," he said, nodding slowly.

"Vodou?" I shrugged, still frowning. "What is Vod— Oh! You mean voodoo?"

He nodded. "These look like traditional Haitian Vodou drapeaux."

I thought they looked like art projects made by talented young people taking classes at the foundation, but I took Max's word for it. I moved on to the next one. "Yikes!" I definitely hoped this one was *not* the work of a kid: It depicted a heart with a dagger thrust through it.

"Ah! Erzulie Dantor," Max said, as if encountering an old acquaintance.

"Who?"

"Erzulie is the goddess of love, beauty, and sensuality."

I looked again at the stabbed heart. "No way."

"Erzulie Dantor, however, is the Petro aspect of Erzulie. Her dark side, you might say. Vodou has a complex and practical view of the world and of human nature." He gestured to the dark goddess' symbol. "She represents the feelings of jealousy, heartbreak, and vengeance that can be wrought by love."

"Wow, and I thought Yahweh was a vengeful god," I said, looking again at the cruel image.

I wasn't surprised that Max knew something about voodoo. After three hundred fifty years of travel and study, he knew about a lot of things—particularly mystical, magical, and spiritual things.

I turned away from the exotic voodoo art to look at the opposite wall, which was lined with photographs. There were pictures of Martin Livingston, several of which were already familiar to me, since they had been reproduced on the foundation's Web site. There were also pictures of the foundation's board of directors, its most important donors, and it employees. I noticed that there was a photo of Jeff in which he still had hair.

And there was a photo of Darius Phelps.

"Max," I said, trying to drag his attention away from the drapeaux. *"Max."*

"Hmm?"

I pointed to Darius' picture.

"We're in the right place." I felt a chill creep over my damp skin as I stared at the familiar face in the photograph. "No doubt about it. This is the man I saw last night."

7

I flinched in surprise when a nearby door was flung open.

"There you are!" said Jeff with false brightness. I could tell he was annoyed that I had spent so long on the phone. He'd probably been stalling, trying to convince his boss I was reliable while simultaneously wondering why I hadn't come upstairs yet. "Did you get lost?"

Max said quietly to me, "I'll wait here."

I took one more look at Darius Phelps' photograph, noting that he had been a handsome man in life—something that hadn't been so readily apparent last night, when he was three weeks dead and physically maimed.

Then I turned and walked through the door that Jeff was holding open for me. Using my ace-in-the-hole immediately, in hopes of compensating for my tardiness, I said in a clear voice as I entered his boss' office, "I'm sorry that call took so long. I was talking to the production office of *The Dirty Thirty*. Michael Nolan, the show's star, has had a heart attack, and they've got to reschedule the filming of my scenes." I handed Jeff his cell phone. "Thanks for letting me borrow this."

"No problem." Jeff closed the door and turned to the

woman who was rising from her chair behind her desk and extending her hand to greet me. "Catherine, this is Esther Diamond."

My first surprise was that she was white. I had just sort of assumed that Jeff's boss at this important African-American institution in Harlem would be black.

She was also younger than I expected, given that her husband would be about sixty-five now, if he had lived. She was a very well-groomed woman, which made her age hard to guess accurately, but I thought she was probably in her early forties.

I reached across the desk to shake her hand and smiled. "Dr. Livingston, I presume?"

"How witty," she said, stone-faced. "I never hear that."

I glanced at Jeff. He gave me a pained look.

"Do call me Catherine," she said in a cool voice as she withdrew her hand. "I insist." She looked down at her well-manicured fingers with a barely perceptible expression of distaste, then reached for a tissue.

"It's very hot outside," I said by way of apology as she wiped my sweat from her hand. "And I'm not dressed for the weather, I'm afraid."

Jeff said quickly, "I explained to Catherine that you came straight here after an all-night location shoot after I called you earlier today, and you haven't had time to change out of your costume for the hit television show that you're working in."

A few moments ago, I thought that *I* might have spread it on a little too thick. Now I stopped worrying.

Catherine gestured gracefully to a couple of chairs in front of her desk. "Please have a seat."

Since I had spent too much time in these high-heeled boots in the past twenty-four hours, I accepted the offer gratefully. Jeff sat down next to me.

Catherine's spacious office was lined with bookcases

that were filled with well-ordered volumes, top to bottom, without a speck of dust in sight. There were wonderful African masks and batiks on the remaining wall space. My sweeping glance around the room briefly revealed all sorts of interesting objects decorating the shelves of the bookcases. Her desk was piled high with books and papers in neat stacks, as was a nearby coffee table that sat in front of a small couch. A long piece of colorful, geometrically patterned cloth was spread across the back of the couch.

"That's beautiful," I said, pointing to it.

She smiled, looking friendly for the first time. "It's kente cloth. Also known as *nwentoma*. It has been popularized and misappropriated now, of course, but it's originally native to the Akan people of Ghana and the Ivory Coast." She nodded toward the cloth that draped the couch and said with pride of ownership, "That piece is genuine and dates from the early twentieth century."

"Very special," I said politely.

"The ribbons of green color symbolize growth and spiritual renewal. This derives, of course, from green being the color of planting and harvest, of life renewing itself with each cycle of the agricultural seasons. The yellow symbolizes royalty and wealth, so this cloth may have belonged to royalty, or to someone connected to royalty. However, yellow can also symbolize fertility. Thus, combined with the green, this may have been a gift to a new bride, expressing a hope for fecundity and perpetual renewal of her womb. Alternatively, it may have been a celebratory gift to a new mother—a woman of status, obviously, since it was a costly item."

Boy, and I had thought Max could sometimes prattle on too long without encouragement. He was an amateur compared to this woman.

Still, since I wanted a job from her, I feigned interest. "You can tell all that from the colors?"

So she talked about the colors some more (red was associated with bloodshed and sacrifice, purple with women, blah blah blah), and then she talked about the symbolic meaning of the pattern (more of the same), and *then* she talked about the legend of how kente cloth had originated (two guys got the idea from a spider's web).

Frankly, I was starting to wonder if her husband had died of boredom.

Still, it wasn't that difficult to guess what had first attracted Martin Livingston to her. She was a good-looking woman with a well-maintained figure that was shown off to advantage today by a sleeveless sheath dress. Her smooth blond hair was pulled back in a stylish chignon, and her makeup was skillfully applied with a light hand. A lot of men would look twice at her. And if Martin had also shared her loquacious fascination with "ritual weaving and the symbolic visual language of traditional African cultures," then the marriage was probably a match made in heaven.

I, however, was finding Catherine's company a bit of an endurance test. I was just starting to think I didn't really want this job after all, since it might mean bumping into her on a regular basis, when she gave a rueful little laugh and said, "Oh, dear, I've done it again." She smiled at me. "You must forgive me, Hester."

"Esther."

"I tend to get carried away when the conversation turns to a subject that I find so interesting."

I refrained from pointing out that it wasn't a conversation, it was a monologue. A long one.

Jeff said to me, "You'll learn a lot, working here."

"Indeed," I said, hoping that my gaze would turn him into stone.

"Ah, yes," Catherine said. "That brings us to the subject at hand. I gather from Jeff that your filming schedule allows you enough time to take over the responsibility for some of his workshops that he has abdicated this summer?"

Ouch. I resisted the urge to look at Jeff to see if he was wincing.

"Yes. I'm waiting for the production office to re-schedule me for another scene or two, but that will prob-ably be a nighttime shoot. And my other job is mostly at night, too."

"Other job?" they said in unison.

"I'm a singing server at Bella Stella."

Jeff said in surprise, "You're waiting tables?" Appar-ently he'd assumed my *D30* gig was a steady thing.

"And singing." I said pleasantly to Catherine, "Maybe you've heard of Bella Stella? There was a mob hit there about two months ago. Chubby Charlie Chiccante got it right in the chest and died while I was waiting on him during the dinner shift. The story was in all the tabloids."

Sometimes I just can't help myself.

Catherine's carefully blank expression didn't change as she looked from me to Jeff. As if she were silently ac-cusing him of that murder, he held up his hands and said, "Hey, I was in LA two months ago."

She looked at me again. "My, what interesting stories of the actor's life you will be able to share with our stu-dents here at the Livingston Foundation."

Jeff jumped in. "Does that mean you're approving her as my sub?"

"I don't have time to look for someone myself, Jef-frey. Nor do I know anything about acting. So I'll have to trust your judgment." She added, "Besides, thanks to how unreliable your first choice was, we need someone immediately, don't we?"

"Esther's reliable," he said.

"I'm reliable," I said.

"Actually, she was my first choice," Jeff lied, "but her shooting schedule at the time meant she couldn't do it. But now Frank is out of the picture, and Esther's available. So it's all good."

"If you say so." Catherine turned to me. "Jeff will show you around and explain how things work here. When he's not available—which is often, I'm afraid, ever since he took this other job—you'll probably have to come to me for whatever you need. I'm terribly busy, but will fit you in as best I can. Sadly, our administrator died unexpectedly a few weeks ago, so things are in disarray until we can replace him."

"Darius was the administrator here?" I blurted.

Her facial register of emotions was subtle, but I saw that she was surprised. "You knew Darius?"

"Not exactly." If Jeff could lie, so could I. "But Jeff was telling me earlier about his death. Very sad. He was only thirty-seven?"

Jeff gave me a sharp glance but remained silent.

"Yes," Catherine said, revealing some sadness. "He was still a young man. It was a terrible thing. And we're quite lost without him, I'm afraid. I didn't realize how much we relied on him here until he was gone."

I said, "A ruptured intestine, Jeff told me." Now my former boyfriend turned his head and gave me a hard stare. "How did it happen?"

"I don't know much about it." Catherine shook her head. "I gathered that it was one of those anomalous tragedies. The sort of unpredictable physical disaster that can strike a person at any time. Even someone with access to good medical care in a wealthy society."

"Had he been complaining of any symptoms?" I asked.

She seemed to search her memory. "Not as far as I know. Jeffrey?"

Jeff shrugged. "I hardly ever talked to him."

"Was there a police investigation?" I asked. "I mean, someone so young dying so suddenly like that . . ."

She gave me a look that indicated she found the question peculiar. "I haven't heard of any police involvement." She looked inquisitively at Jeff. He didn't notice, because he was looking at me.

I asked, "Did Darius get along well with everyone here?"

"I believe so." Catherine's cool tone hinted that I was fast wearing out my welcome now.

I knew I would feel silly asking my next question, but I also didn't want to face Max's disappointment if I didn't ask it. "Did he have any enemies?"

"You seem very . . . *interested* in his death, for someone who didn't 'exactly' know him," Catherine observed.

"We met once, and it was a very memorable occasion," I said truthfully. "Did he ever mention being afraid of anyone?"

"No."

"Did he have any unusual religious practices? Or, um, interesting hobbies?"

Catherine said, "Jeff, I believe you have a class shortly?"

"Yes, I do." He stood up quickly. "Let's go, Esther."

"Was Darius dating anyone?"

Jeff's hand slid under my elbow, and he pulled me to my feet. "We've taken enough of her time, Esther."

"I'm sorry." I smiled at Catherine. "I tend to get carried away when the conversation turns to a subject that I find so interesting."

"Thanks, Catherine." Jeff hauled me to the door. "And this will work out well this time. I swear."

He opened the door and shoved me through it.

I came eye to eye with a large snake. Its sleek head weaved toward me as its tongue flicked out at me.

I choked on a frightened gasp and staggered backward on my high-heeled boots. Losing my footing, I fell against Jeff, who staggered backward, too, as my weight hit him. We careened into the chairs we had just been sitting in. One chair fell over with a clatter, taking Jeff with it. My ankle turned as I tried to save my balance, and I flew sideways over Jeff and hit the floor. I banged my head on the corner of Catherine's desk. The pain was excruciating.

I lay there in a fetal position, eyes squeezed shut, sucking in noisy gasps of air between my teeth as I tried not to pass out or burst into tears.

"Esther?" I heard Max call, sounding alarmed.

"Ungh," was the only response I could manage.

I flinched and opened my eyes when I felt something touch me, but relaxed when I saw it was Max. He squatted down, helped me sit up, and tried to examine my head.

Then he said, "How many fingers am I holding up?"

"I don't care." I closed my eyes again.

He said patiently, "I'm trying to ascertain—"

"I know." I touched my skull gingerly. "I think it's just pain. Not a concussion." I opened my eyes once more, and I saw that Jeff was hauling himself slowly to his feet.

"What the *hell* . . . ?" Then Jeff saw the snake. "Oh!" He looked at me. "Maybe I should have warned you about that."

"You think?" I snapped.

I'm not hysterically phobic, but—like a *lot* of people, I thought irritably—I'm scared enough of snakes to have a strong startle-reflex if I suddenly come face-to-face with one without warning.

Holding my hand over my aching skull, I glanced up at Catherine, who was standing nearby. She looked down at me with an expression that suggested she doubted my mental stability. Her gazed moved over me, and I realized that in my fall and subsequent agonized huddling, my tiny vinyl skirt had ridden up to my waist. The flimsiness of Jilly's purple fishnet stockings ensured that everyone in the room had an excellent view of my underpants.

The skirt was too tight for me to pull it down while I was in a sitting position, so I tugged on Max to signal to him that I wanted help standing up. With his assistance, I rose to my feet, then straightened my little skirt while he averted his gaze.

"Mambo Celeste," Catherine said. "Are you all right?"

There was a short, heavyset black woman standing in the doorway. Her expression was wide-eyed with astonishment as she stared at me, apparently as stunned by my tawdry appearance as she was surprised by my dramatic reaction to her entrance. There was a big, thick snake draped around her shoulders. Both of her hands protectively cradled it, as if my antics might disturb or harm the reptile—which was at least six feet long, maybe eight.

"Hmm? Oh. Yes, I'm fine." The woman patted the snake and spoke to it soothingly. "And Napoleon is all right, too, aren't you, *mon petit?*"

She spoke with a slight accent, and she gave the snake's name a distinctly French pronunciation.

All of my attention had been claimed by the snake's face coming straight at me when Jeff had opened the door and shoved me through it. But now that I got a good look at Mambo Celeste, I was a little surprised that she had faded into the background even for that shocked instant. A broad and round woman, she wore a colorful, floor-length dress of beautiful, brightly patterned blue, black, and white cloth sewn in a pattern of cascading folds that emphasized her girth with regal results. A scarf of matching material was wrapped around her head. Beaded earrings dangled from her ears, and a simple gold cross hung around her neck. I thought she was probably somewhere in her fifties. Her face was jowly and lined, and she looked like someone who frowned more often than she smiled.

"I'm fine, too, thanks," Jeff said sourly. "But you should stop carrying that damn snake around the building, Celeste. People get startled, go figure."

"*Mambo* Celeste," she corrected him coldly. "And I did not know there were strangers here."

"*I'm* not a stranger," Jeff said, "and I don't like bumping into that thing. Neither do half my students."

Mambo Celeste's eyes flashed. "Napoleon is not a *thing*. And if people are afraid of him, it is only because they do not understand."

Jeffrey scowled. "What *I* don't understand—"

"Jeffrey," Catherine said anxiously.

"—and what my aching sacroiliac doesn't understand . . ." He rubbed the recently-insulted portion of his anatomy. ". . . is how you can think it's a good idea to have a reptile that's taller than *I* am on the loose in a building that's always full of kids!"

"Jeffrey, this isn't the time—"

"For God's sake, Catherine, what if that thing suddenly gets hungry? Or feels threatened?"

The snake turned its head and looked at Jeff. He noticed and, perhaps as creeped out by this as I was, seemed to lose his train of thought.

Max sought to ease the tension with a polite question. "Your pet appears to be a boa constrictor, I believe?"

"He is not a pet." Mambo Celeste seemed determined to be disagreeable.

"He is a servant of Damballah," Catherine said, giving Jeff an admonishing glance, "and, as such, should be treated with reverence."

"Who's Damballah?" I asked, gingerly probing my scalp.

Catherine, who was about to answer, looked surprised when Max said, "Ah! He is perhaps the most powerful of the Vodou loa, and his origins are very ancient, going all the way back to the Great Serpent whose seven thousand coils brought forth Creation. Damballah is earthly and very wise. His wife is Ayida-Wedo, the Rainbow, a goddess of the sky. Like Damballah, she is also represented by a snake." He smiled courteously at Mambo Celeste. "Is my summary correct?"

"Who are you?" she asked suspiciously.

"I beg your pardon!" He removed his straw hat. "In all the commotion, we skipped introductions, didn't we?"

Jeff said to Catherine, "This is Dr. Max Zadok, a friend of Esther's."

I said to Max, "This is Dr. Catherine Livingston. My new boss, I guess."

Max nodded to her. "My pleasure, Dr. Livingston."

"What is your field, Dr. Zadok?"

"I studied science and theology at Oxford University," he said, wisely omitting the awkward detail that he had graduated more than three hundred years ago. "And what is your field, doctor?"

"Cultural anthropology, religion, and folklore," Catherine replied. Which perhaps explained her verbal incontinence over the old piece of cloth decorating her couch.

Looking at me with open distaste, Mambo Celeste said to Jeff, "And who is this . . . *woman* you have brought here?"

"Esther Diamond," I said. "I'm a new workshop teacher here. Temporarily, anyhow. I hope we'll be friends."

Her expression suggested that she'd rather weave kente cloth with her toes than befriend me.

"Mambo Celeste—er, a mambo is a Vodou priestess," Catherine said, addressing me, the ignorant one. "Mambo

Celeste honors us here at the foundation by teaching Vodou practices and by leading rituals. I direct the foundation's programs in traditional cultures and syncretic religions, which educate young African-Americans about their rich heritage. As with our programs in music, drama, literature, and art, we encourage our students—whether children, teens, or adults—to explore forms of self-expression beyond the commercialized contemporary pop culture that's already familiar to them."

I said, "What's a syn . . . syncret . . ."

"A syncretic faith," Catherine said, "is one that combines and adapts two or more existing religions into a single new one. Syncretic religions were the focus of my Ph.D. research—which is also how I originally got involved in the Livingston Foundation."

"Is that how you met your husband?" I asked. "When you started working here?"

Catherine ignored the personal question in favor of lecturing me some more. "Examples of syncretic faiths in the New World include Santería, which emerged in Cuba; Candomblé, which is an Afro-Brazilian religion; Shango and Brujería, which respectively developed in—"

"And I guess voodoo is the best known of these?" I interrupted, sensing that I could be in for another lengthy monologue if I wasn't careful.

"Vodou is the more proper traditional term," she said. "It developed in Haiti, arising out of various traditional West African religions that came to the New World with captive slaves, combined with the Roman Catholicism of the slaves' French masters."

"The loa whom I mentioned," Max said to me, "are Vodou spirits who correspond loosely to Catholic saints. And you will perhaps have observed that the mambo wears a Christian cross."

"So you're loosely Catholic?" I said to her.

Mambo Celeste looked at me as if my skirt were up around my waist again. Jeff looked heavenward, as if seeking forgiveness from his Maker for having brought me here.

Max cleared his throat. "We were admiring the beautiful drapeaux in the hallway. Did those come from Haiti?"

"No, they were made by members of Mambo Celeste's spiritual community." Glancing at the snake-draped woman with a smile that struck me as slightly patronizing, Catherine added, "The mambo serves a devoted group of followers."

"What are they following?" I asked, watching Napoleon's head rise and fall sinuously in front of Mambo Celeste's face as his tongue flicked in and out a few times. I wished he would take a nap or something.

"They follow the rituals." Mambo Celeste eyed me with disdain. "They serve the loa."

"Vodou worship involves propitiating and invoking the favor of the loa," Max said to me, "which is a pantheon of spirits that includes ancestors, natural forces, and representatives of human nature. Worshippers make appropriate gifts of food, beverages, shelter, and money, and they pay homage with respect, deference, and love." He gestured to Mambo Celeste and her twining reptile. "A mambo or a houngan—er, a priest—is an accomplished intermediary who can intercede with the loa on behalf of the community. A mambo is someone who has trained with dedication, studied devoutly, and made great personal sacrifices to be closer to the spirits."

Looking rather pleased with this description of herself, Mambo Celeste looked curiously at Max. "Are *you* a servant of the loa?"

"I am a respectful friend of all faiths," Max said. "And an eager student of anyone willing to share wisdom and knowledge."

Mambo Celeste smiled a little, and for a moment, she almost didn't look unfriendly. "Perhaps you would like to join my community in a ritual one day?"

"I would be most honored to do so!" Max beamed at her.

She glanced at me with distaste, then said to him, "I suppose you may bring your friend, if you wish. But she must dress with more respect."

"Er, I'm standing right here," I pointed out.

"Hmph."

While I gently explored the sore spot on my scalp again, Catherine said, "Were you coming to see me about something, Mambo Celeste?"

"Ah. Yes."

Catherine said to me, "Well, as you can see, I have other matters to attend to. And your students are probably waiting for you downstairs."

Since Napoleon seemed to be getting restless, I was only too happy to vacate the room. "Jeff?"

"Right." His eyes were also on the snake. "Let's go teach a class."

"It was nice to meet you, Dr. Zadok," Catherine said, dismissively. "Perhaps you'll come to one of the foundation's art exhibitions or public lectures someday."

"I look forward to it." He added to Mambo Celeste, "And to meeting you again, I hope."

Once we were out in the hallway with the door closed behind us, Jeff said quietly to Max, "Well, you've certainly got hidden talent. I never saw that old witch warm up to anyone so fast—let alone a white person."

"Hmm." Max paused to study Darius' photo again, then followed us to the stairs. "I certainly agree with your concerns about her roaming this building with an unrestrained boa constrictor. But a mambo is a learned and powerful woman, and that merits our respect."

"She's pretentious and nasty," Jeff said dismissively

as we started down the stairs. "That Creole accent she talks with? *Please.* Her family emigrated here from Haiti when she was a teenager, fleeing Duvalier. She's been in New York for nearly forty years. You can't tell me that 'authentic' accent isn't put on—or at least consciously retained."

"Oh, an accent can be a hard thing to shed," Max said. "It's just the way a person learned to speak a language. It feels familiar."

Jeff paused on the steps as he listened to Max's accented voice. "Sorry, Max. I didn't mean to be rude. I just don't like her."

As we reached the ground floor, I said, "And I gather she doesn't like white people?"

"Hell, no. Catherine's the only white person I've ever seen her be at all friendly to—until Max turned her up sweet, that is." Jeff gave Max an amused glance, then continued, "And, actually, it took a long time for her to accept Catherine."

"What do you mean, 'accept'? Catherine's the boss," I pointed out.

"Oh, she's only the boss since the old man died. Here, this way." Jeff led us to a set of swinging double doors and pushed them open.

"The old man? You mean Martin Livingston?"

We followed him into a hallway that had classrooms on either side of it. The foundation was obviously a busy place in summer. We passed an art class, a tribal drumming class, and a room full of women who seemed to be planning an event. Fortunately, the drumming class seemed to be wrapping up.

Jeff was saying, "Yeah. Martin was a lot older than Catherine. It was a May-December thing. Also his third marriage." He glanced at me. "But maybe you knew that already? You seem to know a lot about *Darius,* after all."

We stopped outside the doorway of a room that had

about fifteen teenagers in it. I heard one of them say, "Hey, there he is now," and realized this must be our class.

"What's going on, Esther?" Jeff looked puzzled. "*Did* you know Darius? Why did you come here today? And why were you asking Catherine all those questions about him?"

"I'll explain after class." I exchanged a look with Max. "And we'll have some questions about Frank as well as about Darius."

Max asked, "Who's Frank?"

Jeff said, "The guy who was filling in for me before Esther."

"Ah," said Max. "Of course."

Jeff frowned, looking even more puzzled. "Why do you have questions about Frank? And what's he got to do with Darius?"

"Later," I said. "The students are waiting." And punctuality was a cardinal virtue of our profession. I was once ninety seconds late for a rehearsal on my first Equity job. The producer took me aside and gave me a memorably stern lecture about it. Ever since then, I had been religiously punctual as an actress; and I didn't like starting off on the wrong foot with these kids by showing up late for my first session with them.

Jeff nodded and entered the room ahead of me. "Sorry, folks! I had to take my new coteacher upstairs to sign some paperwork before we could get started today."

I realized I would indeed have to go back upstairs to sign paperwork at some point, now that I was working here. But not today. Catherine Livingston and I had already spent enough time together for one day.

"This is Esther Diamond, and, as you can see . . ." Jeff gestured to me, bulging out of my low-cut leopard-print top and barely covered by my tiny red skirt. "She's very shy and modest."

The kids laughed and I rolled my eyes. Then Jeff explained that, actually, I was wearing my *D30* costume, having come straight here from filming, and they looked suitably impressed. Apart from all being African-American teenagers, they were an eclectic-looking group. A few of them were dressed in well-pressed preppy summer cottons, several were in Afro-Caribbean ethnic wear, some of them wore gangsta drag (and how anyone could possibly think those sagging trousers and baggy shirts looked cool would forever baffle me), and some dressed exactly like the kids that Jeff and I had each grown up with in the Midwest.

Jeff also introduced Max, who took off his hat and gave a little bow to the group. "I am neither an actor nor an acting teacher, but since I have accompanied Esther here, may I remain and serve as your audience today?"

"What is he, then?" one of the baggy-clothes boys asked me with a bold grin. "Your pimp?"

"Down, Jamal," Jeff said mildly.

"He's my bodyguard," I said. "In case any young men make disrespectful comments to me while I'm dressed like this."

The rest of the kids enjoyed this noisily, and Jamal laughed, too. They seemed like a nice group.

Jeff suggested that Max take a seat. Then, rubbing his lower back again, he asked if any of the kids had any painkillers with them. A girl named Shondolyn had a jumbo-sized bottle of ibuprofen, and I cadged a couple of pills, too, since my head still hurt. And then we got down to work.

It was an improvisation class, so we mostly played various theater games for the next ninety minutes, exploring different ways of doing each exercise and solving new problems, and then discussing how to apply what we had just learned to other acting situations—including scripted work.

Since my outfit so boldly proclaimed the profession of the character I was portraying on *D30,* we played with that a lot, mostly by using it as a communication-challenge exercise. In some of the games, I picked a different reason, other than the obvious one, that I would be dressed like this, and the students playing the scene with me had to figure out—without my telling them, just based on our interaction—what that reason was and behave accordingly. For example, in one scene, I was a cocktail waitress, in another, I was wearing the worst-ever bridesmaid's dress. Then we reversed the game, so that the students playing scenes with me had to give me enough clues, in our interaction, for me to figure out what rationale *they* had selected for me to be dressed this way (in one scenario, I turned out to be a lion tamer).

Most of them were enthusiastic, engaged kids, and we had a lot of fun. So I was really glad that Jeff had offered me this opportunity.

After we wrapped up the class, Jeff and I stayed behind to answer a few students' questions while most of them drifted out of the room, laughing and chatting. Max waited for us by the open door. I was by now feeling ravenous and hoped we were going to question Jeff over a (very) late lunch, rather than set off immediately for the spot where I had seen Darius attacked by gargoyles. I was about to ask Jeff if he had time for a meal, when Max gave a startled cry.

"Esther! The huntsman!"

"What?"

I looked over at Max and saw that he was pointing down the hallway, in the direction from which we had come earlier.

Jeff said, "Huntsman?"

Max cried, "A young man armed with a sword!" And he set off at a run.

8

I set off after Max.

Jeff followed me. "What's going on?"

"Max!" I cried. "Stop!"

The sword-wielding young man hadn't threatened me last night, but that didn't mean I thought it was a good idea to run after him and jump on top of him. Which seemed to be Max's plan.

Shoving past startled students, Max disappeared through the swinging double doors at the end of the hall. I ran after him, apologizing to students as I pushed them out of the way, then I plunged through the double doors, too, letting them slap shut in my wake. Right behind me, I heard Jeff give a howl of pain.

Max ran across the lobby of the building. The man at the reception desk who had initially welcomed us here today looked worried now. As Max disappeared through another set of swinging doors on the other side of the lobby, the man called out, "Is there a problem?"

Behind me, Jeff cried, "I don't know! Esther! What's going *on?*"

I dashed after Max and through the double doors, hoping that Jeff, hot on my heels, would be more cautious this time.

Directly ahead of me, Max cried, "Halt!" and seized his quarry by the shoulder. They were the only two people in this corridor.

I caught up to Max and found him wrestling with . . . a boy who looked about twelve years old. The kid was wearing a white fencing jacket and carrying a French foil with a protective rubber tip on its point.

The boy looked more startled than alarmed by this sudden seizure. He was wrestling with Max and saying, "Whoa! What is your *problem?*"

Jeff caught up to us. "What are you *doing?*"

Max said to the boy, "In the interests of safe and rational discourse, I must ask you to lay down your weapon."

"Max!" Jeff said. "Let him go!"

"Max, let go," I urged, putting a hand on his arm. "This isn't the huntsman."

"What *huntsman?*" Jeff snapped.

A young man came through the doorway of a nearby room. I suddenly realized that I heard the click and clash of metal blades coming from that room—the sound of swords hitting each other.

The young man's face registered surprised recognition when he saw me. "What are *you* doing here?" Like the boy, he wore a white fencing jacket. He carried a rapier in his hand.

Startled, I pointed at him in dumb silence.

Max looked at him. "The huntsman?"

I nodded.

The young man, who was athletically lithe with a stern face, close-cropped black hair, and mocha skin, said to me, "You can't come in here dressed like that! What's the matter with you?"

"I haven't had time to change," I snapped.

Jeff said, "You two know each other?"

"*No,*" we said in unison.

The boy in Max's grip said impatiently to the young man, "Biko, will you tell this dude to let me go?"

To the boy, Biko said, "We do not refer to elders as 'dudes.'" And to Max he said, "Take your hands off this boy right now." Biko looked about eighteen years old, but he had the presence and gravitas of someone twice that age.

Max immediately released the boy. "Oh, I do beg your pardon."

Biko looked at the kid and nodded his head toward the open door. The boy obeyed the silent command and, with a look over his shoulder that indicated he thought we were all crazy, went into the room from which Biko had just emerged.

"A fencing class," I said, realizing what the sound of clashing swords and the white jackets meant.

Biko frowned at me. "What are you *doing* here?"

"This is most embarrassing," Max said. "I fear we've gotten off on the wrong foot. And I am to blame."

"I'll say," Jeff muttered.

Biko looked at him. "Are these people with you, Jeff?"

Jeff sighed. "Yes." He made brief introductions. "Esther Diamond, actress. Dr. Max Zadok, madman. Biko Garland, fencing instructor."

"Why are they here?" Biko asked him, ignoring the introduction.

"I'm filling in for Jeff," I said.

"Oh, that's right." Biko nodded. "The gladiator gig. Scheduling conflicts."

I looked at Jeff, too. "Gladiator? That's the kind of 'athlete' you're playing?"

"Biko helped me prepare for the audition," Jeff said. "I needed some sword fighting moves."

"Gladiators didn't fight with rapiers," I said.

"The rapier is the weapon I'm best with," Biko said calmly, "but it's not the only one I know how to use."

"Is that why you took it hunting with you last night?" I said. "Because it's the one you use best?"

He looked at me, then at the two men, then back at me. His face didn't give away anything, and I wondered what he was thinking. Then he said, "Class isn't over. These kids need my attention."

He turned to reenter the training room.

Max said, "Were you hunting a zombie, by chance?"

Biko froze, and all three of us looked at Max in surprise.

"A *what?*" Jeff said.

"A *zombie?*" I said.

Biko just stared at him, frowning.

"Well?" Max said. "Was that what you were hunting last night?"

"Biko, man," Jeff said. "I'm sorry about this. I don't really know these people. I'll get them out of here now, and we won't even talk about this again. Okay?"

Jeff took my elbow in a firm grasp and tugged. I jerked my arm away from him, looking from Max to Biko. I repeated, "A zombie?"

"Reanimation of the dead," Max said. "Exactly what we were talking about this morning."

"Holy shit," Jeff said. "You really *are* a madman."

"I don't like people cursing around these kids," Biko said absently, still staring at Max.

Jeff ignored that. "Max? Esther? Shall we *go* now?

I said to Max, "Now you're saying I saw a *zombie* last night?"

Biko's gaze flashed to me.

"Are zombies a sign of the apocalypse?" I asked, feeling confused.

"God, what *are* you into these days?" Jeff asked me in horror.

Biko said to me, "You saw something last night?"

I looked at Max. He nodded.

I looked at Jeff. He was staring at me as if seriously rethinking the wisdom of letting me spend time with his students.

Then I looked at Biko and said, "I saw Darius Phelps last night. About a block past where I saw you."

Biko look puzzled. "You mean you saw his body?"

"No, I mean I saw him. Walking and talking." I added, "Sort of."

"You didn't see Darius," Jeff said firmly. "He's dead."

"Jeff's right." Biko nodded. "It couldn't have been Mr. Phelps. He's . . ." His gaze shifted to Max, and he drew in a sharp breath through his nostrils. "No." He shook his head. "No *way*."

Max said to him, "Wait a moment. If you weren't looking for Darius Phelps, then what *were*—"

Jeff said impatiently, "Darius is *dead,* I'm telling you. I was at the funeral."

"What was he buried in?" I asked suddenly, turning to Jeff.

"A *coffin,* Esther. Like most people."

"No, what was he wearing?"

"How should *I* know?" Jeff said.

Biko said, "It was closed-casket funeral. But I heard Dr. Livingston saying that he'd asked to be buried in his tuxedo."

I gasped and clasped my hand over my mouth.

"Figures," Jeff muttered. "He was a pretentious bastard."

"Oh, my God," I choked out, feeling cold again.

"I know, I know," Jeff said. "Don't speak ill of the dead and all that. And, yes, it's too bad the guy died young. Even so, I don't see why I should have to start pretending I liked him, just because he's dead now. I never pretended when he was alive, after all."

"*Max,*" I said. "A tuxedo!"

"Yes, my dear." He patted my arm.

"A zombie?" I said, trying not to think too hard about the fact that I had been alone in the dark with him. It. Whatever. "You really think so?"

"As soon as I saw those drapeaux upstairs," Max said, "it seemed an inescapable conclusion."

"Whoa, time out," Jeff said. "How does gaudy folk art lead you inescapably to the conclusion that—that—that . . . Christ, I can't even say it, it's so crazy."

"That Darius Phelps is a zombie now?" Max concluded for him. "Well, it is, of course, possible that he was reanimated by some other means—"

"Oh, like *what?*" Jeff said. "Who the hell goes around reanimating corpses?"

"Various cultures throughout the ages, Jeffrey," Max said patiently. He was accustomed to being disbelieved. "Whether seeking immortality or using the dead to terrorize others, reanimation has been the study of many mystical practitioners. It has also been the solace of billions who have believed in the resurrection of Jesus Christ, and of those who believe that they themselves will be resurrected on Judgment Day."

"Or when the Messiah comes," I added, not wanting my team to be left out of the discussion.

"But you're not talking about someone who's been resurrected by God Almighty," Jeff pointed out.

"No, indeed," Max said. "I believe a much lesser—but nonetheless formidable—power is behind the reanimation of Darius Phelps. And although many possibilities exist for explaining this phenomenon, it seems rather foolish to ignore the one staring us in the face. Mr. Phelps, after all, worked in a community where Vodou is practiced."

"Watch it," Biko said. "You're stepping on dangerous ground now. My sister is a servant of the loa."

"I am most respectful of her faith," Max said. "But

every power may be used for evil ends, when in the hands of the wrong person. And since there is a tradition, on the dark side of Vodou, of raising zombies from the grave . . . My hypothesis is that this is the fate of the unfortunate Darius Phelps."

Jeff asked with somewhat malicious interest, "Are you accusing Mambo Celeste of doing it?"

"Traditionally, such a thing would be abhorrent to a mambo," Max said. "More to the point, we are far from being able to accuse anyone, Jeffrey. We have very little information at the moment. But it does occur to me, all things considered, that we are probably looking for a bokor."

Biko made a startled sound. He was gazing wide-eyed at Max.

"A what?" I said.

"A bokor," said Max.

"A dark sorcerer," said Biko, nodding slowly. "Someone who practices black magic."

Max eyed him. "I gather I am not the only one to whom this possibility has occurred?"

"No," Biko said. "Not the only one."

"But you were not aware of Darius Phelps' transformation. So what led you—and your sister, I presume—to this suspicion?" Max paused before asking, "What exactly you were hunting with deadly intent last night, Mr. Garland?"

The young man let out his breath. "I think you'd better call me Biko."

"You were hunting last night?" Jeff said. "In *Harlem?*"

Biko nodded. "Yes." He looked from Jeff to me, and then to Max. "I was hunting baka."

After a moment of puzzled silence, Jeff said, "Back of what? Back of where?"

"No," Biko said. "Baka." He enunciated slowly. "Ba-ka."

I gasped so hard that I choked. All three men looked at me. "That's what he said!"

Looking at me with an expression that I remembered well from our days as a couple, Jeff said, "Yes. Just now. He said 'baka.' So what, Esther?"

"No! I mean Darius! That's what *he* said. *Ba . . . ka . . .*" I looked at Biko. "I thought it was just nonsense syllables. He wasn't coherent at the time. But it's a word? Baka?"

"Yes."

"I'm not familiar with it," Max said.

"The baka are the deadly tools of a dark sorcerer—of a bokor," said Biko. "They're evil spirits. They can take the form of small monsters or of—"

"Gargoyles!" I said.

"Oh, come on," said Jeff.

Biko considered my comment. "Yes, I suppose you could say the baka look a bit like gargoyles. Or, at least, some of them do."

"Wait, you were out hunting *gargoyles* last night?" Jeff shook his head. "Okay. That's it. All *three* of you are insane."

"That must be what I saw!" I said to Max. "That must be what attacked Darius. Baka!"

"That doesn't make sense," Biko said.

"Oh, you think?" said Jeff.

Biko ignored him. "If a bokor raised Darius from the dead—"

"Are you *listening* to yourself?" Jeff said.

"Then why would he—or she—send baka to attack him? Er, it? Um—"

"Whatever," I said. "I don't know. Could there be two bokors? At odds with each other?"

"Oh, dear." Max looked alarmed. "Two warring bokors? That could be very messy."

"Oh, Harlem has survived worse," Jeff said philosophically.

Biko gave him a contemptuous look. "You only say that because you don't know what a bokor can do."

"Why were you hunting the baka?" Max asked curiously.

"What on earth makes you think these things exist?" Jeff asked him.

"How did you get involved in this?" I asked.

Biko's expression was a mixture of anger, sadness, and revulsion. "My sister Puma and I . . ."

"Yes?"

"Well . . ." He looked at all three of us. "The baka ate our dog."

"I find pet death very disturbing," I said.

"*I* find the idea that you're buying into this crazy bullshit very disturbing," Jeff said.

"Here we are," said Max. "I believe this is the place."

Biko had to finish teaching his class, but there was clearly a lot that we needed to discuss. So he had advised us to go to his sister's nearby shop, on West 123rd Street, and wait for him there. He called her on his cell phone and told her to expect us, then he went back to his students while we left the building.

Jeff, who was appalled by this whole business, had not intended to accompany us. But Max wanted to question him about Darius and also about Frank. So, aware of Max's silent glances imploring me to convince him to join us, I asked Jeff if he'd like to go to the hospital with me, after we were done meeting with the Garland siblings, to visit Michael Nolan. I conscientiously did *not* imply that if he made a good impression, Nolan might help him get an audition for the show. (In fact, I thought

there was a better chance of Fiorello LaGuardia being turned into a zombie than of Mike Nolan helping
another actor get work.) But, as expected, Jeff leaped
to the conclusion that he wanted to reach; and, for the
sake of the greater good, I didn't correct his optimistic
assumptions. So he walked with us to Puma Garland's
shop.

Now Max read aloud the sign in the window of the
small storefront. "Puma's Vodou Emporium."

"So I guess I can understand where Biko's getting
his crazy ideas," Jeff said, looking at the shop window
without enthusiasm. "But as for you two . . ." He shook
his head.

" 'There are more things in heaven and earth, Hora-
tio, than are dreamt of in your philosophy,' " I quoted.

"Whatever."

Alerted by her brother, Puma Garland was waiting
for us inside the shop. An attractive young woman with
a robust, hourglass figure, she was dressed in blue jeans
and a flowing shirt of brightly patterned material. Puma
wore her chin-length black hair in bouncy curls, and she
accented her look with gold hoop earrings and beaded
bracelets. She was obviously older than Biko, probably
in her mid-twenties.

And the moment he saw her, Jeff's whole attitude
about this venture changed. He took her hand when she
introduced herself to us, looked into her eyes, and said,
"We've come to help you."

"Oh, good grief," I muttered.

Puma flashed straight white teeth in a pretty smile,
then turned to Max. "You must be Dr. Zadok?" She
shook his hand. "And you're Esther Diamond?" She
blinked a little at my outfit, but she was welcoming, even
so.

"Hi," I said. "I'm really sorry about your dog."

Her face fell.

"Oh, nicely played." Jeff gave me a quelling look.

Puma rallied quickly. "Biko says you've seen the baka?"

"Yes. Last night."

She took my hands and squeezed them in sympathy. "You're lucky to be alive. They're very dangerous."

Recalling the dismemberment I'd witnessed, I said, "Yeah, that was my impression."

The shop's telephone rang. "I'm sorry, I'd better get that," she said. "Make yourselves comfortable, and when I'm done with this call, we'll talk."

The caller turned out to be a supplier evidently trying to resolve a shipping error, and the conversation lasted for a while. Trying to ignore the rumbling of my empty stomach, I looked around the shop. It was small and crowded with merchandise, but well-ordered and appealing.

There was a display of charms and potions for attracting love, luck, and money, as well as for protecting oneself against negative forces, enemies, and evildoers. There were colorful drapeaux for sale on the walls, similar to the ones I had seen at the Livingston Foundation. The items available for a worshipper's personal voodoo altar included candles, offering bowls, crystals, incense, and spirit bottles.

"What's a spirit bottle?" I asked Max.

"It's a tool for communicating with the loa." He picked up a pretty bottle decorated with beads and delicate paint. "A mambo or a houngan has the power to call a spirit down into the bottle, where it will converse with worshippers who wish to question it. Or an experienced worshipper who prepares mentally and spiritually may call a loa into the bottle and commune with it there."

"That seems very accommodating of the loa," I said.

"They can be called into other objects, too." Max pointed to some masks that were decorated with shells, paint, feathers, jewelry, and sequins. "You can hang such a mask in a room that you wish to protect. If you want to shield a child from illness and harm, for example, you might hang a spirit mask in his bedroom and call the appropriate loa into the mask."

"You were right," I noted. "This is a practical religion."

The Catholic influence on Vodou was evident in the many pictures of Catholic saints for sale in the shop, as well vials of holy water, crucifixes, and rosary beads.

There was a bulletin board near the front door with flyers and notices pinned to it. Patrons of the shop were invited to attend traditional rituals, as well classes and lectures about Vodou. A calendar of the Livingston Foundation's activities for the month of August was posted. And various mambos and houngans in the tristate area offered their services: divination, healing, casting spells, consulting the spirits, constructing charms, concocting potions, helping people find happiness and ward off evil, and spiritual cleansing.

Elsewhere in the shop, I examined a prepackaged ritual kit for beginners, but decided I wasn't that interested when I saw the price tag; I'm a working actress, and I live on a tight budget. I also looked at some divination tools (including animal bones), spell kits, and protective amulets. There was a big gourd rattle decorated with cowry shells. I enjoyed playing with it until I read on the label that its rattling noise was not made by beads, beans, or pebbles, as I had supposed, but by snake vertebrae.

"What *is* it with voodoo and snakes?" I said, putting the rattle down quickly.

"In many faiths of the world, dating back far into prehistory, snakes represent wisdom, strength, and fertility." Max added, "But there is no denying the negative reaction to snakes that our distant primate past instills in many of us."

I poked around a large selection of whole and powdered herbs—some common, some exotic. Wondering what Jeff was studying so intently, I wandered over to him. He was looking at a machete and some ritual knives that were displayed inside a locked glass case.

"Do you suppose these are for slaughtering animals?" he asked me.

"*Sacrificing* animals," Puma corrected him. She had just gotten off the phone. "Like us, the Vodou loa must eat and drink to stay strong. And if they are strong, then they guide us, protect us, and bring us good fortune. So we must nourish them."

"How often does this nourishing occur?" Jeff asked cautiously.

"Around here, animal sacrifices are only made on special occasions. Most of the time, we offer grain, rum, tobacco, produce, and that sort of thing."

"Oh. Okay." Jeff relaxed and smiled.

"But I think we'll have to offer an animal sacrifice soon," Puma said with a worried look.

"What?" Jeff blurted.

"Everything is out of balance. Angry loa have been set loose in Harlem," Puma said. "We must propitiate the spirits and seek their protection with a generous offering and a major ritual. Or else we will all suffer the consequences of their wrath."

9

"I can scarcely imagine how painful this subject must be for you," Max said to Puma. "But may I ask you to recount how your dog met its fatal end?"

Jeff gave Max a warning glance, then said to Puma, "Unless it's too upsetting for you."

She smiled warmly at Jeff. He smiled back, his bald head shining like a new penny. I hoped the gladiator job was worth having shaved off all his hair.

"It's all right," she said. "After all, you've come here to help, haven't you? And to figure out what to do about the strange things happening in this neighborhood?"

"Indeed," said Max.

"Then you need to know. Things have been . . . out of balance lately," Puma explained, "You see, Vodou seeks balance between opposing influences. Light and dark, good and evil, life and death. These things are all aspects of human nature and part of us, not separate or alien. So we have gods of death and vengeance, just as we have gods of life and love. We serve them all, because they all claim a place inside each one of us."

"Very practical." I thought it was unlikely that death or wrath would vanish from human experience, so I could see the sense in a religion that accepted these forces within its theology and sought balance between the extremes.

"But lately," Puma said, "things seem all out of whack. When I perform my Vodou rituals at home each morning, asking for good luck and blessings, I feel that the spirits are distracted and agitated."

Jeff's expression was a visible struggle between trying to look politely interested in a pretty woman's earnest comments and trying not to roll his eyes in open skepticism.

"The natural harmony . . ." Puma seemed to search for a more accurate word. "The . . . direction . . ."

"The flow?" Max suggested tentatively.

"Yes! The normal *flow* of spiritual energy seems . . . disrupted or . . ." Puma shook her head and frowned. "Out of balance. I don't know how else to describe it."

"You're doing very well," Max said.

Jeff flashed him an incredulous look but said nothing.

I met Max's gaze, recalling what he had told me this morning about the flow of mystical energy being reversed or misdirected. He gave a little nod in response to my inquisitively raised brows.

"Anyhow, Biko stayed late the other night at the foundation, to do some extra training by himself," Puma continued. "And when he was leaving, he heard someone in trouble across the street from the foundation, near the gates of the park, crying out in the dark. So he went to help, of course."

"Of course," said Max.

"The boy's got more guts than sense," said Jeff.

I imagined that the Garland siblings' mother had raised them to be the sort of people who did indeed help without hesitation when they heard someone cry out in the dark. The woman had, after all, named her daughter after the bold and resourceful mountain lion and her son after the brave activist who had galvanized resistance to apartheid in South Africa before being slain by his enemies in the 1970s. Those names were a lot to live up to, and I thought that Puma and Biko came across as people who made the effort.

Puma said, "And there on the sidewalk, right outside the park, Biko saw . . . these growling *creatures* attacking a man."

I drew in a sharp breath through my nostrils and looked at Max again.

"He described them to me." Puma gave a shudder. "Horrible little monsters with fangs, claws, pointy ears, hairy legs, and greenish skin. They had glowing red eyes and foul breath."

"That's exactly what I saw!" I said.

Jeff gave me a censorious look, as if I were encouraging Puma in a warped delusion.

"Biko fought the creatures and chased them off," said Puma.

"How was the victim?" Max asked.

"He was confused and panicky. Weeping and sweating. Actually . . ." She bit her lip. "Biko said the man had wet his pants."

"Whoa," Jeff said. "Messy."

"Who was he?" I asked. Not Darius Phelps at any rate. Until meeting me today, Biko hadn't known that Darius was up and about. So to speak.

The victim also probably wasn't a zombie, I suddenly realized. If, like Darius, zombies didn't bleed, then chances were they also didn't sweat, weep, or urinate.

Puma replied, "Biko didn't recognize him, and the man wasn't coherent. He just babbled hysterically about demon possession, dark rituals, and the walking dead."

"Jesus," said Jeff. "Heavy."

"What did Biko do?" I asked.

"You know what boys are like." Puma shook her head

in exasperation. "Instead of staying with the victim, Biko went chasing after the creatures—which I guess we all agree are baka?"

Max and I nodded. Jeff shifted his weight and looked at the voodoo dolls displayed near the cash register.

"But your brother didn't catch the baka, did he?" said Max.

"No. And when he came back to the spot where he'd left the victim . . ." She spread her hands. "The man was gone."

"Then the victim wasn't wounded in the attack?" Max asked.

Puma shook her head again. "Just scared and disheveled, according to Biko."

"Well, having seen those creatures myself," I said, "I can understand why the man ran away." And even though Biko was armed with a rapier, I still had to give him a lot of credit for going after the baka.

Max was stroking his beard thoughtfully. "Hmm. Exactly which night did this happen, Puma?"

She thought back. "Monday."

"Was the victim African-American?" When she nodded, Max asked Jeff, "And is your colleague Frank, the missing substitute teacher, also African-American?"

"Huh? Yeah." Jeff shrugged. "So what? This is Harlem, Max. *Most* people here are Af. . . ." His eyes widened. "Okay, wait a *minute*. You're not thinking—"

"Oh, I get it." Following Max's train of thought, I asked Jeff, "When did Frank start playing hooky?"

"The day before yesterday. Tuesday." Jeff added, "But that's got nothing to do with—"

"So Frank stopped coming to work at the foundation the day after Biko found a terrified man being attacked by mysterious creatures in the same neighborhood." I said. "Doesn't the coincidence even make you curious, Jeff?"

"No, of course not! Because Biko's story is crazy—no offense intended, Puma—and because there are a *lot* of reasons Frank might be missing. His absence does *not* have to be because he was attacked by demon spawn!"

"Missing?" I repeated. "What do you mean, *missing?*"

"Calm down. I *don't* mean 'missing.' I mean . . . out of touch. All right?"

"Who's Frank?" Puma asked in confusion.

Jeff said, "Frank Johnson. My sub."

"Pardon?"

I explained to her who Frank Johnson was. Then I said to Jeff, "Define 'out of touch.' "

He sighed. "Okay. Fine. Catherine called Frank on Tuesday, after he didn't show up to teach class. She tried him again yesterday, after he missed class a second time. No answer, no reply. Both times. That's why she called me today. After I heard from her, I called him, too, and left him a message." Jeff shook his head. "He hasn't called me back, either."

"Given his reaction to the attack that night," Max said, "the victim may have been terrified into a hysterical retreat."

"Frank's dodging calls because he has screwed up, that's all," said Jeff.

"Does he screw up a lot?" I asked.

"Well, I didn't think so, obviously, or I wouldn't have asked him to sub for me," Jeff said snappishly. "But I guess I was wrong."

"If Frank Johnson is indeed the victim Biko rescued," Max said, "then he may have information vital to our investigation."

"*What* investigation?" Jeff said.

"We must speak with him," said Max.

"Lots of luck. I just told you he's not returning calls."

"Then we should go to his home," Max said.

"I'm not sure where he lives," Jeff said. "Somewhere in Hamilton Heights, I think."

"Hey, that's in the Thirtieth Precinct!" I said brightly. They all looked at me.

"Never mind," I said. "You were saying?"

Jeff pulled out his cell phone and flipped it open. "Look, if it'll make you people happy, I'll call Frank again. And I'll say . . ." He looked at Max. "What will I say?"

"We want to know exactly what happened on Monday night."

Frank was still not answering his phone, so Jeff left him a rambling message. "Look, man, don't worry about the Livingston classes. It's cool. I mean, I've found someone to fill in for me. You. Me. Anyhow, the workshops at the foundation are covered. But I need to ask you about Monday. Did you happen to see anything, uh, a little out of the ordinary that night? Or were you—oh, I don't know—attacked by green gargoyles with bad breath, for example? Call me back. It's important."

As he hung up, I said, "Smooth. Very smooth."

"Like you could've done better."

Puma smiled warmly at him. "Thank you so much, Jeff. I know you didn't really want to call him, and I appreciate it."

That helped. He stopped sulking.

"With Frank still unavailable and Biko still at the foundation, perhaps we should continue with Puma's recitation," Max suggested.

Jeff hoisted himself up to sit on the sales counter, next to the cash register. My feet were starting to hurt again, so I gratefully sat on a tall stool that Puma brought out from behind the counter. Max declared himself comfortable standing where he was.

Puma continued her tale. "Biko looked for the victim, but there was no sign of him. So he came home and told me what had happened. I suppose it seems like jumping to conclusions, but given everything he told me, and the imbalance I had been feeling during my rituals . . . I had a strong feeling that my brother had seen baka."

Max nodded. Jeff closed his eyes and looked like he was trying to imagine himself elsewhere. I kept listening attentively.

"So the next night, Biko took his sword and went out hunting in the same area. He figured if the baka came out to attack someone else, he'd find them. But he phoned me after about two hours to say it was starting to seem like a waste of time, so he was coming home." Fear and revulsion crossed her face as she said in a low voice, "I don't know if they realized he was hunting them, and hid and stalked him. Or if they picked up his scent, recognized it from the night before, and followed it. Either way . . ." She shuddered again.

I gasped as I realized what she meant. "They followed him home?"

Puma nodded. "We had a little mixed breed dog. Maybe twenty pounds. His name was Gilligan. He always comes . . . *came* to the shop with me. Gilligan was getting old and slept most of the time. I've still got his daybed here, behind the cash register. And his little food and water dishes." Her face crumpled briefly, then she cleared her throat. "Biko always took him for his bedtime walk. Gilligan was gentle and easygoing, and he sure didn't move fast anymore, but he and Biko were barely outside the door of our building that night when Gilligan went *crazy*. I'd never heard him bark like that. So I looked out the window of the apartment right away—we live on the second floor—and I saw that little dog take off down the street like a bat out of hell. Faster than he had run in years! My brother had dropped the leash and was staring after him. I don't blame him. Gilligan *never* ran, so he took Biko totally by surprise.

"And then I *knew,*" she said. "Because it had to be something really strange to make Gilligan act like that. Something out of this world. So I was out the door like a shot, down the stairs, and out onto the street, running after them. Biko was already half a block ahead of me. It was dark, so I couldn't see Gilligan, but I could sure *hear* him. He was barking his head off!"

Puma took a shaky breath and continued. "Then I could hear him attacking something. And since he was the friendliest dog in the world—loved kids, loved other dogs, even loved cats—I knew he'd only do that if he'd met with something truly evil."

"The baka," I murmured, totally immersed in her tale.

"So I'm running down the street, and I can hear barking and growling and howling. Biko's shouting, and I'm shouting, and then . . . then Gilligan gave this horrible *wail,* and . . . Oh!" She covered her mouth with her hand and lowered her head, unable to continue.

Jeff looked dumbfounded and glanced at me, as if hoping I'd know what to do now.

Max pulled a clean white hanky out of his pocket and handed it to Puma. "Here, my dear. Take this."

"Thank you, Dr. Zadok." She sniffed, wiped her long-lashed eyes, and swallowed hard. "I caught up to Biko, but we couldn't find Gilligan. Not at first. But then . . . we found the trail of blood."

I made an involuntary sound, picturing the scene.

She continued. "It was dark out, but there was some light from the streetlamps, and Biko's got good eyes. We followed the trail into the park. And we found what was left of Gilligan, right by that big stone staircase that leads up to the old watchtower." She struggled with the memory for a moment, then said, "They had eaten most of his little body."

Feeling almost as if I could see what Puma had witnessed, I covered my eyes with my hand while she finished her story.

Gilligan's collar lay nearby. The Garlands had taken that to remember him by, then had scrounged a big enough piece of plastic from a park garbage can to wrap up what was left of their dog. They had taken Gilligan's remains to a twenty-four-hour animal clinic and paid for proper disposal.

Puma gave a watery sigh as I looked at her now. "He lived a long and good life, and he died quickly and bravely, fighting something evil. I guess that's not so bad, all things considered."

"No, indeed," Max said gently. "I hope the same words might be said of me, one day."

After a moment, she said in a firmer voice, "So last night, Biko went hunting the baka again." She shivered a little. "It had to be done, of course. But I was so scared for him, I was pretty relieved when he came home without having seen them." She looked at me and added, "But you saw them."

"I'm glad I didn't know about Gilligan at the time," I said honestly. "I'd have been even more scared than I already was."

Jeff said skeptically, "Esther, you're telling us you *really saw* these things? These growling, green gargoyle things that, uh, ate Puma's dog?"

"Yes, Jeff, I really saw them. I *fought* with them."

He looked appalled. "Why did you do *that?*"

The phone rang, startling us all. The caller was Biko, telephoning to tell his sister that his class had just ended. He had to put away the training equipment and pack up his swords, and then he would come straight here.

After she hung up the phone, Puma set aside her sorrow and briskly offered us cold drinks, which we accepted with gratitude. She pulled some bottled water and canned soda out of a little mini-fridge behind the sales counter. I felt so sticky and dirty by now, I wanted to pour my water over my head, but I settled for drinking it. Thirstier than I had realized, I drained it within minutes. My empty stomach responded gratefully to the feeling of something—even if it was only water—filling it.

Since Biko would be here soon, Max proposed that we wait until he arrived before we dissected the events of last night or discussed what to do next, so that we wouldn't have to repeat anything after he got here. Clearly eager to change the somber mood of the group, and perhaps also motivated by the natural instincts of a merchant, Puma encouraged us to ask questions about the stock in her shop while we waited for her brother.

Jeff seemed interested in some of the voodoo dolls that were stocked within easy reach of his perch on the sales counter. There were wooden dolls, as well as ones made of different colors of cloth: red, brown, blue, green, tan. They had yarn for hair, and they wore a variety of little outfits, such as smock dresses or drawstring trousers. One even wore a suit and had little spectacles on its painted face.

"Hey, here's one that looks like you," Jeff said to me, holding up a pale burlap doll with tangled brown yarn hair and button eyes and wearing a smock dress.

"I fail to see the resemblance," I said.

"I've also got one that looks a bit like Dr. Zadok," Puma said, pointing it out.

I looked at the little figure, which was clad in garish green-and-purple trousers. "Well, the white hair and beard, I'll grant you," I said. "But Max would never wear those pants."

"Hmm." Max regarded the voodoo doll with interest.

"Don't show Esther one that looks like me," Jeff said to Puma. "She might start sticking pins into it."

"There's always that possibility," I agreed.

Looking at the Max-like doll, Jeff asked doubtfully, "Do people really do things like that?"

"Oh, of course," said Max.

"What's so 'of course' about it?"

"It's sympathetic magic," Puma said.

"Sticking pins into a doll to torment a person sounds pretty *un*sympathetic to me," said Jeff.

She smiled at this sly witticism. " 'Sympathy' means an affinity between two things. In this case, a magical association, so that what happens to one thing affects the other thing in a similar way."

"It's pretty far-fetched," Jeff said.

"It may be the oldest form of ritual magic." Puma seemed relieved to have a topic to take her mind off the menacing mystical influences looming over Harlem. "Paleolithic hunters painted pictures on their cave walls that showed them killing and honoring their prey. They believed that the magic associated with this ritual art would help them achieve success in the hunt." She smiled and added, "At least that's one theory about cave paintings."

"And another theory is that they didn't have cameras back then, so they *painted* the story of their big day out on the savannah," Jeff said, flirting with her. "Hoping to impress the girls back at the cave."

She smiled again, responding to his charm.

I was less susceptible, since I was well acquainted with the neuroses and vanity that came *with* Jeff's charm.

Puma said, "But sympathetic magic does go back thousands of years."

I asked with a slight feeling of dread, "Do you have a Ph.D. in anthropology, too?"

She looked puzzled by the question. "No. I have an undergraduate degree in business."

"Oh, good," I said.

Max took up her theme. "Sympathetic magic, evoked through effigies and fetishes, was and is practiced in cultures all over the world. Poppets like these—" He gestured to the voodoo dolls. "—were common for centuries in European sympathetic magic."

"Do you mean witchcraft?" Jeff asked.

"For the most part."

"In fact," Puma said, "the voodoo doll was adapted from the European poppet."

"Hmm." Jeff examined the doll in his hands. Then his gaze moved to a nearby display of Catholic ritual objects. "So what's the foundational text in Vodou? The Bible?"

Puma shook her head. "There isn't a foundational text."

"Really?" I was surprised. "Nothing like the Koran? The I Ching? The Book of Mormon?"

"No. Vodou developed as the religion of slaves—people who weren't taught to read or write," Puma explained.

"But the slaves revolted and drove the French out of Haiti two hundred years ago." Jeff said to me, "It was well worth the effort, but it was a brutal conflict, and Haiti's happy ending *still* seems a long way away."

Thinking of Haiti's grinding poverty in our era, and particularly of the massive 7.0 magnitude earthquake that had devastated the country and killed a horrifying number of people, I thought it did indeed seem to be a nation bereft of its just rewards as a society where slaves had overthrown their captors and founded a free republic.

"Even today, Haiti's literacy rate is only a little more than fifty percent," Puma said. "And it was much lower in the nineteenth century. So Vodou is an oral tradition, not a written one. The rituals and beliefs have been passed down verbally, for many generations, right up until our current-day mambos and houngans—who will leave behind their knowledge orally, too."

"So that's the only way you can learn about it?" Jeff asked. "In person?"

"Oh, there are books *about* Vodou; just no books *of* Vodou." Puma added, "And actually, there aren't that many *good* books about it. Nowhere near as many as there are about other major religions. It's always been misunderstood and misinterpreted by outsiders, and until pretty recently, it was dismissed as a superstition rather than respected as a religion." Being a canny shopkeeper, she added, "I've got some of the better books about Vodou in stock, if you're interested."

"How major a religion *is* voo—Vodou?" I asked curiously.

"There are an estimated sixty million practitioners worldwide."

"Wow! I had no idea." Jeff looked at me. "They've sure overtaken *your* tribe."

"Yes, but we're the Chosen People," I said, "which is an exclusive club."

"I was raised slightly Methodist," Jeff told Puma. "So this is unfamiliar territory to me. And Mambo Celeste, the voodoo priestess who works at the foundation—"

"Yes, I know her well," said Puma. "She and I studied Vodou under the guidance of the same houngan."

"You and that—that—that—er, Mambo Celeste studied with the same teacher?" I asked in surprise. "I mean, with the same priest thingy?"

"Houngan, Esther," Jeff said with exaggerated patience. "Houngan."

Like he knew the lingo.

"Well, not at the same time, of course." Puma was probably thirty years younger than Celeste. "But we did have the same teacher."

"So you're a mambo, too?" I asked.

"No, I'm not." She shook her head. "I considered that path very seriously when I was younger, and I've been involved in the local Vodou community since my teens. My mother was worried at first. Like a lot of people who only know what they've seen in bad movies, she was afraid that Vodou was some sort of devil worship or crazy cult. Once she understood it better, though, she supported my faith, even though she didn't share it. But she wouldn't agree to me becoming an initiate—training to be a priestess, that is—until after I went to college and got a degree. She was strict about that. And she was right, too. By the time I finished school, I realized that I didn't have a true calling to become a mambo, and my real path unfolded before me." Puma's gesture encompassed the shop around us. "I combined my passion for Vodou with my talent for business."

"Was your houngan disappointed?" Max asked curiously.

"Oh, no! He encouraged me to follow my bliss."

"And is he still among us?" Max asked.

"He's still alive, if that's what you mean," she said. "But he's   still here in New York. He went back to his birthplace in Haiti to help people after the earthquake. He had recently turned seventy, and we were all so worried about him going, given what conditions were like down there after the quake. But he felt a calling to restore the spiritual center of people's lives there after all that they had lost." Her expression glowed with affection and respect. "We don't hear from him very often, but once in a while he lets us know that he's all right. And I think he intends to stay there."

"He was Celeste's teacher?" Jeff said with a frown. "It, uh, doesn't really seem like she took after him."

"Not many people do," Puma said tactfully. "He's a remarkable man."

"It sounds like it. But, to be honest, the impression that Celeste has given me of her religion," said Jeff, "is that it's mostly about having a pet snake."

"Well, snakes are venerated in Vodou," Puma said.

"But I guess it's fair to say that carrying one around the way she does . . ."

"And such a *big* one," I said.

"Is a silly and dangerous affectation?" Jeff suggested.

Puma said to me, "You've met Napoleon?"

"Yes. Earlier today."

"Between the baka and the mambo's boa constrictor, you've have a rough twenty-four hours, haven't you?" she said sympathetically.

That seemed like an understatement to me, but I grunted in agreement. "Surely she doesn't walk around the city with Napoleon draped over her shoulders? Or get on the subway? I mean, if she can get on a train with a seven-foot long boa constrictor, while the MTA balks at letting *Nelli* on public transportation—well! That's just not fair!"

"Who's Nelli?" Jeff asked with a frown.

"Max's dog."

"The mambo doesn't carry the snake around town," said Puma. "Napoleon lives in the hounfour."

Max said, "Actually, Nelli is—"

"What's the hounfour?" I asked Puma.

"It's a Vodou community's social and spiritual center. You might call it the temple or the meetinghouse."

"And where exactly is this hounfour?" Napoleon's home seemed like a good place for me to avoid.

Jeff said, "In the basement of the Livingston Foundation."

"I don't think Napoleon leaves the building unless he needs to see his veterinarian or something," said Puma.

"Then I'll just stay out of the basement."

"Good plan," said Jeff. "That's what I do."

"Still," I said, "you'd think she'd need a license or something, for a reptile that size."

"He wasn't nearly that big when she got him," Puma said. "I sometimes wonder if she feeds him too much."

I had a sudden mental image of the mambo feeding rats to her squirming boa constrictor, and I made an involuntary sound of disgust.

"Are you all right, Esther?" Puma asked with concern.

I decided maybe I should pour some cold water on my head after all. "I need to use the restroom."

"Of course." She led me behind the counter, through a doorway that was covered by hanging beads, and into the stockroom behind the shop. She pointed to a door on my left. "Right there."

"Thanks."

Inside the bathroom, one glance in the mirror confirmed that I looked every bit as haggard as I felt. My snarled hair hung in greasy clumps, my skin was pale with fatigue and shiny with perspiration, my lips were chapped, and the remnants of Jilly C-Note's mascara was caked around my eyes. I really did look like a crack whore now. My tight, low-cut shirt had big dark patches under the arms, where I'd been sweating. I suspected I was beginning to smell like a pachyderm, and I thought that by the time I got home, I would need surgical assistance to pry the push-up bra off my tender flesh.

If Lopez could see me now, he would surely be cured of his attraction to me.

And if my mother could see me now, she would thank God that at least she had *one* daughter who had turned out all right: my sister Ruth, who was a hospital administrator in Chicago and had two kids, a standard-issue husband, and no leopard-patterned clothing of any kind.

I thought longingly of my shower and my bed, but suspected that I was still hours away from seeing either of them. Wishing that Puma kept a garden hose in this bathroom, I did the best I could with paper towels and cold water, then I rejoined the others.

10

I didn't want to think about the mambo's snake any-more, so I was relieved to find that Jeff had changed the subject by the time I returned.

"So how would I create sympathetic magic with this?" he asked Puma, holding up the doll that he claimed looked like me.

I resumed my place on my stool. "I trust that you're asking purely out of intellectual curiosity?"

"Well, you wouldn't do it with *this*," said Puma. "These dolls are novelty gifts, not real poppets. Some-thing like this is a fun impulse buy for someone who comes into the shop to browse out of curiosity, not really knowing anything about Vodou. The voodoo doll is an icon that they recognize, and if they see one that they think looks a little like themselves, or a family member, or a friend, they get a kick out of it and buy it. And, of course, once they've decided to buy something . . ." She grinned. "Well, then I see what else I can talk them into buying."

"I should employ such a strategy at my bookstore," Max said with admiration, "but I lack the talents of a true merchant."

"Hmm." I started wondering where Biko was. This

shop was only a few blocks away from the foundation. He should be here by now.

Puma said, "These dolls are good sellers for me. Especially with the European tourists who come here on guided walking tours of Harlem." She added with a rueful expression, "So it's worth putting up with Mambo Celeste giving me a hard time about the dolls whenever she comes here."

Ah, the mambo again. Yay.

"Why does she give you a hard time?" Jeff asked. "Dolls seem pretty harmless. Especially compared to some of the stuff you carry." He nodded toward the glass case that contained the ritual knives.

"Well, I guess you could say she's very traditional." Puma added in a spurt of candor, "And a little rigid. Also opinionated." She shrugged. "Mambo Celeste thinks a poppet is out of place in a respectable Vodou emporium. So she doesn't approve of me selling them—or of there being so many of them on display. She thinks it gives people the wrong idea."

"Well, *that's* hypocritical," Jeff said. "Although I mostly avoid it, I've been down in the basement of the foundation, where she does rituals, and I've seen her altar. There are dolls on it."

Puma shook her head. "Dolls on Haitian altars represent the loa. They're not poppets, and they've got nothing to do with black magic or cursing people."

"Ah!" Max nodded vigorously. "Of course!"

Jeff muttered, "More of the 'of course' chorus."

"I had forgotten!" Max told me, "It has been quite some time since I had the privilege of studying with a houngan."

"You've studied with a houngan?" Puma asked with interest.

"Many years ago. And for less time than I would ideally have wished. So my knowledge is both limited and,

er, rusty," Max said. "But I do recall now that the voodoo doll and its associated dark magic is strictly a mainland practice."

"Mainland?" I repeated.

Puma said, "The European poppet became the voodoo doll by way of New Orleans, not Haiti."

"Is voodoo different in New Orleans?" I asked.

The mention of New Orleans voodoo made me think
of another of the Big Easy's famous features: food. Jam-
balaya, gumbo, red beans and rice . . . My empty stomach
grumbled.

"Some of the customs are different, and the focus
isn't identical," Puma said. "Traditional Haitian Vodou
emphasizes religious ritual and spiritual connection,
while New Orleans voodoo tends to emphasize magic.
There are more similarities than differences, but the differences are there. I deal with both traditions here in the
store, since there's a lot of crossover."

"Which is understandable!" Max was clearly enjoying talking shop, as it were, with a knowledgeable practitioner of Vodou. "After all, both traditions developed
among West Africans enslaved in French Catholic soci-
eties in the New World."

Puma nodded. "And there was contact between the
two communities."

"Well, if Celeste doesn't like you having money-
making voodoo dolls in the shop just because it's not
her brand of voodoo," Jeff said, "why don't you just tell
her to mind her own damn business?"

"Because she's a mambo. She has dedicated her life to
interceding with the spirits and helping people, and she
deserves my respect." Puma added, "Also, she spends a
lot of money here."

"Ah." Jeff nodded, obviously persuaded by the final
reason. He held up the poppet of "me" again and contemplated it. "So I guess Celeste's disapproval isn't be-

cause these are tourist souvenirs? It sounds like she'd grumble even if you were selling real poppets."

I had the impression he was thinking of buying the doll just so he could wave it around at the foundation and annoy the mambo.

"Well, you can't exactly sell a real voodoo doll," Puma said.

"Is it illegal or something?" he asked.

"No, it's not that," said Puma. "The real thing is very specific and personal. It's not something you can just go into a shop and buy. For one thing, you need to incorporate physical items from your victim into the doll. Strands of the real person's hair or their fingernail clippings. That kind of thing."

"How the *hell* would you get hold of someone else's fingernail clippings?" Jeff asked with revolted fascination. "Wait. Never mind. I don't think I want to know."

She smiled. "It probably requires some dedicated effort." Giving him a flirtatious look, she added, "But that's only if your intended victim if an enemy. If, instead, you're creating a poppet to make someone fall in love with you, then incorporating some of their bodily fluids into the doll is your best bet. Sweat, saliva, semen, and so on."

"You know, if someone's collecting another person's, uh, secretions and smearing them into a burlap doll," Jeff said, "maybe it's time to seek psychiatric help."

I could not help but agree.

"Well, people do seek professional help for these things, but not from shrinks. From priests and priestesses," Puma said. "To curse or charm your intended victim, you would probably bring the nail clippings— or whatever else you'd collected from the victim—to a voodoo king or queen. That's the New Orleans equivalent of a mambo or a houngan. They'd fashion a poppet for you, usually out of wax or cloth, incorporating the physical bits of the person that you've provided."

"Okay, I see why this is something you can't go into a shop and buy," said Jeff.

Max added, "Through the ritual, the physical detritus that has been collected, and the power of the sorcerer, the poppet develops an affinity with the victim. In a mystical sense, it *becomes* that person. Thus, whatever happens to the doll also happens to the victim."

Jeff said to me, "Hey, wouldn't it be great if we could get a voodoo queen to make poppets of casting directors and then charm them into giving us work? Or curse the poppets of critics who gave us bad reviews?"

"Do the two of you work together?" Puma asked us.

I saw her glance at the clock on the wall. Like me, she was probably wondering what was taking Biko so long.

"Not really." Jeff explained that we had done *Othello* together about five years ago and told her that I would be teaching some of his workshops at the foundation for a while because of his current scheduling conflict. He added, "I've been teaching there, on and off, for years."

"I've been involved there for years, too," said Puma. "It's funny that you and I have never met before. But then, the foundation has so much going on, both on site and elsewhere."

"And I haven't actually been around for a while," Jeff said. "I've been living in Los Angeles for the past couple of years and only came back at the start of this summer."

I was a little surprised by that. When Jeff had mentioned LA earlier, while we were in Catherine's office, I assumed it was a short trip, not a long stay. However, I really had no idea what he'd been doing since leaving New York four years earlier with the short-lived road company of *Inferno: The Idi Amin Musical*.

Studying his face now, Puma said, "Actually, I thought you looked sort of familiar when you came into the shop. I think I saw you at Mr. Livingston's funeral."

"I was there," he said with a nod. "I left for Los Angeles pretty soon after he died."

"How did Martin Livingston die?" I asked, recalling that the foundation's Web site hadn't given any details.

"Massive stroke," said Jeff.

Puma added, "It was very sudden."

"And unexpected?" Max asked.

My gaze met his as I recalled that Darius Phelps' death three weeks ago had also been unexpected.

"It took everyone by surprise," Jeff said. "Martin wasn't a health fiend, but he kept in shape and took good care of himself."

"But a stroke can happen to anyone, can't it?" I said, glancing at Max. "Even people who seem to be in good health? And he wasn't a young man anymore."

"Here today, gone tomorrow," Jeff said, looking morose. "One night he was at an awards dinner. Just another celebrity-filled occasion in a billionaire philanthropist's daily life."

I wished Jeff hadn't used the word "dinner." It reminded me again of how hungry I was.

He continued, "According to people who were there, Martin looked fine. But then suddenly he collapsed in the middle of the festivities. And three days later, he was dead."

I frowned. "It took him three days to die?" I had assumed that his death by sudden, massive stroke meant he had died instantly.

"Yes," Puma said. "He passed away at Harlem Hospital. My mother was still alive then—she died last year of cancer—and she was one of the nurses taking care of him there. She said he was out of his mind during the three days he spent dying in the hospital. Ranting and raving. Seeing things. Saying crazy stuff. And *strong*, too—much stronger than you'd expect a man in his condition to be. Even with sedation, they had to keep him in restraints. But they couldn't stop the internal bleeding. Finally, he went into cardiac arrest."

"A grim way to go," Jeff said.

"And so unfair," Puma added, "when you consider how much good he did. I mean, he certainly changed *my* life."

"In what way?" Max asked.

"For one thing, a scholarship from the foundation paid for part of my college education," she said. "And another Livingston scholarship will be paying for part of my brother's education. Biko's starting at Columbia University this fall."

"Hey, good for him," said Jeff.

"The reason I was able to open this shop was because I got a no-interest loan from the foundation. Mr. Livingston was passionate about wanting to see independent African-American businesspeople thrive in Harlem." Puma continued, "The foundation is also where Biko discovered fencing, and that sure turned his life around."

"Oh?"

"My little brother—and where *is* he?—was a really smart, independent, strong-willed kid, but he didn't have a focus for his energy. My father was long gone, and my mother worked overtime at the hospital to support us. Biko was becoming so wild and restless by the time he was twelve years old, we were really worried about how he'd turn out. I was trying to get him interested in Vodou, but it just wasn't his thing. Anyhow, one day I dragged him to the foundation with me for a Vodou ritual he didn't want to attend. He saw some boys with swords in the building, and that made him curious enough to go watch the class, and that was it! From that day onward, if he wasn't at school or at home, we always knew where he was: training. My mother never had to worry about him again." She smiled at the memory.

"That much have been a great relief to her," Max said, "as well as a source of pride."

She nodded as she continued, "After a couple of years, the fencing instructor went to Mr. Livingston and said that Biko had reached a stage where he really needed private instruction from a top coach. The foundation paid for that, and also paid for him to compete in tournaments—some of which he won. And because of that, part of his college education is also going to be paid for by an athletic scholarship." Puma concluded, "So Mr. Livingston made a huge difference in our lives. And we're not the only ones. Not by a long shot."

"Martin contributed a lot to the world," Jeff agreed.

"And speaking of Biko . . ." Puma picked up the telephone, pressed a speed dial button, then held the receiver up to her ear. A few moments later, she turned her head to stare at it with a puzzled expression.

"What's wrong?" I asked.

Still staring at the receiver, she replied, "He answered his phone, said, 'Not now,' and hung up."

"Did you sound as if he was in danger?" Max asked.

She shook her head. "No. Just distracted. And also like he doesn't want me to call him back."

"Then we should patiently await his arrival," Max said. "He will no doubt explain when he gets here."

"I suppose you're right." She put the receiver back in its cradle.

"What sort of man was Martin Livingston personally?" Max asked Puma, returning to the previous subject.

"He was a man of many fine qualities," she said carefully.

He noticed how measured her response was. "But?"

She shook her head. "I don't like to speak ill of the dead. Especially since they may be listening."

I asked Jeff, "Did you know him well?"

"No. He was personally involved in the foundation, but he didn't run the day-to-day operations. I spoke to him a few times, but that was about it. He was gregarious and seemed like a nice guy." Jeff asked Puma, "Why didn't you like him?"

"I didn't say I didn't like him," she said firmly.

"Ah." His expression changed. "He put the moves on you."

Puma scowled at him but didn't deny it.

"What do you mean?" I asked Jeff.

"Martin had quite a reputation. Some people described him as a ladies' man," said Jeff. "Other people called it sexual harassment."

"He made a pass at you?" I asked Puma with some surprise. Also some distaste. Martin Livingston would have been about forty years her senior.

Puma cleared her throat, looking uncomfortable. "He was a man of, uh . . . vigorous appetites."

"Did he try to force himself on you?" Max asked, aghast.

"Oh, no! No, nothing like that." Puma looked at each of our faces, then sighed. "All right. Fine. Mr. Livingston grabbed me once, when I went to his office alone to thank him for paying a tournament fee and travel expenses for Biko to compete. My mother usually went to thank him, but she was having her first battle with the cancer back then—I guess this was about four years ago. So I went instead. And since she was sick, I didn't tell her what happened. I didn't want her to get up out of her bed and go storming into the foundation to give him a piece of her mind. Which she would have done—and in her pajamas, too!" Puma smiled for a moment as she remembered her mother's feisty nature, then continued, "I jumped out of my skin and shoved him away when he tried to kiss me. But I think I was more startled than shocked. I knew his reputation by then. He made passes at lots of women. Anyhow, it was embarrassing, but he certainly didn't get rough or mean about it. He sort of laughed it off. And he never tried it again. Although . . ."

"Although?" Max prodded.

Puma looked at me. "You know how some men can just . . . make you uncomfortable? Because they stand too close when they're talking to you, or keep touching you when there's no reason to?"

"Yes. I know." What woman didn't?

"It was like that. It was never threatening, but it was . . ."

"Intrusive?" I suggested.

She nodded. "I hardly knew Mr. Livingston, and I didn't see him often. Sometimes at a special event at the foundation, or once when he came to see Biko compete in a tournament. That kind of thing. But when I did see him, the way he looked at me . . . Well, I always wound up, oh, checking my neckline, thinking maybe it was too low or that my bra must be showing. You know the sort of look that I mean?"

"I do. I get that look from some of the wiseguys when I'm waiting tables at Bella Stella." Since they tipped me well, and I needed the money, I put up with it; I had to be practical. And since Martin Livingston's generosity was so important to the Garland family, Puma had to be practical, and so she had put up with it, too. I said, "But that kind of thing seems a lot more reprehensible coming under the guise of philanthropy."

"Oh, the philanthropy was genuine," Puma said quickly. "He really was a good man in many ways. He cared very deeply about Harlem and the African-American community here, and he did a lot of good. In other ways, though . . ." She shrugged. "Well, everyone has their flaws, and at least his weren't cruel or destructive. Just, uh . . ."

"Sleazy?" I suggested.

"I was going to say rambunctious."

"Oh, I think Esther nailed it," Jeff said. "Sleazy." He had his own flaws, but rampant promiscuity and ogling women to the point of making them uncomfortable had never been among them. And I could see that the idea of the old man pestering Puma bothered him. I recognized the signs of Jeff's attraction, having long ago been a recipient; he was definitely drawn to Puma.

An interesting dilemma, considering how uncomfortable he seemed to be with her religion.

Then again, I was a secular Jew interested in a practicing Catholic who thought I might be a dangerous lunatic. So I should probably eschew snarkiness about other people's love lives.

Turning my thoughts resolutely away from the cop who wouldn't date me, I said, "And being filthy rich probably made it easier for Martin to indulge in his, er, hobby." After all, more women would fool around with a sixty-year-old billionaire than with a regular joe of the same age. That was the way of the world.

"Like I said, he had a reputation for that kind of thing." Jeff said to Max and me, "I think I told you that Catherine was his third wife? Well, they say his first wife got tired of his philandering, so she left quietly in exchange for a huge settlement. The second wife supposedly knew what she was getting into and looked the other way. I guess there are compensations if your cheating spouse is rich and important. But then his hot and heavy affair with Catherine turned into the real thing, and so he left his wife for her. And that divorce, they say, was *really* expensive."

"I don't like gossip," Puma said with a frown.

"I do," I said shamelessly. "When did he marry Catherine?"

"The wedding was six years ago," said Puma.

"And two years ago," I said, "he died and made her a wealthy widow." I wondered whether Catherine counted herself bereaved or lucky.

"Well, she's a lot wealthier than any of us, certainly," Jeff said, "but not nearly as wealthy as his two ex-wives."

"Oh?" That seemed odd.

"He was, you know, a *philanthropist* by the time she married him. So his fortune's all tied up in the foundation and managed by the board of directors."

"You mean that Catherine didn't get anything?" I asked.

"According to the grapevine at the time . . ." Jeff smiled apologetically at Puma, who was again frowning with disapproval. "She got their penthouse, personal possessions, and some money. Everything else went to the foundation."

"I heard she's selling the penthouse." Puma clapped a hand over her mouth, as if startled that this bit of gossip had popped out. Then, looking sheepish, she added, "They say she can't keep it up on the money he left her."

"I was at their place once for a fund-raising party, talking to rich guests about my work at the foundation," Jeff said. "Just the property taxes on that penthouse would probably be enough to feed Haiti for a month." He added to me, "Martin was generous, but not self-sacrificing. He liked living large."

I recalled something else Jeff had told us back at the foundation. "You mentioned that Mambo Celeste took a long time to accept Catherine?"

He nodded. "You bet."

"The mambo doesn't really like, uh . . ." Puma paused awkwardly.

"White people. We know," I said. "Though she seems to like Max."

"I tried to establish a rapport with her," he said modestly to Puma.

"To give Catherine credit," said Jeff, "she patiently put up with rebuffs from Celeste for a long time."

"Because of her interest in Vodou," said Puma. "I guess she thought they'd have a lot in common. But Dr. Livingston's approach is . . . you know, so academic. So dry. She can talk all day about what we believe, but I don't think she can really *understand*."

"Celeste got less rude after the wedding. Maybe Martin put his foot down," said Jeff. "Or maybe Celeste just figured the marriage meant Catherine was there to stay, like it or not."

"They seem friendlier since he passed away," Puma said. "I think the mambo feels some compassion for Dr. Livingston now, since they're both childless widows."

"Oh, come on," Jeff said. "Celeste's husband didn't die, he left her. It was years ago, but everyone knows about it."

"*She* likes to call herself a widow," Puma said primly. "I try to respect that."

It was not difficult to imagine why a spouse might have left the sour-tempered, snake-wielding Vodou priestess. I exchanged a glance with Max and saw the same thoughts written on his expression. But we kept our mouths shut.

"Anyhow, I think Celeste's just being practical," said Jeff. "The board of directors manages the money and makes the major decisions, but they don't pay attention to the daily operations or care about the hiring and firing. Celeste must know that if she's unfriendly to Catherine, now that for all practical purposes Catherine's the boss, then there are plenty of other voodoo priests and priestesses who'd probably be happy to work at the foundation in her place."

It was clear from Puma's expression that she didn't

like this ungenerous interpretation of the mambo's behavior, but she evidently also didn't have a good enough
argument against it to say anything.

"Did your houngan work there, too?" Max asked
Puma.

"No, he was always too busy serving his own clients."
She explained to Jeff and me, "It's like serving parish-
ioners, except that since there's no official church or
salary, people pay their mambo or houngan for help, if
they can afford to offer something." Then she continued,
looking at Max, "He also used to spend part of almost
every year in Haiti even before he moved back there
after the earthquake. But Mambo Celeste was here all
year round, and the foundation is where she focused her
efforts."

The front door of the shop opened, and we all turned
to see Biko enter. He had an unusually long athletic
bag slung over his back; I supposed his swords were in
there.

"Finally!" his sister said. "Where have you been?"

He flipped over the standard placard that hung on
the front door so that people approaching the shop
would see a CLOSED sign in the window. Then he locked
the door.

"What are you doing?" Puma demanded. "I'm not
closed!"

"You are now," Biko said, joining us all near the cash
register. "We have to talk, and we definitely don't want
to be overheard."

Studying the young man, Max said, "Something has
happened, hasn't it? Something that delayed you."

Biko nodded. "A cop showed up at the foundation.
He was coming downstairs when I was leaving. He'd
been in Dr. Livingston's office, talking to her. And he
zeroed in on me as soon as he saw me. I think it was
the swords that attracted his attention," he said with a

puzzled look. "Anyhow, he flashed his badge and asked a lot of questions. It took some time."

"Oh, no." I wiped a hand wearily across my face. "Was his name Lopez?"

"I didn't catch his name," Biko said. "But he did look Latino."

"About six feet tall, slim, black hair, blue eyes?" I said. "Really good-looking?"

"Really *tired* looking," Biko said. "Like he hadn't been to bed. But I guess girls would call him good-looking. Anyhow, yeah. That's him." He frowned at me. "You know him?"

"Detective Connor Lopez," I said with resignation, wishing I hadn't gotten him involved in this. I'd really had no choice at the time, but now that we were talking about, oh, zombies and baka and bokors, I had a feeling that I was going to regret having called on him for help last night.

"*Connor* Lopez?" Jeff said. "Okay, who wants to go out on a limb and guess how he got blue eyes?"

Puma asked, "What did he want, Biko?"

With a sharp glance at me, Jeff added, "Yeah, why was the *really good-looking* cop asking questions at the foundation?"

Biko took a deep breath as his gaze swept our faces. "Darius Phelps' grave has been vandalized, and his body is missing."

11

I felt a combination of shock, revulsion, and doomed inevitably as I absorbed Biko's statement. Then I asked, "Lopez told you this?"

"The cop? Yeah."

"And what did you tell him?" I asked.

"Nothing."

I said in surprise, "He didn't ask about last night?"

"Oh, he asked me *lots* about last night," said Biko. "I told him I was home in bed. And that my sister could back me up on that."

"Biko!" his sister cried, her volume rising enough to make me wince. "You lied to a police detective?"

"Don't give me a hard time, Puma." Biko looked defensive. "I couldn't exactly say, 'I was out hunting the baka that ate my dog, officer,' now could I?"

"Hmm." Puma looked perturbed. "No, I suppose not."

"What else did Lopez say?" I asked.

"He mostly asked me a lot of questions about Mr. Phelps."

"What kind of questions?"

They turned out to be pretty much the same kind of questions that I had asked Catherine in her office. I assumed that Lopez had posed those question to her, too, before encountering Biko.

"So I just kept saying that I don't know anything about Mr. Phelps' death—which is true—and that I was at home and in bed last night." Biko leaned against the counter and let his shoulders slump. "But I could tell he didn't believe me about that part."

"Man, you need to learn to lie better," Jeff said critically.

"No, we must not blame young Biko if Detective Lopez was unconvinced by his answers," said Max. "He is not an easy man to dissuade. And although he is pursuing an erroneous theory, I do not for a moment suppose he will *cease* to pursue it until he is satisfied that the matter is resolved."

"What theory? What pursuit?" Jeff said. "How do you and Esther know this guy?"

"I propose," said Max, "that we proceed with an orderly narrative of last night's events, then move on to discussing relevant theories, avenues of attack, and possible solutions."

"Good idea," said Puma. "And since I guess I'm closed now, why don't we go sit in the storage room in back? There's a table and some chairs in there."

"Esther and I can't stay, Puma." Jeff looked at the clock on the wall. "We have to go visit someone in the hospital."

"That'll have to wait," I said.

"But we're already late," he pointed out.

"For God's sake, Jeff," I snapped. "Sucking up to Mike Nolan for ten minutes is not as important as figuring out what to do about the strange things that Biko and I have seen!" I added to the others, "But before we do anything else, we need to order some food."

Biko gave me an incredulous look. "I've just found out—from a *cop*, no less—that no one knows where

Mr. Phelps' three-week-old corpse is. And you saw him walking around Harlem last night. Do you really want to *eat* now?"

"I also saw him get maimed by the baka," I pointed out crankily. "And, yes, I want to eat now."

"Do I have to stay for this conversation?" Jeff asked me. "I can already tell I'm going to hate every part of it."

"You can leave whenever you like," I said, knowing he wasn't going anywhere. As long as the prospect of meeting *D30*'s lead actor loomed on the horizon, nothing short of an attack by crazed gargoyles would get rid of Jeff—the thought of which reminded me of the attack that Biko had witnessed. I said to the young fencer, "Can you describe the victim you rescued Monday night?"

"The man that I found the baka attacking? Sure. He was, uh . . . Well, for one thing, I'd swear he was *alive*, Esther."

"Yes, I thought about that," I said. "Tears, sweat, urine."

"Very good," Max said to me, nodding with approval.

"Actually," said Biko, "I was going to say that he was breathing and his skin was warm."

"Oh," I said. "I guess that works, too."

Jeff said wearily, "What did he look like, Biko? Max and Esther have got this theory that . . . Never mind. Just tell us."

"He was about thirty years old, I guess. No more than five foot eight, I'd say. Skinny."

Jeff sat up straighter and stared at Biko.

The young athlete continued, "He had a voice sort of like a public radio announcer, and he wore his hair in twists."

Jeff's shoulders slumped suddenly and he lowered his head.

"Jeff?" I said.

He didn't answer, just reached into his pocket, pulled out his cell phone, and called someone. A moment later, holding the phone to his ear, he said, "Frank, call me. I mean it. We have to talk about Monday night." He closed his phone and put it back in his pocket.

"One mystery solved." I explained to Biko whom he had seen being attacked. "You didn't recognize him from the foundation?"

"No. I mostly stick to the training room. And it sounds like this guy Frank Johnson was brand new and just teaching one class a day on the other side of the building from me. So it's not really surprising that I hadn't seen him before." Biko asked Jeff, "Does your friend live near the foundation?"

"I'm not sure where he lives," Jeff said morosely. "He's more of an acquaintance than a friend. Especially after this week."

"He may live in Hamilton Heights," I said to Biko.

"In that case, since the classes he teaches are all in the daytime," said Biko, "what was he doing right outside the foundation late at night?"

"Good question," I said. "One that we can discuss while I'm eating."

"How can you think of food at a time like this?" Jeff demanded. "I'm missing my meeting with Michael Nolan!"

Puma looked puzzled by this non sequitur. But I knew that if Jeff asked her out, she would learn. Indeed, she would learn that and, oh, so much more.

Feeling my stomach rumble, I said tersely, "Except for one mini-bagel this morning, I haven't had anything to eat in almost twenty-four hours, and it's been a hell of a marathon. If I get any hungrier, I'll start eating these dolls!" I picked up the one that looked like Max and tossed it at Jeff. It bounced off his shoulder, and Biko caught it. The kid had good reflexes. "I want carry-out. I don't care what. I just want *food*."

Jeff sighed. "Okay. Fine." He added to Biko, "Don't even try to argue with her when she's like this. Take my word for it and just do what she wants."

"Shall we all have dinner?" Max suggested cheerfully. "My treat."

"All right," said Jeff, turning on a dime. "I'm in." Actors rarely turn down a free meal.

"Oh, but first I should ask," Max said. "Are any of you Lithuanian?"

They all looked at him blankly.

Shrewdly sensing the consternation that his question had caused, Max said, "I assure you that I have no hostility whatsoever toward Lithuanians. But it's wisest to ask the question *before* we break bread or attempt to work together."

Jeff asked me, "What is he talking about?"

"No one really knows." I had meant to ask Max about this odd foible before, but the few times the subject had come up, we were always too busy fighting Evil to discuss it.

"Dr. Zadok," Biko said, "do we *look* Lithuanian?"

"Here in the New World," Max said, "where the admirable values of your society so often lead to replacing the walls of the Old World with sturdy bridges built between people of different backgrounds, that is not a question that I would venture to answer."

Jeff said to me, "No, really. What *is* he talking about?"

"As far as you guys know, do you have any Lithuanian ancestors?" I prodded.

They all shook their heads.

"Then it doesn't matter what he's talking about," I said.

"Excellent!" Max beamed at them. "Let's get dinner!"

"But you and Esther are our guests, Dr. Zadok," said Puma. "Biko and I will buy dinner."

Max argued graciously, pressed his point, and won. Biko phoned in a food order to Miss Maude's Spoonbread Too and asked them to deliver it. Puma insisted on providing our beverages out of her little refrigerator.

While we waited for the food, Biko recounted his most recent evening of hunting the baka. "I think I found signs of them—the half-eaten remains of a couple of pigeons, and some really big claw marks nearby—but I didn't see them." And then he'd met a hooker who turned out to be an actress looking for her colleagues.

"You might have been a little more detailed in your warning to me," I pointed out.

"You'd have thought I was crazy," he said dismissively. "Or playing a twisted joke on you."

"Fair point."

"Anyhow, I didn't see anything after I met Esther," Biko said. "I guess she got all the action last night."

I took up the story and gave them a full account of my night. Trying to get over rough ground as lightly as possible, I portrayed Lopez simply as a police officer who knew my true identity and could therefore help me in my time of need.

"Now that you've involved the cops," Jeff said, "I don't suppose there's any chance that you'll just let them handle this?"

Max and I were about to remonstrate, but we didn't need to. Biko said irritably, "Are you *deaf*, man? Esther told everything to the cops, and they laughed at her. The only one who even took her seriously is the one who thinks she fell for a practical joke!"

"He might being taking her more seriously today,"

Jeff shot back, "now that he knows Darius' body is missing."

"The cop thinks he's dealing with body snatchers," Biko argued. "Not a zombie!"

There was a sharp knock at the front door, making us all jump. Happily, it was just the delivery man from Miss Maude's.

"Thank God," I said. "Food!"

Biko looked at me. "We're taking about body snatching and zombies, and *you*—"

"Get the door," I said. "I'm hungry."

Max paid for the food while Puma and I took the carry-out bags back to the stockroom and laid the food and beverages out on the table in there. Too tired and hungry to wait for anyone else, I helped myself and was already eating when the others sat down with me.

With multiple establishments each boasting they had the best friend chicken in Harlem, I had no idea if Miss Maude's claim was any more or less true than the others, but it sure was darn good chicken in any case. I also ate mashed potatoes, string beans, collard greens, and cornbread stuffing. I ignored the feel of Jilly C-Note's tight skirt cutting into my waist, reminding me that I would again have to appear on camera in this revealing outfit. I had *earned* a hearty meal.

And despite Biko's earlier criticism, I noticed that he, too, ate plenty. He smiled sheepishly when I pointed this out.

Puma said, "This boy has a hollow leg. Especially after he's been training."

"If I may raise the pressing subject of Darius Phelps without ruining anyone's meal?" Max asked tentatively.

"Well, you obviously won't ruin *Esther's* meal," said Jeff, eyeing the way I was packing it away.

"Go ahead, Dr. Zadok," said Puma.

"All things considered," Max said, "I believe we

should work from the hypothesis that there is a bokor among us who has summoned baka and who has raised Darius Phelps from the dead. All for some as yet unknown purpose or goal."

"I agree," said Puma.

Jeff's expression suggested he was rethinking his interest in her. "Are you people even going to *consider* another theory?"

"Like what?" Biko said.

"How about whatever theory Esther's cop friend is working on?" Jeff suggested.

We all looked at him.

His gaze swept our unresponsive faces, and he sighed. "Okay. Never mind. Forget I spoke."

"You're not a believer," Puma said kindly. "That's all right. You don't need to feel bad about it."

"I don't feel bad about it!"

"You haven't seen the things that Esther and I have seen," said Biko.

"Fine. Let's run with that. Great. A bokor has raised Darius from the dead," Jeff said in exasperation. "Why would anyone do that? And why *Darius*, of all people? Max, if you had ever met him, youd'd know there couldn't be a less likely candidate for . . . for whatever you're talking about."

"What sort of man was he?" Max asked curiously.

"He was *not* a guy to dance half-naked around a voodoo altar with a bottle of rum," Jeff said.

"Please don't be condescending about our rituals," Puma said coolly.

"Hey, *I'm* that sort of guy," Jeff assured her. "Well, if the music's good. I mean, I'm game for anything. Within reason."

"Yes," I said between bites of chicken, "but if we could depart from the fascinating subject of yourself and return to what Darius was like?"

"He wore suits with vests. He overarticulated his consonants. He kept hand sanitizer on his desk. Darius was a guy," Jeff continued, "who listened to Mahler, went to poetry readings, and talked about the 'nose' on his cabernet."

"Yeah," Biko said absently. "I was kind of surprised to find out he was straight."

"I don't know much about zombies," I said, "but I'm going to guess that being erudite—or gay—doesn't automatically disqualify someone from becoming one."

"No, indeed," said Max. "In fact—"

"What makes you so sure he was straight?" Jeff asked Biko. "Don't tell me you asked him?"

"No, I walked in on him and Dr. Livingston one night at the foundation."

"Walked in on them?" Jeff's eyes bulged. "As in . . .?"

Biko nodded. "They were, uh, giving her couch a workout."

"What two consenting adults do in private is none of our business," Puma said firmly.

"They weren't in private," Jeff pointed out. "They were at the foundation."

"Their mistake." I urged Biko, "Go on."

The lad helped himself to more fried chicken. "It was late at night; I'd been training alone, and I was just leaving the building. I thought I heard Dr. Livingston upstairs in her office, and it sounded like she was in pain or calling for help."

"Oops," said Jeff.

"So I go running up there, expecting to find her bleeding to death or something . . ."

"Oh, no," I said.

"And there she was with Darius. Both of them . . . well, not expecting company, obviously. It was pretty embarrassing."

"When was this?" I asked curiously.

"About a year ago."

"So she was a widow at the time," Puma said, "and perfectly entitled to have a boyfriend."

"Were she and Darius still involved when he died?" I felt rather sorry for the blond anthropologist who'd lost two men in the space of two years. Even if one of them was a notorious womanizer and the other was a wine snob.

"I don't know." Biko shrugged. "I don't even know if they were *involved* back when I walked in on them. Maybe it was a one-time thing."

"Well, were there rumors about them?" I asked.

"I don't pay attention to gossip," said Biko.

"That's a family failing," I noted.

"*I* pay attention," said Jeff. "Darius died a few weeks after I got back from LA, and everyone at the foundation was talking about him then—the way you do when someone's kicked the bucket unexpectedly like that. No one mentioned anything about him and Catherine having an affair."

"So maybe what Biko saw," I mused, "was indeed a one-time incident."

"Or maybe they had a thing going," said Biko, "but they kept it quiet."

"And you can see why they might do that," said Jeff. "There are internal politics at the foundation, like any other organization. So if Catherine and Darius were together, maybe the two of them made a point of keeping that off the radar. They both seemed like pretty private people, anyhow." He thought about it and added, "In fact, except for what I've already told you, I don't really know anything else about Darius."

"Me, neither," said Biko. "And he's been at the foundation for about four years."

"Did he have any family?" Max asked.

"There was a sister at the funeral," Puma said. "From Chicago. I got the impression they weren't close. Otherwise, the attendees were mostly people from the foundation and from his golf league."

"He played *golf*." There was contemptuous dismissal in Biko's tone.

"We can't all carry a sword, D'Artagnan," I said. "Did Catherine seem very upset at the funeral?"

"That's hard to say," said Jeff. "Well, you've met her, you saw what she's like. She plays her cards pretty close to her chest."

"Cold, is more like it," said Biko. "Mr. Phelps was kind of a cold fish, too."

"Biko." His sister's tone warned him not to speak ill of the dead.

"Being deceased doesn't make someone more likeable, Puma," he said with some exasperation. "And the dead can feel free to listen to me say so, if they want."

"Honestly, I always thought Darius was a pompous ass. And I'm not surprised to learn he was also an opportunist." Seeing my inquisitive look, as I shoveled potatoes into my mouth, Jeff said, "Sleeping with the boss, I mean."

I swallowed my mouthful and said, "Come on, it could have been plain old attraction. Lots of romances start in the workplace, and she's a good-looking woman."

"*I* don't think so," said Biko. "She's all . . . stiff and chilly."

"Oh, color me shocked that an eighteen-year-old boy doesn't see what's attractive about an intellectual woman in her forties," I said. "But Darius might have."

Biko shrugged. "Whatever."

"Anyhow, even though I'd much rather not have met Darius' zombie," I said, "better me than her, I guess."

Puma gasped. "Oh, yes! I mean, can you *imagine*?

Having relations with a man . . . and then meeting his walking corpse? How awful!"

"Which brings me back to my original question," Jeff said. "Why raise the dead? And why Darius? If, for a minute, we go with this crazy theory that you're all stuck on, and say that Darius is a zombie now . . . Why him?"

"Excellent question." Max patted his mouth with a paper napkin. "Why Darius, indeed?"

"Opportunity?" Puma suggested. "He had a nondenominational funeral."

"Does that make a difference?" I asked.

Max nodded. "Without the inclusion of Vodou rituals, his corpse presumably was not prepared with any of the usual precautions against zombiism."

Jeff froze in the middle of reaching for more green vegetables. I noticed that he was eating grilled salmon and avoiding the fried food and starches that I was gobbling. It occurred to me that his gladiator outfit was probably skimpy.

"There are usual precautions against zombiism?" he asked.

"Oh, indeed!" Max said with enthusiasm. "Traditionally, for example, the family of the deceased often kills the corpse a second time, in order to protect it from being raised by a bokor and enslaved as a zombie."

"How do you kill a corpse?" Jeff asked in appalled fascination.

"Oh, usually you would plunge a knife into the heart of the cadaver," Max said. "Alternately, you might behead the corpse in its coffin."

Puma made a sound of assent and nodded.

"I just *had* to ask." Jeff set down his fork. "I think I'm done eating."

"You could also shoot the body," Puma said. "Or inject it with poison."

"Or strangle it," said Max.

"It's a whole buffet of choices," said Jeff.

"You shouldn't let that salmon go to waste," I said. "It looks good." After the things I had experienced lately, I didn't see any point getting squeamish over methods of killing a body that was *already* dead.

Jeff said to me, "Be my guest."

"Thanks." I took a bite of the fish. It was tasty, so I lifted the filet onto my plate. "I have a question, Max. I was alone in the dark with Darius last night. If he's a zombie, then why didn't he try to eat my brains or something? Isn't that what zombies do?"

Biko gave me a wan look, and paused in his eating.

"Oh, not at all!" said Puma. "People just get that idea from the movies."

"Sure, blame the entertainment industry," Jeff muttered. "It's all some actor's fault that Esther's wondering why no one has ripped open her skull and consumed her brains."

Biko sighed and pushed his plate away.

"Zombies aren't villains," Puma said emphatically. "They're victims."

"But they can be dangerous," Max interjected.

"Yes, that's true," Puma agreed. "More mashed potatoes, Dr. Zadok?"

"Oh, yes, thank you. Just a small amount, please."

"Zombies don't eat brains," Puma said. "They don't eat at all. They're not human anymore."

"Ah. I get it." I nodded. "Which is why they also don't bleed, sweat, cry, and so on. But even if Darius wasn't, er, hungry last night, why didn't he attack me? Was it just because he was disoriented and weak after *being* attacked?"

"He would only have attacked you if commanded to do so. Which clearly was not the case," Max said. "Zombies aren't evil, they're just the living dead. They can, of course, be used for evil purposes by their master, but they are inherently neither good nor bad. They are just tools and have no will of their own."

"And *that's* why someone raises the dead," Puma said to Jeff. "To have a docile, obedient slave."

"A person no one will search for," Max added, "because they're not missing. They are no longer part of this life."

Puma explained to me, "A zombie is not a demon or monster, it's a dead body whose soul the bokor steals and whose body the bokor reanimates with black magic."

"After exhuming it from the grave?" I said, finishing Jeff's salmon.

"*Robbing* the grave is more like it," said Biko.

"Ah, and that suggests a possible answer to Jeffrey's question of why Mr. Phelps was chosen as a victim," Max said, looking pleased with the realization. "Darius' death was recent, and a bokor needs a fresh corpse when he raises a zombie from the grave."

"Oh, absolutely," Puma said. "A zombie should be raised within a few days of burial. After all, decomposition would make it so . . . *messy*. Body parts dropping off, teeth falling out, skin rotting away. And the stench of decay would be hard to conceal."

I suddenly felt very full.

"I suppose you could wait longer if the body was embalmed," Puma added doubtfully. "But a bokor's rituals are bound to be based on rural Haitian practices, where most buried bodies rot and start being consumed by parasites quickly."

"I think I'm done eating," I said faintly, feeling a tad queasy.

"Are you sure?" Jeff said to me. "Because we can always go out and sacrifice a goat for you, if you're still feeling a bit peckish. The night is young."

I laid down my fork and pushed my plate away as a strong memory assailed me.

"Are you all right?" Puma asked me. "You suddenly look a little . . . green."

"Darius smelled funny," I blurted.

Jeff made a sound. "That's a little too much information, Esther. I don't really want sensory detail on the experience."

"He *was* dead at the time," Biko said charitably. "He didn't have a body odor problem in life."

"Hmm. Yes, even with a relatively prompt post-burial exhumation, thus allowing very little time for decomposition before the bokor's magic would halt—or substantially decelerate—nature's progress . . ." Max nodded with a thoughtful expression. "Yes, I think a certain amount of odor should be expected, even so. The zombie is no longer a living being, after all, and dead tissue does smell . . . different."

Biko said, "So if they smell funny, don't breathe, don't sweat or bleed, and so on, they should be easy to identify, right?"

"Oh, yes," Max said. "Under normal circumstances, I would think so. Keep in mind that Esther's brief encounter with the zombie last night occurred in very frightening and confusing conditions. If, by contrast, the creature simply walked into this room right now . . ."

We all looked toward the door, as if afraid of seeing the late Darius Phelps suddenly enter it.

"It would be much more obvious that Darius is no longer a normal man," Max said. "As is often the case with reanimation of the dead—"

"Often?" Jeff repeated. "How *often* do you meet dead people, Max?"

"Not now, Jeff," I said.

Max continued, "His skin would probably be sunken and dull, his eyes glassy and unblinking, his expression blank. His movements would be clumsy and unnatural, his speech slow and slurred."

"Since zombies have no thoughts or will, they don't speak unless spoken to, and they don't move or do anything unless ordered to," Puma added. "And if you try to talk with a zombie, it will seem confused and disoriented, because it has no memory and no normal cognitive functions."

"Most of that describes the, uh, individual that I met last night," I said. "I thought his disorientation was because, you know, he had just lost a *hand*."

"Okay, time out. I believe that you saw something really weird last night, but it's time to get off this zombie train to nowhere," Jeff said to me. "How about this theory instead? You did see Darius on the street last night, but he wasn't a zombie. He was reanimated by technology, not by voodoo."

"What sort of technology animates a three-week-old corpse?" I said with a frown.

"Let's say someone dug up his body and installed robot parts inside him."

"But how did he answer my questions when I spoke to him?"

"Computer programming."

"And how did he manage to struggle against the baka?"

"Remote control."

"And what *about* the baka?" I said. "What were *they?* Robots with bad breath, drool, and dirty claws?"

He thought it over. "They were mutant dogs."

"Good God, Jeff," I said. "Were all your brains in your *hair* when they shaved it off?"

He looked self-conscious and ran a hand over his bald head. "You don't think this look works, do you?"

I said to Max and Puma, "Okay, now there's something else I don't get. If zombies are just tools, serving the will of the bokor, then what was Darius doing wandering the streets by himself?"

"That is a puzzle," Max agreed.

"It's also kind of surprising that he could tell you his name," Puma said with a frown. "Zombies are supposed to be empty inside, with no . . . Oh, wait! I've got it!" In her excitement, she leaped out of her chair, startling us all. She looked at Max, "When is a zombie most dangerous?"

"When its bokor commands it to commit violence or mayhem," Max said promptly.

"No, I mean, when is it most *unpredictable?*"

Max looked puzzled for a moment, then his expression cleared and he rose to his feet, too. "When it is awakened!"

"Yes!"

"Whoa! How do you *awaken* a zombie?" I asked. "You've just said they're the living dead, with no will or soul."

"There are various ways to awaken one, in theory," said Max. "If the zombie tastes salt or meat, for example."

"But I thought they don't eat or feel hunger?" I said.

"If it makes them unpredictable," said Biko, "I'd say that's a good reason not to feed a zombie, hungry or not."

"Another way a zombie may awaken is if it hears someone it knew in life calling it by name. But again, that's a theory," said Max. "I have never actually seen a zombie or studied with a bokor."

"The essence of it is," Puma said, "that the zombie has an experience that reminds it of being alive. And so it awakens."

"In much the way that a specific taste or smell can evoke a powerful memory within a living person, so that the person feels transported back to the place or event in question," Max said. "Alternately, something may go wrong with the bokor's spell, and so the zombie begins to slip free of the sorcerer's control. All magic is notoriously unpredictable, after all, and dark magic especially so, because it is governed by such mercurial influences."

I said, "So you think Darius, er, woke up?"

"Quite possibly," said Max.

"I don't like to hear myself asking this," Jeff said, "but what's so dangerous and unpredictable about an awakened zombie?"

"Well, instead of an empty vessel just serving the bokor's will," Puma said, "now you have a soulless creature trying to exercise its own will, without morality, self-control, or memory. And there's no telling what it'll do or what might happen."

"So now that he's awake, Darius won't just go back to his apartment and open a bottle of wine?" Jeff asked.

"No. He may be drawn to places or people that were familiar to him in life," Max said. "But, as Puma has indicated, he is devoid of reason or awareness. Whatever he does, he will not behave as if he were still alive."

"Oh, my God," I said slowly. "Max, I think I know why the baka attacked Darius!" I recalled the way the two little creatures had made a swift beeline across the street that night to the spot where they assaulted Darius. They were *hunting* him. "If he awakened and, er, wandered away from home—"

"Or fled captivity," said Puma.

"Then maybe the baka were *sent* after him," I said.

"Ah!" said Max. "To retrieve him for the bokor?"

"Yes."

"Or maybe the bokor wanted to get rid of the evidence before anyone saw his runaway zombie and started asking questions?" Biko suggested. "Maybe the baka were sent to dismember Mr. Phelps and scatter the parts!"

"Okay, what do you say we put away these leftovers?" Jeff said loudly.

I took a deep breath. "So what we're saying is—"

"What do you mean 'we'?" said Jeff as he and Puma rose to start packing up the food and throw away our paper plates and plastic utensils. "*I'm* voting for the robot theory."

"It's a stupid theory, man," said Biko.

"Okay, then I'm voting for the detective's theory," Jeff shot back, folding aluminum foil over what was left of the chicken.

Puma frowned. "What's the detective's theory again?"

"I don't know," Jeff said. "But it's got to be better than *this*."

"Let's get *our* theory straight," I said. "Darius dies of a freak medical problem, and there happens to be a bokor in the neighborhood who decides to raise him from the dead, wanting a slave who'll be completely obedient to his or her will. Is that what we're saying?"

"Actually, I think we should consider the possibility that the death was not accidental," Max said.

We all looked at him in surprise.

Then Jeff said, "It was a ruptured intestine, Max. If there had been anything suspicious about it, the doctors would have told the cops. And the cops would have started sniffing around Darius' life—including his workplace. But nothing like that has happened."

Max said, "A bokor powerful enough to raise a zombie from the dead and conjure baka could, I'm sorry to say, commit murder and make it appear to be natural causes."

This statement had a sobering effect on us all.

"Mr. Phelps might have been killed?" Biko said. "Deliberately?"

"Perhaps," Max said.

"To *make* him a zombie?" When Max nodded, I said, "That's awful! Why would someone do that?"

"I suspect," Max said, "it may be that someone has been raising a small army of zombies and needed at least one more—and quickly, too."

"*Excuse* me?" said Jeff.

"The disturbance in the directional flow of mystical energy that has been building steadily in this locale is consistent with Darius' reanimation," Max said, "but not explained by it. Not entirely, that is."

"Why not?" I asked.

"Because it is too powerful to be the result of one isolated incident. Something more is happening than just the mystical enslavement of Darius Phelps." With a frown of concentration on his face, as if focusing on the disrupted spiritual flow of this dimension from his folding chair right there in Puma's Vodou Emporium, he said, "I believe there are more zombies out there. And I believe the bokor has raised them to assist with some devastating plan that is unfolding even as we speak."

12

"I don't think it's the best possible idea for us to bring Max in there with us," Jeff said to me in a low voice.

"He wants to see Nolan," I said.

"But—"

"He's coming with us," I said firmly. "You, on the other hand, are entirely expendable if you keep irritating me."

Jeff gave a disgruntled sigh but dropped the subject.

We were entering the hospital where Nolan was a patient, a few blocks away from Puma's shop. I didn't want to make a bad impression on the *D30* production office by missing my visit altogether. It was early evening now, well past my afternoon slot on the visitation schedule; but I figured better late than never. I also thought that the sooner I introduced Jeff to Nolan, the sooner I could shed him; his skepticism was getting a trifle shrill. Meanwhile, Max wanted to interview Nolan and assure himself that the heart attack was exactly what it seemed to be, rather than a devious voodoo assault that mimicked natural causes.

Apparently crack whores weren't that unusual a sight at the hospital, since the nurses on staff scarcely even blinked at my appearance. Or perhaps they just had very low expectations of the sort of person likely to visit Nolan. In any case, my name was on the security list that the *D30* production office had given the hospital for its star's private room, and my two companions and I were told where to go.

Puma, who had already been anxious about angry spirits and voracious baka when we'd first met, was now totally freaked out by the prospect of an army of zombies being raised in Harlem as part of some major dark mojo that Max believed was in the works. So she was going to consult Mambo Celeste about holding a community ritual to appease the gods and seek their protection. It should be done soon, Puma thought—*very* soon. Meanwhile, she would also try to learn if the ruptured intestine that killed Darius might have been magically inflicted on him.

With zombies and baka on the loose in this neighborhood, Biko didn't want his sister walking home alone from the store, even though it was still light out. So he would help her close up the shop, take her home, and then meet us at the hospital. Max wanted to see the places where Biko had encountered baka during his recent nocturnal adventures, as well as the spot where I had met Darius' zombie. And since I wasn't keen on making that tour after dark, I wanted to get this visit to Nolan over with in a hurry and get back outside while there was still some evening light left.

The door to Nolan's hospital room was guarded by his personal assistant, a plump, anxious, bespectacled woman whose appearance suggested that, like me, she hadn't been home since the actor had fallen ill last night.

She checked off my name on her list. "You're late."

"Sorry," I said.

"*Very* late."

"We were unavoidably detained," Max said. "Please accept my humble apologies. The fault is mine, I fear."

"And you are?"

"Dr. Maximillian Zadok," he said, taking off his straw hat. "A specialist from Oxford University."

"A specialist? Oxford? All right, you can go in, too."

"And I'm Jeffrey Clark." Oozing charm, my old boy-friend said to Nolan's twitchy assistant, "You've had quite a day, I'll bet. Maybe you want to go get yourself a cup of coffee or something while we visit with Mike?"

She was too accustomed to actors to be flustered by his flirting with her. "I can't. He likes me to be within shouting distance at all times." She looked down at her notebook. "Jeffrey Clark? Your name's not on my list."

Jeff nudged me. I said, "He's with me."

"Hmm. Well, there've been two no-shows already, and Mike's cranky about how few visitors he's had so far. The star of *Criminal Motive* was hospitalized for exhaustion last year," she said, naming an Emmy Award–winning drama in the *Crime and Punishment* franchise. "Mike found out how many visitors *he* had while he was in the hospital, and now he's keeping score. We've only been here one day, and we're already way behind." She said to Jeff, "So I guess you can go in. It'll help the tally."

He beamed at her. "Thanks."

It was a good thing that I hadn't really expected a brush with death to change Nolan's personality, since it took only a few seconds at his bedside to establish that this was indeed not the case.

He told me I looked like shit, then glanced at Jeff and Max and asked me, "Who the fuck are they?"

I introduced them to him. Jeff, a dedicated self-promoter, immediately tried to engage him in conversation. Nolan interrupted him, without apology, to shout for his assistant, demanding that she come straighten his pillows for him.

Jeff again tried to strike up a conversation. Nolan again interrupted him, asking me, "Are those for me?"

"Huh? Oh!" I realized he was nodding to the two books tucked under my arm. "No. This is some, uh, research I'm doing."

They were books about Vodou. Puma had given them to me when I left the shop a little while ago, insisting I take them free of charge. She thought they might help me better understand the ritual we'd be attending soon.

So you didn't bring me anything?" Nolan was looking at me as if he'd just learned I was a shoplifter. "Not even a card?"

"I was mugged after you collapsed last night," I said wearily. "My purse was stolen." It was as good an excuse as any.

"No shit? Jesus." He shook his head. "The cops need to do a better job around here."

That struck me as the sort of sentiment that the star of *The Dirty Thirty* should probably keep to himself.

Nolan looked weak and pale, but he certainly didn't seem to be at death's door. He also talked like he expected to be back on the set within a few days to finish shooting our final scene together. If he felt any curiosity at all about why I was wearing my costume while visiting him, he concealed it manfully.

I glanced at the clock on the wall, figuring that ten more minutes was a reasonable length of time for this visit. The next time I looked at the clock, I was appalled to find that only three minutes had passed since my previous glance. Could a voodoo curse slow down the passage of time inside this hospital room, I wondered?

Max questioned Nolan about his health, his symptoms, what he remembered about his collapse, and his diagnosis. After a few more minutes, during which time I kept my gaze fixed on the agonizingly slow revolutions of the clock's second hand, Max fell silent. When I met his eyes, he gave me a cheerful little nod, indicating that he was satisfied.

Jeff started chatting with Nolan again, and for all his own self-absorption, he was smart enough to recognize by now that the way to Nolan's heart was to pretend to be fascinated by him. A certain natural revulsion had prevented me from mastering this technique with Nolan myself, but Jeff was made of sterner stuff. Before long, Nolan was yammering away about himself in an animated manner, clearly delighted to have as attentive an audience as Jeff.

When I announced, with considerable relief, that it was time for us to go, Jeff's face fell. So I added, "I mean, Max and I have to go. But if *you'd* like to stay . . ."

"Sure, he'll stay," said Nolan, not about to let his captive listener escape so easily.

The two men gave us a quick wave of farewell, and Max and I left.

As we exited the room, Nolan's assistant tried to block our path. "You're supposed to stay a half hour," she hissed. "That's the rule!"

"We can't stay," I said. "Places to go, bokors to stop."

"What?"

"I want credit for this visit," I said.

"You show up hours late and stay barely fifteen minutes, and you want credit?" she said incredulously. "You're going to have to come a second time."

"That's not fair!" I protested.

Max said, "One of our party is remaining behind. Will that suffice?"

She blinked. "Oh! The cute bald guy is staying?"

"You *like* that look on him?" I said.

She picked up her pen to make a note on the visitation log. "Okay. How long is he going to stay?"

"Probably until Nolan gets well and checks out of the hospital," I said.

I got credit for the visit.

As we rode the elevator back down to the main floor, Max said to me, "Mr. Nolan clearly suffers from an excess of choler. I do not find it surprising that his temperament has affected his health."

"So you think his heart attack was strictly due to natural causes?"

"All things considered, it is impossible to say for certain, but, yes, I believe so. In truth, based on what he says about his condition, it sounds as if he's lucky the attack wasn't more severe. It may not be wise for him to return to work as early as he evidently intends to."

I nodded in agreement, though I wasn't sure who had the strength of will to stop Nolan, if returning to work too soon was what he decided to do.

Biko was waiting for us outside on the sidewalk. His sword case was slung over his back. Although there were plenty of people around and it would be light for a little while longer, I was still glad he was armed, since we were about to go visit baka stomping grounds.

"Got rid of Jeff?" he asked.

"Yes."

"Good. He's not a bad guy, but he really doesn't seem to get it."

I thought that statement also accurately summed up Jeff as a boyfriend, but I said nothing.

We weren't very far from the spot where Biko and I had met, so we started our investigation there. Biko showed us the half-eaten pigeon carcasses he had found last night. We also studied the claw marks that were nearby.

"It was the baka," I said with certainty when I saw the thick scratch marks on the cement wall that Biko pointed out. I felt a chill run through me, despite the evening's muggy heat. The hand that made these marks would have been nearly as big as mine, and the claws could easily eviscerate a dog Gilligan's size. "These marks weren't made by a person or a pet."

"No, indeed," said Max, examining them intently.

We went next to the area where I had seen the zombie and the growling gargoyles, and where Lopez and I had later found the severed hand being eaten by carrion feeders. There was no evidence here of anything that had happened last night. I was just about to say so when someone coming out of one of the row houses shouted loudly.

"*You!*"

We all looked up.

A white man in his fifties, balding and wearing wire-rimmed glasses, shook his fist at me. "The cops were here all morning and half the day because of you! What did you *do?*"

"Friend of yours?" Biko said to me.

I recognized the voice. "That's the man who wouldn't call for help for Darius!"

"Get *out* of here!" The man ran over to the garbage cans on the sidewalk, picked up a lid, and brandished it at me. "We don't want your kind around here!"

"Oh, dear," said Max.

"Yo, mister," Biko said sternly to the man. "You talk that way to my sister again, and you'll answer to *me*. Do I make myself clear?"

"Your *sister?*" the man blurted.

"*Yeah*, my sister," Biko said. "She was mugged here last night. Are you the jerk who just shouted at her when she was calling out for help?"

"She wasn't . . . She . . ."

Biko started walking forward. "Are *you* the guy who let *my* sister get mugged right outside your own house and wouldn't help her? *Are you that guy?*"

"Uh . . ." The man wisely chose to go inside, where he

locked his door—and probably shoved a piece of heavy furniture in front of it, too.

"Hmph." Biko glared at the closed door. "Maybe the next time a woman in the street is asking for help, that loser will do more than shout at her and slam his window shut."

We searched the area, but the cops had cleaned up all signs of what had happened there. So we accompanied Biko to the north end of Mount Morris Park where, very near the Livingston Foundation, he showed us where he had found the baka attacking Frank Johnson. Though the fading summer light was very dim by now, we were able to find some scratch marks on the pavement, similar to the ones we had seen a little while ago. We walked through the darkening park to the south end, and Biko showed us where he and Puma had found Gilligan's body. Only a large dark brown spot on the cement revealed evidence of what had occurred there.

"His blood," Biko said quietly.

"My dear fellow." Max patted his shoulder.

Ahead of us was a large expanse of grass, then a steep, rocky hill that was thick with shrubs and trees. The hill was high, ascending well above the roofs of the townhouses that surrounded the park. An old stone staircase led up the steep slope, curving to its shape, sweeping gracefully and disappearing up into the night-shrouded foliage that crowded around it. Wondering where those steps went, I looked farther up. Above the dark outline of the trees against the twilight sky, I saw the top of what looked like some sort of fantastic treehouse. Max and I had noticed it much earlier today, from a distance, soaring just above the treetops.

"What is that?" I asked Biko, craning my neck and pointing up to it.

"The old watchtower," he said. "The last one left in

New York. It's so old, it's been obsolete for more than a century."

"Watchtower for *what?*" I asked.

"Fire," said Biko. "In the eighteenth and nineteenth centuries, Harlem was mostly farm country—can you picture *that?* In those days, they had tall watchtowers around New York, like this one. Someone would be posted at the top of the tower to keep an eye out for a fire starting. When he saw one, he'd alert people by ringing the big bell that hung below him in the tower. After the switchover to fire alarm boxes, the towers went out of use and mostly got torn down. This is the only one still standing." After a moment, he added, "Mr. Livingston told me that. He was talking about restoring it one day, but the foundation always had so many other projects it wanted to do first."

"Out of use for more than a century," I mused. "It must be falling apart by now."

"Yeah, I think it's in pretty bad condition." Biko chuckled and added, "If you go up there in the daytime, you'll see that it looks like the world's best jungle gym. When I was little, I always wanted to climb on it. But my mom told me she'd skin me alive if I ever went anywhere near it. Too dangerous. And by the time I was old enough to come to the park without Mom or Puma, I guess I just wasn't stupid enough to try it. It always looked to me like the spiral staircase would collapse, or the iron bars would fall off, or that big bell would tumble down on my head."

"Hmm." Max nodded.

After a moment, we all turned by silent consent and walked out of the park, disappointed not to have learned anything new from this outing. My feet were killing me, and I was so tired that I didn't think I could make it all the way to the subway. Max must have noticed my drooping shoulders and weary pace.

"I must take Esther home," he said to Biko. "I should have done so well before now."

I was about to protest that Max didn't need to escort me, but then I remembered that I didn't have my subway card, money for a cab, or the keys to my door.

"But I think, Biko," Max continued, "that you, Nelli, and I should rendezvous later and go hunting by night for baka and zombies."

A man and woman who'd been in the process of passing us on the sidewalk paused and gave us a hard stare. Whether it was because of what Max had just said, or because of my outfit . . . Well, I supposed that either reason would have been sufficient for their sudden decision to cross the street and continue their walk well away from us.

"Who's Nelli? Oh! Your dog, right?" Biko shook his head. "Dr. Zadok, after what those baka did to *my* dog—"

"Nelli is very large, and combating creatures such as the baka is her life's work," Max said. "Although I am reluctant to put her in harm's way, knowing now how ruthless the baka can be when facing a canine opponent, I feel that it would frustrate her—even insult her—to omit Nelli from our expedition. It would also be wise of us to recruit her to this endeavor, since she is well-equipped for detecting mystical adversaries."

There was a brief pause while Biko translated this in his head, and then he agreed with Max's proposal. Since the baka had so far been encountered in the vicinity of the park, the two men agreed to meet at the foundation later to commence their hunt. After we all exchanged phone numbers, Biko went home, and Max escorted me to Malcolm X Boulevard, where we caught a cab.

Fortunately, he was so absorbed in thinking about the mysterious problem at hand, he forgot to be frightened in the taxi until we ran a red light while crossing a major thoroughfare. And only a few minutes after that, we were descending from the cab outside my apartment in the West Thirties, near Tenth Avenue.

I got one of the neighbors to buzz me into the building, then Max followed me up to the second floor, to my front door. Using his mystical abilities, he placed his hand on the doorknob, took a slow breath, uttered a few words in another language, and turned the knob.

"There you are, my dear!" He opened the door and gestured for me to go inside.

"Max, I just realized," I said, "You've never been here before."

"Indeed, I have not."

"Come on, I'll give you the grand tour."

He protested briefly, considering how exhausted I was. But I spent so much time in his home, I wanted him to at least know what the inside of my home looked like. So I insisted he come inside for a few minutes.

"Ah, very nice!" Max said when I turned on the light.

Actually, it was an old apartment in poor repair, mostly furnished with charity-shop furniture and hand-me-downs. But it was home. "Thank you."

Max looked around while I poured him a glass of cold water. The kitchen flowed into the living room, the two rooms being partially separated by a counter. A small table for four people was perched halfway between the two spaces, neither of which was large enough to hold the whole thing comfortably. The bathroom door was on one side of the living room. There was another door near it that led onto a very small balcony; it overlooked a claustrophobic space between four close together buildings and offered no privacy, but it was nonetheless a balcony.

I had two bedrooms—a fact that had made Lopez almost green with envy on his first visit here. But the second bedroom would scarcely have passed as a walk-in closet in most other cities. In fact, now that I no longer had roommates, that was precisely what I used it for. I kept a large supply of rehearsal props and costumes in that room, as well as the overflow of my own clothes that didn't fit in the small closet in my bedroom.

Max beamed at me and said courteously, "I like your home, Esther. It's very welcoming."

"It's rent-controlled," I said. "Otherwise, I'd probably be living in a phone booth an hour outside of the city."

Seeing Jeff today reminded me of how things had been back when I was dating him. "I moved in here with two other girls from Northwestern University after I first came to New York. One girl slept in the back bedroom—which is only big enough to fit a twin bed, nothing else. So she had to keep her clothes in the bigger bedroom, which the other girl and I shared."

"Where are your former roommates now?" Max asked, taking a seat in the overstuffed chair that we three girls had purchased together at a Goodwill shop five years ago.

I sat on the couch. "One quit acting and applied to law school after we'd been here about a year. The other one left about eighteen months after that. She got married to a doctor and moved to the suburbs. She's never officially quit the business, but she's got a baby, she's teaching part-time, and she hasn't gone for an audition since before she got engaged." I shrugged. "I don't think she'll want to come back to this life later on."

"Two out of three? A high attrition rate."

"Not really. That's what this life is like. A lot of people who start out acting wind up doing something else. One out of three of us sticking with it is probably a high percentage compared to the field overall."

"Ah, but you are gifted," he said. "As well as committed and driven. And these are qualities that cannot be measured by percentages."

I smiled, liking his description of me.

Max set down his glass and rose to his feet. "You need your rest, my dear. And I must go collect Nelli and prepare for our nocturnal expedition."

I rose and followed him to the door. "Be careful, Max. There's danger on the streets at night even apart from baka and zombies."

"I will be accompanied by a skilled swordsman," he reminded me.

"Ah, yes. There is that. Good night, Max. I'll see you tomorrow, I suppose?"

He nodded, wished me good night, and left.

I locked the door and latched the chain. Then, remembering that the keys to my home were in the clutches of the baka, I pushed a heavy chair in front of the door.

I stripped off my clothes and dropped them on the floor. I knew I should make a list of all the things I needed to do in the morning before returning to the Livingston Foundation (such as call a locksmith and cancel my credit cards), but I was just too exhausted to think about it right now.

I headed for the shower, and I stood under the running water, soaping, scrubbing, and shampooing until I finally felt clean. By then, I was starting to run out of warm water. I emerged from the shower, wrapped my hair in a towel, dried myself, and put on my bathrobe.

I was plodding toward the bedroom, planning to go straight to sleep, when I noticed the flashing light on my answering machine.

"Oh, right." I hadn't answered calls on my cell phone since it was stolen last night, so anyone trying to reach me would probably wind up calling here and leaving me a message. I pressed the playback button and listened to my calls.

There was one from my mother. This was inevitable. She always managed to call when I was having a rot-

ten day. It was some sort of psychic gift. There was little chance, realistically, that she would *fail* to call on a
day when I'd been arrested for prostitution, mugged by
gargoyles, and spooked by a big snake. And since my
mother wasn't precisely a person who focused on the
sunny side of things, I was glad I had missed her call.

There were a couple of calls from the *D30* production
office. One had been made before I'd called them from
Jeff's cell phone. The other call reminded me that I was
scheduled to visit Nolan that afternoon.

"Whatever," I muttered.

There was also a call from Thack, my agent, who'd
heard about the confusion on the location shoot last
night and wanted to make sure I was okay.

And then there was one from Lopez. My heart gave
a little skip. Maybe seeing me last night had made him
reconsider . . . Maybe calling him for help hadn't been
such a bad idea, after all.

He had made the call shortly before I arrived home. I
smiled when I heard his familiar voice say, "It's me."

Then I stopped smiling.

"The Two-Five called me. They just found your purse.
Nothing seems to be missing. I don't know where you
are, so I'll pick it up tonight and hold onto it until I hear
from you." A pause. "I know about the Livingston Center, Esther. You and I need to talk."

13

The following morning, feeling much more human now that I was clean and rested, I called my bank and reported that my credit card was missing. I doubted that the drooling gargoyles who had taken my purse had used its contents for a spending spree, but better safe than sorry. Apart from that, since Lopez's message said that nothing seemed to be missing, I decided not to worry about the rest of the bag's contents until I got it back and could check for myself. Meanwhile, at least I knew it was in safe hands.

I phoned Thack, my agent, to let him know I was all right and to nag him about getting me some auditions. Once I finished the *D30* shoot, my professional life would consist entirely of waiting tables and teaching some summer acting workshops until the kids went back to school.

Perhaps this was a petty personal concern, what with zombies rising from the grave and Max predicting that some sort of apocalyptic event was imminent. But I had bills to pay and a struggling career to think about, and these problems weren't going to go away just because a bokor was on the loose.

Thack answered my call with exclamations of surprise

and concern. "Esther! A whole day without answering your cell! My God, I thought you must by lying dead or unconscious somewhere in Harlem!"

"No, I just misplaced the phone." Given Thack's tendency to react dramatically to things, I decided to leave it at that.

He asked, "Did you get lost wandering in the dark after the crew packed up the set without waiting for the actors to return from their break? And how *dare* they do that! It's lucky you weren't all murdered!"

"Oh, no, we were in a nice neighborhood." Well, except for the supernatural creatures that were running around at night. "Anyhow, I have the impression that things on the set just descended into panic and confusion when they realized the show's star was having a heart attack right there and then."

"Well, I've met Mike Nolan," Thack said. "And, frankly, it couldn't happen to a more deserving actor."

"I can't argue with that," I said. "He expects to be back on set in a few days, but that seems a little unrealistic to me."

"Either way, the *D-Thirty* team are saying they want *you* back to finish the episode," Thack said. "You've made a good impression there. Congratulations!"

"Thanks. But it'll probably only be another day or two of work. So is there anything else going on?"

"Not really. You know what the business is like in August. Quiet as a graveyard!"

I wished he hadn't phrased it quite that way. "Uh-huh."

He continued, "But I'll call you as soon as anything turns up."

I kept my tone professional as I said good-bye and hung up. Then I sighed and fought off a feeling of gloom, trying to look on the bright side. At least I was teaching some of Jeff's workshops this month; practicing my craft—whether I was taking some classes or, on this occasion, teaching them—was always a good way to hone my skills, stay sharp, and keep improving.

The phone rang, and I answered it. As if summoned by my thoughts, the caller was Jeff, checking in from his day job as a gladiator. He wanted to make sure I knew what time I needed to be at the foundation today. I assured him I did, and we discussed what sort of exercises I would work on with the students.

Then he said, "And you're not going to talk to them about . . . other stuff, are you?"

"Other stuff?" I poured myself another cup of coffee. "Are you saying I *shouldn't* tell the kids that the foundation's administrator has become a reanimated corpse and that I saw him being attacked by evil monsters the other night, right before I was arrested for prostitution? Do you mean *that* kind of 'other stuff,' Jeff?"

"Are you still sleep-deprived?"

"No."

"Then knock off the sarcasm," he said irritably. "I don't want you getting *either* of us in trouble with Catherine or with parents by telling those kids about the crazy stuff that you were talking about yesterday. Is that so unreasonable?"

Actually, it wasn't. So I said, "Okay. Got it. I know where the line should be drawn, and I'm not going to freak out—or amuse—a bunch of teens by talking about things that, believe it or not, I know better than to discuss in public."

"Okay. Good. That's settled, then." It was clear from his tone that he still favored any theory *except* the one that the rest of us had agreed upon yesterday.

Nonetheless, I asked, "Have you talked to Frank Johnson yet?"

"He hasn't called me back."

"Call him again," I said.

"Esther—"

"*Please*, Jeff. It's important."

"Fine. I'll call him on my next break. Satisfied?" He sighed. "Now if we can move on to saner subjects before I have to get back to work, I'm also calling to thank you. I owe you."

"For what?"

"For introducing me to Mike!" he said, as if that should be obvious. "What a great guy!"

"You like him?" I said doubtfully.

"He's going to talk to the show's casting director about me."

Ah. In that case, yes, Jeff liked him. Jeff could bring himself to like Simon Legree, if the cruel slave master helped him get an acting job.

"He's going to do that for you?" I asked.

"Yeah!"

"Great! I'm glad to hear it, Jeff."

I didn't have the heart to tell him that I would bet real money against Nolan doing anything of the sort. For one thing, I knew from past experience that Jeff was perfectly capable of believing he had heard a verbal promise when, in reality, there had merely been a reluctant nod or noncommittal shrug in response to his asking someone for a professional favor. I also thought that baka would fly through midtown before Nolan would trouble himself to do something generous for another actor, let alone an obscure one who had nothing to offer in return except gratitude and loyalty.

"So who knows?" Jeff said with a smile in his voice. "Maybe you and I will wind up working together on *The Dirty Thirty* sometime."

"I'd like that." I was being honest about that, at least. Jeff was very talented, and he was great to work with. This was, in fact, the reason I had fallen for him five years ago. And being dazzled back then by my own exciting new experiences as an actress in the Big Apple, it had taken me a while to realize that working with Jeff was the *only* time I was in love with him. The rest of the time I was just rather fond of him in an exasperated way. And I still was now, I realized. "But I don't think we're likely to meet on the show, Jeff. I'm just doing a guest spot and have only one more scene to film."

"Really? From the way Mike talked about you, I thought—"

"He *talked* about me?" I said with reflexive revulsion.

"Yeah. I got the impression from him that there was a rapport between you two."

"What?" I believed in zombies and dark magic, but I found it hard to believe that Michael Nolan hinted that he liked me.

"Or, uh, maybe he meant more that it was a rapport between your characters," Jeff said uncertainly. "It sounded to me as if he was pleased with the scenes you two have done. He seems to think that you and he—or, I guess, your characters—are interesting together."

"Oh. Well. That's good to know." It had never occurred to me that Nolan had noticed me *or* my character. I supposed I should feel flattered that he felt some professional respect for me. But I was skeptical that he did. The notion was probably just Jeff's imagination at work again. "In any case, I'm not scheduled to do any more work on the show after this episode."

"Oh," he said. "That's too bad. But, hey, you got a guest spot on a hot TV show. Here's hoping I get one, too."

"Is that what you were doing out in LA?" I asked. "Trying to get into TV?"

"Yeah. Nothing was really happening for me here, so I moved out there when I got cast in a TV pilot, but the show didn't get picked up. I wound up doing three more pilots that year, but nothing panned out." He sighed. "The second year, I couldn't even get auditions anymore. So a few months ago, I decided it was time to come back to New York."

Falling right into my old habit of trying to encourage Jeff about his career, I said, "And you got work almost as soon as you came back. So returning to New York was a good decision."

He gave a morose little grunt of assent.

I urged, "So tell me about this gladiator role."

"You don't think the shaved head looks good on me, do you?"

"Are you working in a play?" I asked.

"*Other* people think this is a good look for me. What don't you like about it?"

"This conversation is starting to feel all too familiar," I said wearily.

"Is it the shape of my head?" he asked. "Do you think my skull is bulbous?"

I made a heroic effort to be patient with him. "Tell me about the job. Does it involve combat scenes?"

"I've been thinking about getting some head shots this way, to show more casting directors that I can do this look." He asked anxiously, "Do you think that's a bad idea?"

I gave up and snapped, "You know, *you're* the reason I decided not to date any more actors! Are you aware that men in other professions don't do this to women? I mean, do you think Lopez has ever dragged me through a marathon of talking about his voice or his appearance, the way you used to do? Do you think he frets to me about—"

"Who's Lopez?" Jeff asked.

I realized what I'd said. "No one. Never mind."

"Why does that name sound—Oh! Do you mean *Connor* Lopez? The *really good-looking* cop?"

"My point is—"

"The guy who sprung you from the slammer, right?"

Eager to distract him, I said, "I don't like the bald head. It doesn't suit you at all."

"So *that's* why the guy got out of bed in the middle of the night to get you out of jail. I thought it sounded a little above and beyond the call of duty," Jeff said. "You're dating him?"

"No."

"Does Max know you're dating him?"

"I'm not dating him," I said.

"Are you going to tell Biko and Puma you're involved with this cop?"

"I'm not involved with him!" Since the silence that met my emphatic statement was fraught with skepticism, I added, "I went out with him a few times. In the spring. That's all."

"Well, he sure must have been pissed off the other night, then."

"No, he was very nice to me, actually." All things considered.

"Ah." There was a wealth of understanding in that monosyllable. "I get it."

"You get *what?*"

"He dumped you."

"It was, er . . . a mutual decision," I lied. Yes, Jeff was right; but his assumption stung my pride.

"Come on, Esther. The guy goes to a precinct house at some ungodly hour, after months of not seeing you, to ask other cops for a favor that *had* to be a little embarrassing for him."

"Well . . . yeah." I shifted uncomfortably on my chair.

"And he wasn't chewing iron and spitting nails?" Jeff snorted. "Obviously, he feels guilty about dumping you. Why else would he help you out *and* be nice about it?"

"Maybe he likes me," I said defensively.

"Then why did he dump you?"

My shoulders slumped. "He thinks I'm deranged."

"Really? Wow. Who can plumb the depths of *that* mystery?"

"Is there any other reason you called?" I said. "Or are we done now?"

"One other thing. Do you know if Puma's dating anyone?"

I sighed. "I met her for the first time when you did, Jeff. How would I know?"

"I'm thinking of asking her out."

"Whatever."

"The voodoo stuff's a little strange, I admit. But I'm pretty open-minded about religion." He added slyly, "I used to be involved with a Jewish girl, you know."

"Uh-huh."

"Anyhow, I like Puma. She's got something. You know what I mean?"

I did, but his comments about Lopez had annoyed me. So all I said was, "Can I hang up now?"

"You're not jealous are you?"

"Jealous? *I* dumped *you*," I reminded him.

"No regrets?"

"Certainly not since you shaved your head," I said.

"That's harsh."

"I have to go now. I've got calls to return. There are other people besides you who want to belittle and abuse me today, Jeff."

"Hey, how *is* your mom?"

"Good-bye."

Jeff had guessed right again. As soon as I ended my call with him, I phoned my mother. I told her I was fine, and that I hadn't returned her (as she told me) cell phone messages because I'd lost the phone. Then I said that I was on my way out the door and couldn't talk now. Naturally, this didn't work.

"How on *earth* did you manage to lose your cell phone?" Her tone implied it must be my fault.

"I had a fight with a gargoyle," I said wearily.

"I don't like ethnic slurs, dear."

"Did you call for any particular reason, Mom?"

She wanted to know when my episode of *D30* would air. "Although I've recommended that they not let their children watch it, based on what you've told me about your role, some of our friends and relatives would like to see it."

I explained, as briefly as possible, why the episode was in limbo at the moment. "So I don't know when it's going to be on television."

"Ah! Well, perhaps it's all working out for the best," she said.

It was so unlike my mother to see the bright side of a bad situation, I asked, "What do you mean?"

"Presumably you'll get paid for your work, even though the episode hasn't been completed?"

"Yes."

"But since it's incomplete, maybe it won't be aired." Her tone was bright with relief and satisfaction as she concluded, "So you'll earn a nice paycheck, but you won't actually appear on TV as a homeless bisexual junkie prostitute."

"My episode might never air. Gee, I hadn't thought of that, Mom." I felt like going back to bed and pulling the covers over my head. "I'm so glad you called."

"So am I, dear."

"I have to go."

"Have you met any nice young men lately?"

"Bye, Mom."

Next, figuring I might as well get it over with, I called Lopez. To my relief, I got his voice mail. I left a message thanking him for retrieving my purse and asking him, whenever it was convenient for him, to leave it with the receptionist at the Livingston Foundation.

Since I really didn't want to discuss the foundation, Darius Phelps, Biko, or anything related to these subjects with Lopez, I was hoping I could get my purse back without actually having to talk to him. After all, this was already turning into a trying day for me, and I hadn't even left my apartment yet.

Jilly C-Note's costume was still lying on the floor where I had dropped it last night. I picked up the purple fishnet stockings and the push-up brassiere, and I put them into a bucket with cold water and a generous dollop of soap for hand laundry. I would let the items soak until late tonight, and then rinse them when I returned from my shift at Bella Stella, which is where I would go directly from the Livingston Foundation later today.

I sniffed Jilly's boots, inside of which my abused feet had been sweating too much lately. I made a face as I discovered that the boots needed a serious remedy. Using a trick I had learned from another actress, I put a solid air freshener inside each boot to absorb the unpleasant odor. The boots should smell fine by the time I had to put them on again.

Then I put the leopard-print shirt and red vinyl skirt into a bag. I would drop them off at a dry cleaner while doing my errands today, and I'd request twenty-four-hour service. That cost more, but I wanted to be sure of having the outfit in hand by the time I got rescheduled for filming.

I had a spare set of keys I could take with me today, and I could use my Equity card as my ID to cash a check at the bank, so that I'd have some cash on me until I got my purse back. I got my daypack out of the closet and packed these things into it, as well as some other supplies I'd need for the day, including bottled water and some healthy snacks. This was cheaper than buying food and beverages while I was out and about. Besides, if I was going to wear Jilly's outfit on camera again, I shouldn't indulge in any more fried chicken.

I decided to wear the same sleeveless white blouse, black capri pants, and sensible shoes to the foundation that I would also wear to work at the restaurant tonight; that way I wouldn't need to bring a change of clothes with me or need to return to home later.

Before I finally left the apartment that day, my gaze fell on the two books that Puma had given me. I shrugged and packed them into the daypack, too, figuring I might as well get some reading done on the subway ride to Harlem.

Today's acting class at the foundation involved rehearsing two- and three-person scenes from various plays. Some of the kids were ambitious enough to tackle Shakespeare, and we worked on articulating the text and exploring the rhythms, as well as examining some of the more unfamiliar vocabulary. Another of the challenges for an actor doing Shakespeare is figuring out what to do while the *other* guy in the scene has a speech that lasts for thirty lines—which happens often in Will's work.

"You've probably already heard Jeff say that acting is reacting?" I said to the kids. "Well, onstage, as in life, you're not doing *nothing* when someone is talking. You're listening. Or refusing to listen. You're thinking about what the other person is saying. Or trying to ignore it and not let it get to you. Or . . ." I glanced at a girl whose eyes were barely open. I remembered her name from yesterday, since she had given me a couple of painkillers for my aching head. "Or maybe, like Shondolyn, you're struggling not to fall asleep while someone else is doing all the talking."

Shondolyn blinked and jerked herself awake as the

other kids laughed. But, to my surprise, instead of laughing with them, or even looking sheepish, she got teary-eyed.

"I'm sorry, Miss Diamond," she said in a shaky voice.

"Call me Esther." I hadn't meant to embarrass her into tears. "Don't worry about it, Shondolyn. Friday afternoon, hot day, substitute teacher droning on and on . . ." The kids laughed again, but awkwardly this time. "Bound to happen."

She cleared her throat. "I need to be excused for a minute."

"Sure," I said in bewilderment as she fled the room.

I noticed that the boy named Jamal, once again dressed in baggy hip-hop clothing, involuntarily rose from his seat, his expression serious and concerned as he watched her leave. He moved uncertainly, as if wanting to go after her, then stopped himself and sat back down, but his gaze remained fixed on the door through which Shondolyn had departed. I wondered if he was the cause of her tears. A young lovers' quarrel, perhaps?

"Okay, everyone," I said to the students, who were restive in response to Shondolyn's distress. "I want you to think about what I've just said as you run through your scenes with each other again. I'll be back in a few minutes, and we'll see if what I've talked about is helping you."

I left the room and went directly to the place I thought I was most likely to find Shondolyn. Sure enough, she was in the ladies' restroom. But she wasn't crying, as I expected. She was cursing and punching the wall.

Tough girl.

She looked embarrassed when she saw me. "Sorry." She went to the sink, turned on the tap, and started splashing cold water on her face.

"That's all right," I said. "I just came to see how you are."

"I'll be okay in a minute." She sounded tired.

I hadn't worked with kids before, so I hoped I wasn't taking the wrong approach. Starting with what seemed to be the most likely cause for her distress, I asked, "Is there someone in the class that you're uncomfortable with, Shondolyn?"

"What?" She ripped off a paper towel from the dispenser and started patting her face dry. "No."

She was a very attractive girl, with a lot of poise and style for a teenager. But I noticed now that she looked exhausted and there were dark circles under her eyes.

I said, "You haven't, uh, quarreled with anyone in the group?"

"No, Miss Dia—Esther. No, it's nothing like that. It's just . . ." Tears welled up in her eyes again. She brushed them away angrily. "I just feel like I can't take it anymore."

I put a hand on her shoulder. "Take what, Shondolyn?"

"I'm so tired," she said, still sounding angry. "I can't sleep. It's been bad for weeks, and lately it's getting worse. So now I've got a headache almost all the time. I think it's just because I'm so *tired*." She added apologetically, "It makes me pretty bad-tempered, too."

The headaches must be why she had been carrying that bottle of painkillers yesterday. I hadn't thought about it at the time, but I realized now that not that many teenage girls went around with a jumbo-size bottle of ibuprofen in their purses. "Has your mom taken you to a doctor?"

She nodded. "He gave me some sleeping pills."

"Did they help?"

She said irritably, "I don't take them. My mom thinks I do, but I don't." She added, "Don't tell her, okay?"

Worried that I was out of my depth, I nonetheless said, "Okay. But, Shondolyn, why don't you take the pills?"

"I'm scared I won't be able to wake up if I do."

I frowned. "You mean . . . you're afraid of dying in your sleep?"

She looked at me like I was an idiot. "No. Why would I die in my sleep?"

Then what are you afraid of?"

She took a breath. "The nightmares."

"Nightmares?" I repeated.

Considering the hormonal roller coaster that teens experience, the conflicting pressures they feel from their peers and their families, and the way they're so often forced to straddle the fence between childhood restrictions and adult problems, I thought that nightmares might easily just be a side effect of adolescence.

But as Shondolyn spoke about her dreams in recent weeks, I realized she was experiencing something strange in her sleep. The girl relieved her anxieties in a rush of uninhibited honesty, the words tumbling over each other to get out of her mouth. Maybe it was because I was a stranger who listened without interrupting or judging her, or maybe it was just because she had reached a breaking point. In any case, she told me about her nightmares in vivid detail.

And in her dreams, I discovered, this girl had seen the baka.

Having seen them myself, I recognized them quite clearly from her description—which included their dirty claws and their stinking breath.

She had also seen the walking dead in her dreams: glassy-eyed men with dull, sunken skin who didn't breathe or talk, and who moved in response to commands from an unseen master.

"It's freaking me out!" She scowled and kicked the nearby garbage can. "I can't stand it anymore!"

I could understand why she feared sleep—and why she was forcing herself to stay awake at night, to the point of hurting her health and her temperament. I could also understand why her mother thought that sleeping pills and time were probably the answer to her problem. The images haunting Shondolyn probably convinced her mom that she was a sensitive and impressionable youngster going through a troubled phase, and if her family was supportive and patient, it would pass.

Whereas I feared she was being menaced by the mysterious bokor who was summoning dark forces. And the next thing she said convinced me of it.

"I also hear names in my sleep. I can't remember most of them, but there's one that sticks in my head: Mama Brigitte." Shondolyn looked at me. "I've never met anyone with a name like that. Why is it in my dreams?"

Thanks to the reading I had done on my way here, I recognized the name. And because of that, I suddenly felt so cold, I almost wished that Puma hadn't given me those books.

"I want you to go see a friend of mine. Right now," I told Shondolyn. "Her name is Puma, and she runs a voodoo shop that's only a few blocks from here." I wasn't sure where Max was, and I thought this girl needed immediate help.

"Whoa!" Shondolyn resisted as I tugged on her arm, trying to drag her out of the bathroom. "No way am I going to some voodoo shop! I'm a good Christian!"

"So is Puma," I said. "In a sense. She'll explain." I hoped the Catholic paraphernalia in the shop would reassure Shondolyn. "Puma studied with a respected, uh, priest and teacher. I want you to tell her what you've just told me—"

"You're not coming with me?"

I was leading her down the hall toward our classroom now. "I have to finish teaching this class. But I don't want you to go anywhere alone. I'm going to ask Jamal to escort you to Puma's shop."

Shondolyn curled her lip. "That boy with the baggy pants and sloppy shirts?"

Apparently Jamal's interest was not reciprocated. Well, this was his chance to prove to her that he had strength of character, even if he lacked fashion sense.

I said, "He'll be glad to be asked. I think he likes you."

"He can dream *on*."

At the door to our class, I summoned Jamal, advising him to bring his daypack with him. Then I said quietly to Shondolyn, "Puma can probably explain some of the images in your dreams, and she'll give you something to protect you." No doubt the houngan had taught Puma how to use some of those amulets and herbs in the shop. And we'd need to locate Max, in whose powers I placed the most faith.

Jamal's shoulders straightened and his eyes lit up when I explained that I wanted him to escort Shondolyn to Puma's shop and to protect her—this, in particular, seemed to appeal to him. Shondolyn looked as if only her fatigue kept her from rolling her eyes. I gave them my cell phone number and told them to call me as soon as they reached the shop. Then I sent them on their way.

Only after they were gone did I realize that I still didn't *have* my cell phone. "Damn!"

Some of the kids paused in their rehearsals and looked at me.

"Sorry," I said. "Uh, let's get back to work."

While teaching the rest of the class, I tried not to speculate frantically on why Shondolyn was dreaming of Mama Brigitte, a dark and dangerous loa who was the wife of Baron Samedi, the Lord of Death.

14

"**A**pparently there was some commotion after you left my office yesterday?" Catherine said to me.

I was in her office again today. I looked up from the employee paperwork I was filling out so that I could get paid and also so that I could work with the kids. There were various forms I had to sign guaranteeing that I didn't have a criminal past and that I wouldn't lead my students astray. I felt very glad that no record existed of my recent arrest.

"Commotion? Oh!" I recalled Max's mad dash through the building in pursuit of the boy with the sword as Jeff and I ran after him. It seemed like a long time ago. I supposed that the worried receptionist had told Catherine about it. "Max and I thought we saw someone we knew. We were wrong."

"My, you do keep things lively, er . . . Esther." She'd had to glance quickly at one of my employment forms to recall my name.

I decided not to tell her that I had sent a student to a voodoo shop today. Despite her enthusiasm for the syncretic faiths of the New World, Catherine would no doubt realize that the girl's family might not approve, and she might feel obliged to reprimand me. So, in the spirit of not looking for trouble unless it came looking for me, I said nothing.

After I had finished teaching the class today, I'd checked at the reception desk. Lopez hadn't dropped off my purse yet. The receptionist—whose name was Henry—had let me use the foundation's phone to call the shop. Puma assured me that Shondolyn had arrived safely and that I had done the right thing by sending her there. Max and Biko were also there, and between Puma and Max, they were figuring out what ailed the girl and finding a solution. Shondolyn had dismissed Jamal, who had seemed worried about her and disappointed about being sent away; but he had left after the girl made it clear that she didn't want him there.

Ah, rejection. I knew the feeling.

Which reminded me of something. "I understand that a police detective came here yesterday to see you?" I said to Catherine.

"Goodness, word travels fast," she responded with a cool look. "Yes. Like you, the police officer had questions about Darius Phelps' death. And I gather that . . ." She paused for a moment, evidently wrestling with distaste. "That is, the detective informed me that Darius' grave has been robbed and the body taken."

I feigned shock. "Do you have any idea who would have done such a thing?"

"As I told the detective, no."

I met her eyes. "Do you have any idea *why* someone would take his body?"

She looked surprised by the question. "Perhaps it was stolen by someone who provides cadavers to medical schools. Or by a necrophiliac. Or by a gruesome prankster."

I was a little sorry I had asked.

Catherine added, "Or perhaps someone is trying to raise a zombie."

I blinked. "Pardon?"

"When I mentioned this yesterday, the detective looked almost as surprised as you do right now. But given my field of study, it's natural that this would occur to me. And, I confess, I am rather curious to learn whether that was the intention."

I glanced involuntarily at the nearby couch and decided that what Biko had witnessed there was probably just a one-time incident. Or perhaps an episode in a very short-lived fling. Even for a woman who was prone to concealing emotion, Catherine seemed so detached when talking about Darius' missing body that I found it hard to believe they'd recently been lovers, or that there'd been something serious between them in the past.

She concluded, "But I suspect we will never know the intention of the thief or the fate of the corpse. Surely a missing body cannot long claim the attention of the police at this time of year, given the increased violence that typically accompanies a summer heat wave."

I thought it likely that Lopez was pursuing this case on his own time, but I left that subject alone.

I asked her, "Are you familiar with any actual instances of, er, zombiism?"

"Of course," she said. "There are well-documented examples in Haiti."

"Really?" That wasn't what I had expected an academic to say.

"Certainly. The cases are controversial—"

"No kidding."

"—but widely discussed. The most famous case is that of Clairvius Narcisse, a Haitian man who died in the 1960s, was buried, and then returned to his village in the 1980s. Shortly after burial, he had been exhumed from his grave by a bokor—a dark sorcerer—who then forced him to work as a slave on a sugar plantation, alongside many other zombies."

"There were other zombies there?" I asked.

"According to Clairvius Narcisse, yes. However, Narcisse escaped after the mysterious bokor died, and neither that man nor the plantation were ever identified." Catherine shrugged. "Such stories are typically impossible to verify in all their particulars."

"Was the man who returned to the village really the same one who had died years earlier?" I tried not to think about what the zombie must have smelled like after all that time.

"According to various witnesses, he was the same man who had been buried," she said. "But one obvious reason that folklore all over the world is full of stories of the living dead, the undead, and restless spirits is that a percentage of people over the millennia have been buried alive."

"Buried alive?" I repeated in horror.

"Oh, yes," she said casually. "Without modern medical equipment or trained personnel present, someone in a state of coma, hypotension, or deep narcosis may well be considered dead and in need of burial."

I asked in confusion, "So was Narcisse alive or dead?"

"Alive, obviously," she said. "Only people mistakenly presumed dead get out of their coffins and walk away, Esther. The *actual* dead stay put."

Not quite. Darius Phelps had been pronounced medically dead in New York City in the twenty-first century, and *he* was still walking around. But I thought my telling that to Dr. Livingston might be sharing a little too much. Especially if I wanted to keep my new job here.

"If Narcisse was alive all that time, why didn't he go home sooner?" I asked. "How did he wind up enslaved as a zombie for years?"

"He was presumably subjected to powerful hallucinogenic drugs that affected his memory as well as his ability to exercise his own will. Only after the bokor who had enslaved him died, and thereby stopped dosing him with drugs, did Narcisse start recovering his wits and eventually make his way home."

"What about the other zombies that he mentioned?" I asked. "Did they escape, too, after the bokor died?"

"No one knows." She spread her hands. "As I said, such cases often remain shrouded in mystery and doubt."

"What sort of drugs would have such an effect on Narcisse?" I wondered.

"Oh, folk medicine and various ritual practices are full of interesting pharmacology," she said with enthusiasm. "In addition to nerve toxins derived from animals, there is a rich variety of botanical poisons and hallucinogens. An ethnobotanist could tell you much more about this than I can, of course."

However, her limitations apparently weren't going to prevent her from indulging in another monologue. "Calabar beans, which are used in some forms of African witchcraft, cause paralysis while keeping the victim conscious. Without an antidote, a dosage can easily be fatal." Barely pausing for breath, she continued, "A plant known as datura, which grows in Haiti, can cause hallucinations, delusions, and amnesia. That is probably what was given to Clairvius Narcisse. In Candomblé, which is an Afro-Brazilian syncretic religion—"

"What do you think happened to Darius Phelps?" I asked, hoping to avoid a recitation of the whole canon.

"Pardon?" She looked puzzled.

"Well, his grave is empty now," I said. "And you mentioned zombiism."

"I mentioned it as a matter of intellectual curiosity. Realistically, Darius' body was probably taken by someone whose motives are crass and perverse," she said coolly. "But if the body snatcher is motivated by the dark side of traditional Vodou beliefs and is intent on raising a true zombie from the dead through magical invocations and rituals . . ."

"Yes?" I prodded.

"Then the thief is a disturbed and deluded individual who needs help more than he needs punishment. And I hope the police will realize that, if they catch him."

"Or her." I took the plunge. "Do you think Mambo Celeste could conceivably be invol—"

"What? No. Absolutely not," Catherine said firmly. "A mambo is a guide, a healer, and a teacher."

"Anyone who reads the daily news knows that religious leaders in other faiths go astray and do bad things," I pointed out. "So why couldn't a mambo?"

"Obviously, a mambo *could,* just as anyone could. But is it feasible? No—at least, not in this case. I know Mambo Celeste well, and although she is a . . . an unusual personality, shall we say, she is dedicated to her faith and conventional in her practices." As if thinking of Napoleon, Catherine amended, "Er, *most* of her practices."

"But—"

"If you're imagining Mambo Celeste prowling a cemetery by night to dig up Darius Phelps' body, well . . ." She shook her head. "No, it really is too ridiculous for words."

I shrugged. "If you say so."

"I do." Her phone rang. She answered it, listened for a moment, and said, "No, I'll come down for it." She hung up and said to me, "There's a delivery at the reception desk for me. Shall we walk down together?"

I said apologetically, "I've taken up too much of your time again." I rose to my feet, figuring that fetching the package herself was her way of getting rid of me.

"Not at all." She opened the office door and gestured for me to exit ahead of her. "I always enjoy discussing such interesting subjects."

In the hallway, I looked at the pretty Vodou drapeaux that had attracted my attention yesterday. Today, thanks to the books Puma had given me, I recognized some of the printed names which had previously meant nothing to me.

"Legba," I said, reading the name aloud.

"Papa Legba," Catherine corrected me. "He guards the crossroads between the physical world and the spirit world, the intersection where the human and the divine can communicate—if Papa Legba allows it."

"This pretty symbol that covers his flag . . ." I traced the shape of the design with my finger, seeing it more clearly now that she had defined it. "It's a cross, isn't it?"

Catherine nodded. "Representing the crossroads. It's the vévé of Papa Legba."

"The what?"

"The vévé—the symbolic design. Each loa has a unique one." She explained, "To invoke a loa during a ritual, the practitioner draws the spirit's vévé on the ground, using flour or ashes or perhaps colored chalk."

Looking at an attractive vévé in bright colors on the next flag, I read the name aloud. "Ogoun."

"Ah, yes." Catherine stood beside me as I admired the drapeau. "Ogoun is the loa of fire, war, and male fertility."

"He sounds aggressive," I said.

"Like all the Vodou loa, his nature is complex," she said. "Ogoun has a hot temper and can flare up angrily if aroused. He's a patron of warriors and workers. He's strong and masculine, and he fights for freedom and justice. On occasion, he can also be quite sexual." She concluded with a smile, "And like many of the loa, he likes his rum."

We moved on to the flag that had startled me yesterday, the one depicting a dagger piercing a heart.

"Erzulie Dantor," said Catherine. "The Petro aspect of Erzulie."

"That's what Max said. I gather the Petro aspect is sort of a dark side?"

"Yes. The Rada are the benevolent family of loa to whom worshippers pray most of the time, to raise luck and invoke healing," she said. "By contrast, the Petro loa are angry, violent, and dangerous. And just as we all have our dark sides, there is a Petro counterpart to most of the Rada loa."

I followed her down the hallway and began descending the stairs with her. Thinking of Mama Brigitte, the loa whose name haunted young Shondolyn's dreams, I asked about her more famous husband. "Is Baron Samedi a Petro spirit?"

"Ah, the Lord of Death." She shook her head. "No, he's a Gédé loa. They oversee the realm of death and watch over the deceased."

The deceased—like Darius Phelps? As I continued walking down the stairs, I wondered if there was a connection between his zombie and the lady loa in Shondolyn's dreams.

"And Baron Samedi's wife, Mama Brigitte?" I asked. "Is she in the same line of work as her husband? Dealing in death?"

Catherine paused to look over her shoulder at me in evident surprise. Yesterday, I hadn't even known what a loa was; now I was asking about a very specific one.

"I've been doing a little reading," I said.

"Good for you!" There was a touch of condescension in her tone, though she seemed sincere. "Given your newfound interest in Vodou, do you plan to attend the ritual on Sunday?"

"Ritual?" I repeated.

"Yes." As we reached the ground floor, she explained, "Mambo Celeste has decided it's time to hold a community ritual. She came to see me today, shortly before you did, to schedule it. There's far too much going on at the foundation tomorrow for it to take place then, but the day after should be fine."

So evidently the mambo had heeded Puma's request. I knew that Max would want to attend, and I thought the ritual would be a good opportunity to scope out the local Vodou community for suspects—or for the bokor's potential victims.

"Shall we see you there?" Catherine asked.

"I look forward to it," I said.

At the reception desk, Catherine accepted a small package from Henry, the nice man who greeted visitors and sorted the mail. He told me, before I could ask, that my purse still wasn't here.

Catherine was obviously about to ask me what this exchange meant when, instead, her attention was attracted by a new arrival at the front door.

"Ah, your friend is here again," she said without noticeable warmth. Frowning, she added, "And he seems to have brought a small horse with him."

I turned to see Max and Nelli enter the building. Biko came in behind them, carrying his fencing gear.

"Ah, Esther!" Max smiled. "I hoped we would find you here."

Upon seeing me, Nelli gave a little *whoof!* of pleasure and trotted forward to greet me, her tongue hanging out of her massive jaws and flicking bits of dog spittle around the floor as she crossed the lobby.

I patted Nelli's head in greeting and said apologetically to Catherine, who was looking at her with an expression of mingled distaste and apprehension, "She's very hot."

"Indeed!" said Max, joining us. "The temperature outside is grueling. How do you do, Dr. Livingston? It's a pleasure to see you again."

"Dr. Zadok. Biko." Catherine glanced at the two men briefly, then returned to eyeing the dog.

"Allow me to introduce my canine companion," Max said to the anthropologist. "This is Nelli."

Catherine said, "I'm afraid we don't really allow . . ."

Nelli slobbered on her in friendly greeting.

"Oh, dear," said Max, gazing with dismay at the large smear of dog drool that now stained Catherine's silk skirt. "My apologies. Will this help?" He produced a crumpled hanky.

Catherine regarded it with almost as much disgust as she'd just shown for Nelli's saliva. She cleared her throat and, in an impressive display of self control said, "No. Thank you. Fortunately, I keep some spare clothing in my office. I think I'll just go . . . change." She beat a fast retreat and disappeared up the stairs.

Cheerfully oblivious to her sartorial solecism, Nelli panted happily as Biko scratched her ears. I realized he probably missed his dog.

Biko said to me, "Puma has convinced the mambo to hold a ritual. Day after tomorrow."

"I know. Dr. Livingston just told me." I moved away from Henry's desk and, once we were out of earshot, I conferred with my companions in a low voice. "How's Shondolyn?"

Max said, "Puma and I are both convinced the child has been targeted by the bokor—though the reason for this is currently a mystery to us. We are working on protective measures but, given the evident strength of our adversary, that may not be enough. Therefore, I consider it essential to her safety that she be removed from this vicinity. Fortunately, she has relatives in Maryland with whom she can stay. We have just come from walking her home, where she will speak to her mother about it."

"Good," I said with relief. At least that was one innocent we could get out of harm's way. "Did you three find anything during your hunt last night?"

"Nelli picked up some scents that really excited her," Biko said.

"Unfortunately," said Max, "one of those scents turned out to be a young man delivering Chinese food to a residence."

I said critically to Nelli, "Can't you tell the difference between kung pao shrimp and a zombie?"

She wagged her tail.

"Hey, you want to keep your voice down?" Biko said to me as he glanced in Henry's direction. "Anyhow, we did come across a few signs. More claw marks. A disemboweled squirrel. Stuff like that. Mostly around the park. And then . . ." He gave Nelli an exasperated look. "Our fearless familiar freaked out on the steps leading up to the old watchtower."

I glanced at her. She was looking intently at Biko now, her tail still twitching a little.

"She was snuffling around like crazy," Biko said. "Then she started barking, howling, growling, and going nuts. Running up and down the steps the whole time."

"Hey!" That certainly sounded relevant. "And then what?"

"Then," Max said regretfully, "a patrolman came upon us and told us to leave the park or he would arrest us."

"We're lucky it was *just* a patrolman," Biko said. "With the racket Nelli was making, I'm surprised no one sent a fire truck."

She started panting and wagging her tail again, her beaming facial expression suggesting that making noise and attracting attention had been exactly what was required of her.

Biko said judiciously, "Working with animals is tricky."

"Indeed," said Max. "But at least we have an obvious starting place for our next nocturnal investigation."

"Will you be leaving Nelli at home this time?" I asked.

"She will guard Puma by night," Max said, "while we are out hunting."

"Good plan," I said.

"And you?" Biko asked me.

"I'll be waiting tables in Little Italy tonight," I replied. "And I'm scheduled for a double shift tomorrow, since I've been away from the restaurant for a week."

"Lame," said Biko. "We're fighting Evil in Harlem while you're downtown waiting tables and collecting tips?"

"I have bills to pay, D'Artagnan," I said. "Besides, brute force really isn't my strong suit. If you're planning to kill the baka when you find them, you don't need me for that. Not with a sword in your hand and a mage by your side, while a trusty canine familiar guards your sister." I paused. "Wow, put like that, you should have your own TV show."

"Yeah, well, before I become a big television star, I've got to go teach a class. I'll see you two later." Biko raised his fist. "Be cool, bro."

Max raised his fist and bumped it with Biko's. "Peace out."

"I see that you two have been getting along well," I said to Max as Biko walked away.

"He's an excellent young man," Max said with approval. "And he has been kind enough to instruct me in some most engaging local dialect."

I decided I should use the foundation's phone to call Lopez and find out when he planned to drop off my purse. I didn't want to hang around this lobby for no good reason. I was just about to say so to Max when Nelli suddenly went stiff all over and started growling.

Her hair stood on end, her ears were pricked alertly, and her posture was so erect that it made her look even bigger than she was.

Startled by this sudden and unusual shift to an aggressive attitude, I followed the direction of her gaze—and saw Mambo Celeste entering the lobby with her immense snake draped around her shoulders. Nelli's growling got louder.

"Max," I said. "Take Nelli outside."

Recognizing the danger, he tugged on the dog's pink leash. "Nelli, come!" He tried to pull her toward the door. *"Nelli."*

Nelli didn't even seem to hear him. She started trembling with emotion, her hostile gaze fixed on the snake.

The mambo's eyes flew wide open when she saw Nelli standing in the lobby while Max continued tugging futilely on the leash. When she realized Nelli was growling at *her*—or, rather, at her snake . . . Instead of holding still or backing away slowly, either of which would have made sense, she instead shook her fist at Nelli and started shouting in Creole, the French dialect of her native Haiti. Her agitation bothered Napoleon, who started squirming.

The mambo's shouting, fist-shaking, and swaying motion, combined with the snake's increased activity, convinced Nelli that the threat she thought she perceived was real and immediate. She lunged forward a few steps and started barking ferociously at Napoleon.

"Nelli, no!" I snapped. Then I yelled at the mambo, "Shut *up!* Hold still! You're upsetting the snake *and* the dog!"

Henry, the receptionist, was neither young nor athletic, but he was brave. He picked up a tall, skinny wooden sculpture that decorated the reception desk and brandished it at Nelli, maneuvering himself to stand between her and the mambo, whose shrieks had now reached decibels that competed with Nelli's agitated barks.

Max yanked so hard on Nelli's leash that he lost his balance when she lunged again, and he fell down. Startled by this, Henry backed up a step. This accidentally brought him into direct contact with Napoleon, whose neck was eerily stretched out toward Nelli as he stuck out his tongue to catch her scent. Frightened by the contact—or perhaps mistakenly believing the snake was attacking him—Henry turned around with a startled cry and hit Napoleon with the wooden sculpture.

The snake recoiled so violently from this blow that his flailing weight made the mambo lose her balance and stumble sideways into the reception desk. Perhaps disoriented by the mambo's staggering, Napoleon started trying to coil around her head and shoulders, evidently trying not to fall off his familiar perch.

Nelli's barking grew hysterical, and she lunged toward the snake with violent determination. Max maintained his grip on her leash, so she dragged him laboriously across the floor as she struggled to get closer to the mambo and the coiling boa constrictor.

Trapped between the ferocious dog and the snake that appeared to be attacking the shrieking woman, Henry was waving around his wooden sculpture and screaming in panic, unable to decide which animal to strike first.

"Stop!" I shouted at him. Then I wrapped my arms around the dog's neck. "Nelli, *no!*"

As she lunged forward, my foot tangled with Nelli's leg. Fearing I was about to break my ankle, I scrambled desperately to move my foot into a less dangerous position. I felt something tug and then snap as it caught on my shoe. Nelli howled in shock, and I felt warm liquid gush down my bare ankle and onto my shoe. I looked down and was horrified to see blood all over the place.

Nelli staggered for a moment, yelping in pain. I realized that, in my scrambling, I'd accidentally torn off her dewclaw, a residual toe that grows on a dog's foreleg.

"Nelli!" I cried, racked with guilt and still afraid she'd tangle with the snake if I let go of her.

Bleeding, yelping, and barking, Nelli staggered forward a few more steps. Wrestling with the frightened snake, the mambo fell onto the reception desk. This trapped part of Napoleon's body under her considerable weight, and I could see the snake go into full panic mode and start fighting for its life. The mambo's resultant shrieks competed with Henry's screams as he continued waving around the wooden carving.

Biko came dashing into the lobby with his sword. From his perspective, it evidently appeared that we'd all been attacked by a lunatic with a lethal sculpture, and now a wounded Nelli was trying to defend us. So he lunged forward and shoved the point of his rapier against Henry's chest. "Drop it!"

"No!" Henry howled in response to this new attack.

"Biko!" Catherine Livingston shouted from somewhere nearby. "What are you *doing?*"

"Drop it!" Biko moved his arm and Henry cried out, evidently feeling the tip of the sword prick his flesh.

The chubby mambo was still lying across the desk, fighting with the boa constrictor. Catherine was shouting. Biko was stabbing a man who was brandishing a piece of art. Max was being dragged along the floor. I was clinging to a hysterically barking Nelli, and there was blood all around us.

This, then, was the scene that greeted Lopez as he entered the lobby of the Livingston Foundation with my purse in his hands.

15

"**P**olice!" Lopez shouted. "Everyone *FREEZE!*"
I'd had no idea his voice could be so piercing.

"*Police! NO ONE MOVE!*"

Henry and Catherine fell silent. Biko froze and looked at Lopez, a comically surprised expression on his face.

Nelli was still panting anxiously and growling, but she ceased barking. Even the mambo's shrieks reduced in volume.

Still clinging to the dog, I was shoved aside and fell down. Nelli yelped in surprise as she was seized from behind, and then she started choking. I looked up to see her dangling from Lopez's grasp on her pink collar, her front feet flailing in midair as she gasped and coughed.

"Biko! Stand down," Lopez ordered. "Right now!"

Biko lowered his sword and backed away from Henry, but he turned a hard stare on the man.

Lopez glanced at the wooden sculpture. "*Drop it.*"

Henry dropped it. Catherine gave a little moan as it cracked and splintered upon hitting the hard floor.

Looking at the shaking, sweating older man, Lopez said in a clipped voice, "Go sit down."

Henry nodded and staggered over to the wall, where he slumped down into one of the lobby chairs, at a safe distance from both Nelli and Napoleon.

Still holding the struggling dog, Lopez said urgently to me, "Is this your blood?"

"Huh? What? Oh!" I shook my head, still disoriented. "No, it's Nelli's."

He turned his attention next to Mambo Celeste. An extraordinary expression crossed his face as he watched her struggle with her writhing snake. He lowered Nelli to the ground and, keeping one hand on her collar, he used the other to reach for his holstered gun.

"No!" Catherine, Max, and I all cried at once.

"It's her pet," Catherine said. "It's just frightened."

"Good God." Lopez left his gun in its holster and instead used his free hand to reach down, grab Max by his shirt, and haul him to his feet. "Can you control your damn dog?"

"Well, now that she is somewhat calmer, I believe—"

"She needs a vet." Lopez handed Nelli's leash to Max.

"Nelli!" Max cried in alarm, realizing that her blood covered the floor.

"My vet's just a few blocks away," Biko said. "I'll take them."

Lopez said to Biko, "Hand me that sword."

Biko looked shocked. "I can't give you my *sword!*"

Moving swiftly, Lopez seized the weapon from the appalled young man and headed for the struggling mambo.

Biko said in horror, "Hey, don't *touch* that thing with my—Oh, *man . . .*"

Unable to bear the sight, the lad looked away as Lopez poked the writhing snake sharply with the rapier.

Napoleon responded sensibly to this new attack by slithering away from the mambo and fleeing. Seeing the snake on the move again, Nelli barked.

"NO!"

Nelli flinched at Lopez's tone and lowered her head. Moving with disturbing speed, Napoleon had already reached the far wall and was frantically trying to climb it, intent on escape. He kept falling down and trying again. I was torn between pity and revulsion.

Lopez returned the rapier to Biko and then grabbed a pretty batik cloth that was draped over the small table that stood next to Henry's chair. He knelt by Nelli's side.

Realizing his intention, Catherine protested, "You can't use *that!* It's—"

"Shut up." He wrapped Nelli's bleeding paw with the material as he said to Catherine, "You and that woman have five minutes to get that snake into its cage. If I don't see it safely contained by then, I'm calling animal control to come get it."

Nelli's dewclaw lay near me. I moved away from it and climbed laboriously to my feet.

Lopez finished wrapping Nelli's paw. He ignored the dog's attempt to lick his hand as he rose to face Catherine, who was still standing there frowning at him. He said to her, "Now you have four and a half minutes."

She gave him a coldly affronted look, opened her mouth, and drew breath to speak. I thought she was going to threaten to complain to his superiors, and I recalled that she was a billionaire's widow and probably well-connected. But, meeting Lopez's hard gaze, she evidently changed her mind. After a pregnant pause, Catherine closed her mouth, looking sullen as her shoulders sagged slightly.

She turned on her heel and walked swiftly to the reception desk, where she took the gasping, cursing Mambo Celeste by the shoulders and tried to get her to calm down. Then, moving like people who were a lot more familiar with snakes than *I* ever wanted to be, the two women picked up the squirming, disoriented boa constrictor and carried him out of the lobby.

Lopez said to Biko, "Lock that sword away some-place safe, then take Max and his dog to your vet."

The young fencer nodded and went to do as ordered.

When Max attempted to thank Lopez for his help, the exasperated detective interrupted him. "Get that man a glass of water or something, would you?" He pointed to Henry, who still sat slumped in a chair. "He looks like he's going to faint."

"No, no, I'm all right," Henry said faintly. "It was all just a little . . . overwhelming. I've never liked that snake. And this dog is . . . Well, she's awfully *big*, isn't she?" His gaze shifted and he pointed to something. "Oh, look, miss. I think your purse has arrived."

"My purse!" I said to Lopez, "Oh, thank you!"

I scooped the bag off the floor, where he had dropped it, and began investigating its contents. My wallet, money, ID, various plastic cards, apartment keys, and cell phone were all there. "Oh, thank God! It would have such a nuisance to have to replace all this stuff!" It would have cost money, too, and I didn't have money to waste.

Lopez went downstairs to the hounfour to make sure Napoleon was properly contained. Max began apologizing at length to Henry for the disturbance while a sub-dued Nelli sat beside him, her injured paw wrapped in its colorful makeshift bandage. When Henry felt able to stand up again, he decided to retreat to the restroom and compose himself there.

Meanwhile, I sat down on the stairs and listened to my voice mail messages. There had been a number of calls since the phone was taken from me, but it turned out that they were all ones that I already knew about, so I deleted the messages.

Biko returned from stowing his fencing gear. He and

Max hurried for the exit with a limping Nelli, pausing only to ask if they'd see me at Puma's shop later.

"No," I said. "By the time you're done at the vet's, I'll be on my way to the restaurant." And since I'd be at Bella Stella all day Saturday, we agreed to meet here at the foundation again on Sunday before attending the Vodou ritual downstairs.

Since I had been reunited with my phone, I decided to call the *D30* production office to let them know I was taking calls at this number again. I also wanted to make sure they knew I had indeed paid my required visit to Michael Nolan.

I spoke with the same woman who'd taken my call yesterday. I still didn't know her name. But she knew mine.

"Esther! I was just about to call you!"

"I visited Mike," I said firmly. "I was unavoidably detained, but I did show up and do my time. Er, I mean—"

"Yes, I know. He mentioned that."

"He did?"

"I talked to him earlier today. He's checking out of the hospital today and plans to come back to work on Monday."

"What?" That seemed awfully soon to return to his demanding work schedule. "Are his doctors agreeing to that?"

"I don't have the impression that he and his doctors have reached a consensus yet," she said carefully. "But Mike's determined. And, well, we do need to finish the episode."

"Ah."

With Nolan chomping at the bit and with his character at the center of an unfinished episode in a tightly budgeted TV series, the production staff would certainly go *find* a doctor willing to declare him ready to return to work, if need be. The *Crime and Punishment* empire had a lot of experience at keeping the wheels of production rolling forward. So if they said they would start filming with Nolan again on Monday, then I believed them.

"When do want me back on the set?" I asked.

"Can you hang on for a second, Esther?" Without waiting for my reply, she put me on hold. A couple of minutes later, she came back on the line. "I've got Mike on the other line. A doctor has cleared him to return to work."

"That was fast." I was tempted to get the doctor's name, so that I could make sure never to entrust my own medical care to him.

"We'll need you on the set at six o'clock Monday evening. All right?"

I would have to go straight to the *D30* set from the foundation, where I was scheduled to teach a class that afternoon. "No problem," I said, glad I could feel confident that Jilly's abused costume would be ready by then. "Where am I going?"

"The same location Mike got sick. You remember where it is?"

"I doubt I'll ever forget," I said sincerely. "So we're still doing the original scene?" The one where I would spend most of my time on my knees in front of Nolan.

"Yes. Oh, and Esther? Mike is waiting on the other line because he wants to talk to you."

"He does?" I said in surprise.

"Yes. Anyhow, unless something changes and you hear from us again, we'll see you Monday evening," she said cheerfully. "Now hold for Mike Nolan, please."

"Hello?" I said when I heard the line click.

"Who the fuck is this?" said Nolan's familiar voice.

I resisted the urge to hang up on him. "Esther Diamond. You wanted to speak to me?"

"Oh, right."

He was still at the hospital, but he had just finished checking out and was now waiting for the arrival of the car that would take him home. And he wanted to talk to me about the scene we'd be filming on Monday. Mostly, he seemed to be concerned that I would screw it up.

After a few minutes of listening to him giving me unsolicited advice and unwanted direction, I decided it was time to change the subject. "I want to thank you, by the way, for how nice you were to my friend yesterday evening."

"What friend?" he said.

"Jeff," I said. "Jeffrey Clark."

"Who?"

"The man I brought with me to visit you last night," I said.

"The old guy from Oxford?"

"No, the bald man who stayed with you after I left."

"Oh, right! Nice guy." There was a pause. ""His name was Jeff?"

Apparently the bonding had been a little one-sided.

"I gather you offered to speak to the show's casting director about him," I said. "That was very good of you."

"Huh?"

"You're going to talk to the casting director about Jeff," I reiterated.

"Why would I do that?" He sounded puzzled.

"So that Jeff can audition for him."

"Jeff's an actor?" There was surprise in Nolan's voice. "I thought he was a fan. I thought that's why he asked you to introduce us."

"He's an actor," I said. "And you're going to talk to—"

"Oh, come *on*, Esther. I can't go pestering the casting director on behalf of every aspiring actor who talks his way past security to meet me."

I gave it one more shot. "Jeff Clark's not aspiring. He's very accomplished. He—"

"Forget it," Nolan said. "I'm not a charitable institution."

I sighed and dropped the subject. I felt a little sorry for Jeff, but Nolan's reaction wasn't exactly a surprise to me.

"Well, I hope you continue feeling better, Mike," I said as I saw Lopez reenter the lobby. He looked around the empty area and then walked over to me. "I'll see you back on the set on Monday."

"Another thing I was thinking about," Nolan said. "When you're kneeling in front of me and you say—"

"I've got to go," I said, looking up at Lopez. "Bye."

As I ended the call, Lopez asked without enthusiasm, "The set of *The Dirty Thirty?*"

I nodded. "We're resuming filming of my episode on Monday." I recounted the news I'd just received.

"Are you kidding?" He sat down beside me on the stairs. "That guy had a heart attack less than forty-eight hours ago. Is he crazy?"

"I have a feeling he's afraid to miss work. The show has two other talented costars and a strong supporting cast," I said. Actually, for all that he was a jerk, Nolan was a compelling performer and his antihero character was very popular, but I didn't underestimate the neuroses of a self-absorbed star. "I'll bet that Nolan is worried he'll lose the spotlight if he gets written out of a few episodes because of his health."

"Even so," Lopez said, "you'd think that the risk of dying young would scare him more."

I smiled at my practical companion. "You don't know actors."

"I'll take your word for it."

More than ready to stop discussing Michael Nolan, I asked, "Is Napoleon locked up?"

"They call him Napoleon? I'd say he's about two feet taller than his namesake. Anyhow, yeah, he's contained." Lopez added, "And his cage is nicer than my first apartment."

"Then you'd think he would spend more time in it." I put my cell phone away. "It's such a relief to have my purse back. Thank you so much!"

"No problem."

"Where did the cops find it?"

"In a garbage can right outside the Harlem Market."

I knew that place. A few blocks south of here, it was a semienclosed space with market stalls where the vendors sold African souvenirs: tribal masks, leather goods, clothing, decorative objects, drums, and music. "I wonder how my purse wound up there?"

"Probably dumped deliberately," Lopez said. "Whoever had your bag didn't want to get caught with it, and I think they didn't really know what to do with it. So they probably figured its contents would get stolen and scattered pretty quickly if they left it at such a busy location."

"I'm lucky that didn't happen." I clutched the bag gratefully to my chest.

"One of the market vendors found it. He called the cops."

"Really? I should go thank him!"

"Not a bad idea," Lopez said. "Maybe more guys would report petty crime if they thought a pretty woman would come around and thank them for it."

The silence that descended between us after he said this lengthened until it grew awkward.

I gazed across the floor of the lobby. Nelli's blood was smeared all over the place, and the cracked wooden sculpture lay where it had fallen. I would have enjoyed seeing Catherine or Mambo Celeste have to clean up the mess, but I assumed the foundation employed a janitor or a cleaning service.

Feeling Lopez's sidelong glance, I gestured to the wreckage. "Uh, I can explain this."

He shook his head. "No need."

I looked at him. "Really?"

"Well, in one sole building, we have a huge snake and a woman too silly to keep it in a cage where it belongs, Max and his neurotic dog, a teenager with a sword, and—oh, yes—*you*." He shrugged. "I'd say the results were inevitable."

"Hey, *I* tried to prevent this from happening."

"Yeah, that was my first thought when I got here and saw you wading through blood and giving a half nelson to a hysterical dog the size of a minivan: Esther must be trying to prevent trouble."

"Prevention wasn't going as smoothly as I would have liked," I admitted. "Not all of us can manhandle a dog that size by her collar, Stud Muffin."

"You should never get that close to the teeth of a dog that's not in its right mind," he said seriously. "If she had bitten you by accident . . ."

"It all happened pretty fast," I said. "I don't like that snake, but that doesn't mean I think we should let our dog kill it. Anyhow, I'm not so sure Nelli would have won."

"You couldn't have talked Max into getting a kitten?" he said with some exasperation.

"Nelli has special qualities." Seeing his skeptical expression, I added, "They're not immediately apparent, I grant you."

"Well, I suppose she's slightly more cuddly than a seven-foot-long boa constrictor." He grimaced. "What do you think they feed that snake?"

"I don't know, and I don't want to know."

"And, Jesus, the way he attacked that woman—"

"Mambo Celeste," I said.

"The way he attacked Mambo Celeste when he was

scared . . . Well, you'd think she'd reconsider her choice of house pet now."

"She won't," I said with certainty. "He represents Damballah, a sacred . . . something or other."

I was suddenly very tired of this place, and I looked forward to spending tonight singing old favorites to cheerful tourists in a noisy restaurant downtown. And as another silence descended between us, I also suddenly recalled how many things I didn't particularly want to discuss with my companion.

"Well, thanks again for bringing my purse. I really appreciate it." I got to my feet. "I have to go to the restaurant now. Bye."

"Nice try." He pulled me back down beside him. "We have to talk."

"I'll be late for work," I lied.

"We've got Bella Stella under surveillance," he pointed out. "I know what time your shift starts."

"Surveillance? That's a waste of taxpayer money," I said. "The restaurant's full of tourists at this time of year. All the wiseguys are on their summer vacations."

"Fair point," he said. "Get any postcards from Lucky Battistuzzi lately?"

"One," I said, refusing to apologize for my friendship with the semiretired hit man. "He's enjoying his tour of Sicily."

"Ah, yes. Visiting the sights, enjoying the food, reminiscing about the good old days with other retired Mafia killers." He shrugged. "I'm just guessing, of course."

"He went there to recover from a broken heart," I said crisply. "But since *you* seem able to move on from a woman so easily, you probably can't understand that." I rose to my feet again. "Now if you'll excuse me, I'm going to work."

"Wait just a damn minute." He rose, too, looking irritable now. "Who got out of bed in the middle of the night as soon as you asked for help? Who faced a firing squad of laughing cops to get your arrest erased? Who's been driving the Two-Five crazy for the past couple of days because of what happened to you in their precinct?"

"Oh, you'd drive them crazy about that no matter *who* got mugged and found a severed hand there."

"Well . . ." He backed down a little. "Okay, that's probably true."

"Anyhow, now we're square," I said tersely.

He frowned. "We're square for *what?*"

"We broke up, then you got me out of jail." Jeff's interpretation of events had stung more than I'd realized. "So we're even now."

"How are we *even?*" he asked in bewilderment.

"You don't owe me anything else."

"I didn't 'owe' you *that*," he snapped.

"Fine," I snapped back. "Then I guess *I* owe *you* now."

"What's the *matter* with you?"

"Tell me the truth." Still smarting from the humiliation of Jeff's comments, I said, "Did you help me the other night because you felt guilty?"

"Guilty? About what?"

"About dumping me," I said impatiently.

"What are you talking about? I *didn't* dump you! I . . . I . . ." His blue eyes suddenly blazed with surprise in his dark face, and a look of sheer astonishment replaced his angry expression. "I dumped you?" After a stunned pause, he sat back down on the steps, looking thunderstruck. "Oh, my God. I hadn't thought of it that way. I guess you're right. I, uh . . . I *dumped* you, didn't I?"

I folded my arms across my chest as I looked down at him. "It's always good when we can clear up these little misunderstandings."

"I dumped you," he repeated, looking at me in amazement.

"And obviously that's something I particularly enjoy hearing repeated. Go on, say it again," I said, as he continued staring at me. "It makes me feel so warm and fuzzy inside."

He was still looking at me with a bemused expression.

"Lopez?" I prodded.

Lost in his own thoughts, he gave a little start. Then he sighed. "I'm sorry. I had no idea that you felt that way. I mean, that you thought I had dumped you."

"You *did* dump me."

"Well, yes, I know that *now*."

"How could you not know it before?" I demanded.

He made a vague gesture. "I didn't think of it as dumping you."

"God, I had no idea how much of a . . . *guy* you could be," I said in disgust.

"Honestly, I thought of what happened as . . ." He ran his hands over his face, then he rested his chin on them as he contemplated something invisible. "I thought of it more like . . . I don't know . . ." He shrugged as he searched for an example. "*Born Free,* when they decide Elsa really can't be domesticated and they've got to let her go."

"What?"

"Or *A Beautiful Mind,* when they realize they've got to lock up Russell Crowe."

"I'm not liking the comparisons," I said.

"It's like wanting peanut butter so much that you eat it in your dreams. But when you're awake, you know you'll go into anaphylactic shock if you touch the stuff." He gave himself a little shake and stood up. "Do you see what I'm saying?"

"Something about food allergies, mental illness, and a fear that I'll attack livestock?"

"Exactly."

"What the hell are you *talking* ab—" I gasped as he

suddenly backed me against the wall and braced his hands on either side of me.

"I didn't dump you," he said quietly, his gaze locked with mine. "I gave you up."

"Oh." The word came out on a wispy breath.

"*Now* do you see?" His dark lashes lowered as his attention shifted to my mouth.

"Um . . ."

"And I didn't come to Harlem at three o'clock in the morning to get you out of jail because I felt guilty." He leaned closer to me.

"No?"

"No." His lips hovered near mine.

My fingers curled into the fabric of his lightweight summer jacket as I closed my eyes, enjoying the soft tickle of his breath on my cheek and the anticipation of the moment.

My heartbeat got louder, drowning out everything else as he whispered, "I came because you asked me to."

The sound of a polite cough penetrated my senses.

My eyes flew open and I looked over Lopez's shoulder as he whirled to face the intruder. Catherine was standing a few feet away. She gestured to the staircase that we were half blocking.

"Sorry to interrupt," she said in a cool voice. "I need to get to my office."

"Of course." Lopez turned to me. "We should leave."

"You two know each other, then?" Catherine raised her brows and looked at me. I suspected that my face was flushed. "You didn't mention that when you asked me about his visit, Esther."

Lopez gave me a sharp glance.

I decided that changing the subject immediately was my best available option. "I'm so sorry about Nelli's behavior." I shrugged and spread my hands. "I guess she's never seen a snake before."

Catherine said, "I don't want that dog coming here again."

"No, of course not," I said. "I'll speak to Max. And I'm sorry about the mess in the lobby." However, I thought Mambo Celeste should apologize for at least half of that.

"Dr. Livingston," Lopez said, "it's not a good idea for a snake that size to be in an uncontrolled area with a handler who can't manage him."

"We weren't expecting an attack from a vicious dog on our own premises," she said crisply.

"Nelli isn't vicious!" I protested. "She's just, uh . . . high-strung."

"A dangerous trait in a dog that size," said Catherine.

She had a point, and Lopez's glance warned me not to get into a fruitless argument with her about it.

"There are a lot of people roaming around this building," he said to her. "Including kids. Do you really want to risk someone getting hurt—and the legal problems that will come with that? It would be safer for everyone, including you, if you'd just insist that Napoleon stay in his cage."

"Thank you for your concern, detective. Now if you'll excuse me, I have a great deal of work to do. Goodbye."

As Catherine ascended the steps, Lopez watched her with an exasperated expression. Then, as her footsteps faded, he turned to look at me. For a moment, he seemed to be running through a mental list of things he wanted to discuss, trying to decide which topic to broach first. But then he glanced upstairs again, and his expression turned sheepish.

"Sorry if I've embarrassed you in front of your new boss," he said.

A sudden image entered my mind of Biko barging

in on Catherine *in flagrante delicto.* I snorted with unexpected laughter. Then I covered my mouth, recalling that the third person in that story was dead now.

Lopez looked amused and puzzled at my reaction.

I waved away his concern about embarrassing me. "Oh, she's in no position to be critical. After all, Biko found her and Darius having sex in her office."

"When?" He looked suddenly alert.

"About a year ago."

"She was having an affair with Darius Phelps?"

I shrugged. "I don't know. But I have a feeling it was not an *affair* so much as just an instance of two single colleagues, both working late, alone together at the office—or so they thought. Biko was practicing late that night, and I gather Catherine was, er, very noisy." Lopez's reaction made me laugh again. "No, she doesn't really come across as someone who'd lose herself in passion, does she?"

He smiled. "People are full of surprises. Especially women." When he looked up the stairs again, his expression was thoughtful. Then he returned his attention to me. "What do you say we get out of here?"

I nodded, tired of the atmosphere at the Livingston Foundation and eager to leave. "I'll get my stuff."

16

As soon as Lopez opened the foundation's front door for me and I exited the building, a wall of heat and humidity hit me like a physical blow. "Ugh!"

"Yep." He loosened his tie. "Violent crime is up all over the city." He pulled a pair of sunglasses out of his breast pocket and put them on. "Especially domestics. Ain't love grand?"

"Ah, how I've missed the small talk of a cop," I said. "Other people just say things like, 'It's another scorcher today.'"

We moved away from the building and crossed the street, then walked beside the park. Silent and brooding behind his dark glasses, Lopez took off his light summer jacket and slung it over his shoulder, then unfastened the top couple of buttons on his short-sleeved cotton shirt. Since I had a daypack with me as well as my purse, he made a gesture offering to carry the daypack for me, and I handed it over.

Despite the smothering heat, there were kids in the Mount Morris Park playground, some Rollerbladers on the paths, and a number of people walking their dogs. It was a sunny Friday afternoon in summer, and people were determined to enjoy it even if they roasted for it.

We heard music coming from inside the park and as we got closer to the sound, I saw a crowd of people gathered to watch the break-dancers who were practicing there.

We admired the dancers for a few minutes, then we moved on, walking inside the park now. The atmosphere between us was charged, thanks to the private scene which I had started and he had nearly finished before we were interrupted by Catherine.

I'd been well aware of feeling hurt and forlorn that he'd broken up with me, and I'd certainly missed him since then—even though we'd been involved too briefly for that to make much sense. But until Jeff poked the hidden sore spot with the unerring accuracy of an ex-boyfriend, I hadn't realized that I also felt humiliated.

That pain, at least, was cured now. Yes, Lopez had broken up with me; but he hadn't stopped *wanting* to see me. For reasons which were all too human, his unguarded confirmation of this made me feel better.

On the other hand, the reasons he wouldn't date me still hadn't changed. And, considering the current circumstances, those reasons were still relevant, despite our mutual outburst a few minutes ago. In any case, since I had to be at work soon, I thought we should probably get started on the argument he had come here to have.

I said, "I know that Darius Phelps' body is missing."

He didn't miss a beat. "Who told you? Biko or Dr. Livingston?"

"Why didn't *you* tell me?" I challenged.

"I couldn't get hold of you," he pointed out reasonably.

"Oh. Right."

"So now I'm missing out on the big double-take I was hoping for, since you already know he's gone."

I peered at him suspiciously, but his sunglasses hid his expression. "How long has the body been missing?" I asked.

"I don't know yet. It's a huge cemetery and Darius apparently hasn't had any visitors since his funeral. So no one realized he was missing until I asked them to look." He added, "This case is making me think pretty seriously about getting cremated when my time comes."

"And the hand we found? Was it his?"

"No."

That surprised me. "How do you know?"

"I was right about the hand being only a few days old. And Darius Phelps has been dead for a little over three weeks." Lopez shook his head. "So it can't be his hand."

Oh, if only that were true.

"Can you identify it through fingerprints?" I asked.

"No hits yet."

That must mean that Darius had never been fingerprinted when he was alive. And I assumed the police weren't going to attempt a DNA comparison; in their minds, nothing credible linked the days-old hand in Harlem with the weeks-old missing corpse.

Thinking about the nature of mystical zombification, I said tentatively, "What if decomposition stopped a couple of days after Darius died?"

"How?" Lopez shook his head. "He wasn't even embalmed—and that doesn't stop decomposition, anyhow, it just slows it down. No, wherever Darius is now, he's still decomposing, like any other dead organism."

"Not necessarily," I said glumly.

Lopez lowered his head to look inquisitively at me over the top of his sunglasses.

That look made me feel unequal to the task of sharing my theory with him. So instead I said, "This means you think there's a separate victim?"

"Actually, I think there are *several* victims. As soon as the director of the cemetery learned yesterday morning that Darius' body was missing, he offered full cooperation with a thorough survey of the whole place. So far, they've found four other empty graves." He caught my elbow as I stumbled. "All right?"

Max was right! Someone was raising an army of zombies! Or at least a small platoon of them.

"Yes, I'm fine." My voice sounded breathless. "Are the other, er, victims from Harlem, too?"

"No, they lived all over the city. They're not all African-American, either. And they died of different causes. One died of an accidental head injury, one of a chronic illness, one was shot by a drug dealer, and one punched his own ticket."

"He did what?"

"Uh, committed suicide."

"It sounds very random," I said, puzzled.

"It is. I don't think there was any connection between any of them in life." He gestured to a park bench in the shade. "Want to sit down?"

I nodded and took a seat. He sat down beside me and removed his sunglasses, then lifted his head and closed his eyes, enjoying the momentary breeze that fluttered through the heat-soaked park and ruffled his black hair. I looked at the smooth, dark golden skin of his throat, gleaming with a faint sheen of perspiration, and thought about the moment in the lobby when he had almost kissed me.

Eyes still closed, he said, "I think the connection occurred after they died. As corpses, they all have relevant factors in common."

"Huh?" I said, still staring at him.

He lifted the fabric of his pale shirt away from his chest and flapped the material gently a few times, inviting cooler air to touch his torso. "For starters, of course, they were all buried in the same cemetery. It seems to be the grave robber's hunting ground."

Lopez let go of his shirt, opened his eyes, and looked

at me. I did my best to assume an intelligent facial expression.

He continued, "And in death, they all fit the same profile as Darius. That is, they died in the prime of life and within the past month." He tugged on his tie, removed it, and stuffed it into the pocket of his jacket. "And they didn't have local families, so there was no one to visit their graves or notice anything odd."

I frowned as I thought it over. "Is the bokor finding them through their obituaries?" It seemed so . . . mundane.

"What's the bokor?"

I realized I had been thinking aloud. "I meant the grave robber."

"Why was Max at the Livingston Foundation today?"

I knew what Lopez was doing. The quick topic shift was intended to surprise me into an unguarded answer. This was something that I had *not* missed about him.

"He came to visit me," I said.

"Why are you working at the foundation?" When I didn't answer, he said, "Imagine my surprise when I went to see Dr. Livingston yesterday and she remarked that I was asking questions similar to the ones a new employee had been asking that same day—an actress whose name she couldn't remember."

"I'm filling in for a workshop teacher there."

"I won't even bother asking how or why you tracked down Darius Phelps' place of employment," he said. "I probably should have seen that coming. And, once you got there, you couldn't resist asking questions about him. Fine. But for God's sake, when you found Biko at the foundation, why didn't you call me?"

"Why should I have called you?" I asked blankly.

"Because he was part of whatever crazy stunt someone was playing in the dark with a severed hand the other night!"

"Oh! You think ...? Oh, no. No," I said. "You've got it all wrong. Biko wasn't playing tricks that night. He was looking for the creatures that I saw."

"So he *was* out and about?"

Oops. I suddenly remembered that Biko's official story about that night was that he was at home in bed. He'd be annoyed when he found out I'd blown his alibi. Oh, well. Spilled milk. Besides, Lopez hadn't believed him anyhow.

"He was looking for the creatures that killed his dog," I said. "The same creatures that I saw that night."

Lopez leaned back on the bench and studied me through narrowed eyes, trying to decide if he believed me. He didn't bother asking why Biko had lied to him about that night; he could figure that out easily. I thought he was trying to figure out whether Biko had also lied to *me*. After a long moment, he said, "So you found out who Darius was and where he worked, and you found the kid with the sword."

"Yes."

"So what are you looking for now?" he asked.

"Well, for one thing, I want to track down the creatures I fought with that night. Biko wants to find them, too. He wants to stop them before they kill any more pets—or do worse than that. And I think that's a good ide—"

"*Stop* them?" he repeated. "Esther, whoever killed his dog and stole your purse needs to be locked up, not run through with a sword by a kid who thinks he's the Count of Monte Cristo."

"They weren't people."

"They sure as hell weren't gargoyles."

"Actually—"

"Even if your purse was taken and Biko's dog was

killed by . . . Let's say, by a couple of very strange *animals*, okay?"

I nodded, since Lopez was making an effort to meet me halfway.

He continued, "It's dangerous for *everyone* to have a teenage boy wandering around with a weapon, looking for someone to attack."

I decided it wouldn't relieve Lopez's concerns if I told him that Biko was accompanied by Max and Nelli.

After studying me for a moment, he said, "Oh, God. Please tell me you're not out prowling the streets by night with that kid?"

"Of course not," I said virtuously. "I wait tables at night."

"Oh. Right. Good." He let out his breath. "Suddenly, for the very first time, I'm *glad* you work in a restaurant where wiseguys keep getting whacked. At least I know where you are then."

Hoping to get him off this subject, I asked, "What do you think is being done with the missing bodies?"

"There are a lot of possibilities, and they're all pretty disgusting." He returned to an earlier question. "Why have you taken a job at the foundation?"

"I wanted the work. Waiting tables isn't as fulfilling as you might think, officer." I added, "And I like the kids."

He nodded, accepting that. Then he said, "Look, the bottom line is . . . I'm not thrilled about you being at the foundation."

"Thanks to my sensitivity to your every subtle inflection, I guessed something of the sort."

"No, seriously. I'm not sure it's safe for you to be there."

I looked at him again. "Oh?"

He gazed out across the park with a troubled frown on his face. "Something's not right there. I don't know what it is yet, but it's like . . . like hearing a melody slightly out of tune." He stared into the distance for a moment longer, bothered by something he couldn't identify or pinpoint. Then he shook off his pensive mood and said again, more matter-of-factly, "Something's not right. And until I know what it is, I'm worried about you spending time there—even apart from whatever crazy scheme Max may be dragging you into."

"*I* kind of dragged *him* into this," I said.

"No wonder Dr. Livingston doesn't like you."

"I don't think she likes anyone," I grumbled. "But I do agree with you that something's not right around here." I thought of Shondolyn and added, "And I'm a little worried about the kids who hang out at the foundation."

"With a boa constrictor on the loose there, I'm worried about them, too."

"I want to keep an eye on them. At least until we know what's going on and . . . and I'm sure they're not in danger."

He looked at me. "Well, I know by now I can't talk you out of that. But if you're going to keeping going there, then I want you to promise me you'll be careful and keep your eyes open, and *call me* if you need help."

"Agreed." I appreciated that he'd decided not to press me about certain subjects. Even though that was only because he was hot, tired, distracted, and in no mood to deal with the sort of answers he was probably afraid I'd give, if pushed. Which reminded me . . . "I need to ask another favor."

"Go ahead." He smiled wryly. "If you put on your hooker outfit again, I'll probably do anything you want."

The memory of wearing Lycra and vinyl in this heat prevented that comment from being as tempting as it might otherwise have been.

I pointed upward, through the leafy trees that climbed the steep rocky hill that was nearby, to the dully gleaming roof of the old iron watch tower that sat high above the park. "Will you take me up that hill?"

He looked up at the tower. "Why?"

"Because you're armed."

He turned his head sharply. "Excuse me?"

After today's misadventure in the foundation's lobby, I thought it was entirely possible that what had excited Nelli's interest on those curving stone steps last night was the scent of a snake living in the vicinity. But I thought it was equally possible that the dense shrubbery concealed baka or zombies, so I didn't want to climb that hill alone and unprotected. I also thought that investigating the area by day in the company of a cop with a gun made a little more sense than sneaking up there at night with a sword.

"Esther?" he prodded.

I didn't want to explain to him about Max, Biko, and Nelli's nocturnal activities, nor to discuss our theories about supernatural creatures.

So I said, "Biko told me about that old watchtower, and I want to see it. But it's so overgrown and isolated, I don't think it's a good idea for me to go up there alone, even in the middle of the day. So will you walk me up there?"

"Sure." Looking surprised and relieved that I was making such a normal, ordinary request, he rose from the bench and extended a hand to help me up. As we crossed the pavement together and approached the curving stone steps, he asked, "What *is* the old watchtower, anyhow? I don't know this neighborhood."

As we began ascending the old stone stairs, many of which were in need of repair, I related what Biko had told me about the tower.

"In other words," Lopez said, "we're climbing a long, steep, crumbling staircase in hellish heat to see a dangerous ruin that might fall on top of us while we're looking at it?" He grinned at me. "I'm so glad you invited me along."

I was surreptitiously trying to spot baka claw marks or anything else that might explain what had excited Nelli last night. But I'm no tracker, and the stairs were in such bad shape and so littered with fallen leaves, clumps of moss, rocks, and broken sticks that just trying not to trip and fall was occupying most of my attention. Lopez kept his hand under my elbow to steady me, but even so I stumbled a couple of times.

The surrounding flora and foliage was so dense that, halfway up the hill, it was easy to forget that we were in Manhattan. As I eyed the dense bushes and surrounding trees, I was very glad to have an armed cop at my side. In addition to my fear that mystical monsters lurked in those bushes, I realized that much more mundane dangers could easily lurk there, too. I'd be nervous if I were here alone, even without the menace of baka running loose in the neighborhood.

We reached the crest of the hill without my seeing anything suspicious, let alone anything that I thought Lopez should shoot. To my surprise, we emerged onto an old stone plaza. It was about as long and wide as a basketball court. Many of the paving stones were broken, and others were missing altogether.

"I *love* this city." Lopez looked around the crumbling old hilltop plaza with a pleased smile. "New York is full of so many surprises. I never would have guessed this was up here."

"Now aren't you glad you came?" I said.

"That all depends on whether this thing falls on top of us." Squinting against the harsh sunlight, he looked up at the nineteenth-century watchtower that rose above the tree-shrouded plaza. "Actually, it's not in such bad shape, is it?"

The imposing tower, which was quite tall, was a hollow octagonal structure made of long iron bars, poles, and rods. At ground level, the outer edge of the tower was defined by a cage made of evenly spaced vertical bars; I was briefly reminded of my jail cell in the local precinct house. A spiral staircase inside the cage ascended to an enormous bell that hung suspended about fifteen feet off the ground. The iron staircase continued past the bell, circling the tower all the way up to the lookout platform at the top of structure.

Gazing up at this elegant and impressive iron framework hidden here on a forgotten, overgrown hilltop in a city park, I was in complete agreement with Lopez. I just loved New York.

"You must get to see a lot of stuff like this, as a cop," I mused. "Hidden things, obscure pieces of the city that most other people just walk past."

"Back in the days when I was on patrol, I did. Sometimes I kind of miss that. Getting to know a neighborhood and its people really well." Still gazing upward as he strolled around the tower, he said, "Since I became a detective, though, I mostly just see crime scenes when I'm on the job. And they're usually not very scenic."

"This structure looks sort of familiar . . ." I realized what it reminded me of. "It's sort of like a starter-kit for the Eiffel Tower, isn't it?"

He chuckled at the description, then said, "Here's a gate. This must be how the watchman got in, in the old days." Lopez gave it an experimental tug. He looked a little disappointed when it didn't open. But, like a responsible police officer, he said, "I'm glad to see there's a good lock on it. Kids might try to get in there to climb around."

"Kids of *any* age," I noted, coming around the tower to join him at the gate. "I can see I would have trouble keeping you out of there, if not for that lock."

"Well . . . yeah." He smiled sheepishly. "And I was

the kind of kid who would have found a way in there anyhow."

"Somehow, that doesn't surprise me." Looking at the lock on the gate, I remarked, "That looks shiny and new. Maybe someone *did* get in here."

"Or maybe the parks department is just being smart and making sure it doesn't happen."

Lopez's phone rang. He pulled it out of his pocket and looked at the LCD panel. "It's my dad. He doesn't call me very often."

I knew that, by contrast, his mother called him all the time.

"I should probably take this. Excuse me." Lopez set down my daypack and flipped open his phone. *"Hola, papá. Que tal?"*

Lopez started to relax and lean back against the iron bars of the tower. Then he made a face and moved away from them when he realized how hot the bars were, having been in the sun all day. *"Bueno . . . Sí . . . Por qué? Cuál es el problema?"*

I knew his father was from Cuba, but I hadn't known that the two of them spoke to each other in Spanish.

As Lopez stepped away from the tower, he frowned a little at something his father said. *"Yo? No, no . . . No puedo, papá."* He said more emphatically, *"Porque estoy muy occupado."*

Actually, I realized, I hadn't known Lopez spoke Spanish at *all,* though it probably should have occurred to me. Indeed, listening to him arguing gently but firmly with his dad about something now, it was clear that he was completely fluent in the language. His parents must have raised their three sons to be bilingual.

It was a reminder of how little Lopez and I actually knew each other.

I also realized, as I listened to him speaking fluidly in a language I didn't know, that I found him incredibly sexy at the moment. The Spanish words flowing musically from his mouth sounded mysterious and romantic to me . . . even though, based on the few words I understood, I had the impression he was trying to refuse to do something his father wanted him to do. His speaking in a foreign language seemed to fit so perfectly with his exotic looks. His black hair gleamed like onyx under the harsh sunlight, his dark golden skin glowed in the heat, and his long-lashed eyes flashed with blue fire as he started arguing more fiercely. His shoulders moved with oiled grace beneath his thin cotton shirt as he paced around the sun-drenched stone plaza . . .

Okay, I needed to look *away* now.

I took a sobering breath of muggy air and reminded myself that this was guy who wouldn't even date me! In fact, this guy had *dumped* me.

He was, I was pretty sure, talking to his dad about his mom now . . . and here I was, getting turned *on* by the conversation. Just because his words were all in Spanish . . . rolling off his silken tongue like melting honey and—

"Oy." I turned away.

Conversations in Yiddish had certainly never had this effect on me.

I needed to think about something else. Humming softly to myself, in hopes of drowning out the tummy-tickling sound of Lopez using words like *encantado* and *semana,* I started poking around the plaza looking for leftover baka food or other signs that the creatures had been here. It was a big area to cover, but Lopez's argument with his father was taking a while, so I had time to look over the whole place.

I got excited when I found some splotches of red on the paving stones—so excited that I even forgot about Don Juan for a few moments. But the color of the scattered blotches was too bright to be blood, I realized after my initial reaction. It looked more like faded red paint or chalk. There was also melted candle wax. Not far from these marks and wax droppings, there was a large blackened area with ashes around its edges.

"Ah."

Not baka or zombies, I realized. Partiers. A bonfire, some candles, some . . . red whatever. If the group was large enough that they didn't have to worry about being mugged by night in this isolated spot, then it was a great place for a party: a big, private, open-air plaza beneath the skeletal beauty of the old iron watchtower. And after the trees lost their leaves for the winter, there would be good views of the city by night from this spot.

But the start of autumn was still more than a month away, and the summer sun was merciless up here. I decided it was time to suggest to Lopez that we be on our way.

As I returned to his side, to my relief, he broke into English. "All right, *fine.* Okay. I'll do it. Yes." He sighed. "I just said *yes*, didn't I?"

Apparently English was the language of surrender in the Lopez family. Based on what little I knew about his mother, this didn't really surprise me.

"Two hours, start to finish," he said firmly. "From the moment I pick her up at the station until the moment I drop her off there again. That's all I can spare. Make sure she understands that."

I caught his eye and pointed toward the stone steps. Lopez nodded to me and raised a finger, indicating he'd be done momentarily.

"*Sí . . . Sí, entiendo.*" In response to his father's next comment, he said ironically, "*De nada, papá.*"

I felt my insides fluttering again. Even when being ironic, he sounded sexy in Spanish.

Oh, get a grip.

Lopez ended the call and pocketed his phone. "Sorry."

"No problem." I made a sympathetic face. "Parents."

"Exactly," he said wearily.

I decided not to mention the Spanish thing. He might not even realize that I hadn't known he spoke the language, and I was seriously concerned that I'd turn into some sort of gushing nudnik as soon as I opened my mouth on the subject.

"My dad can be a little . . . old-fashioned about certain things," Lopez said as he walked over to my daypack and scooped it up. "My mom complains about it, but I swear to God she encourages it."

"Is there something wrong at home?" I asked carefully, not wanting to pry, but nonetheless curious.

"No, no. Nothing like that." As we approached the uneven, rocky stairs, he said, "Here, you'd better take my arm." We began descending the steps together. "When something's actually *wrong,* my parents go to church. Or they retreat to their bedroom to discuss it quietly behind a closed door. Long dramatic arguments occur in our family strictly over stupid stuff." He paused. "We have a lot of long dramatic arguments."

Making my way carefully over a broken step with Lopez's help, I asked, "What was *this* stupid stuff?"

"My mom wants to go to some fancy new store on the Upper West Side tomorrow, and my dad can't take her, so he wants me to take her. Even though, between my *actual* job and the other cases I'm helping out on, whether my help is wanted or not—such as the Twenty-Fifth Precinct's lonesome severed hand . . . I'll probably be working fourteen hours tomorrow and don't have time for this. But I'm the son who lives in the city, so I'm the one who has to do it."

Wondering if I was missing something, I asked, "Is

there some reason your mom can't shop on the Upper West Side in broad daylight without an escort?"

"That's where we get to the part about my dad being old-fashioned. There are naked men in this store, so he doesn't want my mom going there without a husband or son at her side."

"Naked men?" I repeated. "In a store?"

"They're not *naked* naked," Lopez said. "Watch your step." He helped me over a rocky patch. "The men are wearing—I don't know—thongs· or loincloths or something."

"What sort of store *is* this?"

"Would you believe it's a gourmet grocery store? And it's all the rage."

"Well, with naked employees, I guess it would be."

"I doubt my dad ever even removed his shirt in front of my mom before their wedding night," Lopez said. "So the idea of her nibbling samples of gourmet delicacies served by mostly naked men at some Upper West Side food emporium is *way* outside his comfort zone."

"Maybe she just shouldn't have told him she was going."

"Oh, are you *kidding?*" he said in disgust. "That would take all the fun out of it for her."

"Ah. I get it"

Now I understood why steam was practically coming out of Lopez's ears. His mother enjoyed this little game with his father, which was perhaps the sort of thing that helped keep the sparks alive in their (I gathered) contented long-term marriage. But tomorrow, their game was going to cost their youngest son at least a couple of hours of valuable work time. And so—especially since he was overloaded this week—he felt like throttling them both for it.

When we reached the bottom of the steps and were once again back in the busy, bustling park, I said, "And now I really do have to leave for my shift at Bella Stella."

"I'll walk you partway to the subway," he said. "I've got a few more questions for Dr. Livingston if she's still at work, and then I want to stop in at the Twenty-Fifth Precinct, where I'm getting more and more popular every day, of course."

His mentioning the precinct reminded me that Lopez had resources that Max and I didn't.

"I just thought of another favor I need to ask," I said.

"If it involves another steep climb, the answer is no."

"A man who was teaching workshops at the foundation is missing. His name is Frank Johnson, and no one has seen or heard from him since Monday night." Since Lopez was already concerned about my presence at the foundation, I didn't mention that Frank was my direct predecessor. "He's not answering his phone or returning messages. Can you find out where he lives? Or find out if he's . . . all right?"

"Missing since Monday night?"

I nodded. "He might be going about his daily life and just ignoring calls from the foundation. I mean, I hope he is. But just in case . . ." Seeing Lopez's intent expression, I asked, "Why are you looking at me like that?"

"No reason."

"No, *tell* me," I insisted.

"I'm thinking," he said with some reluctance, "that the hand we found lying in the street could belong to someone who was last seen alive on Monday night."

"Oh." I feigned distress, which wasn't hard to do at this point, and nodded.

As we exited the park, Lopez told me that as long as I was working at the foundation, and until we really knew what was going on, he wanted me to keep his cell phone number on speed dial.

I agreed, and I accepted my daypack from him as he returned it to me. We stood together awkwardly for a moment, and then I said good-bye and turned to go.

"Oh, hell," he muttered.

Lopez reached for me, pulled me into his arms, and kissed me. He was a little rough, and then very gentle.

And I could swear I tasted Spanish words on his lips. Then he rested his forehead against mine. "You'd better go."

"Right," I murmured. "After all, you know what time my shift starts."

"I do." He kissed me softly again, then let me go.

I practically floated all the way to the subway station. When I got there, luck was with me. I caught a downtown train immediately. Only as I was standing in the crowded moving train, aware of the silly expression that was probably still on my face, did reality start to set in again.

I was sure the severed hand belonged to Darius Phelps. However, unless I personally introduced Lopez to Darius' zombie, I knew there was no way I could convince him of my theory. Meanwhile, I felt very worried about Frank Johnson, and Max really wanted to talk with the man.

So if Lopez's theory—that the hand might belong to Frank—motivated him to find out what had happened to the missing instructor, well, I supposed that worked out well for everyone.

After a few stops, I changed trains and caught one that would take me to Little Italy. There was an empty seat on this train, and as soon as I sat in it, I saw that my shoes and ankles were still covered in Nelli's blood, now dried to a rusty brown color. I realized some of her blood was on my left hand and both of my knees, too. I'd need to clean up when I got to the restaurant.

I was already in danger of being late, and washing off

the blood would take some time. So I decided to tidy my hair and start putting on my makeup while I was still on the subway train. Since my mind was on other things—including the memory of Lopez's lips pressed again mine, moving seductively as his breath caressed my cheek—I did quite a bit of rummaging around in my purse before I realized my hairbrush wasn't in there. Nor was my makeup.

I sat staring into the depths of my handbag with bemusement. The baka had not stolen or destroyed any of the items that I had worried about: money, phone, ID, keys. So why had they taken my hairbrush and my . . .

Cold fear exploded inside my torso and rapidly spread outward to engulf my limbs.

The baka who had stolen my purse served the bokor. So if personal items of mine were missing from its contents, then the bokor must have those. And some of my hair could certainly be extracted from my brush.

The mysterious dark sorcerer now had the ingredients needed to make a voodoo doll whose fate I would share.

17

On Sunday afternoon, as bad weather was moving into the area, Jamal was waiting for me outside the Livingston Foundation. He was wearing yet another baggy outfit, so I supposed Shondolyn had been too preoccupied to convey fashion advice to him the other day. As the boy approached me, I saw that his forehead was shiny with sweat from standing around on the sidewalk waiting for me to arrive.

The sky was overcast today and the air felt heavy with tension. I thought the suffocating temperature ought to break, given that the sun wasn't out and there was a fair bit of wind today; but, no, it was still unbearably hot outside. I wore a sleeveless cotton dress and sandals, and my hair was in a topknot, but I was still sticky and wilting.

"I heard there was gonna be a big ceremony here today," Jamal said to me. "So I thought you might show up, since you're into this voodoo shit."

I was about to protest that I wasn't even remotely into "this voodoo shit," but I decided to hold my silence when I realized how unconvincing that would sound. Not only had I sent Shondolyn to Puma's Vodou Emporium for help, as Jamal well knew, but I was also currently wearing a rather large, unattractive, and some-what smelly gris-gris bag around my neck.

After receiving my frantic phone call on Friday, Max and Puma had worked together to concoct this protective charm for me. Max and Biko had brought it to me at the restaurant later that same night. Since then, I had only taken it off to shower.

Its comforting presence around my neck, however, did not keep me from worrying that every little itch, twinge, or twitch that I felt was terrifying evidence that the bokor had made a poppet in my image, using my hair and makeup, and was now tormenting it—and me—with lethal intent.

Jamal said to me, his expression a mixture of concern and accusation, "Dr. Livingston says Shondolyn is gone."

"Gone away to stay with relatives," I said with a nod. I had talked to Max at length yesterday, and he said that Puma had received a call from the girl saying she was leaving for Maryland that same day and would probably stay there until she had to return to New York to start school in a few weeks. Her mother had informed the Livingston Foundation that she was withdrawing from the summer sessions due to health issues.

Being targeted by the bokor was certainly a threat to health, I thought. Also to longevity.

Jamal asked me, "Is Shondolyn going to be all right?"

"I think she'll be fine, now that she's gone away for a while," I said. "This . . . atmosphere wasn't good for her."

"You mean the weird shit that's going on."

"That depends on what weird shit you're talking about."

"There is *strange* shit wandering around this neighborhood at night," Jamal said earnestly. "Those crazy people in that shop that you sent Shondolyn to—they seemed to know about it."

"Do you know about it, too?"

"I've seen some things," he said. "I don't know what's going on, but I know this, ma'am. You shouldn't be around here after dark. Especially not alone. You feel me?"

"Yes," I said.

"And I guess you're right, it's probably better for Shondolyn to be outta here."

"For the time being," I said. "But this weird shit will get its ass kicked, and then Shondolyn will be back, when it's safe for her to come home."

"Well, I guess that's okay, then." He looked at some of the local Vodou worshippers who were entering the foundation now. "I ain't gonna stay for this voodoo thing."

"Okay."

"See you in class." He raised his fist in a little farewell gesture. "Keep it real."

"Er, Jamal," I said. "Just a tip about the kind of guy Shondolyn likes."

He eyed me suspiciously but didn't refuse to listen.

"Different clothes," I said. "Get some tight jeans, some button-down shirts in your proper size, and some boring shoes."

"What? No way!"

"If you want her to look at you and see a guy she might be interested in," I said, "that's what it's going to take."

"Shit." He looked like he was seriously rethinking his interest in the girl. Shaking his head, he walked away.

Behind me, Biko said, "Hi, Esther. Making friends and influencing people?"

I turned to face him and saw that Max was with him. My greeting to them both disappeared in a sneeze. I waved a hand in front of my face, and my eyes watered.

"Are you okay?" Biko asked.

I coughed a little and gestured to the lumpy brown leather pouch that hung from my neck. It was the size of a baby's fist. "Whenever I move suddenly, something escapes this gris-gris bag that irritates my system. I think it must be the cayenne pepper."

"Hmm, we may have used a little too much of that," Max said with concern. "Still, better safe than sorry."

I saw Puma about half a block away, coming from the direction of her shop. She was wearing a white skirt and blouse, and she had a white bandana tied around her head. She waved when she saw us, and picked up her pace.

I realized as she greeted us that most of the other people I'd seen arriving for the community ritual were also wearing white. I, however, was in an apricot-colored sundress.

"Puma, should I have worn white?" I asked. No one had mentioned a dress code.

"What you wear doesn't really matter," she said. "It's what's in your heart that counts."

"Shall we go inside?" Max suggested.

"I'm waiting for Jeff," Puma said, "but I guess he can find us. I told him we were going to meet in Biko's training room."

"Jeff is coming?" I said in surprise.

"If that boy wants to date me, then you bet he's coming," she said. "He doesn't have to share my faith, but he should understand that it's a big part of who I am."

"After you, ladies," Max said.

Puma took my arm as we proceeded inside. "Listen, Esther, before Jeff asks me out—and I've decided he *is* going to ask me out—I want your blessing. I won't go out with him unless I have it."

"Why do you want *my* blessing?"

"Well, you and I are friends, and you and Jeff used to

go out. So it wouldn't be right for me to start seeing him without your blessing."

"Did Jeff tell you about us?" I asked.

She snorted with laughter. "No one had to tell me anything, girl. It couldn't be more obvious if the two of you wore matching T-shirts saying, WE'RE EXES."

Startled by this revelation, I looked over my shoulder at the two men accompanying us down the hallway toward the fencing room.

Seeing my inquisitive look, Biko said, "I think the T-shirts would be overkill. Not needed."

"No, indeed," said Max.

"Oh," I said. "Well. Hmph."

"So do I have your blessing or not?" Puma asked.

"My blessing *and* my condolences," I assured her.

Biko said, "Spoken like an ex."

As we entered Biko's training room, which was spartan in its minimalist tidiness, Puma said to Max, "I guess you left Nelli at home?"

"Yes. After her severe reaction to the boa constrictor, she is not welcome at the foundation." Max added worriedly, "However, I believe she would not have been able to attend today's ritual, anyhow. She seems to be feeling under the weather."

"What's wrong?" I asked.

"She's very sluggish. To the point of being difficult to wake, let alone coax outside for a perambulation. Nor is she interested in her food dish, her water bowl, or any of her toys."

"That doesn't sound like Nelli," I said with concern. "Maybe she needs to go back to the vet, Max."

"Or maybe *someone* gave her too many treats again last night." Biko's accusing glance at Puma left us in no doubt of the probable culprit.

"I'm sorry if I made her sick," Puma said to Max. "She just always seems to be so hungry."

"I think it's more likely that her injured paw has gotten infected," I said, feeling guilty about being the one who had inadvertently wounded her.

"Well, if she is not back to her usual self by morning," Max said, "I will definitely take her to the animal clinic."

I told them all what I had learned from Lopez about the bodies that were missing from the same graveyard where Darius Phelps had been buried, confirming Max's suspicions that additional zombies had been raised. I also said that I had explored the area of the stone steps at Mount Morris Park by day without finding anything.

Biko and Max thought they had spotted a baka in the park late Friday night, but it had quickly eluded them. And they had seen nothing since then.

"I've been reading the books you gave me, Puma," I said. "And I'm wondering what we're going to do about these zombies. According to my reading, we can't, er, de-zombify them without a lot of special ingredients that I think are going to be hard to find." I read from a list that I had made during one of my breaks at the restaurant. "Human blood drained from the left foot. Powder from a ground-up human femur. A live chicken. A dead sea snake. The skin of a banana eaten by someone who's recently recovered from a fever. And this is just a partial list!" I shook my head and concluded, "Harlem will be *swarming* in zombies by the time we manage to collect all the supplies we need."

"Ah, the good news there," said Max, "is that we can free the zombies from their enslavement simply by dispatching the bokor."

"How *simple* do you really think dispatching a bokor will be?" Biko said skeptically.

"I mean to say, when the bokor falls, the zombies created by the bokor will fall, too."

I said, "So stopping the bokor is the thing to focus on, then." I tore up my shopping list with relief.

Puma asked, "Speaking of the bokor . . . Do we think Esther was targeted deliberately? Or is she just unlucky because her purse was stolen by the baka?"

"Excellent question. Unfortunately, without more information, either possibility is feasible." Max added to me, "It is my hope that the gris-gris pouch will protect you. But you must notify us immediately if anything unusual happens, or if you start to feel peculiar."

"I've felt peculiar ever since I met Darius' zombie," I said. "But I understand what you're saying."

Max said, "I think the most interesting thing that we have learned recently is simultaneously also the least surprising."

"That I used to date Jeff?" I said.

They all looked at me.

"Never mind," I said. "Go on, Max."

"Under the influence of hypnosis—which had the unfortunate side effect, as Puma noticed, of making Nelli exceedingly hungry—Shondolyn recalled additional names from her troubled dreams."

"Besides Mama Brigitte?" I said.

"Yes. Baron Samedi, for example. This was to be expected," Max said. "The bokor must make offerings to the Lord of Death, without whose blessings no one can raise a zombie."

"And why would the Lord of Death *let* anyone raise a zombie?" I demanded. "Doesn't he want to, you know, keep the dead on his team?"

"Baron Samedi is a trickster," Puma said. "He does what amuses him. And the bokor's offerings to him may be very generous."

"However, most of the names Shondolyn recalled were those of Petro loa," Max said.

"Petro," I said. "Those are the violent, dangerous spirits, aren't they?"

"Very dangerous," Max confirmed. "Dark, angry, and unpredictable. In some cases, genuinely evil."

"Marinette was one of the Petro loa that the girl named," Puma said. "Marinette is a sworn servant of evil. Invoked strictly for black magic."

"This is, of course, the sort of spirit we would expect to find the bokor serving and petitioning for favor." Max added, "Even so, our adversary is daring."

"Also ambitious," said Puma.

"How so?" I asked.

"The darkest Petro demand a very high price for their blessings," Puma said. "Permanent, steadfast devotion and, more to the point, expensive sacrifices and rich offerings."

"In exchange," Max said, "they can work impressive feats of magic and confer great power on their worshippers."

"But invoking them is perilous," Puma said. "They can turn on their followers."

"The Petro loa may even kill a servant who disregards a vow to them or who breaks a pact with them," said Max.

"So that's why you think we're looking for someone who's daring and ambitious," I guessed. "The bokor has chosen dangerous partners in hopes of securing great power."

"But a crucial unanswered question," Max said, "is why has the bokor exposed a teenage girl to these influences? What is the goal or the intention?"

Biko said, "Whatever it is, it probably intersects with the reason zombies are being raised."

"I do wish we could communicate with Jeffrey's missing colleague," Max said anxiously.

"I've convinced Detective Lopez that it's important to track down Frank Johnson," I said. I had left a phone message for Lopez earlier today asking for an update, but he hadn't called me back yet.

"The cop?" Biko looked doubtful. "Is that such a good idea, Esther?"

"We must pursue every possible avenue for finding Mr. Johnson," Max said. "His information could be critical. Well done, Esther."

"You see?" I said to Biko.

"Whatever."

"Meanwhile," said Max, "if I am correct in my theory and Darius Phelps was murdered, then my researches in recent days have led me to understand how it could have been done."

He had our full attention now.

"Poor Darius may have been murdered via a fairly arcane form of sympathetic magic," Max said.

Considering that I was pretty sure the bokor now possessed strands of my hair, I didn't like being reminded that sympathetic magic could be fatal.

"You begin by taking wrappings from food that the victim has partially eaten," Max said. "Such as sausage casings or banana leaves. There are no doubt many equivalents in contemporary New York, including sandwich wrappers and cannoli tubes. In any case, you fill the wrapping with certain rare ingredients, exercise dark magic to create a mystical bond between the object and the victim, and then you, er . . . stomp on the object. Linked in sympathetic symbiosis with the victim's intestine, this causes a rupture."

"That's disgusting," said Biko.

I clutched my gris-gris pouch and prayed that it was working effectively to ward off the bokor's dark magic.

Then I realized what Max's theory meant. "Darius knew the bokor," I said.

"I believe so."

How else would the killer have obtained the victim's partially eaten food? And, indeed, why go to that much trouble unless . . .

"It was personal," I said aloud. Based on the number of empty graves Lopez was discovering, the bokor didn't need to kill an acquaintance to create a zombie. Bodies were available. "So *killing* Darius was the point. Creating a zombie after the murder was just sort of . . . a bonus."

"A maliciously satisfying one, no doubt," said Max. "Few murderers have an opportunity to enslave the victim after death."

"If Mr. Phelps knew the bokor," Puma said anxiously, "then that means *we* might know the bokor, too."

"I'm glad I've got a sword," Biko muttered. "And when I find out who created those creatures that killed Gilligan . . ."

"Well, I know who gets my vote," I said. "The nasty voodoo priestess who doesn't seem to like anybody, and who could easily have an agenda of her own."

"What?" Puma shook her head. "No! Absolutely not. She's a *mambo.*"

"I wish everyone would stop saying that as if it makes her a saint," I said irritably.

"She's not a saint," Puma said. "But I can't believe that she's an evil bokor who's committed murder."

"That's because you have trouble believing ill of people," I said. "And although that's an admirable trait, it's not very practical."

Jeff entered the room. "Ah! So this is where they keep the beautiful women!"

Looking upset, Puma said, "We should go downstairs. It's almost time for the ceremony to begin."

She brushed past him and ran out the door.

Jeff looked puzzled. "Did I do something wrong?"

Biko said to me, "I don't like Mambo Celeste, either,

Esther. And that snake gives me the creeps. But she's been a mambo a long time around here. And Puma studied with the same teacher as she did. I just don't know." He shrugged. "And now we'd better go attend the service, or Puma will be hurt."

He followed his sister out the door.

"Hi, Biko," Jeff said. "Bye, Biko."

"Max," I said. "Are we really going to attend a ceremony where someone who might be an evil bokor is raising spirits? Doesn't that seem a little dangerous?"

"Our adversary is secretive," Max said. "And secrecy is the usual nature of a bokor. If Mambo Celeste is the guilty party, she will not risk revealing that identity to her community by doing anything untoward at a public ceremony. I believe her behavior at the ceremony will be exemplary, either because she is innocent, or else because she is determined to seem so."

"All right." I resigned myself to it. "I guess we might as well go downstairs now." I took Max's arm and exited the room. On our way out the door, we greeted Jeff.

Following us, he said, "I'm getting the impression that I've missed a lot."

"You have. But do you really want to know what?" I said.

"Come to think of it, no." He obviously had other things on his mind. "I wonder if Mike Nolan has talked to the casting director about me yet?"

I didn't feel like talking about that right now, so I ignored the implied question.

When we reached the lobby, I stumbled to a halt and stared in surprise. "Lopez?"

He saw me and walked over to us. "I thought you would be here."

He wore khaki slacks, sandals, and a white cotton shirt, open at the neck. He looked nice, but more casual than usual.

"You're not on duty?" I guessed.

"Not officially."

"Greetings, detective!" Max beamed at him.

"Hi, Max."

"What are you doing here?" I asked.

"Well, on a quiet Friday afternoon, there was a bloody riot in the lobby of this building," Lopez said.

"I *have* missed a lot," said Jeff.

"So when Dr. Livingston told me that people here today would be invoking the spirits, communing with the ancestors, and drinking rum, I thought it might be a good idea to come keep an eye on things."

Jeff stuck out his hand. "Hi, I'm Jeffrey Clark. And you must be Detective Lopez."

Lopez frowned thoughtfully as they shook hands. "Have we met before?"

Jeff shook his head. "No, I'd remember a name like Connor Lopez."

"You look familiar," said Lopez.

"I'm an actor. Maybe you've seen me in something?"

"Oh." Lopez nodded. "Maybe."

"If you guys will excuse me, I'm going to go find Puma," said Jeff.

"We'll come downstairs shortly," Max said to him.

Lopez asked me, "What are you wearing around your neck?"

"I could explain, but then we'd wind up in a long digression that would just give you a headache."

"I withdraw the question."

I asked him, "Did you get my message?"

"Yes. I thought I'd tell you in person. Frank Johnson is alive and well." He paused. "Or, he's *alive,* anyhow. I'm not so sure about well."

"What do you mean?"

"He didn't answer his phone or return my calls," Lopez said. "And because of what you and I talked about, I thought he might be dead. So I got his address and went to his apartment today."

"And?"

"He was home, but he wouldn't open the door. I wound up getting the superintendent to let me into his apartment." Lopez looked puzzled. "He was the same man depicted on his driver's license, and he confirmed that he was Frank Johnson. He was also scared out of his wits."

Max and I exchanged a glance. Lopez noticed.

"What frightened him?" Max asked.

"I have no idea," Lopez said. "I couldn't get anything that made sense out of him."

Thinking we should go talk to him, I asked Lopez for his address.

"Sorry, Esther. He's unlisted. I'm not supposed to give out that information. And based on the way he was behaving today, I think he'd sue the department if I did."

"We understand, detective." Max sighed in disappointment. "But I do wish Mr. Johnson would at least answer his phone."

"Why do *you* want to talk to him?" Lopez asked Max.

"The ceremony is about to start," I said quickly. "Shall we go downstairs?"

Lopez eyed me. "Fine."

We began descending the stairs to the hounfour. Lopez put his hand on my arm so that we slowed down and wound up following Max.

"What's going on?" he asked in a low voice.

"Frank Johnson was behaving strangely the last time anyone saw him," I said carefully. "Max is concerned about his well-being and wants to help him."

"Max should stay away from him."

"Since we don't know how to find him and he won't answer his phone, Max probably *will* stay away from him."

Going down the stairs jostled my gris-gris charm, which made me sneeze again.

Seeing red dust floating out of the pouch, Lopez asked, "No, really. What *are* you wearing?"

"Fine," I said. "*Fine.* Have it your way. This is a gris-gris bag made to protect me from a voodoo curse by an evil bokor. It contains about thirty ingredients. After cayenne pepper, dried lizard gizzard, tobacco, chicken feathers, and frog's toes, I asked Max to stop listing the ingredients for me. Happy now?"

"Okay, you were right the first time," he said. "Now my head hurts."

We walked the rest of the way in silence.

I had never been to the basement before. It was more attractive than I had pictured it. The hounfour was a large open space. The walls were painted a soothing blue and decorated with murals of the Virgin Mary and various Vodou loa.

The only feature marring the scene was Napoleon in his cage. Lopez was right; the snake's cage was nicer than many people's apartments. There was a big tree branch, which the boa was currently coiled around. Beneath the branch, there was a grassy area, some pebbles, and a boulder with a big indentation for a private little pond. Napoleon's head was moving restlessly, and his tongued flicked repeatedly in and out of his mouth.

I looked away, determined to focus on anything *but* the mambo's pet.

The ritual already seemed to be under way, though this was evidently more organic than organized. There were some people drumming, a few other people were singing and dancing, and there was an open brazier in the center of the space full of glowing coals.

"That can't be legal," Lopez muttered. "We're in a basement."

"You're just here to observe and prevent trouble," I reminded him.

There was long iron rod stuck into the brazier, its tip glowing red hot in the burning coals.

I looked at the big altar along the far wall. It was crowded with ritual objects: bottles, candles, dolls representing the loa, spirit masks, a statue of the Virgin, a coffin with a cross on it, a skull, seashells, feathers, flowers, silk scarves, and pictures of Catholic saints. There were dishes of food on the altar, as well as what appeared to be an ample supply of tobacco.

There were a lot of people present in the hounfour, and more were still arriving. Max, Lopez, and I seemed to be the only attendees who weren't African-American. This probably made it easy for Jeff to spot us, despite how crowded the space was by now. He made his way over to us.

"Where's Biko?" I asked him.

"I don't know. Too many people. I can't find Puma, either," he said over the noise of the drumming. "I think she must be getting ready to participate."

"How often do they do this?" Lopez asked me.

I shrugged and shook my head, indicating I didn't know.

Jeff said, "They're doing it now to raise luck and ward off black magic." When Lopez looked at him, he shrugged. "That's what Puma told me."

I explained to Lopez who Puma was. Then, as the volume in the room continued rising, I asked, "How was your field trip with your mom?"

"Don't remind me," he said. "I'm a cop. I've seen a lot of things. I thought I was hardened to depravity. But then yesterday . . . I saw where filthy rich people buy their food, and I felt innocent and shocked."

"Were the men really naked?" I asked, raising my voice to be heard.

Jeff heard the word *naked* and, naturally, leaned closer to hear more. Max was absorbed in observing preparations for the ritual.

"Not as naked my mom would have liked, since she obviously looked forward to telling my dad about it. More naked than *I* would have liked since, oh, I was there with my mother." He smiled wryly. "For that same reason, I scarcely even looked at the mostly-naked women. A missed opportunity."

"What *is* this place?" I asked him. "What's it called? I might have to check it out."

"What are we talking about?" Jeff asked, leaning closer.

"Someplace Lopez went yesterday," I said. "Full of scantily clad store clerks selling expensive food."

"It's called the Imperial Food Forum," Lopez said. "The whole place has a Roman Bacchanalia theme. Food, décor, clothing, music, everything. I think I might have enjoyed if I'd been drunk. And younger. And not accompanying my mom."

I turned to Jeff. "I think it's a creative idea for a first date, Jeff. Maybe Puma would like ..." I stopped speaking as I realized he was staring at Lopez with an expression of dawning horror.

"There was also ... I don't know, I guess you could call it performance art," Lopez said. "A girl with a lute, a guy reciting from the *Aeneid,* a couple of gladiators fighting. And then there was this ..." He stopped speaking and his gaze flew to Jeff. "Gladiators fighting! That's where I've seen you. You were working there."

Jeff started shaking his head. "No ... No, no, no."

I looked at Jeff in astonishment. "*That's* your gladiator role? Entertaining shoppers at the Imperial Food Forum?"

"You were good with that sword," Lopez said, apparently oblivious to the humiliation he had just caused. He really *didn't* know actors.

Jeff looked at me, as if wondering whether he could brazen it out, and then his shoulders sagged in defeat. He said to Lopez, "Thanks, man. Glad you enjoyed the show."

"You must have been cold, though," said Lopez.

"Jeff?" I said.

My ex-boyfriend looked heavenward. "Please, Lord. Take me now."

"Why did you give up the acting workshops at the foundation to—"

"Can we talk about this later?" said Jeff.

Max said, "I believe the ceremony is commencing!"

The drumbeats suddenly got so loud it wasn't possible to hold a conversation. My questions would have to wait until there was a chance of Jeff actually hearing them.

The drums ceased, and a man dressed in simple clothing walked to the center of the hounfour and began reciting verses in French. I recognized the language, but didn't understand it well enough to have any idea what he was saying. After a couple of minutes, Lopez whispered to me, "He's reciting Catholic prayers."

I supposed he recognized it from the Spanish, or maybe the Latin.

I heard a rattle shaking and looked around. I saw Mambo Celeste. She had a gourd-shaped rattle in her hand. It reminded me of the one I had seen in Puma's shop—the one stuffed with snake vertebrae. How fitting, I thought.

The Catholic prayers and the rattling went on for a while. Then the man retreated into the crowd, and the mambo took center stage. To be fair, she made quite an impression. Dressed in a colorful gown and headdress, she had great theatrical style and a level of stage presence and charisma that many professional actors would envy.

There were some ritual libations, saluting of the spirits, and more prayers. Then the drumming began again, and about a dozen young women paraded into the ceremonial space, each of them carrying a colorful drapeau. I recognized a few of the traditional designs by now. Among the loa represented by the flags were Papa Legba, Ogoun, Damballah, Ayida-Wedo, and Baron Samedi.

I didn't recognize any of the young women, though, and I wondered where Puma was.

Someone carried a live rooster into the center of the hounfour and whirled around with it before moving on. I had a feeling I knew what the bird was for. However, according to my reading, sacrifices occurred much later in the ceremony. I was frankly hoping to leave before then, since the ritual would last well into the night.

Now there was a lot of chanting in Creole, and the mambo poured libations with rum, paid obeisance to the drapeaux, and started drawing vévé on the floor, creating the complex designs from memory and by sprinkling talcum powder delicately from her fingers. Mambo Celeste began by invoking Papa Legba and asking him to open the gates to the spirit world. Then she moved on to invoking other loa. The rum pouring, vévé drawing, invoking, and chanting went on for quite a while.

Lopez muttered to me, "I vow I will never again complain about how long High Mass takes."

The celebrants and worshippers were all vibrantly engaged in the proceedings, which followed a sort of organized chaos. I noticed that Max was deeply absorbed and seemed to be enjoying himself.

I saw Baron Samedi prowling around—or, rather, a man dressed up like the Lord of Death. He wore a frock coat with tails, striped trousers, sunglasses, and a formal top hat. His face was painted like a skull, and seeing him wandering around, popping up here and there, made me uneasy enough that I was very glad Lopez was with me.

Finally, we reached the point in the ceremony where almost everyone in the room starting dancing, singing, and chanting; the rum was flowing pretty freely by now. This was the part of the ritual where people lost themselves in dance and awaited possession by a spirit. To be possessed was a mark of favor and a great blessing, a form of religious ecstasy.

However, since I didn't know the language or really understand what was going on, I started to feel restless and ready to leave. Especially since I knew this could go on a while. Max seemed so enchanted by the service, though, that I didn't have the heart to ask him to come with me. But I thought Jamal's warning was well worth heeding: It would be evening by now, and although it wasn't totally dark outside, I still didn't want to leave the building by myself.

So I said to Lopez, "Will you come with me to get a cab?"

"Sure." He turned away from the ceremony with me and put his hand on my back—but then a small explosion behind us made him turn back to the action.

I saw that the mambo was throwing powder into the brazier, and it was creating small explosions.

"Jesus, I think that's gunpowder," Lopez said. "Hang on. I think I'd better deal with this."

"Of course," I said.

As Lopez maneuvered his way through the dancing throng, heading toward the mambo, Max came up to me.

"What is she doing?" I asked him as another explosion made my head start to ache.

"She's asking Ogoun to join us," he said. " He's the loa of—"

"War, fire, and male fertility," I said, remembering what Catherine had told me.

It suddenly occurred to me that the anthropologist

wasn't here. That surprised me. I'd have expected to see her hovering nearby, taking notes.

Then again, maybe after you've done that at a few hundred rituals, the fun starts to wear off. Perhaps she had decided to stay home with a good book tonight.

Lopez was approaching the brazier as the mambo threw another handful of gunpowder into it. He fell back a step and looked a little dizzy for a moment, as if the resultant explosion had affected him.

"What's he doing?" a familiar voice asked me.

I turned to see Jeff by my side. I said, "There you are. You disappeared for a while."

"Should he be that close to the brazier?" asked Jeff.

I looked again. Lopez was standing still in front of the mambo now. Not talking, not making her put down the gunpowder . . . Not doing anything.

Jeff said to me, "He doesn't act like a guy who dumped you."

I had no idea why Lopez was just standing there. He seemed to be swaying a little.

"He didn't dump me," I said. "He gave me up."

"He acts more like a guy who's cutting you out of the herd and putting up a fence to keep the other stallions away from you."

"Huh?"

"We've been in this room since, oh, a different geological era, I think," Jeff said. "And this is the first time he's moved more than eight inches away from you."

I turned to face Jeff. "Tell me about the Imperial Food Forum. I don't understand why you lied to me about it."

"I didn't lie. I just . . . omitted a lot of information and let you think whatever you wanted to think."

I didn't have the heart to tell him I really *hadn't* thought about it. So I said, "I assumed you were in a play."

"I was broke when I came back from LA, and another

actor I know—Frank Johnson, in fact—told me about a job that was available. He said he wasn't right for it, but maybe I might be, since I'd been keeping fit out in LA."

"And?"

"And it was full-time work, and the money was pretty good." He shrugged. "And if the floor show keeps going well, we'll do some TV commercials. And that'll be better money."

"We all do things to pay the bills, Jeff," I said.

"Yeah, well, you've got a part on a great TV show. I'm wearing a thong and playacting with a sword in a glorified supermarket." He made an awkward gesture. "So maybe you can understand why I didn't just come out and tell you."

"*D-Thirty* is the only work I've had all summer," I pointed out. "I've been waiting tables most of the year."

"*Singing* and waiting tables," he said with a teasing smile.

"*Do* you get cold in your thong?"

He gave me a mock punch on the chin, then he put his arms around me, and we hugged. As we pulled apart, Jeff peered over the heads of the crowd and looked into the center of the hounfour again. His expression changed so abruptly that I turned to look, too.

Jeff said, "Holy shit!"

I cried, "No!"

Lopez has stripped off his shirt. Bare-chested and gleaming with a fine sheen of sweat, he knelt before the brazier and plunged his hands into the pile of glowing red coals.

I screamed and tried to lunge forward. In sheer reflexive fear, Jeff kept a firm grip on me, stopping me from moving.

Lopez pulled the iron rod out of the brazier, raised his arms overhead, and held the burning rod in his bare hands, his facial expression completely blank.

18

"**L**opez!" I screamed in horror.

He remained kneeling on the floor in front of the glowing brazier, his naked torso gleaming, his muscular arms raised high overhead as he held the glowing iron rod in his hands. His eyes were half-closed and unblinking, his face relaxed and strangely blank.

"Let me go!" My nose twitched from the irritation of my gris-gris pouch as I struggled with Jeff, frantic to get to Lopez and—and—and . . . Actually, I wasn't sure what I would do. But getting him to let go of the red-hot iron bar seemed like a good place to start.

"Holy shit!" Jeff repeated, still restraining me.

Mambo Celeste was standing next to Lopez. I couldn't tear my gaze away from him to look at her, but I heard her voice raised exultantly and was aware of her swaying in a dance around his kneeling form, her arms spread wide as she chanted and shook her rattle.

His face still calm, almost sleepy, Lopez suddenly leaped to his feet and whirled around in a circle with the glowing rod, twirling it overhead with his hands, then letting it slide down his arms so he could make the thing dance around his torso, moving like a martial artist practicing with a bamboo staff.

That was when I finally realized that he wasn't getting burned. His flesh was unmarred, and he seemed to be in no discomfort at all.

"Whoa!" said Jeff. "He works out, doesn't he? Very flexible."

"Oh, shut up," I said.

I watched in numb shock as Lopez tipped his head back and plunged the fiery rod into his mouth. The crowd cheered, clapped, and chanted with ecstatic enthusiasm as he eased the glowing rod into his mouth, inch by inch, like a sword swallower, until an alarmingly large portion of it had disappeared down his throat.

"Has he ever done this before?" Jeff asked me.

"Of course not!" I snapped, panting with fear and panic.

When Lopez finally pulled the iron bar all the way out of his mouth, it was still glowing.

"How did he *do* that?" Jeff wondered.

Then Lopez held the rod like a spear and, with a guttural war cry, threw it across the room, over the heads of the worshippers. Flying straight as an arrow, it crashed into Napoleon's cage, causing the glass to shatter. The breaking glass and startled cries of the nearby people were loud enough to make me look reflexively in that direction. The boa constrictor was unharmed, but it was frightened enough to move off its branch and tumble out of its cage.

"So now that snake's on the loose in a room packed with people," Jeff said. "*Great.* What was your friend *thinking?*"

"He's *not* thinking! Can't you see?" My heart was pounding so hard I felt dizzy, almost nauseated. "He's possessed!"

"Seriously?"

I felt a hand grasp my arm and turned to see Max

standing beside me, his gaze fixed on Lopez. "He has become a cheval."

"A what?"

"A cheval—er, a horse. That's how it's described in Vodou. He has been mounted and is being ridden by Ogoun, the god of fire and war." Max squeezed my arm reassuringly. "I know it looks frightening, but it's a blessing. A sign of great favor."

Jeff said, "It looks damned dangerous, if you ask me."

Lopez accepted a bottle of rum from a smiling celebrant, raised it to his lips, and tilted his head back. Throat working rhythmically, dark golden skin gleaming, he didn't even pause for breath, but simply drank the whole bottle, draining its contents. When he was done, he tossed the bottle aside, wiped his mouth with his forearm, and—speaking in Creole—demanded more rum. Someone gave him another bottle. He drained that one, too.

"Max," I said desperately, "he'll get alcohol poisoning!"

"Maybe the fire god can handle it?" Jeff said doubtfully.

"There usually aren't any ill effects afterward from being ridden by a loa," said Max.

"*Usually?*" I repeated.

I watched the mambo chanting loudly in Creole and waving her rattle around Lopez as he swayed and his eyes rolled back in his head. As she encouraged him to take yet another bottle of rum, I remembered that I thought she was an evil bokor and a murderess.

"I'm putting a stop to this!" I said.

"Esther, no!" Max grabbed my arm again as I tried to move forward. "That could be very dangerous!"

Jeff grabbed my other arm. "He's right! A lot of

people here are guzzling rum, not just your boyfriend. They seem happy and harmless, but do you really want to risk spoiling their ceremony now that they've had a few drinks?"

"You shouldn't disturb someone who's in the middle of a possession trance," Max warned. "And insulting a loa who has mounted a celebrant is fraught with potential peril!"

"Would this thing hurt Lopez?" I asked anxiously.

"Ogoun has a fiery temper," Max said. "Forcing him to dismount could be dangerous for *you*."

The man dressed as Baron Samedi poured a bottle of rum all over Lopez's arms and torso while the mambo, using a thin piece of burning wood, followed him around Lopez's body, setting the rum alight so that Lopez's flesh was covered with rum-soaked flames. His skin still glowing with fire, he seized the bottle from Baron Samedi and drank more rum.

The mambo rubbed fire and rum into his skin while he drank thirstily, her palms moving along his naked torso and over his shoulders while people around them danced and sang.

"Well, I don't care if the loa *is* offended!" I told my companions. "I want that woman's hands *off* Lopez. Right now!"

"Oh, crap," Jeff said as I tore myself out of his restraining grasp and starting forcing my way through the crowd. The swinging gris-gris pouch made my eyes sting. I ignored the discomfort and stayed focused on Lopez.

"Esther!" Max cried. "Wait!"

"No! This has to stop!" I shoved people aside as I forged a path to the possessed police detective. "It's dangerous! And so is that woman!"

I forced my way into the center of the ceremony and crossed the floor to Lopez's side. I grabbed the bottle of rum as he was about to raise it to his lips again.

"Stop!" I said. "Lopez! Can you hear me?"

He kept his grip on the bottle without any apparent effort, though I was trying hard to pull it out of his grasp. He swayed a little as he looked at me. He seemed to see me, but there was no light of recognition in the blue eyes that met mine.

"Lopez?"

The mambo started shouting at me in Creole. After a moment, she switched to English, telling me to leave him alone, to go away.

When she grabbed me, I shook her off, saying, "Don't touch me! And don't you touch him again, either!"

She grabbed me again, and this time I slapped her hand away. She hissed at me like a cat.

Lopez's heavy-lidded eyes watched this exchange impassively. Then he grinned, slid his free arm around my waist, and pulled me against his naked chest. He ground his hips against mine, and I gave a startled gasp when I felt the unmistakable evidence of his arousal. I suddenly recalled that Ogoun was also the god of male fertility. Flustered and embarrassed—we were surrounded by people—I tried to push him away. It was like trying to move a boulder.

His lips came down on mine, and his kiss was bold and lascivious, his mouth hard, his tongue thrusting and stroking. I struggled, and he bent me backward over his arm until I was disoriented and dizzy, clinging to him for balance as he plundered my mouth with hot insistence, filling my senses with a fog of rum, fire, sweat, warm skin, and hard, flexing muscles. I couldn't breathe or move or find the floor with my feet. My head swam with darkness and heat as he went on kissing me greedily, taking what he wanted and draining me of my will.

By the time he stopped, I was so desperate for air, I thought I would faint. Even so, when he lifted his head, my mouth followed his, craving more punishment from him. He noticed, and it pleased him. He gave my ribs a ruthless squeeze, then laughed and raised the bottle to his lips again, downing more rum. With his head tilted back and his throat working, his hand slid down to my buttocks and he pulled my hips tightly into his again, then thrust against me with graphic intent.

I drew in a sharp breath and struggled again, trying to pull away while I choked on a cloud of cayenne pepper rising from my gris-gris charm. Lopez lowered the bottle to look at me. His smiling lips shone wetly with rum, and his liquor-soaked breath was probably a fire hazard. His long-lashed eyes were seductive with sleepy amusement as he held the bottle to my lips and murmured suggestively to me in Creole.

I didn't understand the words, but the meaning was clear enough. I shoved the bottle aside and, hoping to snap him out of it, slapped him sharply across the face.

He laughed again and let me go. Startled, I staggered sideways into Jeff, whose arms prevented me from falling down. Clutching me, Jeff sneezed in response to my peppery aura, then shoved me away.

"Well, you certainly took charge of *that* situation," he said. "So what's the next part of your brilliant plan to bring him to his senses?"

"Max?" I said sharply.

"I'm thinking, I'm thinking."

"Think faster!"

"This problem is somewhat outside my experience," the mage said apologetically.

Lopez was dancing with a couple of young women now, swaying and writhing cheerfully with them. Ogoun was quite a flirt.

All around us, people were clapping rhythmically, singing, dancing, and smiling. Several people were moving wildly, perhaps in the throes of spirit possession themselves.

"New plan!" I said to my companions. "Max, you distract the mambo. Jeff, you get a bucket of cold water."

"We're going to throw cold water on him?" Jeff said. "*That's* your plan?"

"Anyone with a better idea is welcome to make a suggestion!" I snapped.

"Step back!" Max warned.

He shoved the two of us away from the brazier as Lopez returned to it and reached into its red-hot contents with both hands. He scooped up a pile of glowing coals and washed them sensually over his chest and arms, eyes closed in apparent ecstasy. His skin remained unharmed, though I noticed the falling coals left behind some nasty burn marks on his khaki trousers. Even dry cleaning wouldn't save those pants after this escapade.

"A bucket of water, Jeff! *Now,*" I said. "Let's not wait until he sets the building on fire, huh?"

"Right. Okay. I'll go get—Whoa! What now?"

Lopez staggered backward, moving with sudden awkwardness. Then he stood still, swaying dizzily.

"Is he okay?" Jeff asked.

"Lopez?" I said, stepping toward him.

Looking as if he suddenly found it difficult just to remain on his feet, he put a hand up to his forehead and squeezed his eyes shut. He made an inarticulate sound, then shook his head a few times, as if trying to clear it.

I put my hand on his shoulder. "Lopez? Can you hear me?"

He collapsed like a marionette whose strings had just been cut. One moment, he was swaying dizzily; the next, he was lying at my feet, head thrown back, eyes closed, body inert.

Lopez lay unconscious on the floor of the hounfour, sprawled out atop the remnants of the vévé of Ogoun that Mambo Celeste had drawn there.

* * *

"No! Don't put him down *here*," I said to Jeff as he, Max, and I carried Lopez's unconscious body into my apartment. "Let's put him on the bed."

Max was wheezing from the effort of carrying Lopez up my stairs. He and I each held one leg while Jeff, walking backward, carried the weight of Lopez's torso and shoulders.

"Give me a minute," Jeff said, still trying to put down the limp body. "I've got the heavy part."

"Oh, come on." My back was starting to hurt. "It's just a few more feet. Keep moving."

Max said to me, "The detective is heavier than he looks, isn't he?"

"You're just tired," I said.

We'd had to carry Lopez out of the hounfour, up the stairs, and out of the foundation, and *then* we'd had to carry him down the street until we reached an avenue where we could hail a cab. Stuffing him into the backseat of the taxi had been no easy feat, either; he didn't bend and fold that easily when he was unconscious. And I thought I had strained something when pulling him back *out* of the cab upon arrival at my apartment a few minutes ago.

"No, this guy *is* heavier than he looks." Jeff shifted Lopez's weight in his arms, trying to get a better grip on the limp detective, then started backing toward my bedroom. "Good muscle development. Does he have a personal trainer?"

"Hey! Careful with his—" I winced as Lopez's skull thudded against the doorjamb of my bedroom. "Head."

"Oops." Jeff said, "Good thing he's already unconscious."

"Yes," I said tersely. "Everyone knows that a head injury doesn't really *count* unless you're awake for it."

Max and I shuffled forward awkwardly as the three of us maneuvered the body through the doorway. Lopez's left arm stuck out at an angle that prevented entry. I reached over to nudge it through the door. As a result, I dropped his leg, unable to retain my hold on it with just one hand. My gris-gris pouch bounced against my chest, making my eyes water.

"Goddamn it!" I said. "Where the hell is Biko?" The young athlete's strength would certainly have been useful in this endeavor, but we hadn't seen him since our meeting in the training room.

"And what happened to Puma?" Jeff added as he and Max hauled Lopez to the bed and, with one last burst of effort, dumped him onto it. "I didn't see her at all at the ritual, and she's the only reason I went! We sure could've used her help. She probably has some idea what to do with someone who's become a shovel."

"Cheval," Max wheezed, sitting down on the bed to catch his breath.

"Whatever."

I glanced at Max with concern as I climbed onto the bed beside Lopez and started trying to arrange him more comfortably. "Jeff, get him a glass of water."

"The boy just drank about a gallon of rum." Jeff eyed Lopez. "Do you really think he needs *more* liquids inside him when he's in no condition to use a toilet?"

I said, "A glass of water for *Max*."

"Oh! Okay." Jeff left the room and went to the kitchen.

"I'm still really worried about alcohol poisoning," I said to Max as I looked down at Lopez's peaceful face.

I put my head against his chest and listened. His breathing and heartbeat were steady and even. The temperature of his skin felt normal. He didn't seem to be in any physical distress. But he smelled like a distillery and was dead to the world.

After his collapse, I had realized we would have a hard enough time explaining Lopez's unconscious con-

dition to a cab driver without also having to explain why
he was half-naked; so I had found his shirt and, with
Jeff's help, wrestled him back into it. I unbuttoned the
garment now and pushed it aside, so that I could examine his torso and confirm under calmer circumstances
that he had not suffered any burns or injuries during his
bizarre experience at the Vodou ceremony—where celebrants had assured me with reverence and good cheer,
as he lay unconscious on the floor, that what had just
happened to him was a *good* thing.

Lying on my bed now, motionless but breathing
evenly, his body was smooth and warm. There was a light
dusting of black hair across his chest and a thin, faded
scar on his stomach—possibly from an appendectomy.

"No burn marks," I said, torn between relief and
amazement. "Nothing."

"I believe it is likely that the alcohol he consumed
will also have no ill effects," Max said soothingly. "Ah!
Thank you, Jeffrey!" He accepted the glass of water that
Jeff carried into the bedroom.

"I just turned on the AC," said Jeff. "Hope that's
okay."

"Sure," I said absently, realizing it was stuffy in here.
I turned off the air-conditioning whenever I went out. I
couldn't afford to waste money cooling an empty apartment. "Take off his shoes."

Jeff shot me resentful look, then knelt down and wrestled with a surprised Max for possession of his foot.

"No, I meant Lopez's shoes," I said with forced patience. "We need to make him comfortable. I don't know
how long he'll be like this."

"Oh! Right." Jeff sat down on the other side of the
bed and tugged off Lopez's sandals, which he tossed on
the floor.

We had initially argued about where to take our unconscious companion. Scared to death by his oblivious

condition, as well as by having just watched him consume a shockingly large quantity of rum, I'd wanted to go straight to a hospital. But Max had thought it unnecessary, and Jeff had considered it a terrible idea.

"A cop turns up in the ER unconscious and floating in booze?" Jeff had said. "When he wakes up there, how's he going to explain his condition to the staff *or* to the NYPD?"

I didn't want to inflict a professionally damaging situation on Lopez, or possibly even a career-ending one. So, hoping that it was the right decision, I had chosen to bring him here, where I could keep an eye on him while he slept it off.

I leaned over him now and stroked his dark hair away from his forehead. Gazing down at him, I prayed that Max was right and he didn't need medical attention.

"How did this happen to him?" I wondered aloud.

"Yeah, what gives?" Jeff said. "One minute, he was being a cop. The next, he was playing with fire. Weird."

"Spirit possession often occurs very quickly," Max said. "It just usually involves much more preparation—dancing or worship or meditation."

"He wasn't preparing at *all,*" I pointed out.

"Preparation is simply a way of *inviting* the spirit to possess the worshipper," Max said. "It does not necessarily follow that possession will occur. Nor does it mean a spirit cannot choose to possess one who hasn't actually invited it."

Jeff said, "I guess if you're a spirit, you get to do what you want, huh?"

"Within reason," Max said. "Preparing for possession creates favorable conditions for the spirit to manifest. It is an offer to surrender the self and relinquish conscious control." He thought it over for a moment. "The detective was close to the brazier when the mambo threw more gunpowder into it. The resulting explosion seemed to disorient him for a moment, and that evidently created—albeit involuntarily—the surrender of self that invited the loa to take control of him."

"The mambo . . ." I shifted my weight, trying to get into a more comfortable position as I knelt beside our unconscious companion. My gris-gris backed bounced a little. Lopez's slack facial muscles suddenly quivered. He made a little snuffling sound and turned his head away from me.

My heart leaped. "Lopez?"

He was silent and still again.

Jeff said, "I think that thing around your neck irritated him. What *is* it, anyhow?"

I felt a rush of relief. "So he's responsive!"

"Well, not so responsive to getting his head bashed against the doorjamb," Jeff said. "But, yeah. I would say his senses are starting to function again."

I returned to stroking Lopez's hair. He made a brief, faint sound of contentment.

Jeff added, "*All* his senses, I guess."

"You see?" Max smiled reassuringly at me. "To be mounted by a Rada loa can be quite draining, but it's not meant to be harmful. The Rada are benevolent spirits."

I expressed the dreadful fear welling up inside me. "Max, do you think Mambo Celeste did this to Lopez deliberately?"

"No, my dear, I don't. She opened the gateway to the spirit world, but she does not control the Rada. No one does. And although I realize tonight's events were alarming for you, they were nonetheless a very positive sign in the context of Vodou beliefs. The community has been given evidence that Ogoun is watching over them." Max added gently, "He is a warrior and a protector. A fitting match for Detective Lopez."

"He struck *me* as a letch and a drunkard," I said.

"The loa have robust appetites," Max said tactfully.

"They enjoy indulging in physical sensation when they manifest."

Jeff added judiciously, "Pretty athletic, too."

Max gazed at Lopez with a thoughtful expression. "Even so, despite the obviously compatible pairing of Ogoun with our companion, I find it puzzling . . ." He shook his head slightly. "No, *intriguing*. I find it intriguing that an outsider was chosen by the loa for such an honor tonight. A stranger. A nonbeliever. That is most unusual."

Our gazes locked. I realized what Max was thinking. Perhaps tonight's bizarre episode was a heavy hint from the spirit world that he was right and there was indeed more to Lopez than met the eye.

Seeing my inquisitive frown, Max shrugged in silent response. Then we both gazed contemplatively at Lopez's peaceful, oblivious face.

"Well, I'm guessing he's Catholic, right?" Jeff said prosaically, breaking the spell. "And those folks tonight were . . . *sort* of Catholic. So maybe he just really got into it."

"That was nothing like a Catholic service," I said.

"Oh, like *you're* an expert." Jeff began rationalizing what he had seen. As I certainly knew by now, this was a common reaction to mystical events. "Anyhow, people do amazing things in a state of religious ecstasy. Piercing their bodies without bleeding, walking on hot coals, playing with venomous serpents, speaking in tongues . . . How religious is Lopez?"

This question seemed to interest Max, who looked at me with pert curiosity.

"I'm not sure," I admitted, never having discussed the subject seriously with him. "I get the impression that his family is religious, and I know he practices the faith to some extent."

"There! You see?" Jeff seemed satisfied.

"Oh, come on," I said. "His attending Mass once a week does not explain what happened tonight."

"Whatever. And as long as he's all right when he wakes up, I don't really—" Jeff's cell phone rang. "Hey, maybe this is Puma calling, wondering where we are." He pulled the phone out of his pocket and checked the LCD panel. He looked surprised when he saw the caller's name. "Oh! *Finally.*" He met our gazes as he answered the phone and said, "Frank. Thanks for calling me back—after I left you at least five messages."

Max sat up straighter, listening to Jeff's side of the conversation with alert interest. I ceased stroking Lopez's silky hair and clutched his shoulder anxiously, watching Jeff.

"What? Huh? Calm down. What are you talking about?" Jeff frowned. "Tried to *kill* you? Oh, come on."

I gasped. Max hopped off the bed and stood staring at Jeff, his face creased with concern.

"Slow down," Jeff said. "I can't understand . . . The cops? No, course I didn't . . . What are you *talking* about?" His gaze shifted to Lopez. "Er, was the police detective Latino by any chance? Oh, just guessing." Jeff covered the receiver and said irritably to me, "Esther, the next time you sic him on a friend of mine, maybe you should tell me?"

"I didn't *sic* him on Frank, I was worried about—"

"You're not saying this *cop* tried to kill you, are you?" Jeff said into the phone. "Then what are you . . . Uh-huh. Uh-huh . . ." Jeff's puzzled expression transformed into shock. *"What?"*

"What happened?" I asked in alarm.

Jeff shushed me. "When? And he . . . Uh-huh. But, Frank, are you *sure?* Was it definitely . . . Okay. Yes, I believe you . . . No, I don't know, either. Listen, where are you now? Because I'm going to come get you, that's why . . . Come get you to *help* you. Calm down."

He winced and held the phone away from his ear for a moment. The he said to Frank, "Listen to me. You can't just wander the streets. I'll come get you and take you somewhere safe . . . I don't know where. I'll think of something."

"My home," Max said promptly. "It's warded. He'll be safe there."

"I'll take you to my friend Max's place," Jeff said into the phone. "It's 'warded,' whatever that means. A good security system, I guess. There is also, I've been told, a big dog there. Uh-huh . . . Okay. We'll be there as soon as possible. In the meantime, I *beg* you to try to calm down, Frank."

Jeff ended the call and stared at his phone with a puzzled frown.

"Well?" I asked. "What happened?" When he didn't move or respond, I prodded, "Jeff?"

"This isn't good." His expression was serious and bewildered.

"*What* isn't good?"

He looked from me to Max, then said, "Biko just tried to murder Frank."

19

"What?" I said.

"I know this sounds insane, but, uh . . ." Jeff spread his hands helplessly. "Frank says that the same young guy who helped him when he was attacked Monday night broke into his apartment a little while ago, armed with a sword, and tried to kill him."

"What?" I repeated, unable to think of anything else to say.

"It's what Frank said."

"Did Biko speak?" Max asked. "Did he give a reason for his behavior?"

"Frank said he didn't talk at all. Just broke down the door and came in slashing."

"What was Biko's demeanor?" Max asked.

"Frank didn't say, but does it really matter?" said Jeff. "Biko just tried to *kill* a guy."

"Max," I said, aghast, "what do we do now? Should we call the police?"

"Probably not a good idea," Jeff said. "At least, not until Frank calms down. Lopez paid him a visit out of the blue, only a few hours before this attack, so now Frank thinks the cops are in on it."

"In on *what?*" I asked.

"I have no idea," Jeff said wearily. "Frank sounds hysterical. Barely coherent."

"Max, what's going *on?*" I asked, my hand still clutching Lopez's shoulder.

"Without more information, it is impossible to be certain. Therefore, Jeffrey, we must go collect Mr. Johnson immediately and take him to safety."

"I guess I'm the one who got him into this by asking him to take over some of my workshops at the foundation," Jeff said with a sigh. "So whatever 'this' is, I suppose I'd better help him get out of it."

I followed the two men out of the bedroom, shocked enough by this development to take my eyes off Lopez for a few moments. "I don't understand. What is Biko *doing?*"

"Let's call him and find out," Jeff said, pulling out his cell phone again.

Had Lopez been right after all? Was Biko a danger to the community, roaming the streets with a sword in search of someone to punish for the death of his dog? I couldn't understand what was happening. An unexplained attack on a frightened mundane seemed totally out of character for the intelligent, responsible young fencer.

There must be some sort of monumental misunderstanding. This just didn't make any sense!

Jeff shook his head and disconnected his call. "Biko's not answering."

"I'll try to reach him, too," I said.

"Good," said Jeff. "Maybe if we tag team him, we'll get a hold of him. I'm going to call Puma, too. If anyone can bring that kid to his senses, it's her. Right now, she's probably still at the ceremony, but she'll check her messages later."   .

"Puma!" I said suddenly. "We haven't seen her all night! And she would realize how confused we are by what just happened to Lopez. She would help us."

Jeff said impatiently, "We need to put Lopez on the back burner and—"

"Jeff, where was Puma?" I said, the truth suddenly clear to me. *"Not there."*

"Of course she was there. She's the one who told me *I'd* better be there, or . . ." Jeff's eyes widened as he realized what I was saying. "Oh, *shit.* You mean she's missing? *That's* why we didn't see her in the hounfour?"

"She wasn't at the service!" I said. "She dashed out of the training room—"

"Because you had upset her," Jeff pointed out.

"—and we haven't seen her since," I said. "Biko left the room a minute or two behind her, and we haven't see him since, either."

"You think something's happened to Puma?" Jeff said, alarmed.

"If something did," I said, "it would explain Biko going berserk."

"I'm calling her." Jeff dialed and held the phone to his ear.

There was a standard amount of friction and exasperation between the Garland siblings, but it was obvious they were close. Moreover, Biko had been the man of the family virtually all his life and, especially now with his mother dead, he obviously took his role as Puma's protector very seriously. I had no doubt that he was capable of rash acts and violence if he thought his sister was in danger.

Jeff frowned and shook his head. "I'm getting her voice mail." He left a message for Puma, saying we were worried about her safety and Biko's whereabouts and asking her to call him immediately. When he hung up, he said to me, "But I don't get it. How would Puma being in trouble explain Biko attacking *Frank?* Puma and Frank have never even met."

"I have no idea why one thing might have led to the other," I said. "So you need to go find Frank."

"Esther is right," said Max. "We must get a clear account of events from Mr. Johnson."

"Lots of luck with that," Jeff muttered. "Did I mention the word *hysterical?*"

They left to go find Frank. I watched from my window as they walked rapidly away from the building, heading toward Tenth Avenue, where they would hail a cab. (Poor Max, I thought. He'd been in a lot of moving vehicles lately.) Max was clutching his straw hat to keep it from flying off his head, and I noticed some paper garbage tumbling madly across the street. It was getting really windy out there. I hoped that meant the heat would break soon.

I went back into the bedroom to resume my vigil beside Lopez. Sitting on a chair in the corner of the room, I picked up my phone, called Biko, and left an urgent message on his voice mail. Then, with nothing else to do, I called Puma, too. No answer, of course. Where *was* she?

I felt a deep sense of dread as I recalled how trusting of the mambo she was.

Looking at Lopez's slack, motionless body, I tried to take comfort from Max's conviction that the mambo was not responsible for his condition.

If my former almost-boyfriend had been asleep instead of passed out, I would have appreciated this quiet time alone together, as he lay peacefully on my bed while I got to look at him all I wanted, without interruption or arguments. With his body sprawled out in unconscious surrender, his smooth torso exposed by his open shirt, and his face innocent and serene, he would look irresistibly tempting to me under almost any other circumstances. But given the events that had led to his current condition, a heavy weight of fear sat on my chest every moment that I gazed at him now. I knew I wouldn't breathe easily—let alone be able to spare serious attention for Biko, Puma, and Frank—until and unless Lopez awoke and seemed all right.

I wondered again if I should get him to a hospital. I wondered what he would want me to do. I recalled Max's and Jeff's arguments against seeking medical care for him, and I decided to wait. Despite my anxiety and Lopez's oblivion, he didn't seem ill or endangered. So I would give him a little more time to come out of this on his own.

The phone rang, startling me.

Lopez heard it. His head turned and he gave a faint grunt of irritation. His face creased momentarily with a slight frown. I watched him tensely, hoping he'd wake up.

"Lopez?" I prodded.

Still nothing. He just lay there.

I sighed in disappointment and picked up the phone on the next ring. It was Jeff calling to say that Frank wasn't at the arranged meeting place. Jeff had just phoned him to find out why. It turned out that, while waiting for Jeff and Max, Frank had panicked, believing he was being watched or followed, and he had fled into the night.

"Was he *always* this high strung?" I asked.

"I don't really know him that well," said Jeff. "But cut him a little slack, Esther. Someone just tried to kill him."

"That's no reason to go all to pieces," I said critically.

"Anyhow, new plan," Jeff said. "I don't want to spend all night chasing Frank around Manhattan. And Max is worried about his dog—I guess she wasn't feeling so good today—and wants to check on her. So I gave Max's address to Frank. We're going to go there and wait for him."

"Do you think he'll show up?" I asked.

"I'm not sure. But he's scared out of his wits, and we're offering to help him. So I think so." Then he asked, "How's the sleeping detective?"

My gaze slid back to the body on the bed. "Oh, he's still . . ." I gasped when I realized his eyes were open and looking at me. "He's awake! I'll talk to you later."

I ended the call and lowered the phone. My heart pounding and my gaze fixed on Lopez, I was scarcely even aware of the phone hitting the floor as it slid out of my slack grasp.

"Lopez?" I said anxiously.

Lying absolutely still, his black lashes fluttered as he looked around for a moment, taking in what he could see from his current position. His voice sounded normal, though puzzled, when he said, "This is your place."

"Lopez!" I said with relief, realizing he was back. I leaped out of my chair and moved to sit beside him on the bed. I seized one of his hands and held it between both of mine. "How do you feel?"

He turned his head a little on the pillow to meet my eyes as his hand returned my eager grasp. He looked sleepy and confused. "How did I get here? I was . . . in the basement of the foundation, and we were . . ." He closed his eyes, obviously trying to gather his thoughts. "You wanted to leave . . ."

"How do you feel?" I repeated.

"Fine." He opened his eyes to meet my gaze again. "Um, a little tired, I guess. What happened? How did I get here?"

"We brought you here."

"We?"

"Max and Jeff helped me."

He frowned. "Why?"

"Because I couldn't get you here on my own. You were unconscious."

His frown deepened. I could see him trying to remember what had happened tonight. "I've been *unconscious?*"

"You've been dead to the world for . . ." I glanced at the bedside clock. "Almost two hours."

"What the hell happened?" He started to sit up, then winced and put a hand on his head. *"Ow."*

"Do you feel hungover?" I asked, thinking about all the rum he had downed at the ceremony.

"What? No, of course not." He made a gesture indicating he wanted help sitting up. Once in an upright position, he swung his legs over the side of the bed and took a few deep, steadying breaths. "Oh, no wonder you asked that. Jesus, I smell like a barrel of rum, don't I?" Then he put his hand on his head again. "Agh."

"You're sure you're not hungover?" I asked again, doubtfully.

"I'm sure. Someone hit me on the head." He took my hand and put it against his scalp. I felt the slight lump there.

"Oh!" I realized guiltily how he'd gotten it. "Sorry."

He looked even more confused. *"You* hit me?"

"Not exactly."

I was surprised to realize that he seemed completely sober. Even with Max's assurances that he wouldn't have alcohol poisoning, I had assumed he would be very drunk—or at least hungover—when he finally regained consciousness. I realized now that when Max had said there would be no ill effects, he'd meant *none*.

I asked, "What's the last thing you remember?"

"Uh . . ." Still rubbing his aching head, he thought about it. "I was going to take you outside to find a cab, but then . . . Oh, *right*. That idiot woman started throwing gunpowder into the brazier in a closed room full of people. So I went to stop her, and . . . and . . ." He shook his head. "That's it. I don't remember anything else." Looking down at the burn marks scattered across his khaki pants, Lopez touched one and said, "I must have been standing too close to the next explosion, and I got knocked out. That must be when I got this bump on my head, huh?"

"Um, actually—"

"But why do I stink of rum? Did someone pour a bottle over me thinking it would wake me up?"

"You won't like what I'm about to tell you," I said.

"In that case," he said with weary resignation, "I should probably pull myself together first." He slid off the bed and stood up.

"Wait." I was a little worried about him being on his feet only moments after regaining consciousness. "Are you *sure* you feel okay?"

Looking fairly normal, albeit tired, he said, "Yeah. Actually, for someone who was knocked out for two hours, I feel surprisingly good. But, uh, I need to get cleaned up."

"Okay."

He was familiar with my apartment, so he went down the hall, through the living room, and closed the bathroom door behind him. I sat on the bed with my chin in my hands, relieved that he seemed to be all right—and wondering exactly how much to tell him.

Everything, I decided. I should probably tell him everything.

He had made quite an impression at the Vodou ceremony. People were bound to talk about what had happened tonight. And I didn't think Lopez would want to find out about his possession trance from a stranger or a suspect; he should hear about it from me. He still wouldn't like it, but it was better than his getting broadsided by someone else who'd seen him dancing half-naked around a Vodou altar with a bottle of rum and a fistful of hot coals.

Meanwhile, Puma was probably in danger, Biko was trying to kill Frank Johnson, and we thought the bokor had murdered Darius. With lives at stake, it seemed like it was time to pony up and tell Lopez what I knew, even though he wouldn't like that, either.

He finished his ablutions and returned to the bedroom, using a hand towel to dry off his neck and face. Then he towel-dried the front of his hair, which was dripping a little. Still slightly damp, but now looking surprisingly bright-eyed and bushy-tailed, he stood in the doorway and smiled at me as I sat on the bed.

"Thanks for helping me out tonight," he said. "Thanks to Max and Jeff, too. I guess they left after they carried me in here?"

His shirt still hung open and, staring at him as he stood in the doorway of my bedroom, I forgot what I had intended to say. So I just nodded dumbly.

He stared, too. After a long moment, he started to speak, stopped, cleared his throat, and tried again. "There's something we have to talk about, but I can't remember what."

"Maybe the bump on your head made you forget?"

My voice was husky, and my heart was starting to beat harder. Since meeting him, after all, I had thought often of him being in this room with his chest naked and his gaze pinning me to the bed.

"No . . ." he said slowly, his voice soft. "I don't think it's . . . my head." He took a breath. "We shouldn't be in your bedroom."

"Where should we be?" I asked.

"You shouldn't be on the bed."

"Okay." I slid off the bed, joined him by the door, and looked up at him. "Is this better?"

His black lashes were wet and spiky, his blue eyes intense as his gaze moved over my face. "Um . . ."

Lopez started breathing harder as he dropped the towel and lowered his head toward mine.

His phone rang, startling me. He froze, scant inches away from kissing me. I could tell from his conflicted expression that he was going to have to take the call. I started to back away from him, but his arm slid around my waist, stopping me.

His gaze locked with mine as he fumbled in his pocket for his cell. "This'll just take a second." He flipped open the phone and said, "Lopez."

I leaned against him and slid my arms around him, feeling his naked skin under my palms and the warmth of his bare chest seeping through my cotton dress. I also felt him stiffen with surprise as he listened to his caller, his dazed, heavy-lidded expression suddenly growing alert.

"When?" he said. "And you're sure it's him? Uh-huh. Okay." Looking at me with obvious regret, he said, "Yeah, I'm on my way."

I sighed with disappointment as he hung up and slipped the phone back into his pocket. "Police business?"

"I'm sorry," Lopez whispered. He pressed his forehead against mine, his hands caressing my arms. "I've got to go."

I made an involuntary sound of protest and kissed him. He kissed me back.

"No, really, I've got to go," he breathed against my mouth, starting to sound dazed again. "They didn't even want to call me."

"Hmm?" I inhaled scent of his skin, still tinged with rum, and nuzzled his neck.

He tilted his head back and tightened his hold on me. "If I don't go, they'll use it as an excuse to . . . to lock me out of . . . Mmm."

"Out of?" I breathed into his ear.

"What? Oh." His hands were on my back, searching for the zipper of my dress. "Out of the case."

"It's on the side." Our lips met again as I tugged on his hand to show him where to unfasten my dress.

Lopez started kissing my neck—then he coughed a little. He gave up on my zipper and raised both hands to the back of my neck to untie the thin brown string that held my gris-gris pouch in place. "Okay, the bag of peppered frog toes has to go. How can you wear this thing?"

"No, leave it." I reached up to move one of his hands back to my zipper.

"Esther . . ."

I kissed him again, getting things back on track. He made a sound low in his throat and got serious about what we were doing.

Until he sneezed. Then he gave a resigned sigh, still holding me tightly, and whispered, "I have to go."

"What case is so important?" I grumbled as I pushed his shirt aside and nibbled on his shoulder.

"What?" he said faintly, his hands moving to my bottom.

I brushed his lips with mine. "The case."

"I don't . . . Oh! The *case.* Right. No. Esther, no. Stop that. Stop right now!" Breathing hard and laughing, he was simultaneously kissing me and trying to push me away. "I'll be dropped off the case like a bag of cement if I don't show up now that they've found one of the bodies."

"Bodies?" Startled, I pulled away to look at him.

"Oops. Sorry." He smiled wryly and touched my cheek. "I guess I'm not so good at pillow talk, huh?"

"What bodies?" I had a feeling I knew.

"Those four bodies that disappeared from the same cemetery where Darius Phelps was buried," he said, smoothing my hair away from my face. "One of them just turned up."

20

"Whoa! They found a body?" I asked, stunned by this news.

"Yeah."

"How could they have found a body?"

"It washed up in Queens." He was watching me intently now. "They figure the body snatcher dumped it in the river."

I couldn't understand what this meant. Why wasn't the dead guy a zombie? How could he just be an ordinary corpse? Had something gone wrong? Had the bokor lost control of the reanimated slave? Or was Max's theory wrong?

If so, then . . . "Where are the others?"

"We haven't found them yet." Lopez prodded, "Esther? Is there something you ought to tell me?"

"Which one did you find?" I asked.

"The guy with the head injury. Why?"

"Was it the head injury?" I wondered. Had it made him unsuitable zombie material?

"Was *what* the head injury?" Lopez asked.

But why would the injury matter? Presumably all the corpses were damaged in some way, after all. Darius had died of a ruptured intestine, and that hadn't prevented the bokor from turning *him* into a zombie.

"Maybe I'm looking at this wrong," I realized.

"Oh?" Lopez's hands were on his hips, and he was studying me with dark suspicion.

"Did this person die before Darius?" I asked.

"He died before any of the others."

"He was the first one to die?" I said. "So maybe *that's* it! Was he the first one to go missing, too?"

"We're not sure yet." Lopez took me by the shoulders and said firmly, "What's going on?"

"If he *was* the first one, then maybe it didn't work out," I said. "Maybe the bokor hadn't really figured out how to do it yet!" It made sense that there might be experiments—and failures. No one was *born* knowing how to raise a zombie from the grave, after all. It was a learned skill.

"Do *what?*" Lopez said impatiently. "And what's the bokor?"

I met his gaze and realized we still did have to talk.

"You're not going to like this," I said.

"I really, really believe that," he said. "Go on."

"Okay. Here goes. And just remember, you *asked* me to tell you this." I took a breath. "I did see Darius Phelps that night. He was raised from the grave by the bokor— that's a dark sorcerer—who's menacing Harlem. Darius is a zombie now."

There was a long pause.

"A zombie," Lopez said at last. "Now why didn't *I* think of that?"

Ignoring his tone, I explained, "That's why there was no blood when his hand was torn off. Zombies don't bleed."

"Ah." He shrugged. "That explains it, then."

I decided just to keep going. "Somehow or other, Darius broke away from the bokor's control and was

wandering the streets that night. The creatures that attacked him are baka. They're deadly little monsters who
do the bokor's bidding. They killed Biko Garland's dog,
and they've been terrorizing Harlem by night."

"I see."

"The night I saw them, they'd been sent to retrieve
Darius. We're not sure—"

"We?"

"Max and I."

"Of course."

"We're not sure what happened to Darius after I was
arrested, but no one has seen him since. And zombies
aren't exactly stealthy, if left to their own devices. So I
think the bokor probably regained control of him while
I was in jail."

"Tough break."

"He's probably under wraps somewhere, at least
most of the time, with the other zombies."

"Yes, probably."

"Anyhow, we're not sure why yet, but the bokor is
raising an army of zombies. Well, a small team of them,
anyhow. I guess five zombies—four, now that you've
found a discarded body—doesn't really count as an
army. But there may be more that we don't know about.
You haven't had time to investigate every cemetery in
the tristate area, after all."

I fell silent, unable to keep going in the face of his
carefully blank expression.

After a long moment, he asked very calmly, "Is that
all?"

"No, there's more." I added, "I was just waiting for,
um, your reaction."

"Reaction? I see." He nodded. "You want a reaction."

"Or I could just tell you the rest," I said in a rush,
sensing the storm was about to break.

"No, no. You want me to *react?* Okay," he said. "How's *this* for a reaction? You know why I had to give you up? This! Right here! THIS! *This* is exactly why I had to stop seeing you! This lunatic, crazy, nutbag garbage of Max's that you swallow hook, line, and sinker!"

"I haven't *swallowed*—"

"A little eccentricity is one thing—in fact, I *like* that you're different. I liked it the night we first met, when you were covered in green body paint and had just destroyed an expensive stage prop with a hammer because you were trying to help someone. I liked it the night I had to get you out of jail because you'd tried to assist an assault victim while you were dressed like a hooker."

"I—"

"But you always go too far, Esther! *Way* too far. You're going to get yourself killed!" Lopez said. "Or *Max* is going to get you killed! And other people will get hurt—or worse—because of both of you!"

The unfairness of that last comment made me angry. "Other people's lives have been *saved* because—"

"I'm not doing this, Esther!" He looked like his head hurt again. "What man in his right mind would fall for a woman who actually *believes* the things that you say to me?"

I tried to calm down. "Okay, this is more of a reaction that I was really looking for. Maybe we should both—"

"Has Max got you out there hunting zombies by night? Are you running around Harlem after dark with an armed teenager and a lunatic old man who's giving you God only knows *what* kind of hallucinogenic drugs to feed these bizarre fantasies?"

"Oh, for God's sake! Max is *not* drugging—"

"I'm warning you right now," he said. "Don't expect me to write more false reports and lie to more cops when I find you and Max knee-deep in missing corpses. I won't keep covering up for you!"

"I'm not asking—"

"And who's watching your back while you're skulking around looking for a body snatcher?" he demanded. "How am I supposed to protect you when you lie to me about what you're doing?"

"I haven't lied," I protested. "I just left out some things. And *this* is exactly why! Just *look* at the way you're behaving now that I've told you!"

"Stop right there," he snapped. "No way is this fight *my* fault!"

"All right, look, I know how crazy it all sounds. Okay? I *do*. And I knew how you'd react. Well, I didn't know you'd be quite this *loud*," I said critically. "But I was pretty sure you'd react badly. And you have."

"You're talking about a sorcerer raising zombies from the grave!" he shouted. "Of course I'm reacting badly!"

"You need to calm down," I said firmly. "There's more that I have to tell you, and I can't talk to you when you're like this."

"No," he said. "*No*. I don't want to hear anymore. Not unless the next words out of your mouth are that you'll end your friendship with Max and submit to drug testing."

I ignored this and said, "What do you think sent Frank Johnson over the edge? He was attacked by the baka!"

"You've been talking to—" His dark brows swooped down. "Oh, Jesus, Esther! You used *me* to find that poor deranged guy?"

"No! I just wanted you to make sure he wasn't dead!" I said. "I was worried about his safety, because I think Darius Phelps was murdered!"

"Well, at least that's one thing you and I can agree on," Lopez said irritably.

"Really?"

"But I'll never prove it."

"Because Darius was killed by a voodoo curse?" I said.

"No, Esther," Lopez said with forced patience. "Because the body is missing."

"Oh! Right."

"And even if I find it, it'll probably be too contaminated by then for forensics to get good evidence." His shoulders sagged. "Maybe there wasn't any evidence, anyhow. That's probably why the hospital is convinced Darius died strictly of natural causes. But *I* don't believe it." He took my shoulders between his hands, and his grip was hard, making me wince a little. "Listen to me. I don't want you going back to the foundation."

"You think the killer is there?"

"And I especially don't want you hunting zombies by night in Harlem."

"But something is coming! Something very dangerous! Why else would the bokor raise zombies and—"

"Stop talking." His expression was angry again. "Just *stop.*"

"That's why the community held the ceremony tonight!" I said. "Because of the dark magic that someone's working in Harlem!"

"*Enough,*" he said.

"No, *listen* to me! At the ritual, you—"

His mouth came down on mine. I was surprised enough to struggle. He gripped me tighter and kissed me harder, his mouth ruthless and punishing. And I realized I didn't *want* to struggle. I surrendered to the angry strength of his arms and the cruel pressure of his mouth. Surrendered and begged for more, kissing him back with all the pent up hunger of the past few months. Where had he *been?* He should have been here all along, damn him.

I had tried so hard not to think about him. Not to imagine *this.* I had failed over and over.

"You should have been here," I said, clinging to him.

"Don't talk," he insisted, his breathing harsh and fast now.

"But—" I grunted in surprised pain when he sank his teeth into my lower lip. Then he soothed my bruised mouth with a long, hot, wet kiss as his hands tangled in my hair, holding my head still for his plunder.

His rum-scented breath clouded my mind as he whispered against my mouth, "No more talking."

He shrugged out of his shirt and dropped it on the floor, still kissing me.

"No more talk," I said with difficulty. Then I gasped as he roughly tore open the zipper on the side of my dress, ruining it. "Oh!"

Instead of apologizing, he knocked me down onto the bed, falling heavily with me. My head was reeling dizzily as his weight pinned me to the mattress and his mouth came down on mine once again.

My eyes suddenly stung, and my nose tickled. Lopez drew his head back and coughed a little.

"Oh, for God's sake," he muttered as he realized what was irritating his senses.

His expression dark with impatience, he grabbed the thin string that was around my neck, yanked it so hard the knot snapped and broke, and tossed the gris-gris pouch across the room. Then he kissed me with rough insistence.

He had never touched me like this before. Out of his head. Not tempering his strength. Not worrying about whether he hurt me. Leaving bruises and teeth marks that would be visible on my skin in the morning.

I clutched his naked shoulders and arched against him as he punished me with his passion and tried to make me regret pushing him this far. As my legs embraced his hips, he pulled up my skirt, tugging on the material until a seam gave way and tore. Then his hands were on my bare thighs, and I didn't care that this dress was in tatters by now.

His back was smooth and warm, flexing with supple muscles. His silky black hair tickled my neck and shoulders as he shoved aside the straps of my dress and feasted on my skin. His belt buckle pressed sharply into my belly, hurting me. I made a sound of protest and reached for it. He grabbed both my arms and pinned them on either side of my head, then kissed me again.

I thought I would faint from lack of air—and I didn't care. I clutched him tighter between my thighs, yearning for everything he could give me. Burning for him. Heat flowed over me and consumed me.

His grip on my wrists was hard enough to hurt. The rum that lingered on his tongue was making me feel drunk. His weight on my chest and his hot kisses made it impossible to breathe. When he lifted his head and looked down at me, I gasped for air and tore my hand out of his grip so that I could reach for his belt buckle. The metal burned my fingers, making me gasp and jerk my hand away. Then he kissed me again, incinerating all other sensation.

Wrestling against the mindless grip of my legs, he rose to his knees, breathing hard, his chest pumping in and out, his lips wet and swollen from our kisses. When I tried to sit up, he shoved me back down, carelessly rough, his eyes glinting with challenge, his dark golden skin gleaming in the lamplight. His gaze stayed locked with mine as he unbuckled his belt.

I was burning for him. On fire for him. Heat licked at my skin. The bed was hot, my body engulfed in fire, the sheets awash in it ...

The dark, angry passion in his face transformed into shock as the bed burst into flames all around us.

"Esther!"

In one fluid motion, Lopez grabbed me, rolled off the

bed, and threw me bodily across the room as he tumbled across the floor. Then he was on feet and hauling me up into his arms while I was still reeling from the fall. Half dragging and half carrying me, he got me out of the burning bedroom and down the hall before I understood what was happening.

"Fire extinguisher!" he shouted.

"Wh–what?"

He seized my shoulders, shook me, and shouted into my face, breaking through my shock with sheer volume, "Where's the fire extinguisher?"

"*Oh.* Oh!" I tried to think. "Ki–ki—" I was shaking with reaction and could barely make my lips move. "Kitch—"

"Kitchen?" When I nodded, he shoved me toward the front door. "Go warn your neighbors! Then get out of the building!" He went into the kitchen and found the fire extinguisher. When he saw me just standing there, he shouted, *"Go!"*

I knew his instructions were sensible and that I should do what he told me. But I couldn't leave him alone in my burning apartment. I just *couldn't.* Even knowing that it was stupid and would make him angry, I followed him into the bedroom.

The bed was on fire, robust yellow flames rising from the mattress as if someone had tossed a firebomb into the sheets. Lopez sprayed the bed with foam from the extinguisher and—to my immense relief—the fire was doused within moments.

The room filled with smoke. I started choking. In the hall, the smoke alarm was shrieking. Waving my hand in front of my face, I stumbled across the bedroom to open the window.

Lopez was breathing hard, coughing, and staring at the bed in appalled amazement. As if for good measure, he aimed the extinguisher at it again and covered the blackened, smoking wreck with a thick film of white foam. Then he looked around the room to make sure nothing else needed dousing.

I dragged a chair into the hallway, climbed up onto it, and silenced the shrieking smoke alarm overhead. Then I opened my front door and went out into the stairwell, where I assured several neighbors who were emerging from their apartments that things were under control and they didn't need to evacuate the building. I reentered my apartment and opened my remaining windows. A robust wind blew into the living room, and I realized with relief that the stifling heat wave was breaking at last—and that this wind would help clear the apartment of smoke pretty quickly.

Lopez came out of my bedroom, still carrying the fire extinguisher. I realized my legs were shaking, and I sat down suddenly. He sat nearby.

There was a long moment of stunned silence as we sat there, catching our breath and waiting for our hearts to stop pounding.

Finally, I got up and poured two glasses of cold water. He accepted the water with absentminded thanks as I sat back down.

He drained his glass, then said, "Did Jeff or Max smoke when they were here tonight?"

"No. They don't smoke."

"Have *you* started smoking?" he asked.

"No."

"Has anyone who smokes been in that bed?"

"No. I mean, that's none of your business. I mean . . ." I shook my head and tried to pull myself together. "Why are you asking?"

"A smoldering cigarette in the sheets is the most logical explanation for what just happened," he said. "I think."

"Oh."

"But if no one's been smoking in your bed . . ."

"Yes?" I said.

"I suppose something must be wrong with the mattress. I mean *really* wrong."

"Bad manufacturing?" I said in a daze. "Flammable materials?"

He nodded. "And spontaneous combustion. Maybe because of, um, unaccustomed friction."

Our eyes met, and I recalled what we'd been doing in that bed when it had burst into flames. I suddenly felt my skin flush.

I cleared my throat and said like a reasonable adult, "Should I call the fire department?"

"No. The fire's out." He pulled his phone out of his pocket. "But I'm going to get an arson investigator over here. We'll find out exactly what happened."

When he finished his call, he said, "I'm sorry, Esther. It's Sunday night. Since this isn't an emergency, tomorrow is the soonest someone will come."

"I can sleep on the couch," I said, as if this were the most important consideration in the life of a person whose bed had just inexplicably burst into flames while she and a man were in it together.

"We need to take that mattress outside. I don't think it'll catch fire again, but since it shouldn't have caught fire in the first place, I don't want it in this apartment all night." He glanced at a text message on his phone. "Then I've got to get my ass out to Queens right away, or I'm off this case." He looked at me. "And all that crap about zombies and bakers notwithstanding—"

"Bokors," I corrected. "And there's only one."

"Whatever," he said. "I want to know what happened to those bodies. More to the point, I want to find whoever scared you half to death in the street that night, stole your purse, and left a severed hand lying around."

Max wanted to find that person, too. But I decided this wasn't a propitious moment to point that out.

In the silence that followed his statement, Lopez seemed to realize he was barefoot and shirtless. He rose to his feet, went into the bedroom, and came out a minute later, wearing his sandals and buttoning his shirt—which looked undamaged by what had just happened.

While he finished fastening his buttons and then tucked the garment into his pants, he said, "It's not too bad, Esther. There's not as much damage in the bedroom as you'd expect. After the arson investigator is done, a new bed and a coat of paint should put things back in shape. You'll probably have to wash all your clothes, though. Smoke gets into fabric."

I sighed wearily and reflected that it was a good thing I'd be getting a paycheck for a week's work in television soon. I couldn't have afforded to replace my bed otherwise.

"Hey." Lopez touched my arm gently. "Are you okay?"

Still seated, I nodded. "Yeah. Just . . . you know. Still stunned."

He leaned over me and kissed my forehead. Then he whispered, "I meant . . . I was so rough. Before."

"So rough you made my bed explode," I grumbled.

He smiled down at me. "Come on. I'll need some help to get that mattress out of that room."

As I rose to my feet, I said resentfully, "Thanks to you, it seems like I'm spending my whole night hauling around heavy objects."

He was willing to do most of the work, and that suited me fine. It was only a double mattress, not queen-size, which made it a little easier to maneuver out of the room, through the apartment, and down the narrow stairs. Outside, we propped it against the stone side of the building, well away from anyone's window. Then

Lopez came back upstairs with me so he could write a notice in thick black marker to warn everyone but the arson investigator away from the ruined mattress.

While he did that, I went back into the bedroom to survey the wreckage with calmer eyes now. Lopez was right; it wasn't as bad as I had feared. At least half the room would need repainting, but the damage had otherwise been limited to the mattress and the bedclothes. I touched my hair and realized how lucky I was that it hadn't caught fire. Or my clothing. There were soot marks on my dress and my skin, but nothing worse. I ran my hands over my body, recognizing for the first time that I hadn't been burned or even singed. Lopez had moved very fast when it happened.

He stuck his head in the doorway. "I've got to go to work now. And figure out how to explain, when I get there, why I smell like a rum distillery tonight." He hesitated. "Are you going to be all right?"

I was looking around the room, still surprised there wasn't more damage. "Yeah, fine," I said absently.

"God, I hate leaving you like this," he said. "Right after a fire and . . . And everything."

That was when I saw it. I gasped in horror and fell back a step, realizing what this meant. What had happened.

"What's wrong?" He was at my side instantly, his hands on my shoulders, looking around the room, trying to see what had just frightened me into such a reaction.

I started shaking. My wide, unblinking eyes were fixed on it, unable to look away.

"Esther?" He shook me gently. "What is it? Tell me."

My throat worked, but only guttural sounds came out. I had no idea how to put it into words anyhow. How to explain to him, of all people, what I had just recognized.

So I pointed in dumbfounded silence.

His gaze followed my gesture, but he was still perplexed. "What? What do you see?"

I took a few sharp, quick breaths, trying to steady myself. Then I crossed the room, stooped down, and picked up the gris-gris pouch that lay on the floor.

He was staring at me, bewildered by my behavior.

I clutched the protective charm to my chest and looked at him.

"Esther?" His voice was puzzled.

I tried to explain. "You took it off me and threw it away. And then the bed burst into flames."

He stood staring silently at me, a baffled frown on his face, trying to work out what I meant.

Then he got it, and his expression changed completely. "Oh, for God's sake! You can't be serious!"

"The bokor took things from my purse," I said.

"A voodoo curse from an evil sorcerer? Come *on,* Esther."

"Personal things! Strands of my hair. Makeup that I use every day." I clutched the gris-gris pouch. "And the *moment* this protective charm was removed from my body . . ."

Looking exasperated beyond endurance, he started to speak—then changed his mind, closed his eyes, and seemed to be counting to ten, willing himself to be calm.

When he opened his eyes again, he was looking at me the way I imagined he looked at petty criminals who were their own worst enemies. "The arson investigator will give us a rational explanation for what just happened, and then maybe you'll come to your senses. In the meantime . . ." He sighed. "I obviously can't leave you here alone. So I guess you'd better pack a few things and—"

"No," I said as I tied the gris-gris bag around my neck. "I have to go see Max." If the bokor was so determined to kill me that my *bed* had exploded in flames, then I wanted to make sure I was adequately protected against whatever might be coming next.

Lopez closed his eyes again. After a moment, he let out his breath. "Fine." He'd evidently run out of energy or will to keep fighting with me about this. "Fine. Let's go. I've got a crime scene to get to."

He was too much of a gentleman to dash off and leave me to find a cab by myself on Tenth Avenue this late at night, even though I lived here and was often on that street alone after dark. But he avoided my gaze, didn't touch me, and scarcely spoke to me as we left the apartment and walked out to the main avenue.

The wind was high now, and the moonless sky was pitch black. I put a hand on my skirt to hold it down as the wind tugged at it, and my hair blew around my face. I glanced at Lopez. He was brooding and withdrawn, and he scarcely seemed to notice the wind tugging at his collar or slipping inside his shirt to make the fabric billow away from his skin.

We stood together in silence on Tenth Avenue until he saw an available cab and flagged it down. When it pulled up to the curb, he opened the door and waited for me to get in.

As he was about to close the door behind me, I said, "Lopez?"

He leaned over and peered into the cab. His face was in shadow, hiding his expression. Apparently he could see my expression though. He gave in and said with weary kindness, "I'll call you tomorrow."

Since weary kindness was *not* what I wanted from him—now or ever—I said, "No, don't bother."

"Esther—"

"You were right before," I said. "We've done enough talking."

I pulled the door closed and gave the driver Max's address in the West Village. And I resolutely did not look back at the ex-would-be lover who watched the cab pull away from the curb and speed down the windswept avenue.

21

"Holy crap," Jeff said when I walked into the bookstore. "What the hell happened to you?"

"Huh?"

Max, who was sitting at the old walnut table with a man who I assumed was Frank Johnson, rose to his feet, his expression concerned. "Have you been attacked by the baka again?"

"Attacked? Oh, *man!*" Frank said, looking panicky.

I blinked. "No."

Jeff asked, "Did the cop go berserk when he woke up? Did *he* attack you?"

"What?" I looked down at myself and realized for the first time what an alarming picture I presented at first glance. "Oh! Um, no . . ."

The side of my bodice was hanging open, the remnants of the zipper dangling limply. Part of my skirt had been ripped away from my waistband, and the torn seam gaped open loosely over my hip. There were black smudges of soot all over the dress and my arms. Probably on my face, too.

Recalling how I had gotten into this condition, my skin grew hot with embarrassment as I realized that Lopez might well have left telltale marks on my neck and shoulders. I nervously pulled my loose, tangled hair forward over my shoulders, hoping to cover as much as I could of the skin that my sundress left bare.

I said, "The bokor just tried to kill me."

"Oh, no, no, *no!*" Frank was on his feet, looking for an exit.

"Hi, I'm Esther," I said to him.

Max said, "Oh! Pardon me." He made the introductions.

Frank was exactly as Biko had described him: A thin man, not much taller than I, who wore his hair in twists. I sensed that his speaking voice was probably very appealing under less stressful conditions; right now, though, it was strained and a little shrill.

"I gotta get out of this town!" he said.

"Where's Lopez?" Jeff asked in confusion.

"He had to go to a crime scene." I sat down and explained.

Max was less surprised than I had been by the news that one of the missing bodies had been found.

"Mr. Johnson was just telling us that he saw four zombies," Max explained to me.

"Do we *have* to use that word?" Frank said.

"*I* don't see why we have to use it," said Jeff.

Max soldiered on. "Including Darius Phelps, there should be five zombies, based on the information we have from Detective Lopez. Since our companion only saw four, it's possible that one of them was out performing a task at the behest of the bokor at that time. Or that the missing zombie had escaped the bokor's control and fled captivity, as poor Darius later did. But another possibility, of course, was that—"

"That the bokor's first attempt at zombification didn't work," I said. "So now there are four zombies and one incriminating corpse that the bokor had to get rid of."

"Precisely."

Nelli walked slowly up to me, the tip of her long bony tail wagging faintly. She was panting heavily, despite the coolness of the air-conditioned store, and her nose was dry as she poked me with it in feeble greeting.

"Max," I said in shock. "Nelli looks *terrible.*"

"Yes. Only the importance of our meeting with Mr. Johnson—"

"Oh, call me Frank, man."

"—has delayed me from taking her to the all-night clinic for treatment."

I put my hand on the familiar's huge head. "I think she has a fever." I touched her bandaged paw. "Is this infected?"

"I don't believe so," said Max. "Jeffrey and I changed the bandage a little while ago, and it seemed to be healing properly."

I cast Jeff an inquisitive glance, and he nodded in agreement with Max.

Nelli sat down and rested her massive jaw on my thigh, squashing my leg into the hard chair that I sat on. I stroked her ears as I said, "All right, out with it, Frank. Then we have to get Nelli to a vet."

"First things first." Jeff, who liked dogs, sat down next to me and stroked Nelli's back soothingly. "Tell us how the bokor just tried to kill you."

"My bed burst into flames a little while ago," I said. "While I was in it!"

"Oh, *shit,*" said Frank, rocking back and forth. "That does it! I'm leaving New York."

"Where was Detective Lopez?" asked Max.

"He was in the bed, too."

"And you were . . . what?" Jeff said. "Ministering to his wounds? Playing gin rummy? Discussing the Middle East peace process?"

"Okay, fine," I said, feeling my cheeks get hot again. "We had argued, and we were making up."

"In the bed," Jeff said, clearly enjoying my embarrassment.

"Yes."

"And did your dress get torn to shreds during the argument, or was it during the making up?"

"Um, the argument. No, the making up." Wishing the floor would open up and swallow me, I said, "Does it matter?"

"Just trying to get the facts straight." Jeff reached over to me and brushed aside my hair. "Is that a hickey? No, it's *several* hickeys. The boy plays rough, doesn't he?"

"Stop that!" I slapped aside his hand.

"Please continue, Esther," said Max, deliberately assuming his most scientifically detached expression.

"Well, uh . . ." I tried to think of how to phrase it. "The occasion, um, called for the removal of the gris-gris bag."

"Oh, dear," said Max.

"And the bed exploded," I concluded.

"Just like that?" Jeff asked.

"Yes." I touched the pouch that hung around my neck and inhaled its reassuring stink. "Max, will this thing protect me now?"

Jeff said, "Well, have any beds exploded into flames since you put it back on?"

"Shut up," Frank and I said in unison.

Max said to me, "I believe it would be unwise for you to remove the charm again until we have confronted our adversary and gained control of the poppet made in your image."

Frank asked anxiously, "Is there a poppet made in *my* image?"

"Has *your* bed caught fire?" Jeff asked him.

Frank had experienced no ill effects (apart from anxiety, terror, and insomnia) in the time between fleeing Mount Morris Park on Monday night and fleeing his apartment this evening after being attacked by Biko. So Max decided that he was probably not in danger from a voodoo doll.

"Nonetheless," Max said, "it would be advisable for all of us to wear some form of protection. Particularly in view of what happened to Esther and Detective Lopez tonight."

Jeff smirked at me. I ignored him.

"Esther," Max added, "there would also certainly be no harm in our renewing the power of your protective charm."

"In the laboratory?" I guessed.

"Yes. Frank, perhaps you would be so good as to continue your recitation downstairs?"

Frank nodded wearily, and he and Jeff rose to follow Max.

We heard a sudden, piercing wail come from the far side of the shop, followed by the slapping and slamming of rapidly opening and closing doors and drawers.

Frank screamed and hid behind me, his eyes rolling in terror. Jeff looked around for a weapon and grabbed the coffeepot.

"What are you going to do with that?" I took the pot away from him, then said to both men, "Calm down. It's just the possessed cupboard."

"The what?" said Jeff.

"That thing tries my nerves," Max said, proceeding toward the back of the shop and downstairs to the laboratory.

"Come on," I said to Jeff. "I'll show you."

Since Frank was clinging to me for dear life, he came along by default.

Along the far wall of the shop there was a massive, dark, very old wooden cupboard. It had a profusion of drawers and doors, and it was about six feet tall and at least that wide. As I understood it, the cupboard was en-

chanted. Or cursed. Or possessed. Whatever. Anyhow, it
could be dormant and inert for weeks at a time, but then
suddenly, without warning, it would act up again.

At the moment, one of its drawers was opening and
closing repeatedly, while thick smoke and a wailing
scream poured out of it.

"Holy shit," said Jeff.

Frank buried his face against my back and started
sobbing.

"I know it's annoying," I said. "But it's really best just
to ignore it."

I gave Nelli a worried look. She disliked the cupboard and usually barked ferociously at it when it acted
up. But she was just staring at it now with glazed, listless
eyes.

"She needs a vet," I said.

Frank paused in his hysteria long enough to lift his
head and look at the dog. "You're right," he agreed.
"She looks worse now than when I got here."

"Esther?" Max's voice floated up from the cellar.

"Coming!" I called. Then I said to my companions,
"Protective charms first. Then a vet for Nelli."

Jeff said, "I am *not* wearing something like that foul
thing you've got around your neck, Esther."

"Yours won't be nearly this smelly," I assured him,
having no idea whether I was telling the truth. What did
I know about voodoo charms? "The bokor doesn't have
strands of *your* hair, after all."

Nelli gave a little groan and decided to lie down. I
cast her another worried look, then turned toward the
back of the shop. There was a little cul-de-sac there with
some storage shelves, a utility closet, a bathroom, and
a door marked PRIVATE. The door led to a narrow,
creaky stairway.

At the top of the stairs, there was a burning torch
stuck in a sconce on the wall. It emitted no smoke or

heat, only light; and it had been burning steadily ever since I had met Max, fueled by mystical power.

My two companions blinked at it in surprise, but chose not to ask about it.

Instead, Jeff said to me, "So how is Lopez? Alert and sober?"

"Yes."

I began descending the steps. Jeff followed me, and Frank brought up the rear.

"Then he's got amazing recuperative powers." Jeff asked, "Was he freaked out by your burning bed?"

"He was alarmed," I said. "*I'm* the one who was freaked out. Lopez expects an arson investigator to explain it rationally."

"That could happen, you know." When I didn't respond, Jeff said, "So are you two back together now?"

"No. He still thinks I'm deranged."

Apparently my tone discouraged further conversation. Jeff said nothing else. We reached the bottom step in silence.

Max's laboratory was cavernous, windowless, and shadowy. The walls were decorated with charts covered in strange symbols and maps of places with exotic names. Bottles of powders, vials of potions, and dried plants jostled for space on the cluttered shelves. Beakers, implements, and tools lay tumbled and jumbled on the heavy, dark furniture.

Frank momentarily forgot his fears and looked around in wonder. "*Cool.*"

Max was at his workbench, burning incense and chanting quietly as he sprinkled something on the charms he was preparing.

Jars of herbs, spices, minerals, amulets, and neatly assorted kinds of claws and teeth sat on densely packs shelves and in dusty cabinets. There were antique weapons, some urns and boxes and vases, several Tarot decks, some runes, a scattering of old bones, and a Tibetan prayer bowl. An enormous bookcase was packed to overflowing with many leather-bound volumes, as well as unbound manuscripts and scrolls.

. "Man, the set designer for *The Vampyre* should see this place!" said Frank.

"Pardon?" I said, resisting the urge to peer over Max's shoulder.

"*The Vampyre.*" Frank spelled it for us. "A friend of mine works for the producer. It's an off-Broadway show they're mounting for a limited run this season. It's a showcase for that actor from that canceled TV series."

"Off-Broadway? This season?" Jeff asked alertly. "Any parts?"

"Not for a brother, man," Frank said with regret. "It's set in nineteenth-century Europe. All white people." He looked at me. "You know, you might be right for it. They're looking for a couple of actresses in their mid-twenties who fit a historical style."

"What's it called again?" I asked. *"The Vampyre?"*

Frank nodded. "Based on the story by John Polidori."

"Who?" I said.

Jeff looked apologetically at Frank. "She's practically illiterate."

Ignoring Jeff, Frank said, "He was a companion of Lord Byron's."

"Oh," I said. "Hence the historical aspect of the production."

Max ceased chanting and said, "Frank?"

I said to Frank, "And they're auditioning now?"

"In a couple of weeks," he said.

Max said, "Jeffrey?"

"Excellent!" I would make sure Thack got me into that audition.

"Esther?" Max said.

"Yes, Max?"

"The charms are ready to be donned."

"Oh, good."

"You want to keep the charm close to your heart," Max explained to the men.

He uttered an incantation as he slipped a thin leather string over each of their heads, from which the charms hung like pendants. The pouches were smaller than mine. There was a distinctly musty odor coming from them. I decided not to ask what was inside the tiny bags.

"I think I feel safer now." Frank closed his fist over his gris-gris bag, took a deep breath, then smiled. "Yeah! I do feel safer!"

Jeff sniffed his pouch. "I comfort myself with the knowledge that Puma will understand. Speaking of which, I've called her four more times. That Vodou ceremony's got to be over by now." He said anxiously, "She's really missing."

"And her brother's gone insane," Frank said.

I gathered that Jeff had explained to him exactly who had attacked him. I asked Frank to explain to me what had happened this evening. While he did so, Max had me sit next to his workbench, so he could modify my gris-gris bag without removing it from around my neck.

Even firsthand, Frank's story still didn't make any sense. Until joining Jeff and Max in the bookstore tonight, he'd never even heard of Puma, let alone had any contact with her. And his only contact with Biko had been on Monday night, when the young man had rescued him.

Yet tonight, for reasons unknown to anyone, Biko had come to his apartment without warning, broken down his door, and tried to kill him.

"Based on Frank's description of Biko's demeanor," Max said, "I now believe that Biko was possessed at the time."

Frank explained to me, "The kid's eyes didn't blink. His face was frozen in a blank expression. He didn't speak. He didn't react when I threw things at him. Not even when whiskey got in his eyes. It was like he was on autopilot." Frank clutched his gris-gris pouch again. "I figured he was on PCP or something. Possession never occurred to me."

"Max, do you mean spirit possession?" I asked, aghast. "Like what happened to Lopez?"

"No. I believe Biko's condition is a form of possession which is sometimes called the white darkness," Max said gravely. "In the grip of this evil influence, the living can be made to do things they would never do otherwise."

"White darkness," I repeated. "Could the bokor inflict this on someone?"

"It would seem so. And it's such a dangerous thing to do that it convinces me that the crisis must be very near."

"Dangerous for *me*, certainly," Frank said.

"For everyone," said Max. "In the throes of possession, Biko—and Puma, if she has also been enthralled— may do terrible things that, as living people rather than as reanimated corpses, they will have to answer for before the law."

"Oh, *no*," I said, realizing what he meant. "If Frank hadn't gotten away this evening, Biko's life would be ruined. He'd be a murderer!"

"Er, *my* life would be ruined even more," Frank pointed out. "I'd be dead."

"Or you'd be a zombie now," I said absently. "The bokor might not waste such an obvious opportunity to replace the corpse that had to be discarded."

"Okay, this is my body that you're talking about killing and raising from the dead," Frank said to me. "So could you speak with a little more sensitivity, please?"

"Lots of luck with that, man," Jeff said.

"Possessing living beings is also dangerous for the bokor," said Max. "Having raised zombies, created baka, and tormented young Shondolyn, the bokor is expending still more power by controlling Biko—of whom control was perhaps gained by possessing Puma first."

Jeff frowned with concern. "I don't really buy this 'white darkness' thing, Max, but I do agree that Biko would be easy to manipulate by threatening Puma."

"This expenditure of power is costly. It must surely require additional obeisance and offerings to the dark loa whose favor the bokor courts." Max added, "And since Biko and Puma are living beings, with friends and responsibilities, their absence has already been noticed."

"Compared to the corpses, who were probably missing for weeks before anyone noticed," I said, nodding. "So the bokor must be getting desperate! Possessing people who'll be missed almost immediately and whose behavior will have complicated consequences."

"The additional danger," Max said, "is that the bokor will consider Biko and Puma expendable once they have served their purpose, and command them to perform a fatal act."

"Kill themselves?" Jeff said, appalled.

Max nodded. "However, clearly one of the tasks the bokor has assigned to Biko is the murder of Frank."

"Tasks?" Frank repeated. "You're calling my murder a *task* now?"

"With that, er, feat still unaccomplished," Max said, "Biko is presumably not yet expendable. So I believe we have time to rescue him."

"What about Puma?" Jeff demanded.

"Without knowing the purpose for which she was possessed, we cannot be sure," Max said. "But I strongly recommend optimism."

Looking at Jeff's worried expression, I decided not to mention the obvious reason Puma might have been possessed: to make Biko vulnerable. Now that he was under the bokor's command, his sister might indeed be expendable.

"Well, I can at least tell you where to start looking for them," Frank said. "In the basement of that building. That's where I saw the zombies."

"Oh, that's so creepy!" I said. "They've been down there all this time?"

Frank said, "I don't know about 'all this time.' I only know what I saw Monday night."

"What exactly happened that night?" I asked.

Frank began by explaining to us that, in contrast to the negative reaction that most people had to Napoleon, he enjoyed herpetology and was interested in the snake.

"You enjoy *what?*" I asked.

"The study of reptiles and amphibians." He added, "I'm a huge Animal Planet fan."

"Uh-huh."

"But Napoleon's owner is a crazy old bitch on wheels," he said. "You know what I mean?"

"I do," I said.

Mambo Celeste had rebuffed Frank's interest in the snake during the couple of weeks he'd been filling in for Jeff at the foundation. Then on Monday, Frank had stayed late after class, using the classroom as rehearsal space for a new audition monologue he was working on. By the time he was ready to leave, early in the evening, the building was quiet and seemed empty. So he gave in to the temptation to go into the basement and observe the snake in its cage.

"Yuck," I said.

"Snakes are beautiful, Esther," he said earnestly. "You just have to learn how to appreciate them."

"Whatever."

Having learned, during his short time at the foundation, that snakes were revered in Vodou, he also felt some interest in learning more about the faith.

"Mambo Celeste cold-shouldered me about that, too," he said. "But at least Dr. Livingston was happy to talk to me about it."

"You mean, talk *at* you?" I said.

"Well, yeah," he admitted. "She doesn't have a sparkling personality, but she's very knowledgeable. A person who's willing to listen could learn a lot from her."

While observing the sleeping snake in its glass cage downstairs, Frank had heard voices chanting in Creole. Giving in to his fledgling interest in Vodou, despite knowing the mambo would react badly if he intruded on her, he had followed the sound by walking out of the hounfour, down a narrow hallway, and toward a room at the end of the corridor.

Curious enough to risk a tongue-lashing from the mambo, he had opened the door a crack and peered inside the room.

"And the first person I saw was one of my students," he said. "A girl named Shondolyn."

"Shondolyn!" I cried at the same time that Max leaped from his chair.

Frank fell back a step, startled by our reaction.

"Go on!" I said.

"Go on!" said Max.

"Uh . . ." Frank looked at us a moment longer, wondering at our excitement, then continued, "I waved to her, thinking that if she was there, maybe I'd be welcome and could sit in on the service."

Though looking directly at him, Shondolyn had not acknowledged him or waved back. That surprised him. Although prone to drowsiness and bad temper, Shondolyn was a pretty good student, and Frank felt he had developed a rapport with her. So he was puzzled that she didn't respond to his silent greeting. As his hand motions grew bigger, it occurred to him that she wasn't ignoring him; she didn't *see* him. Her face was blank and passive as she chanted in Creole—a language, he suddenly realized, she had mentioned in class that she couldn't understand. He also recalled that Shondolyn described herself as a good Christian.

Wondering what the hell this Christian girl was doing standing blank-faced in a Vodou ritual, chanting in a language she didn't know, Frank said her name loudly.

"And that was when all hell broke loose." He shuddered briefly before continuing his story.

Frank heard a woman shriek inarticulately on the other side of the door he was pushing open. Then the door slammed into him, hitting his head and knocking him backward into the hallway. He tripped and fell. He heard a voice inside the room, issuing orders. As he was rising to his feet, four . . .

"I guess they really *were* zombies?" Frank said dispiritedly.

"Yes," said Max.

Four zombies came out of the room. They had cold, sunken skin. Their eyes were dull and unblinking. They didn't speak, though they made some grunting noises.

"And they smelled weird," he said.

I looked at Jeff. "I told you so."

"Ah, how I've missed hearing you say those words," said Jeff.

"How long did you two date?" asked Frank.

Jeff blinked. "Is it that obvious?"

"Oh, please," said Frank, rolling his eyes.

"What happened next?" I asked him.

One of the zombies knocked him unconscious. When he awoke, he was outside and it was nighttime. His mouth was gagged and his hands were bound. Initially disoriented, he realized after a few minutes that he was being carried through Mount Morris Park.

"I had no idea what was going on, but I felt pretty sure they hadn't brought me to the park after dark for a picnic," he said. "And fear lends amazing strength to a man."

Perhaps they hadn't tied his feet because he was unconscious. Or maybe it was because he wasn't a big or athletic man. In any case, he used his free legs to kick and lash out at his stiff-limbed, smelly captors. Although there were four of them, they were surprisingly slow to respond and inept at regaining control of him.

"Zombies do not respond well to the unexpected," Max said. "They're not equipped to solve problems or react to new circumstances. They're created only to obey commands."

"Once I got away from them, I took off running," Frank said. "But these . . . these *things* came out of nowhere and made a beeline for me. These two vicious, growling, stinking little monsters."

The baka had torn at his clothing, chased him around the park, drooled on him, and terrified him out of his mind. They had finally caught him and were, he felt sure, on the verge of killing him when Biko came along and rescued him.

After Biko left him alone to go in pursuit of the baka, Frank had been overcome by terror. He was afraid the zombies would find him, or that the baka would return for him while Biko was hunting them elsewhere. So he had fled.

"Since then," Frank said, "I've been barricaded inside my apartment. Too scared to come out, talk to anyone, answer calls . . . Half the time, I thought I was completely crazy and had imagined the whole thing. The other half of the time . . . I *prayed* I was crazy and had imagined it."

"It didn't occur to you to warn others about this?" I said critically.

"As if anyone would listen," he said. "Come on. You know how crazy it sounds."

Recalling Lopez's reaction tonight, as well as the merriment of the cops on the night I had been arrested, I found it hard to disagree with that. "Even so," I said. "The foundation is full of kids. Shondolyn was in danger. You had a responsibility to—"

"Esther," Max said gently. "Recriminations will not help us decide what to do next."

I made a grumpy noise and folded my arms.

Max said to Frank, "You did not see who led the dark ritual or commanded the zombies?" When Frank shook his head, Max persisted, "But you heard a voice?"

"A woman's voice."

"Did you recognize it?" Max asked.

Frank shook his head. "I was scared and dazed. There was a door between us. A lot was happening. But I'm pretty sure she was speaking in Creole the whole time."

"The mambo," I said with cold certainty.

"She knows I didn't see her," Frank said. "I mean . . . I *think* she knows. So why send the kid to kill me? And if she had doubts, then why wait until tonight to do it?"

"Maybe the cop is the reason," Jeff said suddenly.

"What?" I snapped.

"He goes looking for Frank. So someone *else* goes looking for Frank," Jeff said. "Lopez was poking around the foundation and asking questions, right?"

"Yes," I said. "He was." And on Friday, when I left to go work at the restaurant, he said he was returning to the foundation to ask more questions—after I had told him about a missing teacher named Frank Johnson. I nodded. "I think he started asking about Frank a couple of days ago."

"So maybe Celeste started getting worried about what Frank would say when Lopez got to him," said Jeff.

"And crossing town to find and kill Frank without being noticed, stopped, and exposed would probably be a tall order for a zombie," I said. "So she had to find another way."

Max nodded. "Hence the possession of Biko."

"But how did she know *where* to send Biko?" Frank said, "I don't picture a chubby Haitian mambo or a kid with a sword following that police detective to my place without him noticing."

"You filled out the same kind of paperwork I did at the foundation," I said. "Both of our addresses are on file there now."

As I realized this, I decided maybe I wouldn't go home again until we solved this mess.

"That information is kept in Darius' office," Jeff said. "Since he died, people are in and out of that room all the time, looking for files, getting paperwork, and picking up the slack until his replacement is hired. It's not exactly Fort Knox."

"So the mambo just walked in and looked up my address?" Frank said. *"Shit."*

"The room where you saw Shondolyn is obviously a space used for dark worship," Max mused. "A place to honor the most dangerous of the Petro loa. Traditionally, it could not be done in the hounfour where the Rada are worshipped. That would be a form of sacrilege."

"It would also be kind of stupid," Jeff pointed out. "Whatever Celeste is up to, secrecy is obviously a big part of the plan. Why else try to kill Frank just for seeing that service? And what the hell was Shondolyn doing there, anyhow?"

"White darkness," Max said. "I've questioned, examined, and hypnotized Shondolyn—"

"You've done *what?*" Jeff blurted.

"You missed a lot," I said. "I'll explain later. For now, suffice it to say that we got Shondolyn out of town and away from all this."

"But—but—"

Max continued, "I am certain Shondolyn has no conscious knowledge of attending that service, or of any other involvement in Vodou, dark magic, or Petro worship. But what Frank saw does explain the poor girl's nightmares." He nodded slowly as he met my eyes. "Her subconscious mind has been trying to process the terrifying things she has seen and experienced while in a possession trance. And it appears to have been going on for some weeks now."

"Was the bokor trying to convert her?" I wondered.

"I think it far more likely that the bokor intended to use her for some evil purpose and was preparing her for it," Max said. "Attempting to ensure her cooperation by conditioning her to obedience when in the thrall of possession."

"Or using her to kill someone?" Frank said sourly.

"That may have been the ultimate intention. A well-behaved girl would be an ideal tool for murder, after all, since she would almost certainly catch her victim unaware," Max said. "But I believe we intervened before that could occur. Apart from her nightmares and the resultant insomnia, Shondolyn's life seems to have been proceeding in its normal fashion so far, with no major disruptions and no pattern of long, unexplained absences."

"So what do we do now?" I asked. "I'm tired and want to go home. And since it's probably not safe for me there until we stop the bokor . . ."

"The first thing we must do," said Max, "is destroy the bokor's private altar and purify that space."

"But there could be zombies in that room!" Frank protested. "And who knows what else?"

"For that reason," said Max, "we will prepare ourselves for battle."

"What?" Frank said.

Max put a hand on his shoulder. "This work is not for everyone. You may prefer to remain here."

"Well, *I'm* going," said Jeff. "I want to find Puma."

"I'm going," I said. "I want my poppet."

Looking around at the three of us, Frank gave a defeated sigh. "Fine. I'll go, too."

"Good man!" Max beamed at him.

"But if I'm going back to that place . . ."

"Yes?"

"I'd really like a stiff drink first," Frank said.

"Actually," said Jeff, "that's not a bad idea."

"Ah! I happen to have some rather good aqua vitae here . . ."

While Max poked around his overcrowded shelves, I decided to go upstairs to check on Nelli.

I found her lying by the front door of the shop, groaning softly and panting in distress. I knelt beside her and stroked her head, promising we'd take her straight to a vet before doing anything else.

She growled at me.

"You need a doctor," I said firmly.

Nelli's body started heaving, as if she were having trouble breathing. She was trembling all over. We had waited too long. We needed to take her to the clinic immediately!

"Max!" I called. "Max! Come here!"

I heard his footsteps a moment later. He was carrying a cloth bag—probably full of supplies for the purification he had mentioned—and a machete. His eyes grew round with alarm when he saw Nelli's condition.

"She needs help right away," I said urgently. "I'm going outside to hail a cab. I hope you have a lot of cash on you."

Max nodded as he called over his shoulder, "Jeffrey! Frank! Esther and I must leave immediately! Nelli is in distress!"

Jeff called out that they were coming right away, and I heard their footsteps on the stairs.

Nelli groaned again. Max seized her pink leash from its hook by the door. "Come Nelli. Let's go to the doctor."

She growled again. Her whole body went tense. With my purse slung over my shoulder, I opened the door to step outside.

"I know you find the clinic upsetting," Max said, "but you'll feel much better after they treat you."

He reached down to her prostrate form, intending to clip on her leash. With a ferocious snarl, Nelli tried to bite him. Max leaped back with a cry of surprise and bumped into me, making me lose my footing for a moment. I clutched his arm for balance.

Nelli rose to her feet, snarling viciously. Saliva dripped from her bared fangs. Her hair stood on end. Her eyes glowed with demonic red light.

"Max!"

I dragged him out the door with me and pulled it shut behind us, just as Nelli leaped for our throats, her massive jaws open wide as she howled madly for our blood.

22

I braced my body against the door, praying the thing could withstand Nelli's weight as she hurled herself against it, barking maniacally at us.

"What the *hell* . . . ?" I was panting with terror, my body shaking from the sudden flood of adrenaline.

The door, which was mostly made of glass, shook in its old wooden frame when Nelli flung herself against it again, trying to get to us. Max dropped his bag and his machete and braced both hands against the glass, trying to prevent the dog's violent onslaught from shattering it. The fierce wind whipped his hat off his head and carried it down the street. My hair was blown across my face and got into my mouth.

I turned around and looked inside the shop. Nelli's dripping teeth looked enormous as she raged and snarled at us, her red eyes glowing. I had seldom seen anything so terrifying.

In my peripheral vision, I saw motion at the back of the shop. I looked up to see Jeff and Frank emerge from the stairwell. Max and I started shouting at them to go back, turn around, *go back*.

Seeing us standing at the front door with Nelli press-

ing her nose against the glass barking at us, Jeff must
have thought we had locked ourselves out. He started
forward.

"No!" I screamed. "*No!* Go back!"

"What?"

Hearing Jeff's voice behind her, Nelli whirled to con-
front him. He looked at her—and his puzzled expression transformed instantly into shocked horror.

Behind him, Frank stood in frozen terror as Nelli
made a beeline for the two of them. Jeff shoved Frank
hard, practically throwing him down the stairs, then followed him into the stairwell and slammed the door shut
just in time to escape Nelli's dripping jaws. She threw
herself against the wooden door in a fury; but I had con-
fidence, now that it was closed, that the two men were
safe.

"Max! What's *happening?*" I cried.

Shock washed across his face. "Oh, no! I am a *fool.*"

"Max! What is it?"

"A fool," he raged. "A fool!"

"Max!" I removed my hands from the door to shake
him by the shoulders. "Tell me what's happening!"

"The accident. Friday. At the foundation," he panted.
"Nelli left behind blood and body tissue."

"You mean the torn off dewclaw?"

"I was so alarmed—so distracted—I didn't realize it.
Didn't think!" He beat his head against the glass door.
"Oh, *no.*"

"Blood and body tissue?" I looked at the red-eyed,
snarling dog as she crouched down and made another
run at us. The door shook when she hit it, but it held.
"What does it mean, Max?"

"It means she is in the power of the bokor. It
means . . ." He gestured to the bared fangs and glowing
eyes. ". . . that the bokor can do *this* to her."

My phone rang, making me jump out of my skin. I fumbled in my purse, flipped open my phone with shaking hands, and held it to my ear. "Yes?"

"What the *hell* is going on?" Jeff shouted over the phone.

I explained, and then I concluded, "I guess that's why she's been feeling so sick. The bokor was working dark magic on her." As a mystical being, Nelli had evidently responded to such interference the way a normal dog would respond to an infection.

"Well, what do we do *now?*" Jeff said. "Frank and I are trapped down here!"

I could hear Frank having hysterics in the background.

"You're going to have to wait here until Max and I dispatch the bokor."

"Wait here?" he repeated. "You're going without us?"

"We have no choice," I said, raising a hand to shield my face from the wind. "You did get a good look at Nelli, didn't you? We only have two choices now. Either we stop the bokor, or else we get animal control to shoot Nelli."

"Oh, no!" Max cried.

"So we're going to go stop the bokor," I said firmly.

Max looked at me, and a grim, resolute expression hardened his normally gentle features. "We certainly are," he said in a deadly voice.

"You go get a cab," I said to him. "I'll catch up in a minute."

Max met his familiar's glowing red eyes. "I will not return until I have freed you, Nelli!" He squared his shoulders, collected his belongings from where he had dropped them, and walked down the street. I had a feeling it would take him a while to find a cab at this time of night. Especially since he was carrying a machete.

"Jeff," I said into my phone. "You need to distract Nelli."

"You want me to *distract* the vicious two-hundred-pound dog that just tried to kill me?"

He was exaggerating. She wasn't *that* heavy.

"This street's pretty empty this late at night." It was well past midnight now. "But we can't have Nelli standing here terrifying the few people who do pass. Someone might call the cops. And we especially can't have her breaking down this glass door and killing someone."

"What the hell do you want me to *do?*"

"Just keep her attention fixed on you," I said. "Keep her at the back of the shop."

"Oh, for God's sake!" He gave a heavy sigh. "Okay. Right. Fine."

A moment later, I saw the door to the stairwell open. Jeff stuck out his head and called, "Nelli! Oh, Nelli! Over here, girl!"

Nelli whirled around and went bounding across the shop, roaring with fury. Jeff slammed the door again. The enraged dog scratched on it, barking and snarling.

Fortunately, the possessed Nelli seemed to be as dim-witted as the regular version.

"Good work, Jeff," I said into the phone. "I'll call you later."

"Be careful," he said. "And don't let anything happen to Puma."

"I promise." I ended the call and went after Max.

Thanks to Max's skills, breaking into the foundation in the middle of the night didn't present a challenge. The building was silent and dark. Tonight's Vodou ceremony was obviously over, and all the celebrants were gone.

Once we were inside, we crept into Biko's training room in search of a weapon. Max had his machete, but since our departure from the bookstore had been unexpected, he had brought nothing for me. And I didn't like the idea of facing the mambo, her snake, zombies, the baka, or a possessed Biko without a sturdy means of defending myself.

The weapons in the supply cabinet that Max used his power to unlock were all for young people to practice with, so there was nothing sharp or intentionally lethal there. But as I grasped a heavy wooden practice sword in my hands, I thought it would be pretty useful for beating the stuffing out of a baka.

"I'll take this one," I whispered to Max in the dark.

"Let's proceed." His voice was like steel. Someone had messed with Nelli. Someone would pay dearly for that.

Fortunately, Max's modification of my gris-gris bag had made it less peppery, so now I could move around without it making me sneeze or choke. It bounced harmlessly against my chest as we trotted down the stairs to the hounfour, moving quietly in the dark building.

We passed through the space where I had seen Lopez possessed by a loa hours earlier. The shattered pieces of the glass cage he had destroyed still lay on the floor.

"Where's that damn snake?" I wondered nervously.

We soon found out. We crept down the hallway that Frank had described to the room he had told us would be there. On the other side of the closed door, we heard chanting. Max clasped my hand and squeezed briefly. I squeezed back to let him know I was ready. I let my purse slide off my shoulder and onto the floor so that it wouldn't encumber me. Then with a fierce war cry, Max kicked open the door and plunged into the room, waving his machete. I followed right behind him, with my wooden sword in my hands.

I took a few long strides into the room, then stopped and stared. Mambo Celeste stood before an altar that was draped in red cloth and covered with frightening objects. My gaze briefly took in a dead snake in a jar of fluid, black candles, a desiccated human head, and a black wooden carving of a particularly nasty looking loa. She held Napoleon high over her head, stretched out between her arms, while she chanted. Her face was drenched with sweat, and her arms trembled under the strain of holding the heavy snake aloft.

The mambo whirled around at our abrupt entrance. Her face was a mask of shock. She and Max faced each other in tense silence for a moment.

I realized we weren't alone in the room. Biko and Puma were both there, standing a few feet behind the mambo. I gasped and raised my sword, pointing it at Biko. But it was immediately apparent that he didn't even know I was in the room.

He and Puma stood in identical positions, their arms raised in worship, their blank faces gazing unblinkingly at the eerie altar. They continued with the chant that the mambo had ceased when we burst into the room.

Looking at her now, Max said in a dark, furious voice, "You hurt Nelli!"

The mambo's face contorted angrily and she started shouting at us in Creole. Max ignored her and swept his machete across the altar, destroying several ritual objects with a single blow.

The mambo screamed and threw her enormous snake at him. Max fell to the ground, wrestling with the writhing reptile. Puma and Biko continued chanting, motionless and unblinking. The mambo made a beeline for the door. I blocked her path. When she tried to shove past me, I hit her with my sword.

She shrieked in Creole and then hissed at me. She had done that earlier tonight, when I had been trying to rouse Lopez from his possession trance. Only this time, red mist poured out of her mouth.

The next thing I knew, I was lying in a pool of darkness, and Max was calling my name from far away.

I heard a groan. Then another. Upon hearing the next one, I realized that *I* was the one making that noise. I saw flashing lights, and they made me dizzy. I groaned again. My head was killing me.

"Esther! Esther!"

Someone was patting my cheeks, chafing my wrists, and shaking me gently. It was all very irritating. I tried to shove him away.

It dawned on me that the flashing lights were actually just the dazed fluttering of my eyelids. I willed myself to stop doing that. Peaceful darkness descended.

"Esther!" Max said. "Wake up! Are you all right? *Esther!*"

I opened my eyes, squinted against the candlelight, and saw Max peering down into my face.

"Oh, thank goodness! Esther?"

I tried to speak, coughed, then tried again. "Why am I on the floor?"

"In her escape, the mambo did something that made you pass out."

I frowned . . . and then recalled her hissing a cloud of red mist at me. I shuddered in revulsion. "Oh. Right."

Fortunately, the pain in my head was already fading.

"I believe you must have been unconscious before you hit the floor. You fell with quite a heavy thud," he said. "I noticed it even though I was locked in mortal combat with Napoleon."

"The snake!" I gasped and scrambled up off the floor with impressive speed for someone who'd been barely conscious a moment ago. "Where is it?"

"I have dispatched it." Max rose, too, and gestured in the direction of the altar. "I don't approve of cruelty to animals, but the circumstances were extreme. He was trying to suffocate me."

I saw the snake's head lying at some distance from his body, and realized that Max had killed the reptile with his machete. Napoleon's blood was everywhere.

"That is *so* disgusting," I said with feeling. Then I realized what Max had said right after I regained consciousness. "The mambo escaped?"

"I'm afraid so," said Max. "She fled while you were unconscious and I was wrestling with the snake. By the time I beheaded the creature, I knew it was too late to find the mambo. And I couldn't leave you, in any case. I wasn't sure what she had done to you."

"What'll we do?"

"We shall proceed with destroying the altar and purifying this ritual space," he said. "Then we will search the building for baka and zombies—though I suspect they are not here, or we would have encountered them already."

Puma and Biko stood silently nearby, facing the altar.

"How do we get them to snap out of it?" I asked Max

"We have to destroy whatever substance the mambo used to enslave them. Considering what we know about Nelli's possession . . . Ah. This may be what we're looking for."

Max found two small vials of blood on the altar. He picked them up, smashed them against the floor, then reached into his bag and pulled out a little bottle of holy water. He sprinkled the water over the blood and glass that lay on the floor while he said something in Latin; it sounded like a prayer.

A moment later, Puma swayed dizzily, put a hand up to her brow, and said, "Oh, my *head* . . ." She looked around the room and blinked in astonishment. "Esther? Dr. Zadok! What's going on?"

Biko drew in a sharp breath, bent over suddenly, and clutched his head. "*Ouch.* What the *hell* . . ."

Puma gasped when she saw the altar. "I saw that before ... What *is* this place? What's happened?"

"This is the bokor's lair," I said. "You and Biko have been possessed by the white darkness. But you seem to be coming out of it now."

I thought this was a pithy summary; but a lot of confused questions and outraged demands followed my statement.

While I explained what had been going on, Max was systematically destroying and purifying ritual objects throughout the room. Once the siblings understood the extent of what had been done to them, Biko and Puma joined in. I started looking for a poppet that resembled me. While searching the room, I slipped in some of Napoleon's blood. I shuddered in revulsion and continued my search.

"Esther!" Puma pulled a doll out of an urn that sat before the altar. "I found it!"

"Oh, thank God!" Taking it from her, I scowled when I saw that the burlap doll was dressed in a leopard-skin blouse and a tiny red skirt. "That is so unfair! I was in *costume* that day! She can't really think I go around dressed like that?"

"It's good that you don't get distracted by trivial things in a crisis, Esther," said Biko.

Puma sent her brother a warning glance, then said, "Dr. Zadok? Let's neutralize this poppet."

"Immediately!" While Puma held the doll, Max baptized its little head in holy water. She prayed in Creole, he in Latin.

Then Puma held the head up to me, "Take back your hair and burn it. Not here, but later, in a safe place. When you go home."

I pulled the fragile, tangled bits of brown hair off the poppet, relieved when I discovered that doing so didn't make my own head hurt.

"Now tear open the doll with your own hands and remove the stuffing," Puma said. "Take all the bits home with you and burn them separately."

I did as instructed, then put the messy bits and pieces of my former poppet into my purse.

"Ah-hah!" Max cried. "I found it!"

He picked up a little jar from the overcrowded altar. We all gathered around to peer at it. Inside, there was a dog's claw with some hair and dried flesh attached, as well as a quantity of dried blood.

"This whole dark magic thing is just so revolting!" I said.

Max smashed the jar against the floor, performed his purifying ritual, and then urged me to call Jeff. I did so. Jeff's first question was about Puma, of course. I assured him she was fine.

"As are the rest of us, by the way." I explained what had happened.

Max, Biko, and Puma continued tearing the room apart while I tried to convince Jeff to open the stairwell door and take a look at Nelli. I could hear Frank in the background, predicting that the two of them would die a violent, bloody death if Jeff did what I was asking.

Puma went down the hall to the hounfour to gather some positive ritual objects and bring them in here to start rebalancing the forces at work in this space.

"Why can't this wait until you're back?" Jeff said. "Then Max can be the one to risk his life to check on his dog's mood."

"Max can't wait that long. He's very worried about her." Hearing a deafening silence in response to this, I said to Jeff, "Okay. I'll just tell Puma that we've got to leave the rest of the work here up to her, because now we have to go home and check on Nelli since you're too af—"

"All right," he snapped. "All right. Hang on."

In the background, Frank's voice rose in volume. Then there was a moment of silence. When Jeff got back on the line, he described the dog's demeanor in a puzzled voice.

I said to Max, "Jeff says there's a purple dinosaur in Nelli's mouth now."

"Oh, that's her favorite new toy. She must be feeling better!"

I relayed this information to Jeff.

He said, "Well, she's standing right outside the stairwell door, with her ears perked up and her tail wagging, and that ridiculous thing in her mouth. So it looks like she's back to normal." There was a pause, and he added, "Now she's whining. I think she wants us to come out and play with her."

"Don't disappoint her."

"You're bringing Puma back here, right?"

"Yes. When we're done here."

Cleansing the bokor's dark work space took a lot of time, as did searching the empty building for baka and zombies. So we didn't get back to the bookstore until after four o'clock in the morning. Looking and behaving much like her old self, Nelli woke up long enough to greet us all and show off her new dinosaur toy. Jeff was right, it was a ridiculous thing; but it made her happy. And it was good to see Nelli happy again, after the night's terrible events.

Frank wouldn't come out of the cellar until Biko had apologized for trying to kill him and assured him it wouldn't happen again, and Max had taken Nelli upstairs and put her to bed for the night. Then Frank said it had been nice knowing us all, and he was leaving New York on the very next train to anywhere. He'd give Jeff a call in a week or two to see if this whole evil-bokor-baka-zombie thing had blown over yet.

The rest of us shared a celebratory pot of coffee and

some stale cookies. I realized I was famished. I couldn't remember the last time I had eaten.

"So Napoleon's dead, huh?" said Jeff. "Can't say I'm sorry to hear that."

We had wound up leaving the body where it had fallen, and we left a note about the mess pinned to Catherine's office door. None of us had any clear idea how to dispose of such a large dead animal in summer without causing a nasty stench until the next garbage collection day. I also thought that Catherine's permissive treatment of the snake in life meant that she should damn well take responsibility for disposing of it in death.

"That thing would never even have been in a position to try to suffocate Max if Catherine had been sensible enough to ban such a big snake from the foundation," I said.

Biko said, "Yeah, and knowing Dr. Livingston, that argument's going to work really well with her when she finds a headless reptile corpse in a blood-soaked room in the foundation's basement."

As we had suspected, Puma had been ensnared first, then used as bait to victimize Biko. The mambo had asked Puma to accompany her to the supply room right before the ceremony began. The room was usually locked and Puma hadn't been in there for several years, since the mambo controlled all the supplies used in the hounfour. Puma had entered the room, seen the dark altar, felt stunned and appalled . . .

"And then . . ." She gasped and put a hand over her mouth. "Now I remember! The mambo hissed at me, and some sort of—"

"Red mist," Biko said suddenly.

"Yes!" she said. "Red mist."

"It came pouring out of her mouth?" I said.

The Garlands both nodded. Puma didn't remember anything that had happened after that, until we roused her hours later in the same room. Biko remembered that after he went downstairs, the mambo told him his sister had suddenly fallen ill and he should take her home. The woman had led him back to the same room, and when he saw Puma lying there unconscious, he panicked. He didn't even notice the altar. Just his sister's prone form. Then the mambo had knocked him out, too.

"And you're saying I tried to *kill* that guy Frank?" Biko was stunned and appalled. "God, I can't believe it! And I'm really lucky I didn't get caught. No one would believe this voodoo possession stuff, least of all Esther's cop friend. I'd have been sent to prison!"

"But what was the point of all this?" I wondered. "What was the goal?"

"We still don't have the answer to that," Max said, frowning thoughtfully. "And I believe it's crucial to know."

"Where are the baka?" Puma wondered. "And the zombies?"

"Man, you people are never satisfied," said Jeff. "The dangerous reptile is dead. Celeste is exposed as some kind of dangerous nutbag who'd better never show her face again around here. And Nelli is back to her usual self. That all strikes me as a good night's work." He put his hand over Puma's.

Biko looked at me and rolled his eyes. "We've got two baka and four zombies still lurking somewhere in Harlem. But *Jeff's* satisfied with the night's work, so I guess we'll let it go."

Puma glanced at Jeff, then at Biko. Then she looked at me and rolled her eyes.

"You each have a point," Max said. "As Biko notes, there is still danger afoot. Connected, perhaps, to whatever the mambo's goal was. Or is. For that reason, I suggest that everyone continue wearing their protective charms. Puma, Biko—I made a gris-gris pouch for each of you earlier tonight. Please wear them until we're sure the danger has passed." He looked up at the clock that hung on the wall. "And as Jeff notes, we have put in a good deal of work tonight. I propose that we start fresh after some rest. Due to the inclement weather, the sky isn't light yet, but it will be soon."

I realized how exhausted I was. Although I was nervous about the mambo still being on the loose, I also desperately craved sleep. And I was scheduled to be on a location shoot for *D30* in about twelve hours, so I really needed to get some sleep. I didn't need to look bright-eyed and perky to play Jilly C-Note, but I certainly needed to be on my toes.

23

I awoke late, feeling groggy and exhausted. I hadn't gotten to bed until after seven o'clock in the morning; and it had been, after all, a very eventful night.

Moreover, I'd had to sleep on my lumpy couch. The ruined condition of my bed had actually slipped my mind, until I returned home around dawn and entered my bedroom. That was when I remembered exactly what had happened . . . and also realized that I hadn't seen the flame-ravaged mattress sitting outside the building when I returned home. Someone had taken it during the night. A truly desperate Dumpster diver, apparently. However, even considering the useless condition of the mattress, I wasn't that surprised. The quickest way to get rid of anything in New York was simply to put it outside on the sidewalk. I half suspected that Mambo Celeste could have disposed of the discarded zombie corpse that way.

So, all things considered, I was cranky and crotchety when I woke up, as well as still sleepy.

However, actors who let grass grow under their feet don't get to eat or pay their rent. So I telephoned Thack while my coffee was brewing, and I told him about *The Vampyre*.

"You really want to be in a show about vampires?" he asked doubtfully.

"Thack, I've played a singing rutabaga, a half-naked forest nymph, and a crack whore. Why would vampires be beneath me?"

"All right, I'll look into it and get back to you."

"Don't 'look into it,'" I said irritably. "Get me the audition."

"Somebody certainly got up on the wrong side of the coffin this morning," he said.

After ending the call, I packed up supplies for the day, realizing wearily that I wouldn't return home until the early hours of the morning—at which time, I'd get to enjoy the luxury of sleeping on my couch once again.

Jilly C-Note's boots smelled bearable after a couple of days with solid air freshener sitting inside them. The push-up bra and purple fishnet stockings were clean now, and the dry cleaner had done a good job with the sweat-stained Lycra top and unsavory vinyl skirt that I had dropped off on Friday; luckily, the plastic bag covering the clothes ensured they didn't smell of smoke from last night's mattress fire. I carefully packed the costume into a small duffle bag, along with two water bottles and some snacks, and I left my apartment.

Outside on the street, though reluctant to do so, I telephoned Lopez. I got his voice mail. I wondered if he wasn't available ... or if he had seen who was calling and decided not to answer. I left a message: "I'm on my way to teach class, and I just walked past an empty spot on the sidewalk where my mattress should be. Someone took it last night. So you'd better cancel the visit from the arson investigator, because there's nothing for him to examine."

As I was putting my phone away, a cardboard box blew out of a stairwell and hit me. I was startled, rather than hurt. The wind speed had continued increasing while I slept. It was dark and overcast today, the temperature was cooler, and it looked like we were in for a huge storm. I was glad I had included a rain slicker and a small umbrella when packing my duffle.

I called *D30*'s production office to see if the schedule had changed. They said no. Due to the delays caused by Nolan's heart attack, they couldn't afford to cancel this evening's shoot unless it was raining all night and impossible to film, so I should still plan to be there.

I was walking several blocks east so that I could catch a subway train that would let me off close to the foundation. When I got to a major intersection, I saw that a suicidally brave cop was directing traffic there by hand; the power lines had been blown down by high winds, and the streetlights weren't working. I found a similar situation up at 125th Street in Harlem when I exited the subway some time later.

The sky rumbled menacingly overhead as I walked to the foundation. I thought it was crazy to plan to film outside in this weather; but I also knew there was a lot of money at stake for every day of filming that *D30* lost. So they'd stick to the schedule tonight unless it became physically impossible to do so.

When I arrived at the Livingston Foundation, I was a little surprised at how normal everything looked. You'd never guess that less than twelve hours ago my friends and I had been destroying an evil bokor's lair in the basement and searching the building for zombies.

I was also surprised that I felt no serious anxiety about entering the building now. Mambo Celeste was still on the loose, after all, and this was where she had conducted her dark rituals. However, her work space was destroyed, and her snake was dead. By day, the building looked prosaic, and there were plenty of other people here. Thinking about safety in numbers, I touched the reassuring gris-gris charm that hung around my neck, then went inside the foundation to teach my class.

Considering the weather, I wasn't surprised to find my class was almost half empty. If I were a student instead of a teacher, I'd probably have stayed home, too. Still, we had a good session, and I thought the kids who came were probably glad they had braved the elements and attended.

As class ended, one of the students who lived in Brooklyn said that her mother had just phoned to tell her not to take her usual route home. Most of the lower third of Manhattan had lost power a few minutes earlier, and the girl's parents were worried she'd get stuck somewhere.

"How will you get home?" I asked with concern.

"I'll take the subway to Queens and transfer there." The girl blew out her breath on a sigh and summoned her resolve. "It shouldn't take me *too* much longer to get home than it does by my normal route."

I was startled to hear that a third of Manhattan was without power now, so I logged on to one of the foundation's computers to check current local news. Sure enough, high winds had continued causing power failures all over the city while I'd been teaching the acting workshop this afternoon, and many neighborhoods were now without power.

As thunder boomed overhead, I turned off the computer and went to the window. Still no rain, but the sky was dark gray and roiling. I flipped open my phone and called *D30* again. The connection was full of static, and the harassed production assistant's voice kept fading out while we spoke.

I said, "We're not still shooting this evening, are we?"

Yes, we were. Given the probability of heavy rain, though, they were looking at the prospect of moving the location indoors. Most of midtown and uptown still had power, and since we'd be working in Harlem, that meant the power outages wouldn't affect the location crew.

I refrained from pointing out that I was in Harlem right now and had seen power outages just a few blocks away from here. I didn't think my opinion would count for much when the *C&P* empire was intent on keeping the wheels of production rolling forward. I also didn't want to get my head bitten off by this stressed-out assistant who, in any case, had no power whatsoever over that decision.

She told me the location crew was currently on their way to the Mount Morris Park neighborhood for tonight's shoot. I thanked her, apologized for bothering her, and got off the phone.

Then I checked my messages. There was one from Lopez. I dialed my voice mail and listened.

"That mattress is gone? People in this city really *will* take anything that's left outside, won't they?" he said. "And there goes my hope of proving to you there's a rational explanation for what happened last night. To the bed I mean. There's never a rational explanation for what happens between *us.*"

I smiled wryly, realizing I was forgiving him already for last night's sour parting. I heard him speaking to someone in the background.

Then he said again into the phone, "Sorry, Esther. Things are hopping here. This storm coming in, power outages, traffic snarls, trains stranded, a shooting, some looting . . . What did I want to ask you? Oh, right! What did you *mean,* you were on your way to teach class? I was serious last night when I told you to stay away from the foundation. Listen to me. Before things got crazy here today, I looked into—What?" He was speaking to someone else now. "Okay. Right now? Yes." Then he said to my voice mail again, "I've got to go. Call me as soon as you get this. If I can't pick up, leave me a message. And please tell me that you're not still at that place."

I called Lopez back. A couple of people who passed

me in the hallway glanced at me as I made a sharp sound of frustration when I got his voice mail.

"I *am* at the foundation," I said. "I work here. I can't just not show up." I frowned as I thought about the possible cause for his concern. Maybe, despite our differences of opinion, we had shared some similar suspicions without realizing it. "Listen, Mambo Celeste calls herself a widow, but other people say her husband left her. I'm wondering what really happened to him. I guess this sounds crazy to you, but . . . Is there any chance he was murdered?"

I decided to leave it at that. If there really was something to discuss, we'd talk about it after Lopez had time to get the facts.

I concluded, "Anyhow, I won't be here much longer. I have to go to the *D-Thirty* set soon. Can you believe they're still planning to film tonight, despite everything that's happening out there?" I paused for a moment, then said, "Call me back, if you have time."

I glanced at the clock. I had about an hour before I had to be on the set. Considering that I'd left carnage and wreckage in her foundation building last night, I thought I should probably go upstairs and speak to Catherine about what had happened. I had sort of assumed Max would speak to her, and I preferred that scenario, since I didn't like her. But since I seemed to be stuck here for a while longer . . .

I turned and started walking toward Catherine's office. I reached the double doors leading to the main lobby at the same moment as two teenage boys who were coming in the opposite direction. I was preoccupied, and they were so involved in their conversation that they didn't see me. One of them was gesticulating enthusiastically with his large beverage cup as he pushed his way through the doors—knocking me off my feet and somehow managing to spill the entire contents of his cup on me. It contained a chocolate milk shake.

I gasped at the ice cold sensation seeping through my clothes to chill my skin as I lay on the floor trying to catch my breath. Cold chocolate muck was all over me.

"Oh, my God, miss! Are you okay?"

The two boys hauled me to my feet. Icy chocolate slid down my stomach to my crotch, and down my neck into my bra. A huge glob of it covered the gris-gris bag, which now looked as if it had been *dipped* in the shake.

I made a shrill sound of discomfort and spread my arms, helplessly watching the shake melt stickily into my clothes.

"Miss?" one of the boys prodded.

"Yes," I said. "I'm fine. Just a little . . . *cold*. But the happy part of this accident, of course, is that nothing got on the floor." Every drop of the shake seemed to be on *me*.

Uncomfortable and filthy now, I realized that, although it was far from ideal, I did at least have a change of clothing with me. I'd have to don Jilly's costume in another couple of hours anyway, if *D30* persisted in its determination to film the rest of my episode tonight. And at least I had a rain slicker and an umbrella to keep the costume dry while I was in transit. So I got my duffle and went into the ladies' room. I removed my cold, soggy, dirty clothes and put on Jilly's costume—except for the cruel boots. Though my roped-soled canvas shoes didn't go with this outfit, they were comfortable and still clean, so I kept them on.

The gris-gris bag was so messy and sticky, I gave up trying to clean it while it hung around my neck. I felt considerable anxiety as I removed it, but nothing burst into flames. I tried wiping it off, but the milk shake had seeped into the bag and soaked all the ingredients. Apparently the thing had not been designed with this sort of mishap in mind. I wondered if it even had mojo anymore. Either way, I couldn't put it back on, especially not while wearing my *D30* costume. So I wrapped it in some tissues and stuck it in my purse. I still had it with me, I assured myself. And, after all, the mambo's altar was destroyed, and I had burned the remnants of my poppet before going to bed last night.

Now that I was presentable again, in a manner of speaking, I went to see Catherine.

Her cool gaze assessed my appearance with ironic detachment, and she gave no response at all to my awkward explanation about why I was once again dressed as a prostitute.

Instead, she said, much to my embarrassment, "Goodness, what *are* those marks on your neck?"

I put a hand self-consciously over my throat, realizing I should have used makeup to cover up the marks Lopez had left on me. I had chosen a blouse with a high collar today, so I hadn't expected my skin to be this exposed before I met with *D3*'s talented makeup artist.

She smiled. "So the detective can lose control, after all? I had wondered."

I stiffened, taking offense. Since Catherine had seen us together on Friday, right after the chaos in the lobby, I supposed it was natural for her to assume that Lopez was the source of these love bites. But I scarcely knew this woman, and what had happened in my bedroom was private.

Catherine added, "Perhaps the spirit trance that he experienced at yesterday's ritual unleashed something inside him?" Seeing my surprise, she smiled again. "Yes. I heard about it. How I wish I had been there to see it."

"Why *weren't* you there?" I asked baldly, trying to change the subject. I didn't want to talk about Lopez with her, let alone discuss what had happened to him that evening. "It seemed like the sort of thing that interests you."

"Other things needed my attention."

Since she obviously didn't intend to say more, I moved on to the reason I had sought her out. "Did Max—Dr. Zadok—speak to you about last night?"

Her face wrinkled with distaste. "Yes. His tale was quite extraordinary."

"Where do you think Mambo Celeste is now?"

Catherine shrugged indifferently.

I found her casual attitude odd, given that a trusted employee had been found practicing black magic in her basement, as well as endangering innocent people. I wondered how much Max had told her. Considering Catherine's academic approach to magic and mysticism, Max might have lost all credibility if he had talked about Celeste raising zombies from the grave.

"You and your friends left quite a mess downstairs," Catherine said to me. "Still, it doesn't matter now. The altar is no longer needed."

I blinked. "You mean because the mambo has fled?"

"Because matters have progressed toward their inevitable climax, despite a number of discouraging setbacks. Some of which you caused."

My heart started to beat more heavily. I remembered my first visit to this room, dressed as I was now. The mambo wasn't the only Vodou expert at the foundation who'd become acquainted with me in these clothes.

"It's strange about the poppet." The words popped out of my mouth unbidden, surprising me. It was only in that moment that I realized it *was* strange. "I was told the mambo doesn't approve of voodoo dolls being sold in Puma's Vodou Emporium, where she buys her supplies."

"She was a rigid woman," said Catherine.

"Was?" I said.

"But rigidity can be its own kind of strength."

"Why would someone so strict about Haitian tradition adopt a custom from another branch of voodoo?" I wondered. "A custom she thought gave the wrong impression of the religion? A custom she berated Puma for humoring?"

"That seems a minor deviation from her traditions, compared to the things Dr. Zadok described when he phoned me earlier," Catherine pointed out dryly. "But all people have private desires and deep yearnings which can't necessarily be met in the conventional ways they're most comfortable following."

"I'm wondering . . ." I felt uneasy. Anxious. "Those practices I saw last night, in that room." I heard my phone ring, but my gaze remained locked with hers. "How could that have gone on in your own building without your knowing about it? You and Celeste were close. How it is possible that you didn't—"

"Your phone is ringing," Catherine said. "Aren't you going to answer it?"

Feeling tension spread through me, I reminded myself that there were other people in the building. I didn't really have any clear suspicions yet, just doubts. I tried to organize them rationally as I fumbled in my purse for my phone, glad for an excuse to get out of this room.

"I'll take this outside," I said.

"No need. Please stay seated."

I looked at my phone and saw with relief that the caller was Lopez. "No, you're busy. I'll leave. I just wanted to apologize for . . . you know. Downstairs." I flipped open the phone, as eagerly as if the static-filled communication with Lopez was a protective charm.

Catherine opened a drawer in her desk and reached inside. "Stay," she said.

I tried to rise and found that my legs felt too weak to support me. My knees buckled. I sat back down with a thud.

"Esther?" Lopez said. "Are you there?"

"I'm here," I said faintly, staring into Catherine's cold, dispassionate eyes.

Out of the blue, I recalled that I had once heard evil described as an absence of empathy. Why had looking at her made me think of that?

"Please tell me you're not still at the foundation," Lopez said, his voice faint. "This is a bad connection. Can you hear me?"

"I'm *here*," I said, anxiety welling up inside me.

"You left me a message asking about Celeste's husband. He's alive and well and running a plumbing supply store in Philadelphia. I checked on Friday."

"I'm at the foundation," I said to him.

"I want you to get out of there," he said. "I've been checking on Catherine Livingston, too. When you told me she'd been sleeping with Darius, it got me to thinking. Two men dying of natural causes. Sure, it happens . . ."

I tried to rise again. My legs felt as if they didn't belong to me.

"But three? And all within a decade?" Lopez said. "That's just too much coincidence. Especially given their ages."

"Three?" I said faintly.

Catherine smiled.

"Her first husband died not long after she met Martin Livingston. Same scenario as Martin and Darius. Unexpected death from sudden, catastrophic natural causes in a man previously thought to be in good health." Lopez said, "It's the sort of death that could be arranged by someone who's an expert in exotic folk medicine and ritual poisons—and Dr. Livingston is exactly such an expert. It was the focus of her research before she started working at the foundation."

"What?" I was shaking.

"Martin and her first husband were cremated, and Darius' body is missing, which means I'll never be able to prove anything," Lopez said in frustration. "So you can't repeat this to anyone. Do you understand me?

But I'm telling you, Esther, she killed those three men. I *know* she did. I can see it in her face. She got away with it, and she's gloating. So I don't want you anywhere near her. She's a dangerous woman."

My lips where trembling. My throat felt swollen. My gaze was locked with Catherine's.

"Esther?" Lopez said. "Esther?"

"I'm with—"

There was a deafening clap of thunder overhead, and a blinding bolt of lightning split the gray sky. The lights went out and the phone went dead as rain started pouring down heavily.

"Lopez?" I said into my phone. "Lopez!"

But he was gone. The connection had been lost.

"Oh, goodness," said Catherine. "The city has lost power."

I shook my head, wondering frantically why I couldn't get up. Why couldn't I make my own legs work? "It's probably just this neighborhood."

"No, it's the whole city. It must be." The window was behind her. Although it wasn't yet evening, the sky was so dark, now that the lights were dead, that I couldn't see her facial expression. But I heard a chilling satisfaction in her choice as she said, "Later, you'll see for yourself."

"Later?" My teeth chattered with fear. Why couldn't I *move?*

"When true darkness descends."

"It's you, isn't it?" I was panting with terror now, like a trapped animal. "*You're* the bokor, aren't you? Celeste was just . . ."

"A tool," she said. "In the end, a decoy. You and your friends are . . . dreadfully nosy, Esther. Darius goes missing one night, and the very next day, you, Dr. Zadok, and Detective Lopez all show up, full of detailed questions. Academics aren't *children,* for goodness' sake. I knew what you were after from the moment you arrived here."

"Then why hire me?" I asked, trying with all my might to move my foot.

"I acted in accordance with a wise old saying: Keep your friends close, but keep your enemies closer." In the dim light coming through the window, I could see Catherine shake her head. "You ask me questions about Mama Brigitte, and then—what a coincidence!—Shondolyn's mother calls me the next day to say the girl is leaving town. Good God, did you really think I haven't known every day since you came here what you were up to?"

"I've only been here a few days," I pointed out. "What were you trying to do to Shondolyn anyway?"

"Ah! You still don't know?" She sounded smug. "Well, well. What an interesting evening this will be for you."

I didn't like the sound of that.

"Celeste wouldn't have explored these avenues on her own," I said, breathing hard as I struggled to move my legs. "We should have realized that before now. She was too rigid. Too traditional. Her horizons were broadened by someone with a wider education. Someone who was knowledgeable about many traditions, not just the one. Black magic, ritual poisons, multiple religions, different branches of Vodou, the voodoo dolls that Celeste despised . . ." I nodded with certainty. "It all came from you, you syncretic slut!"

"I don't think I like your tone," said Catherine.

"And setting my bed on fire last night?" I said in outrage. "What was *that?*"

"Setting your bed on . . ." Catherine made a sound of amusement. "Someone set your *bed* on fire? My, what an interesting life you do lead."

"That wasn't you?" I said in surprise. "Then it must have been Celeste."

"You overestimate her. Her skills were limited and, as you should recall, she was quite busy last night."

"Why did she help you? Serve you?" I asked. "Whatever."

"She wanted what everyone wants—influence, importance, respect."

"She thought you could give her those things?"

"I encouraged her to think it. Celeste was never that well liked, you know. Not even by her own houngan. Her gifts were not well-suited to serving others. I was the one who showed her a better path to the recognition she craved."

I heard the past tense again. The sense of finality, of a life story ended. "Where is she now?"

"What a tactless question. Especially when your tone implies you already know the answer."

There were still people in the building. I would scream for help. I was opening my mouth to do so when my throat closed. I gasped for air, unable to breathe.

Catherine pulled her hand out of her desk drawer. I saw that she was holding a tiny little doll, crudely fashioned out of wax. Her fist squeezed its legs into immobility while her thumb and forefinger pinched its throat. Gasping futilely for air, I saw that the doll had a few strands of brown hair—*my* hair—on its little wax head.

There was also a Star of David drawn crudely on the doll's stomach. I thought that was in questionable taste, and I wanted to say so—but I couldn't speak.

"I made a second one," Catherine said. "I believe in being prepared. It's an essential ingredient for success."

She let go of the poppet's throat. Able to breathe again, I inhaled for a scream. Before the air could leave my lungs, Catherine banged the wax doll's head against the desk, and I blacked out.

24

When I regained consciousness, I was in the park, it was nighttime, and I was being carried by four zombies.

I had somehow wound up in Frank Johnson's nightmare.

But unlike Frank, my legs were bound, as well as my hands. I supposed Catherine had learned her lesson after the one that got away.

I felt guilty about Frank's near death experience at Biko's hands as I realized that Catherine had known all along where he lived, but she had left him alone—until *I* started meddling and got Lopez to ask probing questions about him. Before that, Catherine had evidently considered Frank too minimal a threat to expend her attention on.

And what exactly did she need her attention *for,* anyhow? Where was all this leading us?

I had a horrible feeling I was about to find out. My body tilted at a precarious angle, and the zombies started ascending stairs. Moving carefully, since I didn't want them to drop me at this juncture, I looked around and confirmed my suspicion. We were on the crumbling stone steps leading up to the old watchtower. Whatever had excited Nelli the night she had come here, it must have had something to do with this—the smell of zombies on these stairs.

The zombies held me aloft, high overhead, as we ascended. I remained very still, since they didn't seem exactly steady on their feet, and I didn't think I'd survive a tumble down these stairs. I practiced breathing evenly, grateful that I *could* breathe, and wondered how long I had been unconscious.

I guessed a few hours at least. It was nighttime now, the sky pitch-black overhead. The city must still be in the grip of the blackout; the park was completely dark, and as we rose higher through the trees, I could see that the surrounding buildings were also completely dark.

Whatever Catherine was planning, she evidently needed complete darkness for it. She didn't want to be seen.

That didn't seem very promising from *my* perspective.

The moonless, starless sky was a raging sea of thunder and lightning. The noise stampeded through my aching head, and the flashing light was disorienting, making me dizzy as I was carried backward and at an uncomfortable angle up to the forgotten nineteenth-century watchtower atop this steep, isolated hill in the middle of Harlem.

We were in Manhattan, a densely populated borough! Surely I should be able to get *someone's* attention.

As soon as we reached the comparative safety of the broad stone plaza, I made my move. My hands had been tied in front of me, rather than behind. Now I lifted them to remove the gag from my mouth, and I screamed as loudly as I could. Then my heart sank as I realized that no one would hear me over the noise of the thunder. There was no one else in this park, and the surrounding houses and apartments were all too far away. Even *without* the competition of the thunder, I doubted anyone would hear me.

Nonetheless, I screamed again.

"Would you *stop* that?" Catherine's voice snapped at me. "I told them to gag you! What h*app*— oh, for God's sake!"

I was roughly yanked out of the zombies' cold hands and thrown down to the stone pavement. The ground was wet. I remembered that it had been raining hard when I was knocked out by a bokor with a poppet. My tiny vinyl skirt rode up to my waist, the push-up bra stabbed me, and I felt the fishnet stockings tear. If I had known I was going to be kidnapped, I would certainly have worn something else this evening.

Catherine towered above me, wearing a long robe of red silk. I was surprised, because her fashion sense had really seemed more subdued and classic than that.

She kicked me in irritation. "After what happened with Frank Johnson, I told them to tie your legs. But I forgot to specify that your hands should be tied *behind* you so that you couldn't remove your own gag!" She made a guttural sound of frustration. "Take my word for it, don't work with zombies!"

I rolled away from her. Venting her frustration, she followed after me, kicking me again. I grunted in pain.

"It's like working with children!" she raged. "*Delinquent* children! That goddamn *snake* was smarter than these creatures are!"

"So get rid of them," I snapped. "Why keep them around?"

She shrugged. "They do the heavy lifting. I've got brains, not brawn."

"They've got to be hard to keep hidden," I said rubbing my aching ribs where she had kicked me. "Where *do* you hide them?"

"Sometimes in the basement. Sometimes in the woods on this hill. One of the few *good* things about a zombie is that it'll sit in total silence and stillness—not even breathing, obviously—for days at a time. So they're easier to conceal than you'd suppose."

While she talked, I looked around the plaza. There was a small bonfire in the spot where I had previously noticed charring and ashes. And in its dim glow, I could see several vévés drawn in red on the paving stones.

Now I remembered—it was in those books Puma had given me. Red was the color of a Petro ritual.

Catherine, the bokor, was invoking dark gods on this isolated hilltop, beneath the thundering, lightning-streaked sky.

This could only be a *bad* thing. So I needed to stall her. No, it wasn't much of a plan, but it might give me time to think of a better one.

And the best way to stall her was to keep her talking. One of the first things I'd noticed about this woman was how much she *loved* the sound of her own voice.

"Raising zombies from the grave sure couldn't have been easy," I said, struggling surreptitiously with the bonds on my wrists. "That's some major mojo. Plus a lot of logistical problems. Sneaking in and out of grave-yards, digging all that dirt, getting them from the cemetery back to Harlem. You put a lot of talent and hard work into creating these, um, lads."

"You have no *idea*."

"But you failed with the first one, didn't you?" Yes, I rubbed it in a little. There didn't seem to be much point anymore in trying not to offend her.

"It was my first experiment. I was new to raising the dead." She sounded a little defensive. "And I made some mistakes. So that one was unpredictable. Too hard to control. I *had* to get rid of it. Darius was desperately afraid that we'd be exposed because of that one."

"So he was in on it with you?" I was wriggling my ankles, trying to loosen the bonds.

She made a little waggling gesture with her elegant hand. "Sort of."

It hit me suddenly. The poppets. The handsome man whom Jeff and Biko had been sure was gay. What Puma had told us about love spells.

"Oh, my God!" I said. "You seduced Darius with voodoo! You made a poppet of him and—ugh!—rubbed bodily fluids into it! Didn't you?"

"It's not as easy as they tell you," she said. "Saliva doesn't work. Neither does sweat. For a man, it's got to be semen."

Tired of talking to her from my prone position, and also afraid she'd kick me again, I sat up. "You used his semen? Okay, that's too much information."

"I could make you a poppet like that to secure the detective, in exchange for your silence." She added, even as I was opening my mouth to pretend to agree to this proposition, "But you don't need one for him, do you? That was obvious even before you walked into my office in that digusting condition today. Did he do that to you all in one evening? He's really *not* the altar boy he pretends to be, is he?"

"Er, back to the part about letting me go in exchange for my silence," I said.

"Pardon? Oh! No, that was just a flight of fancy," she said dismissively. "I know several languages and dialects, and I have so many esoteric and secret skills, that sometimes I just wish I could use them more often. But you don't need any sort of potion or poppet or charm, of course, because you're going to be dead shortly. So what's the point?"

"How shortly?" I asked with more than casual interest.

She looked up at the churning black sky, where low clouds were gathering directly overhead, flashing with ravenous heat and light. "Very shortly. It's almost time for the ritual to begin."

"Who inflicted the white darkness on Nelli?" I said, desperate to distract her from her purpose. "Was that you?"

"No, it was Celeste. The dog had attacked her snake, it deserved to be punished. She could also incapacitate you and Dr. Zadok at the same time. And so on and so forth."

"Incapacitate?" I repeated. "If Max and I had been one split-second slower to escape, we'd be dead."

"And that would certainly have been a bonus. I really wasn't paying that much attention. Frankly, I rather agreed with you that the snake was dangerous and unattractive. But . . ." She sighed and shrugged. "Did I mention that good help is hard to find? I needed a disenchanted Vodou mambo to assist me, so I made compromises. One does so in all things, you know, not just with men."

"Compromises like enchanting a gay man to sleep with you so you'd have a lover?"

"Have you seen his photo? He was very handsome. And athletic. And—oh!—the *stamina*." Her tongue came out of her mouth for a moment, as if she were licking the memory.

I looked away. "What about your husband? Rumor has it that he had, er, stamina."

"Stamina was not what he had," she said irritably, gazing up at the clouds again. "I looked the other way through a lot of philandering."

"Why?" When I saw the expression on her face, I said, "Oh, right. Because he was a billionaire."

She shook her head. "Men like Martin—well, all men, really—fool themselves into believing a beautiful woman twenty years his junior wants him for himself alone. That was convenient for me, so I let him believe it."

"So it was all about the money?"

"Money and power," she said. "It's *always* about money and power. Or are you still too young to know that, Esther?"

"Max always says that evil is voracious."

"How quaint."

"I still don't understand why you killed Martin, though." There was an obvious reason it had never even occurred to me that she had done so. "You were better off with him alive. Everyone knows you only got a modest amount of money when he died."

"I'll have to give up the penthouse if I don't get more money!"

"Whoops, I guess I touched a sore spot," I said. "So did you not know about the will?"

"I knew, but I didn't think challenging it in court would be so fruitless! Especially not when I made sure he seemed out of his mind in the final days of his life. It should have been easy to convince a judge that he'd been losing his mind for a while. But that board of directors at the foundation . . ." She gave nasty snarl. "It's the old boy system. Every one of them is pals with half a dozen judges. I hadn't counted on that."

"You should have just put up with the philandering."

"I did! But then Martin decided to divorce me!"

"Really? Gosh! Who can fathom the ways of the heart?"

"And two expensive divorces had taught him the value of having his third wife sign an iron-clad pre-nup. So I'd have gotten *nothing* if he'd left me. Nothing!"

"Lopez knows," I said suddenly. "He knows you killed Martin. And that you killed your first husband, too—to attract Martin as a grieving, available, younger widow I suppose? And Lopez knows you killed Darius!"

"Yes, I'm aware of that." She was openly amused at my crestfallen expression. "But it doesn't matter what he knows, Esther, since he can't prove anything. More to the point, he'll be dead by morning, anyhow."

"What?" Forgetting about my furtive attempts to loosen my bonds, I hopped awkwardly to my feet. *"What?"*

"I've administered a topical poison, one that seeps through the skin and induces death by slow paralysis."

"What? *When?* Where is he?"

"He's lying on the floor of the Petro ritual room at the foundation, next to the corpses of Mambo Celeste and Napoleon—neither of whom, I must confess, I expect to miss."

I flung myself against her, wild with rage and anguish. "No! *No!* What have you *done?* You murdering bitch! I'll kill you myself! Noooo!"

She was shouting in Creole. I realized as I felt strong, cold, lifeless hands grabbing me that she had issued instructions to the zombies. They seized me, put my gag back in my mouth, and dragged me—kicking, squirming, struggling, weeping, and howling with rage behind my gag—toward the tower.

Catherine rose, came toward me, and slapped me sharply across the face. As I stared at her with mute, venomous hatred, she straightened her red robe.

"This is *your* doing," she said. "You have no one to blame but yourself. I'm not a fool. I don't actually *want* to kill an NYPD detective. That's far more trouble than it's worth!" She pointed a finger accusingly at me. "But he burst into the foundation after dark looking for *you.* He was uttering insults and threats, and he would have torn the place apart with his bare hands if I hadn't stopped him."

She smoothed her red robe over her summer dress. "I administered what's known as an ordeal poison. Frankly, it's a nasty way to die. But under the circumstances and with such short notice, it was the only reasonable choice open to me."

I growled in rage and lunged for her again. The grip of the zombies holding me was firm, though; I barely moved two inches.

"Be honest with yourself, Esther," Catherine said. "Would he be lying in agonized paralysis awaiting his death now if not for *you?*"

Tears streamed down my face as I realized Lopez would never have gotten involved in this case in the first place if it hadn't been for me. If only I hadn't called on him for help the night I was arrested!

Using the tight grasp of the zombies as leverage, I raised both my legs off the ground, swung from their grip, and kicked out at Catherine as hard as I could. But being bound and held captive made me slow and clumsy. She saw it coming and easily evaded the blow.

"Baron Samedi is coming for your lover!" she said with unholy glee. "The Lord of Death is dancing around him even now, waiting to escort him to the cemetery!"

She said something in Creole. In response, the zombies started to shift me. I seized the opportunity to tear off my gag again.

"And *your* lover?" I shouted over the rising thunder. "The one you had to hex to get him into your bed? Why did Baron Samedi come for him, you murdering bitch?"

She leaned closer to me and smiled maliciously. "Because Darius balked at what we were going to do with Shondolyn. Which was that same thing that, after she was gone, I planned to do with Puma." Her breath brushed my face as she said, "Since you're the one who stole them both from my grasp, it's fitting that you should take over that role tonight."

"What role? What are you doing to do?"

"Human sacrifice."

She produced a key from the pocket of her robe as I gaped at her. Then she used it on the shiny new lock that Lopez—*Lopez!* I wailed silently—had previously noticed on the entry gate to the watchtower.

"You can't do this!" I shouted.

"I'm afraid I must." She gave an order to the zombies, and they started dragging my squirming, kicking, grunting body toward the gate. "I have asked for great power and wealth from the darkest of the Petro loa. I've asked for the ability to nullify my late husband's will, break open the trust, and empty the foundation's coffers of the billion or so dollars that should be mine"

"You're doing all this for *money?*" I blurted. "To woo lawyers and dazzle judges?"

"Power and money," she said. "In the end, they're the only things that matter, Esther."

"The spirits demand a human sacrifice in exchange for *that?*"

"The Petro loa are hungry gods. And I've sought a lot of favors from several of them. They want the most impressive and costly offering there is: a human life."

I looked up at the flashing, thunder-crashing sky, and I thought I saw dark gods looming overhead, come to drink my blood and consume my soul. *"No!"*

Heedless of my screams and protests, the zombies started hauling me up the precarious old spiral staircase that wound around and around the tower, dragging and carrying me all the way up to the lookout platform.

Now I understood the names that had haunted Shondolyn's dreams: Marinette, a servant of evil; Mama Brigitte, who presided over black magic and helped her worshippers acquire ill-gotten gains. The other names in Catherine's personal pantheon no doubt had similar profiles.

I also understood now why she had used the white

darkness to possess my predecessors, to teach them do-
cility and obedience in a trance state. I was making this
process every bit as noisy, slow, tiresome, and inconve-
nient for Catherine as I could. The higher we climbed
and the harder I fought against the zombies dragging me
along, the more I screamed and shouted at the bokor,
the more annoyed she looked. This was clearly *not* how
she had pictured her victim behaving on the big night.

When we reached the lookout platform, she turned
to me and snapped, "Can't you be a bit more decorous?
The gods can hear you! You're spoiling an important
and emotional event for me!"

"Good grief!" I said, gaping at her. "Evil incarnate!
Right in front of me! You're not just evil, you *are* Evil!"

She slapped me again. "Stop your babbling!" She
pointed overhead. "Right there! The dark loa whom I
have summoned are right *there.*"

With my hair blowing across my face, I looked up.
They were indeed right there. Shifting shapes and amor-
phous shadows loomed and writhed overhead, spilling
out of the belly of the crashing thunderclouds directly
above us. The shapes were immense and, although not
even vaguely human, they had a clear form and seemed
to move with conscious intent.

"I have prepared for this night for a *long* time!" Catherine shouted at me as the fierce wind made her red
robe billow. "Ever since that do-gooder houngan left
for Haiti. He was always interfering. It was such a relief
when he left town. You have no idea—"

"*Now* who's babbling?" I butted her nose with my
forehead.

Catherine shrieked and fell back several steps as her
nose spouted blood. With uncontrolled rage in her eyes,
she started hitting me repeatedly while the zombies held
me still.

"Esther!"

Through my pain and terror, through the clash and crash of thunder, through the roaring of the wind and the cold sting of the rain that started falling again, I thought I heard someone call my name.

"Esther! Esther!"

I turned my head away from Catherine's next blow and craned my neck to look down from the platform. I shied back reflexively, not having realized just how high up we were. Then I realized I saw figures scrambling around on the plaza below us. Biko was fighting with the baka down there, while Max tried to get past them to enter the tower. The baka seemed intent on preventing entry. I realized that Catherine must have left them there as sentries.

A bolt of lightning flashed, illuminating the moment that Biko shoved his rapier through the torso of one of the monstrous little creatures, then yanked it upward to gut the thing.

"Ouch," I said involuntarily.

Max tried again to enter the tower. The remaining baka leaped for him., The creature was skewered in midair by Biko's sword. The young fencer beheaded that one, then dashed into the tower after Max. Even above the rage of the thunder and Catherine's screams of protest, I could hear the rattle and echo of the shaky iron stairs as my rescuers ran upward in pursuit of me and my captors.

Catherine yelled something at the zombies. They released me and turned, descending the stairs at their usual measured pace. They'd obviously been instructed to stop Max and Biko. As soon as they let me go, Catherine seized me by the hair and began chanting loudly, her free arm raised toward the thundering black clouds. Despite the obvious collapse of her plan, her face was exultant with religious fervor—and greed. Oh, yes, there was definitely a healthy dose of greed there. As long as she could sacrifice me to her dark masters and get Martin Livingston's immense fortune, then all other problems were solvable, apparently. Including the two heroes racing up the stairs even now to foil her plans.

I decided to be a problem, too. I'm an *actress*. I've trained in stage fighting and I do my own stunts. I can *run* in spiked heels if I absolutely have to. I face casting directors as part of my regular work week. I deal with theatrical agents! So it was well past time to show this murderous academic bitch that it would take a lot more than a few zombies and a little hair pulling to turn *me* into a human sacrifice.

I made two fists and swung my bound hands into her nasty, arrogant face as hard as I possibly could. She shrieked and let go of me. I started hopping away from her as fast as my bound legs would carry me. When I felt her hand on my hair again, I dropped to the platform's floor—ignoring the pain of the hair that tore out of my scalp—and rolled over, kicking at her with both legs.

Below me, I heard Biko shouting, "Darius! Darius, it's me, Biko! Darius!"

"Oh, *no*," Catherine said. "That's how it got away last time."

"If a zombie's name is called by someone who knew it in life," I panted, remembering what Max had told our group in Puma's shop. So *that's* how Darius had wound up wandering the streets the night I had first encountered his zombie. This cold bitch had forgotten for one moment that the lover she had murdered was now an *it*, and she had used his name.

I felt strong hands hauling me upright. I was scared for a moment, until I realized Biko was the one manhandling me. He used his weapon to slice open the bonds around my hands and my feet. Then he lunged in Catherine's direction.

"No!" Max's voice cried behind me.

I whirled to face him. He was staring up at the roiling black clouds and the dancing, menacing shapes overhead. His face was a horrified mask of alarm.

"Biko! No!" he shouted. *"No!"*

Biko halted and turned to look at him.

Max was panting hard, sweating, and red-faced. I realized the climb to this platform would have been a little demanding for him even if he *hadn't* had to fight through baka and zombies to get here.

"We must go! Now! *Now!*"

Biko met my gaze and then, trusting in Max, we ran toward the steps and started down them. Darius' zombie was just standing there, looking confused. It made no protest as Biko shoved it out of the way and then helped me and Max run past it. Three more docile, dazed zombies were in our way, and they each simply moved aside, too, when Biko pushed them.

I noticed foamy white stuff bubbling out of their mouths. "What is that?"

"Salt!" Biko shouted.

I remembered learning at Puma's shop that salt was one of the theoretical ways to awaken a zombie. Thank the heavens it had actually worked!

When we reached the bottom of the stairs, I tripped over a baka corpse. Biko caught my arm and pulled me upright before I could fall flat on my face.

"Keep running!" Max shouted, clambering down the steps behind us. "We may yet be too near!"

We headed for the crumbling stone steps and began descending them.

"No, no! Slow down!" I shouted. "I can't see!" We were going down those treacherous stairs at reckless speed in nearly total darkness, our way illuminated only by the violent flashes of lightning overhead.

"Keep going!" Max cried. "Run!"

"Max!" I protested.

"Faster!"

I took his fear quite seriously, even though I didn't know what caused it. But *my* fear of dying in a fatal tumble down those lethal stairs was real, too. Biko solved my dilemma by grabbing my arm and dragging me with him at top speed, so that our descent was little more than a scrambling, controlled fall to the very bottom of the steps.

Max was wheezing with exhaustion by the time we reached street level. Biko and I paused, seizing Max's arms to support the old mage when we thought he might keel over.

"Must keep going," he panted. "Keep going."

With the two of us supporting him, we made our way across the park and toward the entrance gate as fast as we could. Then we ran across the street and stood outside one of the darkened row houses.

"Here?" Biko said, breathing hard.

It had *better* be here. I couldn't go any farther. Not until I got my second wind.

"Yes," Max panted. "Yes . . . Here . . . Safe . . . I think . . ."

Despite the complete absence of electricity in the city, we would see the lookout platform on the old watchtower quite clearly from here because there was so much meteorological—or mystical—activity directly above it. The thunder made my head ache even at this distance, and the dancing light illuminated the platform so well that I was sure I could see Catherine's blond hair swirling around her head in the violent wind. Her red silk robe was easy to spot as she raised her arms to exalt the dark loa whom she had summoned with the promise of a human sacrifice.

My gaze was still on her when the lightning came straight down from the churning black clouds and made her explode into hot red flames that were then sucked up into the sky. A pale pillar of ashes stood in her place for only a split-second, and then the wind began to disperse it.

"She promised them a human sacrifice," I said in a stunned, breathless voice that scarcely sounded like mine.

"Well," Biko said prosaically, "looks like they got one."

"The Petro loa are deadly dangerous," Max said, still breathing hard. "To make a promise which one cannot keep . . . invites their rage and punishment."

25

"**M**ax!" I cried suddenly.

"Whoa!" Biko did a double-take so big he nearly fell down. "Don't scare me like that! Not *now*. Didn't you just see what we, uh, just saw? I'm a little rattled."

"Lopez!" I shrieked. "Max! *Lopez!*"

I started to run in the direction of the foundation. Biko tackled me and stopped me.

"Lopez!" I wailed.

"He's fine!" Biko shouted into my ear. "He's fine! Lopez is fine!"

"What?" I panted in panic, clutching him. "What?"

He shook me by the shoulders, met my eyes, and said loudly into my face, "Lopez is okay. We found him. Puma and Jeff are with him now. He's going to be all right."

"He is?" I could barely choke out the words, I was so relieved.

"He's *fine*," Biko repeated. "Well, almost fine. A little hardheaded, if you ask me."

I burst into tears and started wailing with relief.

"Uh, Max," Biko said awkwardly. "Could you deal with this?"

"Of course."

Max embraced me and patted my back while I wept copiously against his shoulder. Every so often, he murmured soothing words to the effect that Lopez would be fine.

After a little while, I pulled myself together enough to ask my two companions, "What happened?"

Far from being satisfied by his talk earlier in the day with Catherine Livingston, Max had felt dark suspicions about the woman after ending the conversation.

"So I returned to several questions that have been vexing me," Max said, as we walked wearily in the direction of the foundation. "Why summon so much dark magic? There must be a purpose or goal, and yet we had not yet perceived it."

"Power and money." I glanced at the hilltop, recalling the words of my murderous ex-nemesis. "She said everything is always about that, in the end."

"A simplistic view," Max said. "But then, for all her education and achievement, she did not strike me as a woman of complex insight or emotional wisdom."

"I'm with you, Max," said Biko. "I never liked her."

"I also continued to wonder what Shondolyn had been conditioned for. It must be an important role, since so much effort and risk had been invested in trying to gain influence over the girl. Unable to achieve a breakthrough in attempting to discern whom Shondolyn might be used to harm, I instead began to think about how she might be used as a victim. Which was when the prospect of human sacrifice occurred to me."

"It never occurred to *me*," said Biko. "Not once. And I'm glad. I don't think I want to be the sort of person who gets thoughts like that." After a moment, he said, "No offense intended."

"None taken," said Max.

"Look." I pointed to the hilltop. The angry churning of the black clouds was dying down, the flashes of lightning were fewer and less fierce, and it looked as if the storm gathered directly over the watchtower was starting to break up.

"The dark loa have had their meal," Max said. "They're preparing to depart."

"What are *those?*" Biko asked.

In the intermittent flashes of light overhead, we could see thin columns of smoke curling upward from two spots on the plaza and several places on the spiral iron staircase inside the tower.

"Her creatures," Max said. "Their existence ended when hers did."

"Oh, right," said Biko. "You said once that to dispatch the zombies . . ."

Max concluded, "We would simply have to dispatch the bokor."

"Looks like the Petro did it for us," said Biko. "Even so, there wasn't anything *simple* about it."

"But how did you know about her?" I asked. "Or that I was in danger? Or that she had poisoned—"

"After the citywide power failure, Detective Lopez came to my shop looking for you. Two patrolmen he had dispatched to the foundation to find you had already reported that you weren't there. With no way of reaching you by phone—"

Biko said, "All the towers went down when the power failed. No one's been able to use a cell phone all night."

"Detective Lopez started hunting for you in the places he thought you might be. Your apartment, my shop. He told me his next stop would be the set of the television show."

"The show!" I said. "I'm supposed to be at work!"

"Are you kidding?" Biko said. "We're in a major power blackout, Esther. No one's working except emergency personnel."

I realized that if Lopez was willing to speak to Max

and to the staff of *The Dirty Thirty*, he must have been very worried about me.

I said, "After realizing I wasn't with the cast, he probably suspected that the patrolmen he had sent to the foundation had been hoodwinked." I gave a scant summary of what Catherine had related to me about his behavior when he arrived. "By then, he must have realized I was in danger."

"Meanwhile," Max said, "in his anxiety about you, Detective Lopez was rather more forthcoming than usual. He told me his suspicions about Catherine Livingston. Recognizing that he is a man of very conventional beliefs in certain key ways, I did not precisely share my suspicions with him, but we did come to a mutual understanding that something was wrong at the Livingston Foundation, we both feared for your safety, and we should each try to find you by any means available."

Wow. To trust *Max* to look out for my well-being suggested that Lopez had been at wit's end by then.

"So I proceeded to the Garlands' home, where I asked Puma and Jeff to recount to me again how Martin Livingston had died," said Max said. "Considering the story now from the detective's perspective—his conviction that Martin Livingston's wife murdered him—certain features of the unfortunate event suddenly suggested an obscure method to me."

"A method of murder?"

"Yes. Since Martin's confessed murderer is now dead, we'll never know for certain, but I believe Catherine put a curse on him that is known as 'sending the dead.' It is a particularly dreadful way to die. The bokor sends dead spirits—in many cases, destructive, malevolent ones—to inhabit the victim. The result is often a delusional form of apoplexy."

"A massive stroke accompanied by hallucinations," I said.

"And fatal," added Biko. "Once we realized Dr. Livingston might have killed her husband, and might done it using all the voodoo, Vodou, hoodoo, and other stuff she's learned over the years, a lot of other things fell into place. Max and Puma saw the pattern, and they realized that your life might be the big mojo offering that she was going to make to the dark loa who were bringing storm clouds over the city."

We looked up at the Mount Morris Park watchtower again, where our evil adversary had so recently met her well-deserved end.

"Hey, look," I said. "It's clearing up really fast now."

Instead of looking like the mouth of a particularly turbulent hell, the sky overhead was now starting to look like just a healthy summer storm. Fat grayish-black clouds moved slowly across the vault of heaven, outlined at infrequent intervals by soft flashes of lightning.

Max inhaled deeply, paused for a moment, then said to me, "The flow of life energy here has returned to its normal pattern. All is well again."

"That's good news, Max. I've had enough of the dead coming back to life. They've got a right to rest in peace." I said to him and Biko, "Tell me how you found Lopez."

"We were looking for you," said Biko. "We thought the dark ritual room seemed like the sort of place you might be held prisoner. Or sacrificed. We weren't really thinking of anything as, uh, *epic* as what Dr. Livingston did tonight. Anyhow, we went down there, and that's when we found him, and . . . Oh, *man.*" Biko shook his head. "I swear I screamed like a girl. For one thing, at first, we thought he was *dead*, because Dr. Livingston's poison was paralyzing him. And the setting . . . He was lying next to Mambo Celeste's corpse and not far away from Napoleon's head. Grisly."

"He's a brave man," said Max. "Upon being rescued,

his only thought was of you—of trying to learn your fate. None of us had any idea where you were, you see."

"But how did you cure him? How did you know what poison Catherine would use?"

"We didn't. But realizing that Dr. Livingston's talents for murder, mayhem, and victimization covered a broad territory, we brought a substantial supply of mystical solutions with us, not knowing what sort of problems we would face."

"You saw the salt," Biko said to me. Then to Max, "Boy, are we lucky that worked! And that those zombies didn't turn on us when they were awakened."

"An awakened zombie, though quite unpredictable, is most likely to turn on the person who enslaved it," said Max. "Not some passerby who's just trying to escape a cataclysmic event."

"Good to know," said Biko. "Though I hope I never to need the information again."

"Me, too." Realizing one of our group hadn't been mentioned, I asked, "You left Nelli at home?"

"Yes," said Max. "The storm frightened her terribly, and she's been vulnerable to possession during the course of this investigation. So I thought it best to leave her to guard the fort tonight."

"Oh." I suddenly realized what their story of the night's events meant. "Wait! Lopez still doesn't know I'm all right!"

"We should hasten to the foundation," Max said, quickening his pace. "He will be most eager to see you."

We were approaching the front doors of the building when Lopez came out, moving fast. Puma was running behind him, warning him of the possibility of a relapse. Then they both saw me. Puma stopped speaking and gave a big smile. I saw Jeff bringing up the rear.

Lopez looked stunned for a moment, then so relieved his whole face looked younger. He crossed the distance between us, seized me in his arms, and held me tightly, not saying a word.

I returned his embrace, clinging to him, trying to sink inside of him. I inhaled deeply and realized he smelled rather pungent. I made a little snuffling noise and blinked.

"It's the antidote they gave me." His voice was husky. "It smells weird."

His kiss was long and deep, and then he covered my whole face in kisses before hugging me again. "God, I was scared."

"Me, too. She told me she had poisoned you. She told me you'd be dead."

"Where is she? I need to arrest her." He pulled away and looked at me. "And why are you in your costume?"

"I don't even remember," I said.

"Whoa." He noticed the bruises and love bites around my neck. "Did I do that?" He kissed my neck gently and whispered, "Sorry." He kissed my mouth again, then said, "Now I've got to go arrest Catherine Livingston."

I pointed up to the watchtower. "She died in . . . a lightning strike. I got away."

"She's dead?" When I nodded, he gazed up at the tower with a disappointed frown. "Damn. Just when I finally had plenty for an arrest. She murdered Mambo Celeste, she poisoned me, and you sure *look* like she tried to kill you."

"Well, she's gone now," I said. "And good riddance."

"Are you all right?" he asked with concern.

"Yes." I smiled. "I'm fine."

"I've got a police car around the corner," Lopez said. "Come on. I'll take you home."

"Um, no." I backed away from the hand he put under my elbow, and I shook my head. "No."

"What's wrong?"

I heard the bokor's voice in my head: *"Would he be lying in agonized paralysis awaiting his death now if not for you?"*

This was the second time I'd nearly gotten Lopez killed. The Lord of Death would never have come so close to claiming him tonight if it weren't for me. He'd only gotten involved in this because I had dragged him into it.

"Esther?" he prodded. "Tell me what's wrong."

"I'm not good for you," I said.

He brushed my hair way from my face. "After a day like this, I don't really care. Let me take you home."

"I brought Baron Samedi to your door," I said. "I'm so sorry."

"Who?"

"I think . . ." I said with real sorrow, "I have to give you up."

The rain started coming down. Soft and gentle warm summer rain.

"Detective?" Puma smiled as she joined us. "I'm really sorry to interrupt, but someone's calling your name on your police radio. The one that was in your jacket pocket when we found you."

"Thanks," he said absently, accepting it from her. The radio crackled with static, and now I heard it, too: someone looking for Lopez. The city was in a state of emergency, and they needed to find him.

"And Esther, this was in that room, too." Puma handed me the little wax voodoo doll with the Star of David on its stomach. "It's lost its power, now that she's gone, but you should take it home and destroy it."

"Thank you," I said with relief, recalling how this thing had led to my abduction.

I ignored Lopez's inquisitive look; and he evidently decided not to ask what this bizarre thing was that I was clutching to my chest.

As Puma turned away, Lopez said, "Wait, uh . . ."

"Puma," she said with a smile.

"Puma. Thank you for your help tonight. I think I'd have wound up in the morgue if not for you, your brother, and Max." He reached into his pocket for his card and gave it to her. "You have a friend on the force now."

Puma beamed her beautiful smile at him. "Thank you, detective. But it was my pleasure. It was our duty. And you're Esther's friend, after all."

"By the way, what was in that antidote? I smell a little funky now." He added to me, "They sprinkled it all over me before they poured it down my throat. I was pretty out of it by then."

Puma looked embarrassed and said, "Actually, Max is the one who mixed it. I just . . . uh, excuse me, detective." She went and rejoined Jeff in the doorway of the foundation.

Jeff caught my eye, nodded toward Lopez, and gave me a thumbs up.

"All right," Lopez said. "If you really don't want me to take you home, then I need to go back on duty. By now, they probably think I wandered off a cliff in the dark."

"Going back on duty is a good idea," I said. "Even with the wind dying down, I'm sure it'll take a while for all the power to come back on and order to be restored." Catherine's greed had done an awful lot of damage, both tonight and in the past.

"All right." He frowned, looking puzzled and concerned. "And when things calm down, I'll call you."

"I don't think you should."

Would he be lying in agonized paralysis awaiting his death now if not for you?

He said, "Esther—"

"I don't want you to call," I said.

He sighed in frustration, then looked up at the watchtower, which glinted in the night sky as lightning fluttered in the clouds overhead.

"I'm the only cop here right now, so I'm probably the one who'll get stuck writing it up. There's a body in the foundation's basement that we've got to process, murdered by the woman who died on that hilltop tonight." Looking at the watchtower he asked me, "What are we going to find up there that I don't know about?"

"Besides Catherine Livingston's ashes or charred remains? I'm not sure."

The cops might also find remains of the four bodies that Catherine had stolen from a graveyard, and perhaps some baka remains—and I could only imagine what they would think of *those*. But I decided it would just extend this painful conversation unnecessarily if I mentioned any of that.

Max evidently sensed a cooling of emotion between us. Having made himself scarce earlier, he now joined us. "How are you feeling detective?"

"Almost like normal." The two men shook hands. "Thank you, Max. I think you saved my life tonight."

"I was delighted to help!" Max asked, "What will happen to the foundation now?"

"It may be shut down for a few days as a crime scene, and there'll probably be a minor scandal," said Lopez. "But then it'll go back to normal."

"Catherine was never what made the foundation tick, after all," I said. "It's always been Martin's money."

"And Martin himself, before she killed him," Lopez said a little grimly.

I had made my heart-wrenching decision about him, and now I wanted to get it over with. So I said, "Max, Lopez wants to know what was in the antidote you gave him."

"Ah! It's a fairly complex recipe, concocted to address

a wide range of threats, and some of the ingredients are things which I'm not really at liberty to discuss without a more extensive knowledge of your heritage."

"Excuse me?"

I said to Lopez, "You're not Lithuanian, are you?"

"What?"

"However, the primary ingredients," Max said, "the base of the formula, if you will, is a concoction of excrement mixed with holy water that has been used to wash the external genitalia of an adult human female. The additional—"

"*What?*" Lopez said.

I realized now why Puma had been embarrassed. I suspected she was intimately acquainted with the water she had poured down Lopez's paralyzed throat tonight.

Max blinked at Lopez's tone. "Water used to wash the ex—"

"No, not that part. Though that part is bad enough. *What* female . . . No, I don't want to know. Go back to the other thing you said."

"Ah! Excrement," Max said with enthusiasm. "We used the excrement of a canine familiar—specifically, Nelli—which has the properties of dejecta from both a physical being and a mystical one, and is therefore—"

"Whoa, whoa, whoa! You gave me Nelli's excrement?" Lopez shouted. "While I was lying there paralyzed and helpless, you poured *dog shit* down my throat?"

Realizing that his recipe was not being met with the intellectual enthusiasm that he had hoped to inspire, Max said, "Well, it was also mixed with—"

"Oh. My. God." Lopez looked at me. "I need to go to a hospital. I need an emergency room. I want my stomach pumped. I want a boatload of antibiotics. I want three—no, four tubes of toothpaste. And a gallon of mouthwash. I may want laxatives, but the night is young, so I'll dwell on that question for a while longer."

I said, "So I guess you're leaving?"

"You *knew* this would happen," he said accusingly.

"Well . . ."

"You can get home by yourself," he said sternly to me. "Good night!"

"Er . . ." Max raised his fist in the gesture that Biko had taught him. "Peace out."

As Lopez stalked away, I heard him saying into his police radio that he was on his way to an emergency room for treatment and wasn't immediately available.

Max and I looked at each other.

"You must be very tired, my dear."

"I am. Will you see me home?"

"I would be delighted. It may take us quite a while to get there, though. The city is in chaos."

"Hey, Esther!" Jeff called, coming over to me. "Henry keeps a little portable radio at the reception desk. Puma and I have got it on to a news station that's able to broadcast, and . . . Well, it's pretty upsetting news. You should brace yourself."

"What?"

"Mike Nolan had another heart attack tonight. He's alive, but back in the hospital."

"Oh," I said. "And he was taking such good care of himself, too. It's a mystery."

"I guess this means your scene will be rescheduled again," said Jeff. "And probably rewritten."

"Or my mother will get her wish and the episode will be canned," I said morosely. Once the city was functioning normally, I'd contact Thack about this. And also nag him about *The Vampyre*. After my adventures in Harlem, nineteenth-century vampires sounded very restful.

Jeff said, "I wonder if we should try to get to the hospital tonight?"

"For what?" I asked blankly.

"To see Mike."

I just didn't have the heart to tell him that Nolan had refused to speak to the casting director about him. Let Jeff hear it directly from Nolan

"The hospital? No way," I said. "*D-Thirty* bullied me into one hospital visit with that man, but that's my limit. Anyhow, it's too hard to get around the city tonight. Just getting home will be a challenge for me and Max."

"Cabs are running along Fifth Avenue," said Jeff. "If you walk down a few blocks from here, you can probably get one there and take it all the way downtown."

"Thanks. We'll do that."

I couldn't bring myself to go inside the foundation again; not until the lights were back on and I was sure nothing evil lurked in the building anymore. And certainly not until the cops got Mambo Celeste's corpse out of the basement. On the other hand, this experience had certainly taught me the danger of being careless with personal possessions. So I asked Jeff to go get my purse and my duffle for me. After all, what are old boyfriends for?

Max and I walked slowly toward Fifth Avenue, both tired, and neither of us minding the soft summer drizzle that fell on us. I remembered that I had an umbrella in the duffle, but I didn't bother to pull it out. Jilly C-Note's costume was ruined, anyhow, and I'd just have to think of a plausible explanation for this when I called *D30* to tell them so.

But it probably wouldn't be, "An evil bokor tried to turn me into a human sacrifice for dark loa while I was wearing my hooker costume."

"Max, I have a question."

"Hmm?"

"I know that Catherine Livingston was a ruthless, evil, narcissistic liar, but she said something this evening that I believed." I took a breath. "She and Mambo Celeste had nothing to do with my bed bursting into flames while Lopez and I were, um, in it together."

"Oh?"

"So taking off the gris-gris pouch right before that happened was unrelated. A coincidence."

"And so you're wondering what made the bed explode?"

"Yes."

"Well." Max thought it over. "May one ask, without being too intrusive, what Detective Lopez's mood, demeanor, or intent was at the time?"

"He was, er, agitated. He very angry with me. And also, I think, with himself. He was also very, uh . . ." I cleared my throat. "He felt a compelling urge to remain in my company, but clearly didn't think it was necessarily wise to do so." After a moment, I added, "Oh, and he was supposed to be on his way to work, and I think he felt conflicted about that, too."

"I see. Hmm."

"Max?" I prodded.

"I'm recalling that, at a moment when he feared for your life in Little Italy and wanted light, there was light. And at a moment when the local community needed reassurance from the Rada loa that there was protection at hand, the god of fire and war chose Detective Lopez as his vehicle for manifestation," Max said. "Now you tell me that at a moment when he felt angry, conflicted, and, er, romantically volatile, there was a spontaneous combustion."

"What does it mean?" I asked.

"I don't know, Esther. But this incident does strengthen my suspicion that there is more to your young man than meets the eye, and that it behooves us to monitor him for signs of . . . interesting, albeit, unconscious talent."

"He's not my young man," I muttered unhappily. "I

don't know what to do, Max. It's no good. I've nearly gotten him killed twice, and . . . and . . ." I sighed, too tired even to continue following this depressing train of thought.

"My dear, if I may make a suggestion?"

"Yes?"

He raised his fist and made a little bumping motion. "Keep it real, dude."

I smiled and bumped my fist with Max's. "Peace out."

Glossary

Vodou Terms

baka: an evil spirit in the form of a small monster

bokor: a sorcerer who practices black magic

cheval: a horse; one who is "ridden" by a loa during a possession trance

Creole: a dialect of French and one of the two official languages of Haiti

drapeau: a brightly decorated ceremonial flag that's used to salute the loa during a ritual

Gédé: the family of Vodou loa that deal with death and the dead

gris-gris: a magical charm

hounfour: a Vodou temple or place of worship

houngan: a Vodou priest

loa: a Vodou spirit or deity

mambo: a Vodou priestess

Petro: a family of aggressive, violent Vodou loa

Rada: a family of benevolent Vodou loa

vévé: symbolic designs which represent and invoke the loa

Vodou: a syncretic religion that developed in Haiti, arising from a blend of West African faiths and Roman Catholicism

zombie: a body that's reanimated and raised from the dead to work as a slave

Vodou Loa

Ayida-Wedo: symbolized by the rainbow, she is the wife of Damballah

Baron Samedi: the Lord of Death and guardian of cemeteries

Damballah: the serpent loa who created the world

Erzulie: the loa of love and beauty

Erzulie Dantor: the Petro aspect of Erzulie, this is the loa of jealousy, heartbreak, and vengeance

Mama Brigitte: the wife of Baron Samedi, this Gédé loa presides over cemeteries, black magic, and ill-gotten gains

Marinette: a Petro loa of evil and black magic

Ogoun: the loa of fire, war, and masculinity

Papa Legba: the spirit who guards the crossroads where the spirit world intersects with the physical world